What readers are saying about
Landfall

Her descriptions are exquisite. I don't know if it is just that they touched chords in me about order, simplicity, and forthrightness, or they amazed me that she would be able to acquire so much knowledge about such diverse subjects as sailing, geography, and human nature. But whatever it was, I loved them.

—JOHN THOMAS, Educator and historian

She draws us into the lives of seafaring men…their zest for life, their loves and their fears, and their brutality… Read of a love stronger than any storm cloud that ever rolled over the ocean, deeper than any clear blue sea.

—DOROTHY BLAKEY, Minister for elder care

The Quadrant series is an absorbing tale rich in historical, cultural, and human drama. Raikes' evocative language provides a tangible experience of time, place, and character.

—JUDY BRADBURY, Educator

VOLUME III

the
QUADRANT

"May every road
you take always
lead you home"—
Irish blessing

Kim Ridenour Raikes

LANDFALL

KIM RIDENOUR RAIKES

Designed and Produced by
Maine Authors Publishing
558 Main Street, Rockland, Maine 04841
www.maineauthorspublishing.com

For Malcolm
Traveler, seeker, finder

VOLUME III

Landfall

XXV
EBEN MCCABE
San Francisco Bay—Cape Damaris—Boston, Aug.-Dec., 1844

At first he'd at least put in an appearance, when all hands was called and he was obliged to be present; and there was still some show of his being captain, there on the quarterdeck when he stood to windward. We'd need to tack ship, or maybe reef topsails in the occasional big blows that gusted up the California coast, or in the unpredictable squalls that sprung up around the Line; and I'd duck below to find him pouring over his log, looking at the entries Jim had written, or lying down resting in his berth. His face would be vacant, but calm and still, and his body, though gaunt—the thinnest I'd seen him since his early teens, when he first started hauling cod with me and Pa—would look capable of strength. By shaking him at the shoulder and speaking clearly in his ear—by pronouncing "Ben, it's time t' tack her" or "Time t' take a reef in her"—I could rally him to action; and hauling on his peacoat or oilslicks and sou'wester, he'd take to the poop and stand there for a spell, looking out on all the commotion around him.

Though he never called out an order and hardly even glanced up at the sticks—though every step of the tacking from putting the helm down to swinging the yards to trimming the sails, was left entirely up to Wood Haskett and me—he still had that air of command about him, that broadness of shoulder and squareness of jaw that gave the idea he was at the helm of events; and all hands still looked upon him as skipper—uncharacteristically wooden on deck, but just the same steadier and calmer than in those hectic weeks riding up to San Francisco Bay. That I was determining the day's work and doing all

the navigating, even plotting our course from my own resources—
duties he never would of wholly handed over—no one else knew,
since Haskett was always on deck when I was below; but even if word
had got around, no one would of been too condemning; for all hands
knew the load Ben'd carried since China, the depth of the bond he'd
had with Jim, and the challenges piling up for him at home; and
nobody would of blamed him for slipping under the burden.

Shorthanded, overworked, and heartsore theirselves, every last
one of them related some way or other to the men we'd lost—not
censuring Ben for his extraordinary efforts to find them, in fact
ready to stand up for him when he took the heat in port—they made
way now for his depression of spirit, thinking it the natural outcome
of his failed drive; and of the lot of us who looked on in concern,
only I really feared for him.

By the time we'd crossed the Line and commenced heading
down to cooler latitudes—by the time the crew'd started overhauling
their gear in the dog watch, greasing their boots and lining their pea
jackets with flannel, or making sou'westers that could stand up to the
wind and hail of Cape Horn—he'd begun to complain of pain, hot,
tearing pangs which attacked his back and legs, making it hard for
him to stand and walk; but this too he managed at first to downplay,
taking to the deck with laudanum if he had to, even resorting to his
bolted chair. Hobbling about on the poop on Jim's cane, one hand
on the line we'd triced up for rough days, or sitting all of a heap near
the helm, a blanket about him to keep out the wind, he wore the
same vacant gaze he'd worn since the Bay, the same empty air as
an uninhabited house, or a shell abandoned by its guest; though a
close look at his face showed the eyes of some prey still alive to the
darts and swoops of a beak. Sleeping poor with the pain he felt his
shoulders go next, his arms aching so he could scarcely carry a dish,
and his fingers stiffly lame like one long gone to rheumatics; but even
so he managed to rise every day, and show up on deck at the call for
all hands.

Still caught up in the tragedy that had befallen—wrapped up
too in the concerns of doubling the Horn, on a short-handed ship
heavy-laden with cargo—the crew made shift to work around him;

while Haggai stepped in and filled some of the roles that would of otherwise been thrown to me. The ship without a steward—and too reduced in numbers to spare one—him and Orin carried on the bulk of the work aft; and freed to absorb more of Ben's captainly tasks, I tried not the let them see the true state he was in, always putting papers before him when they cleaned his cabin, or closing his door when they swept the saloon. But when, after six weeks or so from San Francisco Bay—when about the time we lay off Valparaiso, he took to his berth, in too much pain to sit up, it had to be known he was incapacitated; and carefully I let the word out, never hinting how serious off he was, or how long his illness was likely to last, since I hadn't the faintest notion myself.

Not wanting anyone to suppose I had designs on the helm—not wanting to add one speck of further legal complications, and loath, anyhow, to take Ben's place, or to impair his future reputation—I simply kept on in my capacity as mate, as if it was a question of his being laid low for a spell; while the rest fell in with my example, no one taking matters more seriously than I intended. It was simply a matter of the captain's being ill, with some malady known to science, if not us; simply a matter of the mates carrying on to the best of their know-how, a situation that might happen aboard any vessel, in fact that had already happened to us, when he took coast fever on the Indian Ocean. The entire purpose and training aboard Melchett ships was such that the whole went on despite loss to its parts; and mindful of that, we went on pretty much as before, though without a song at the windlass or halyards—the seas getting longer, the days growing shorter, the temperature crisper, and our time, though slower, still steady enough to fetch us a passage.

But when he begun wandering as if in fever, just as we dug in to double the Horn—when he would go drifting back to the San Francisco Bay hills, or rambling on about the plant life he'd seen at the mission—there was no way to hide from those that come aft that we'd lost him; and it was only a question of time till word worked its way forward, and added to the burden of hardship and winter. When I could I sat by him, trying to get him to see me, to make him realize his loss, or the loved ones and responsibilities that still blessed him;

but in answer—if he was even coherent—he simply reckoned up for the hundredth time Jim's stocks, and how long they might last if they was rationed.

"Anotheh keg o' hardtack," he'd chafe, "I should've put aboard two… What possible good did I think I could do with just one?"; then fretfully he'd add, "More wadeh—should've stowed anotheh cask of that too; how long d'ye think it'd last, if they stahted t' ration it as soon as they knew they was lost?" "What day is it now?" meant not what day was it by the calendar—not Sept. 1, 1844—but what day from June 2nd, the day they rowed off—the 91st; then would come recollections of all the accounts of open boats at sea that he carried around in his head, dozens of details and data, him being a champion at such like: thirty days one and forty-two another and fifty-four, the longest he'd ever heard. The other gear he'd stowed in the boat—the compass and sextant, canvas and bucket, the flare, hook and line—he'd take inventory of, wondering if the men'd caught any fish, and trying to remember how frequently it'd rained; then he'd take them to task direct, warning them to keep the chronometer dry, and the canvas inverted over the bucket at night.

Wracked stem to stern myself by Jim's loss—by the knowledge of what he'd be called upon to endure, even if he was ever picked up—I hadn't the heart to shake him out of his drift, to force him to see ahead, rather than back; so I simply set by him and petted him with my hand, trying to reassure him in some way. What I would do for him if he didn't emerge from his daze —what was wrong with him in the first place, beyond the sheer confusion of grief—I was past knowing, being a plain village doctor; but what was happening to Jim was more real than anything else around him—more real than hisself, or the pitch and roll of Cape Horn; and I could only stand by him and wait.

Only once did he show the slightest awareness of what was actually taking place around him; and even that betrayed him in the end. It was off the Diego Ramirez Islands, after nine or ten days of hellish weather—after ten days of head winds instead of the looked-for fair, which even at gale force would of blown us round easy; and I struggled to make headway like I'd never struggled before when he was on deck, and I had the security of simply following his orders. Staggering under the sweep of his duties—faced with the constant run of repairs, and the press of decisions affecting us all, from how far south to beat before risking ice, to whether or not to strike the topgallant masts, safety arguing for it, speed and the cargo against— I'd been borne down by the responsibilities he'd shouldered, especially since I had to admit I'd failed to carry them as well, with the same seagoing instinct and genius.

A saltwater plodder by dint of my nature—a fisherman rather than a sailor, with more of a knack for what lay on the bottom than for what was going on on top—I hadn't his art for swinging a yardarm at just the right moment, when the cant of the wind did most of the work for you; hadn't his hang for trimming the sails, or feeling ahead for the right slant of wind; hadn't his uncanny gift for direction, or his ability to dead reckon, the days without a sighting becoming more frequent as we worked our way deeper into the snow squalls, and my anxiety mounting as to our true position. On tenterhooks we'd come too far south, and was in danger of running amuck with the ice fields, I'd finally caved in and called on Spooner, who in an unprecedented move came aft to double check my work with me; but even so my worry persisted, there being not another sail in sight that I could speak for a swap of latitudes.

When at last one noon around mid-September we raised our first island, an immense crag of ice, indigo blue almost to its peak, and rocking in stately, solitary motion; when soon after we fetched its smaller companions, and confirming my worst fears, a whole field in the distance—I felt myself snapping under their mute threat; felt myself snapping as though they was Ben's fault, as though they wouldn't of appeared if he'd been on deck. Marching below I strode over to his bed, and shook him awake as if he was a child; shook him by the shoulder even after he moaned in pain, and begun to stir under the mat of the covers. "Ben, get up," I commanded, still shaking angrily away, and stomping my foot as though that would help; "get up on deck—thehre's ice all round us; I can't do this without ye—I need ye, Gawd damn it."

To my surprise he obeyed—painfully got up on one elbow, then old habit coming to the fore, found his clothes layered nearby, and pulled them on, lastly hauling on his tarpulin coat and sou-wester, even remembering to hold out his wrists to be lashed; and on deck for a moment he looked like the old Ben, scanning the snow-blur with one hand on the shrouds, and the ice-caked rigging rising around him. But the next thing I knew my hopes was dashed, and I seen all at once I really was on my own—the crew, fed by rumor so far, in one swift glance seeing it too; for the minute he spotted his first cake of ice he cried, not the directions I sought to work us free—not "Sheet home the mains'l" or "Hard up the helm"—but joyfully, jubilantly "Loweh the laddeh! It's them—thank Gawd, it's them!"; and Wood Haskett looking on him aghast, I took him by the arm and steered him back below.

For the rest of the night and following day I shuttled nonstop between him and the deck—between the frigid hazards that threatened the ship, and the raging heat that burned at his brow; for he was in fever now as if the sight of the ice, and the final smash of his sudden hope, had all at once sprung its long-delayed flame. Thinking that if I could just get him home, back home to Maine where familiar surroundings and the honest, confiding faces of young ones might help to heal his broken senses, I battled to bring the ship on her heel, inching her north with the whole crew on the lookout; then back below I ducked for brief spells to bathe him with snow I'd scooped from the deck, or bow my head over him in his daze.

To me it almost seemed—listening helplessly at his side, trying to make sense of the tumbling phrases, or the requests that sometimes come hurling at me—as if he'd somehow taken Jim's place; as if he was feeling what Jim felt, or what he'd felt earlier on in the summer; as if in some unaccountable way Jim was speaking through his voice, relaying some drama on the other side of the Pacific. "It's hot," he'd fret, when all above him on deck the ship hung in a forest of icicles, and the temperature in his cabin hovered at thirty; when the men's hands was splitting from the cold, and their feet breaking out in boils from the constant wetting in bitter water.

Or "It's too still; damn the wind; whehre's the wind," he'd chafe, with *Abigail* half over on her beam ends in the gale, and the thunderous sea-bolts pounding at the hull. "I'm thirsty," he'd crack, and I'd give him water, breaking the layer of ice in his pitcher; but no amount I poured could ever satisfy his need; for no sooner would I clamp the cup back in place than "I'm thirsty" would commence all over again. Hunger, fatigue and pain was equally impossible to relieve; and way out of my depth I could only stroke his hand, and clumsily try to reassure him—Haggai unquestioningly taking over the task and carrying on, whenever I had to look out for her on deck.

As I stooped over him them next days off the Horn, rubbing snow on his brow or listening or praying, I seen for the first time the changes in his face; seen them as I hadn't had time to before, in all the pain and rush of the past months. Looking pretty rugged now from his long spell of neglect, his hair and beard overgrown like all the rest of ours was too, he wasn't unlike some loafer on the docks, worn out and down at the heels and seedy; but what caught my eye wasn't the rough angles he shared with us—that look a carving has when it's only half-finished—but the expression of age, of capsize in the dim light.

Not thirty yet, he nonetheless looked forty, with all them chisels and lines you see on an old face, a face that's stood up to the battering of time and the weather, yet taken on their scrapes the way scrog takes the wind, or the pulp of a tree the rain-rings and dry spells. But more than that he showed surrender, like a ship's beam does when it starts to powder, or a figurehead when it commences to crumble. Looking at him bulky and senseless there in his berth, it was almost like stumbling on some plank on the scrap heap, some board that's been jettisoned as unfit for its task, or set aside to be planed over; like coming on a snowman that's been kicked down by a child, or a lump of clay that's been worked and mashed over.

No terror I'd known over sickness or death was anything like the fear I now felt, as I sat and looked on his derelict timbers: even his lung fever a year ago seeming almost pacific, for that at worst would of ended in merciful death; while this had no end that I could foresee, save some darkly barred asylum window. As if he knew hisself that he was done up—as if he knew he was an unfit timber, he mumbled the terms of his own surrender; murmured "Nothin' I c'n do… nothin' I c'n do… nothin' I cn' do…" till I ached for him, till I longed to take charge of him myself. Other times it was verses from the Bible he spoke, verses I recognized from Sabbath Schools long ago, or texts I had to memorize for meeting; lines from both Testaments of capitulation and loss, not loss of battle or land but of self; but no words come more often than Jeremiah's, not Jeremiah the fighter but Jeremiah the accepting, Jeremiah the stalwart on the scrap heap. For long hours one night I listened to such lines, the hop and skip of images of destruction and re-making, from the basket of figs to the clay on the wheel; then come the quiet "Do with me what you will"; and after that he lay there silent.

If I was fearing for him I was fearing as well for the ship; for she rode them vast seas like a millet seed, a speck—a wisp on whose helm lay my inexperienced hand. Free of the ice we begun at last to run down the torturous miles of our easting, still facing unaccountable head winds, and snow squalls so thick we could barely make out the masts; but it was the giant seas that unmanned my wits, great rolling, darksome, heavy masses, at whose heights we pitched in the blasts of the spray, and in whose pits we reeled without the brace of the wind.

With only eight hands to a watch and the work on deck heavy— with the sails frozen solid and stiff as sheet metal, and the rigging so encased that to start it with bare hands, or to climb it with clumsy, waterlogged boots was a perpetual risk and torture—we was obliged to frequently call both watches; and it was rare for any of us to rest more than a couple hours. Beaten out by the work and exposure the men hardly ever exchanged a word, pacing back and forth on walks made of sand, or ashes taken from the galley; while nobody ever spoke with me either, Ben in his berth dreaming faraway dreams, and Haggai bustling from pantry to galley.

Spinning out twenty hours a day in darkness—straining to hear the ship's needs in the wind, whole choruses of shrieks, moans and whistles roaring in chaotic upheaval—I missed Ben's command like never before, like I'd never thought possible, on old exasperated days; missed his bark, his bawl, his sense of control, the sheer bulk and size of him in the dark. If I could of I would of stood him on deck just for my sake—for the illusion of his protection; but without him I had to come to trust someone; and I found I was dumbly trusting the ship—giving her her head as if she had a will of her own, as if she had eyes that could make out our way—even conversing with her as if she was alive, and could answer me back with a human voice. In fact she did answer me back with sounds, motions, shudders—with progress or lurches or sags to leeward; and I took to actually talking to her out loud—to taking myself seriously whilst I did it, as though I was any less mad than Ben was.

When after a fortnight of struggle we'd finally rounded the Horn and the seas had begun to moderate a little, I fell into a sleep like I'd never had, Spooner kindly standing my watch so I might have twelve hours; and coming back up on deck—finding us bound north once again—the first sound I heard was the hurrah of the men, echoing from the heights of the mainyard, and their song that we was homeward bound at last.

It was just at this time, in about the 58th latitude, as we made ready to run between Patagonia and the Falklands, that Ben gave me the greatest scare of all; and my hopes that he might finally be coming round a little was stove in like a plank on a rockbed. For the past couple of days he'd actually been sitting up, and feeding hisself from Haggai's trays; and I'd come in just the night before to find he'd been up, and fished out Jim's trunk from its nook in the locker. Though the lid was open, things looked to be in place, except for Jim's unmended shirt, which'd been on top, and was missing; and I soon seen Ben'd put it by his pillow, and was sleeping with it the way a child does with a bit of blanket. Seeing how it eased him—how just its nearness seemed to bring peace, the kind of healing sleep he needed—I let it go; just as I'd let go his fetching the log and opening it to Jim's hand earlier this morning.

But now come a strange, uncanny evening, all the weirder for the goings-on about the ship; for somewheres nearby in the long, dark, regular seas, a shoal of whales or grampuses was meeting, invisible except for their breathing; and the sudden reports and gusts of their vapors, rising and falling like the heave of the seas, exploded and sighed in the still night around us. As if that wasn't enough, wisps of fog was trailing about like shrouds and scarves in all directions, the water being warmer than the air; and down below in the forecastle and cabins, eerie noises was drumming in through the hull, whistles and cries like some long-lost mariner's soul, wailing and railing for some deck or haven.

Loosened by the thaw, the ice aloft'd begun cracking, adding to the unnerving clamor; and whole masses and chunks was thundering down on unsuspecting heads without warning. Tumbling up on deck the watch below complained of being unable to sleep; and going below myself for a late cup of tea, I could see at a glance that Haggai was spooked. Not that it was all that grand a feat to spook Haggai: he was, after all, the same man who, when a bolt of lightning once struck a cask of brandy in the general store, took it as an act of the Almighty, and swore off drink forever. But there was plainly something of a large order going on in him now, for he was popeyed as a flounder; and I felt uneasy myself when I seen him.

Coming into the lighted saloon, and finding my tea set sanely at my place at the table, the cup sliding to and fro a little, and the spoon giving a friendly clank with each ride, suddenly cheered me up a degree; but the next moment my heart gave an odd thud; for I seen a light under Ben's door, and the flicker of him moving back and forth; and there come out to me the strains of bright talking that struck me as being not at all natural. Sweeping in with some biscuits, Haggai threw a nod at his room, with "He's up t' some funny business in thehre, mate; asked for a sack o' the pigs' straw, an' I brung it; an' now he's just sent for a pot o' tea, though he wouldn't let me serve it." Thanking him for his vigilance I passed up my own tea, and went and stood by Ben's door for a minute, listening to his hectic chatter; then deciding not to knock, I turned the knob and walked in.

At once I seen he was up and dressed, and looking unaccountably well, despite the dry glitter to his eyes; but my heart, about to rejoice, completely stopped at what I seen next; for there, sitting at the desk, before the cup that only he used, was Jim. Though his back was to me, and he wore his straw hat, the build was unmistakably his; while the red checkered shirt, the white Sunday duck trowsers, the pumps, even the stockings proclaimed him as well. Too walloped to move, or even utter a croak, I just stood there looking at him; but Ben, undeterred, brightly chirped out a greeting, adding "Bring in youhr tea, mate, an' join us."

My heart starting up again in my chest, thumping on with painful lurches and jolts—my wits gradually coming to life in my head, and clanking back into gear with clumsy strokes—I seen that what I'd taken for Jim was a sort of straw man Ben'd made of Jim's clothes, the broad-brimmed hat overshadowing his face; seen next that what Ben'd set out for him was a kind of feast, with half a dozen glasses and decanters and plates—tea, coffee, chowder, tidbits from his own supper, and above all water crowded before him; and not any less stunned than if he was real, I struggled to find what was left of my voice.

"Ben, this won't do," I said, quavering in my heart, but speaking out hard and firm as I could—somehow knowing I must, or risk losing him forever. "This is dangerous…. This ain't Jim, an' you know it."

His eyes—as if stirring, but resisting waking—stared out at me uncertainly in his dumb hurt; but I kept steadily on with my effort. "Only Gawd makes a man…The only life this man's got is in you. Now take it apaht, an' put these things away: if Jim eveh makes it home, he'll need them; if he don't, they d'serve t' be treated with respect, an' left t' rest."

To my surprise his eyes come all the way present, as if he craved my taking command—as if he'd been wanting me all along to take charge, and 'd just been waiting for me to do it; and he obediently nodded, signing he wanted me to do the job. "No, you do it," I stood firm, speaking to him as though he was a child; "you put him t'gether, you take him apahrt; I'll come back an' help ye put things away."

To start him I instinctively begun clearing the drinks, setting all the glasses back on the tray; but as if this was too much—the great crux of the evening, more critical even than his need for Jim's presence—he cried out in protest, "No, no—he's thirsty—he's thirsty—ye can't take these away, he needs them"; and he clutched at the drinks, gathering up the glasses, and tugging pitifully at the decanter. Aghast, wrung with pity, I looked down at his hands, seeing them for the first time in all these long weeks of trial—seeing how their big, square, work-hardened shapes trembled and shook now, as if with old age; and collapsing myself I simply dropped down on the floor by him, and wept with him while he rocked in my arms.

"He's not thirsty anymore, Ben—it's been too long—it's oveh," I sobbed, rejoicing in my heart even as I wept that he'd said "He's thirsty," not "I'm thirsty" as he had in the beginning; "he's eitheh gone, or he's safe; he's not thirsty anymore." Nodding his head at my shoulder he simply wept on, wrenching out his weeks of pain and torture; and when at last he was quiet I left him alone to his task, and went and sat by my cold tea at the table. When I come back I found he'd put everything away in Jim's trunk, except for the straw, which was back in Haggai's sack; and tiptoeing over to his berth I seen he was asleep, without Jim's unmended shirt by his pillow.

Now he begun at last to mend; but he was so run down from prolonged fever and grief, lack of food and erratic sleep, that if possible he was even weaker than before, resting quietly for long spells in his berth, and trying to bring his thoughts up to the present. Every now and again he seemed to know where we was, with a more or less connected train of how we'd got here; but for the most part he was limp and inert as a newborn, taking in what he could in brief snatches, then falling asleep all at once from the effort.

In this state he continued all the way up to the Line; and by that time I knew I'd be at the helm to the end, and had no choice but to order the rest of the voyage. Getting *Abigail* ready for port—scraping her and painting her from the maintruck to the waterline, setting up and tarring the standing rigging, all them hundreds of painstaking physical jobs that needed to be seen to after a long voyage—this sort of thing I knew I could handle, having done it under Ben so many times that I had the whole scenario down pat; but the colossal matter of Ben's documents—the monumental task of his papers: *that* I quailed before like the plague.

Heretofore his desk was the one thing I hadn't touched, as if it was the seat of command of the whole ship, and my intruding upon it would abuse his power; but now, with port three weeks away and Customs looming, I couldn't put it off any longer; and I went through ledgers and drawers from top to bottom, partly to have everything ready for inspection, but more importantly to find out where we legally stood. My heart low, I had a pretty good idea about the latter, even before I broached files and looked up court data; but I soon found matters was even worse than I feared; and up to my elbows one October Line noon, I paused to sip my daily test of the cargo, and take stock of the evidence mounting before me.

First off, there was all the ship's official papers, locked up in a tin safe that could be grabbed in an instant: her certificate of registry and bill of health and sea letter, her bill of lading and manifest and so forth; and amongst them I come upon her certified list of owners—my initial clue that all was not well. It was the first time I realized that both Joseph and Galen had invested in an eighth of the ship—that a percentage of any profit from the freight was automatically owed to their estates, which put Ben in an awkward position with his kin if the tea failed. It was the first time as well I discovered that another eighth was owned by Isaac Howland of Portland—Sal's father and a tough customer, not likely to take a mild view of any lost revenue, especially with all the bones of contention that stood betwixt the Howlands and Melchetts. Though another eighth was mine, and the rest was owned by Ben and Melchett Bros., there was enough of a mess between family, business and in-laws to keep Ben in hot water the rest of the decade; and that was even before taking a look at the owners of the freight.

Thumbing through the mass of freight data, first from Canton, then from Honolulu, I seen how many hands was in the pie of this cargo: Ben having invested in a quarter of the tea, but almost a dozen other entrepreneurs having a hand in the other three quarters, the consignee being Hull and Lombard, the biggest mercantile house in the area, which would demand it in top condition. In addition there was the cargo sold in Honolulu—miscellaneous goods from several sources in Portland—and the odds and ends picked up from the Sandwich Islands, the lot posted to half a dozen local consignees;

so that figuring out percentages of freight and profit, not to mention the tally of Ben's primage, was an undertaking for a genius, even if the main cargo wasn't in condition for sale.

And finally there was the matter of the logbooks: me going all the way back to Canton, and finding our records even worse than I'd thought—the personal log in a jumble of hands, and the official log, though thank God all in Ben's hand and mine, with no interlineations or erasures, nonetheless full of the damning evidence of the deviations, with little or no explanation. Hastily looking things up in Ben's legal dictionaries—wading through all the morass of hypothecating the ship, suing *in personam* or *in rem*, the lot making me lose my appetite for supper—I tried to reckon up where we stood; but the bottom line seemed to be that deviation from course was permissible only in succoring persons in distress, or in case of storms, repairs, or enemy fire, the latter clauses not remotely applicable to us; and to me it looked doubtful whether even John Melchett, up to his eyeballs in settling Joseph's and Galen's estates, could make it stand up in court that our intent to succor our men was the same as our actually succoring them in distress.

Since the insurance on the tea was only valid if we strictly adhered to course, or could show permissible cause of deviation, Ben was liable not only for a stiff fine for wrongful prosecution of the voyage, but for the entire loss of the cargo as well, if the tea failed; and his health being what it was, with the whole crew in the know, there was nothing to prevent him from being sued for mental incompetence as well—me likely to be the chief person called to testify against him in that case. Daily testing the tea, finding it weaker and staler, I knew the only answer was to make port post haste, the voyage already two months longer than we'd expected; and so hellbent was my efforts to keep the sails rap full and every conceivable square inch drawing that all hands on board, from Spooner on down, informed me I was an even worse driver than Ben.

Maybe it was my day at Ben's desk, maybe Ben's illness and the loss of our men; or maybe it was some instinctive vision of greater matters at work outside us; but as we made our concerted run from the Line—

as I looked out from the quarterdeck on all the inter-workings below me—I sensed in my heart that things was about at an end. Though we was going great guns beneath the Gulf Stream cloud banks, and all hands was zestfully manning their stations—though Ben was up on deck now nearby me, out in the sun when there was sun to be had, taking the air from his bolted chair—there was something about all the design and hope of the past, all the achievement and loss of the present, that made me see into the future; something that gave me a degree of perspective about where we was now, and where we was headed.

Like a man on a height, I seen that if we was making good time now, it wasn't just because of my newfound efforts, but because of Melchett principles and methods; because so many of us knew each other's jobs that we could interchange parts and press on; and because we was all kin, shareholders in both the ship and the cargo, and so was committed to mutual success, even in the face of failure. Standing from here, I felt detached enough from the past to see we was part of something unique, part of an endeavor that, despite the perils of legal embroilments and snarl ups, was streamlined and noble and direct, the best tradition of our new country; part of a venture that I could feel in my bones was about to depart forever.

Yet, though I could see for myself where we was heading; though it was plain that bigger ships, manned by a hodgepodge of crews, was going to pander to freights in tramp ports, freights no one aboard had a hand in, any more than they had a hand in the ship; though it was clear that local ventures would gradually cease to be, we still had this voyage, this magnificent vessel, that no portent could take away or diminish; and by some contrariness of nature, if ever I'd felt like a ship master—if ever I'd felt pride in any enterprise that was mine—it was now, on the brink of departure and failure.

Skimming along the Atlantic Coast, standing for a spell longer in Ben's shoes, I seen that this was what it was about, then, this skip and glimmer of possession, this triumphant clockwork of the moment; got a glimpse of his eyes and seen that he knew—that he knew I felt his joy, and looked ahead to the same end. As if all hands aboard somehow shared it all too, our own inevitable failure, yet the supreme success of the moment, the crew pulled together as never before, like men in one last energetic rush of farewell; and at last, on the twelfth of November, ten months from the date we'd set out, we raised Monhegan and the Isles of Mussel Ridge Channel, and hove into Cape Damaris harbor.

Up and dressed and more or less in his right mind, Ben walked down the gangplank under his own power—so worn and thin that Anne's face went white when she seen him; but before she and the rest of his kin could sweep aboard, we was immediately besieged by the families of the missing men, whose craving for news told us more plain than any words that none of them had yet been heard from. Answering their tumult and addressing their needs, which fell naturally enough to Ben, was hard even after our months' preparation; and I waited with held breath to see how he'd weather it, this his first test of authority and reason. Though he must of hoped against hope that by some freak of chance the men'd already turned up, or sent word safe and sound from some Pacific port, there was nothing in his still face that showed his shock; nothing in his quiet sympathy that showed he couldn't bear their loss as well as anyone else, or in his answers that showed lack of logic and order; and I hovered beside him half-fearful, half-awed.

Nor was our tidings the only news that'd happened, all this long passage of time from home; for in the midst of the usual jumble of launchings and clearings, or accounts of elections and a new President, come tales of new faces added to families, or the reports of sudden losses or the inroads of consumption; and all around us was faces wreathed in joy or sorrow, or half-froze in the expressionless look of numb silence, trying to take in the myriad changes.

In their midst swept up Anne with a new babe in her arms, not her child and Ben's but his brother Jared's, who'd married Sally Wingate last year, and sailed with her for the West Indies just a couple of months after we'd cleared. Before I could stop her or intervene to prepare him, she broke the news of their double loss, to yellow fever in Havana—John having sailed down and brung home little Rebecca, whom Jared in his last words 'd given to Ben. Filled with fear that the news would send Ben under again, I simply stood dumbly by at his elbow, looking at the little lass as Anne held her out to him; but the news somehow had the opposite effect that I'd feared; for he took her in his arms in all that pandemonium of homecoming and cradled her to his cheek as if she was the only one in the world—as if he found in their mutual loss of loved ones a kinship that went beyond blood and law. Kissing her wee face, he said to me, in the first coherent sentence he'd spoken in months, "Look how silky her hair is…Jim would of loved her."

Word was soon running rampant about our own voyage, Ben's breakdown and the condition of the tea; but before Anne could get wind I steered her and Ben off the wharf, folks respectfully making way for them and their child, in a wordless show of sympathy for their grief; and soon after we was deluged by the rest of Ben's young ones, who'd broke away from Sadie's grip at the carriage. Whilst he was inundated by them like a surfman by a wave—whilst Tom and Jean was hopping about on his toes, spilling out wildly exaggerated tales of their own return voyage—I took Anne to one side for a minute; and very careful of my words I told her of his illness, and advised her to allow him a week of rest at my cabin, especially in view of the news he'd just had. Since she could see with her own eyes the sense of my request, she gave me a nod with very little fuss; and it was to my place we pulled up a quarter hour later, the chimney a-smoke under the bare wintry trees.

For a while it was bedlam, Sadie stoking up the fire she'd earlier started, when the telegraph signals'd posted our arrival; me and Anne hauling in chests and seabags and boxes; the children swarming up wall and down stair rail, or bouncing their new sister till she howled; and Ben standing dumbly in the midst of it all, till at last he drew up a chair to the fire, and set down with small Becky in his lap. After tea and an exchange of the usual stories, Sadie and Anne swept out the children, with promises to send them for visits one by one; and before long the place was blissfully silent, the fire snapping and crackling on the hearth, and the sea droning distantly on out the windows. Giving Ben my room—knowing there was no way he could bear the sight of Jim's upstairs—I soon had him established, and a chowder going for our supper; and for that night at least we had peace and quiet, and protection from the ill winds that was brewing.

Within a day or two the whole story was out, and the principal actors in it was moving—Hull and Lombard ordering Ben to break bulk, so that they could examine the tea; Isaac Howland taking the steamer from Portland; an insurance adjustor on his way down from Boston; and Melchett Bros. demanding first crack at the log. By the end of a month, when all the dust'd settled—when the tea'd been rejected as I'd expected, and the insurance withheld pending investigations—Ben was served by half a dozen papers, and the trial set in a Court of Admiralty for spring. In between there was mostly talk and speculation, there seldom having been, in the hundred-odd years of the town, a more toothsome series of events to explore; for since the actual legal wheels ground slowly, talk was the only way to keep things in motion, or at any rate, to keep up the illusion of such.

To some, like the families of the missing men, and even a few of those who'd lost out on the tea—Eli Shields amongst them, a long-time friend and backer—Ben was nothing short of a hero; and they as fully supported his decisions at sea as though they'd ended in success. To others, like Melchett Bros.—which remained loyal, but which I knew'd privately censured Ben for the San Francisco Bay run—and some of the charterers of the tea who'd decided to withhold legal action, Ben was simply a man trapped by circumstance and dilemma, who'd done the best anyone could of done, and failed; and to others still, like Isaac Howland, who was a straight-out businessman of the old school, and Hull and Lombard, who had no use for exceptions, Ben was liable for wrongful prosecution of the voyage—unless it could be showed he was mentally incompetent, which was hardly an alternative worth cheering.

Acting as Ben's agent as much as I could, to spare him some of the conjecture and talk, I watched every word that come out of my mouth, with an eye to how it might turn up later on; while Spooner and Wood Haskett followed suit—the three of us having laid plans, even before *Abigail* made port, to protect Ben to the utmost by keeping our words few, as we'd certainly be held accountable in court. Up to the ceiling in Joseph's and Galen's estates—now embarking on Jared's estate as well—John took on Ben's case, and spent long afternoons with us, going over the log and advising us; but how much any of it really meant to Ben, I would of been hard put to say. Throughout all his business he was stoic and quiet, in a sort of a numb state that neither hurt nor helped him; showed up on time, sanely dressed, in his grey coat, with his tin box and spectacles and fresh pens. But he never once, in John's office or out of it, let drop a remark that opened him to me; and I had no more idea what was going on in his head than I had of what might be running through a haddock's.

If he stood up to matters—if he carried things off with no worse an impression that that of a man recovering from long fatigue and fever—it was largely on account of his stay at my place, where the quiet assurance of familiar surroundings gradually seemed to give him some grip; and —more important still—on account of his children, who come by every day one by one to play with him, or to sit on his lap and confide their thoughts. Anne, too, in her own way, with her household news and social doings—with her consideration in not hurrying him, and her tact regarding his business matters, not to mention his loss of Jim, an event which couldn't possibly of grieved her any—was a steady help; while the whole Melchett family from Sarah on down, and old cronies like Jimmy or Bill Worthing, did their part in shoring him up.

But nobody took him out of hisself and brung him to awareness again like his newly adopted daughter Becky, who at eight or nine months was an appealing armful; for he seemed determined to live up to her need, as if she held out some invisible measure; and frequently I guessed, as I watched him play with her, that he was pretending she was his child and Jim's, just as Jim'd often pretended the same thing with Nat.

Having sent out letters to government officials, the harbor masters in New York and Boston, and various consuls in the Pacific begging for news of the missing men, and having received no word by Christmas; having no ship on the stocks, and no ship to captain— *Abigail* in effect grounded till spring, and the time too short anyway to undertake a voyage—he was without something to do for the first time in his life; and this more than anything else seemed to weigh on him, though he never said so out loud.

With Galen's bequest, and dividends that come in periodically from investments like *Charis,* he had money for the present, though by no means enough to meet the liabilities he faced, if he failed to carry the day in court; had his family, his friends, the yard just as before—Melchett Bros. even trying to interest him in a new contract, though they must of had reservations about him. But in spite of the forces working for him, to me he looked directionless and lost—not desperately lost like he had on the Pacific, or those weeks at his desk leading up to Cape Horn, but patiently lost like a ship on the bar, waiting for tides and tow ropes and lighters. There was a blankness to his eyes in place of the old will and drive that persisted even when he played with Becky—a vagueness that recalled a fog mull at sun-up; a total lack of the old bluster and order that'd driven me to drink when he was sailing master, but which I would of given my own wages for now.

Though I knew he was wrestling with the question of what course to chart on land or sea; though I could see he was trying to decide when to move back to his own house, whether to sail again or to build, and how to salvage his reputation as a credible master and shipwright, he seemed unable to make choices; and by year's end he hadn't even moved out of my place. From time to time he tentatively ventured out, like a hermit crab scuttling to a new shell—though never far from the safety of the old; and I'd find him upstairs reading in Jim's room, or out in the stable taking care of Dee, who like him was patiently waiting.

But once, hard on Christmas, I come home from town and found him gone from the house altogether—neither upstairs in Jim's room nor in the barn; found Dee missing too, and the cutter; and on a hunch I turned tail and rode back into town, and spotted horse and sleigh outside the Inn. Stepping inside and running into Jimmy— elbowing late afternoon travelers leaving the dining saloon, and early comers on their way down to the tavern—I climbed up to the third floor for the first time since we'd made port; and marching up to Jim's old door, I knocked—Ben, after a moment's surprise, inviting "Come in."

He hadn't been there long—I could see that by his face, which had the look of a man who's just waked up at sea, with no recollection of how he got there. There was bewilderment on his features, and cautious fear, and delight—all the poignant pain of a hundred associations; and the tentative air of one trying to adjust. He was sitting on the well-worn sofa, before a fire he'd built up on the hearth; but there was no sign of a phantom-like guest nearby him to unsettle my anxious heart—just the cheerful clutter and culch of Jim's things that made me ache myself to see. If I felt Jim's presence, Ben did far more keenly, for his face was a mirror of my hurt; and his hand on the stray jersey he'd drawn into his lap quivered and shook like a limb gone to palsy.

Before I could speak up and urge him to come home with me, he looked round the room and met my eyes; and his lips trembling with the effort, he spoke. "I just… don't know whehre in the world t' go without him," he said hollowly, looking round again as if the walls held some clue, or the jumble of clothes a binnacle pointer. "I've tried, but every time I get hold of an idear, it just slips through my hand like sand."

My heart heavy with the weight of my feeling, I pulled up a chair and set down close to him, so near that our knees was almost touching; but not wanting to crowd him I said nothing in return, simply looked at him and waited gently.

"I… I loved him so, Eben, an' I neveh told him… if I'd even done *that,* I could go somewhehre now, an' staht new…without this ache that stops me." His hand left the jersey and clutched at his chest like it had last year in them spells of stress; and watching its taut shape, I made up my mind.

"Would it help ye t' know that he loved you too?" I offered, not taking my eyes off of his features.

Looking up, he studied my face, as if trying to reckon just what I meant; then letting his glance fall, he tugged at the jersey. "If y' mean that he loved me as a friend," he said hoarsely, "I knew that."

"You know full well what I mean," I said steadily, still looking hard at him; and I waited till he slowly raised his eyes again, and met mine.

For a moment there was simply a dumb look to his face, a wondering look, half-numb, half-dazed; then color sprang to his cheeks for the first time since Hilo, a sharpness to his eyes that was wonderful to see; and an eager shyness took hold of his manner till he shook for all the world like a fourteen-year-old, meeting with success at some country shuffle. "He told you that?" he came at me, ardent.

"Didn't have to," I said dryly, "since I hadn't been born dumb; but he did, aye."

"When?" he pressed me, the word tumbling out, and his eyes shot with the light of a man who hears his hopes met out loud.

"When? Well, that'd be—just b'fore he shipped for Havaner with Tom, two years ago this past fall," I answered, half-fearful I'd opened the door to fresh hurt, half-hoping I'd given him a lifeline to hang onto. "He swore me t' keep it to myself; but now that ye've spoken, I know he would, if he was here."

"Two yeahrs ago," he marveled, eyes hearkening swiftly back to days oft-thumbed, as if he tested each for the testimony imagined so far only in his heart.

"He's loved you from the minute he laid eyes on ye at Toby's, nigh onto three yearhs ago now," I smiled, "not less."

His eyes bright and hot, he held onto my words, the weary hues of his face all a-bask, like some cloud-wrack in March when the sun beckons through. "How could he of been so sure," he murmured, "an' me so slow—why, I neveh once, till—we was in Portland last yeahr b'fore I understood—an' even then, I didn't know what t' do about it."

"Well, he'd had the advantage of experience, I s'pose," I said kindly, meaning only to help him, but realizing immediately my blunder as his eyes shot to search me.

"Then he…he'd gone with others b'fore me," he said, and I could see he'd had his suspicions—could see the jealous glint before he lowered his eyes.

"They only made him sure it was you he wanted, Ben," I said gently, anxiously watching every line of his face.

"Is that how he got sent out by the Rom?" he asked unexpectedly, telling me again he'd done a lot of thinking on his own.

"Aye," I acknowledged, still reading his face.

"I've always wanted t' know, all these years…but he neveh told me; an' I didn't want t' press him."

"He wouldn't of told you till he was sure ye'd accept his feelin's for you. He was terrified you wouldn't—that ye'd send him away like his kin did."

"What…what happened back then, did he tell you the whole story?" he pressed, his hunger for news, and fresh joy for Jim's feelings, winning out over jealousy and hurt.

"Are y' sure you're hale enough t' hear it?" I asked, taking stock of the brilliant red spots on his cheeks, and wondering if looking back was really the best thing for him.

"Oh, Gawd, Eben, don't stop now… You—y' can't imagine how I've waited, how I've wanted t' know him from beginnin' t' end, all this time…"

With his eager gaze on me I cast my mind back—cast it back to the young lad Jim'd been then, that summer's night before he sailed for Havana. "What he told me wasn't much more than a sketch… he was neveh a man of many words, as ye know," I begun, slowly rubbing my brow to ease the ache of my own loss, while Ben leaned ever more eagerly toward me, almost gripping my knees in his anxiety to hear. "But it was him an' his cousin Djemail that got sent out from the Rom together…Djemail bein' the first one t' catch his heart, I would guess. They was just wakin' up t' how they felt about each other; an' they went off one day t' set t'getheh on a hill, I forget its name, overlookin' the lake at Bala, not very fahr from where they was camped."

"Tomen Bala," he said victoriously, as if hearing words hisself from long ago.

"Sounds about right, like I heard it b'fore… One thing sort of led t' anotheh, though nothing much, they was young; but Idris, Djemail's sisteh, who'd followed without their knowin', come upon them there in the holly, an' was surprised at what they was doin'; an' not thinkin', she run back an' told some o' the othehs. Since they was of age, bein' thirteen, they was tried in a court of their elders an' sent out for good…the Rom bein' a lot stricteh about such offenses than ouhr common notion o' them allows."

"I stahted t' guess that's what'd happened t' him," he murmured, now plucking Jim's jersey there in his lap. "It was so plain he could neveh go back to his own people."

"Nor eveh wanted to; he told me that hisself, many times."

"T' think I talked him int' namin' the sloop afteh Idris," he said wryly.

"Oh, he neveh held that against ye," I smiled; "neveh seemed t' harboh hahrd feelin's towards her, at any rate, not since he come hehre…Told me once he blessed her interference, since without it, he'd neveh of met ye."

His face still aglow he looked down at the jersey, smoothing the wrinkled folds of its sleeves. "So that's the story of Djemail," he murmured, his eyes lighted up with eager satisfaction, the kind of light you see in the gaze of an old friend, hearing years of mysteries and puzzles resolved.

"Aye."

I wondered… There was so many times he called on him, those first few months I knew him…at Hannah's, y' know, the night of the fight…and afteh Cuber when he had that feveh… B'sides his fatheh's name, Djemail's was the one I heard most often."

"I shouldn't wondeh; they must of been close, even aside from bein' lovers—thrown t'getheh like dory mates apaht from their people, an' left t' scratch a livin' by their wits."

"Was he with Djemail when he joined the circus?" he asked, as if with a sudden inspiration.

"Aye, the two of them made up an act t'getheh, bareback ridin', as you might expect. I think they kept at it about a yeahr—kept hopin' their folks 'd see their names on the postehs, an' slip int' the tent t' watch 'em perform. But it was a hahd life, the way Jim described it; an' he neveh talked t' me much about it."

"What finally happened, did he eveh say?"

"Djemail took a fall one time from a horse—I guess it broke his neck; he neveh come to again, an' died an oweh or two lateh."

Ben's face went still and tense with the words, as if he hisself could feel them twin losses, loss of people and loss of friend, so early as they come in Jim's life. "Did he leave the circus, then—afteh Djemail...?"

"Not right away, no... An oldeh man there befriended him, not his traineh, but one o' the jugglers, who'd....had an eye on him, ye might say."

He bit his lip as if with envy, but all he said was, still folding the jersey, "So that's whehre he learned t' juggle."

"Aye."

"An' this oldeh man... He was kind t' Jim?"

"I s'pose he was, in an uneddicated way," I said, choosing my words carefully as I went, and trying not to fluster him by noticing his flushed cheeks, or telling him any more than need be. "But he must of been the possessive sort, or so he come across in Jim's talk; an' you c'n about guess how that went oveh with Jamie... since he runs a mile when his freedom's in dangeh. So he packed up one day, hopped the cars t' Livehpool, an' tried his luck with the sea."

A look of recognition flashed over his features, as if he felt on familiar ground. "Aye, the voyages t' Denmark an' Gibraltar—one of the few true pieces of his story he eveh told me in the beginnin'."

"Aye, an' one o' the few smahrt moves he made then as well... I s'pose it was the Rom blood comin' out in him—his wantin' t' see the world; but learnin' his ropes undeh the likes of John Redmond— then pickin' up sailmakin' an' four or five languages—that's whehre he really learned hisself a trade; an' it sure come t' stand him in good stead afteh... not t' mention us," I smiled.

"How does Walker's packet fit in—was he shanghaied sometime afteh he returned t' Livehpool, like everybody's always guessed?" he pressed me, as if in a sudden tumult of questions, and a flurry at the thought of their being answered. "Or was he runnin' away from the law? An' what about that Livehpool barmaid?"

I put up a hand to slow him down, wondering again how much to tell him—balancing the probability of Jim's loss against the chance he might ever make it back to port, and trying to feel in my bones whether he'd want Ben to know, if he ever looked him again in the eye; trying to guess as well whether Ben hisself was really ready to hear my answer, despite the eager hunt of his gaze. With his eyes pinned upon me in anxious attention, as if he understood this was one of the critical points of Jim's life, he even stopped plaiting and folding the jersey; and I felt my way forward with caution

"One question at a time, mate… He come back t' Livehpool from Tunis all right, then got hisself shanghaied aboard Walker's packet—but not for any reason anybody's eveh guessed. It had nothin' t' do with his runnin' away from the law; nothin' t' do with his bein' in trouble with some bahrmaid, or leavin' b'hind a baby he'd fathered—all that speculation we've been hearin' for yeahrs. I b'lieve Jim let them stories float t' keep folks off the scent of the truth, which was that he'd been livin' pretty close t' the edge there on the docks, in cahoots with the crimps an' runners, sleepin' with some of the sailors for money. He'd lure 'em into the boardin' houses, an' receive so much a head for the night; but finally he got fed up with his small cut in the profits, an' stole his fair share from his crimp. T' square the yahrds with him his crimp drugged his dinneh, an' dumped his body aboard Walker's packet—havin' signed him oveh t' the shippin' masteh."

"D'ye mean t' tell me…he was a *hookeh*?" he gaped, in a dumbfounded furor of confusion and hurt, as if he'd never found anything in Jim's past to prepare him.

"You wanted t' know him, Ben… ye can't know him without this."

In his turmoil the jersey, which'd been neatly folded, soon erupted again in a tumult on his knees; and he begun unconsciously tugging at its corners. "I… I just can't imagine Jim sellin' his mind, much less his body—he was such a….a free man," he got out, his voice cracking with the effort. "He could 've…If he'd needed money, he could've made anything out of wood, or gone t' work for a while in a sail loft…you know that."

"He wasn't interested in carvin' or sailmakin', any more'n he was really interested in makin' money," I kept on, watching the struggle of tensions on his face. "He was interested, I guess, in thumbin' his nose at his people—at least at first, when he was still raw from Djemail, when it seemed like he had nothin' more t' lose. He told me he figured if he was banned, he might as well make a good job of it."

A half-reluctant, half-admiring smile broke out on his face in spite of his turmoil. "That does sound like Jim, all right," he admitted, the corners of his lips still twitching and tugging.

"Aye, it does, I thought so m'self…. Lateh on, though, by the end of his stint in Livehpool, I b'lieve he kept on b'cause—admit it or not—he needed a loveh, an' was hopin' t' find one amongst the sailohs."

"You just pointed out how he runs a mile at the idear of losin' his freedom," he struggled.

"He was lookin' for someone strong enough t' make him forget that."

He gazed down at his jersey in silence.

"I ain't tryin' t' excuse him, Ben," I said patiently, "just tryin' t' help ye see him in the light of things as they happened. There's some folks as 're born with that need t' pair up, an' I b'lieve he was feelin' it already thehre on the docks—if he hadn't even b'fore in them days with Djemail. At any rate, don't hold it against him—don't feel betrayed he'd sold out t' othehs; he regretted it as soon as he met ye; an' you don't know how it's galled him since."

By the look on his face I could see he understood—that he nursed a score of regrets of his own that left a bitterness in his mouth; but alls he said was, with a simple acceptance, "So he sailed with Walkeh, against his will… an' finally, he came t' New York."

"Aye, he made fast in New York, an' hated it at once… He hadn't a tuppence in his pockets, his wages havin' all been taken up by Walkeh, all them times he logged him for disobeyin' ordehrs; an' he hadn't any decent papehs neitheh—Walkeh's a' course not fit t' look at, an' Redmond's stolen in Livehpool. The first night off, in some tavern in Wateh Street, he got hisself treated t' a few rounds, then arrested for drunkenness an' thrown into the Tombs; an' not long afteh, hustlin' the streets o' Five Points, he met up with a loseh named Lomond, a crimp on the run with his eye on a new stahrt. As soon as they could they took the steameh t' Boston, an' built up a trade like the one Jim'd had in Livehpool—Lomond the crimp, Slateh an' a couple of othehs the runners, an' Jim an' several good lookin' young men the bait.

"They'd hang around the docks or the bahrrooms, even pose for artists an' circulate their pictures—all them stunts Jim'd tried in England; then they'd steer their prey into the boardin' house, or meet up thehre with the sailors Slater'd run in from fresh ships, an' see to it they had a good time—while Slater an' the rest stole their pocketbooks, rummaged their chests, even filched their very clothes off of the floor. But thehre was a twist t' the set-up this time; for thehre really was somethin' about this fellow Lomond that Jim was true to; an' he tried t' keep up a relationship with him, though it failed in the end—Lomond bein', t' my mind, a ruined man, an' almost crazily possessive."

"So *he* was the one Jim fought with that night," Ben put in, his face a mixture of so many expressions that I could scarcely bear to look at him.

"Aye… The same thing happened as with that juggleh at the circus: Lomond got pretty domineering, an' Jim pretty sick o' dancin' t' his tune. He even got sick o' sleepin' round, by the time they'd been at it a couple months. He's got a noble heart, at bottom; an' he knew what he was lookin' for… knew, by then, he wasn't goin' t' find it that way, an' that he was pretty much trapped by Lomond. What I said earlieh about some folks bein' born t' pair up; well, he must of seen by then he was one of 'em; an' he wanted out of the whole business he'd set up. The whole hierarchy, from the landlord an' ward bosses an' constables on the street on down t' Slateh an' the runners, an' finally t' Jim at the bottom, begun t' stink with pay offs an' betrayals; an' it couldn't of been easy livin' with the enemies they was makin'… Jim was neveh able t' talk much about it."

"How…how in the end did he finally break free…what was it that brought him to us?" Ben stumbled, his hands at last still, and his eyes fixed on me.

"He seen *Charis* by the wharf one day," I smiled, "just like he told us that night at Toby's. He'd waked up unusually early that mornin', d'cided t' leave Lomond in the lurch, an' walked down t' the docks t' mull things oveh… While he was thehre he seen ouhr ship—seen somehthin' in her that made sense t' him, that gave out the hope of direction he needed. She must of looked good t' him afteh what he'd been through; 'tenny rate, he made up his mind t' ship out; to ship out aboard of *her*, if he could. Askin' around, he got youhr name, an' heard you usually had suppeh at Toby's; an' when we come in he marched up to ouhr table, an' got up the nerve t' ask ye for work."

His face all at once simply went numb, went empty of any thoughts of hisself, his needs or his commotion of feelings—as if he was wholly thinking of Jim, of what his life would of been if he hadn't taken him on; as if he was seeing, with a kind of dumbfounded irony, that he was in debt to the likes of Billy Walker and James Lomond, for the fortune of Jim's meeting up with us. The weight and pain of Jim's early years, on top of the stress of his loss at sea, seemed to deepen the very lines of his face; and I felt concerned that I'd said too much—felt convinced that I should let the rest of the story wait, and dole it out some other time. As though he'd read me off he shook his head, and signaled he was ready for more; and setting aside the jersey, he braced a hand on his knee. "So he left us at Toby's an' fought Lomond," he encouraged, his grey eyes defenseless and honest on mine.

"When he come back t' his lodgin's for his trunk, aye."

"Lomond did care, then, about losin' Jim; he must of."

"Eitheh that, or he felt the threat t' his business... He was a jealous bastihd, an' a rabid schemer; an' b'tween the two, he had a hold on them men like no otheh... Jim was lucky t' get off with his life—maybe wouldn't of, if some of the others'd showed up."

"Was it Lomond who jumped aboard t' ask us about him, just as we cast off next mornin'?"

"No, that was Slateh, a regulah hatchet-faced runneh—vindictive as hell, by the cut of his jib."

"Close shave, wasn't it," he breathed.

"It was, aye; an' Jim neveh forgot it."

His face took on an almost rueful humor, as if he was seeing things all at once from a distance. "How different him an' me are," he mused, his eyes on the fire. "He's lived all these yeahrs like a bat out o' hell; an' I've always gone by the book."

"Till Hilo," I pointed out dryly.

"Till Hilo," he admitted freely; and even then, in the midst of our tensions, I realized what a good sign it was that he could see this was the point at which his judgment'd finally faltered—at which he'd failed to make rational decisions, and given hisself up to need and emotion.

"What did he see in me," he marveled, with a kind of detached, whimsical wonder—as if he'd seen himself in comparison to them young bucks on the wharves, and come up short.

"What he seen in *Charis*—a man that could take him on, discipline him, lift him out of the chaos of cheap affairs an' carry him into the steadiness of a marriage."

"He… he *said* that?"

"A' course he did—said it that first night at Toby's, when he rated the crew as likely t' take afteh the ship, an' when he looked at ye with them eyes… But if y' mean, did he eveh put it into plain words, in the form of a confession t' me—well, he did, afteh that month he spent at youhr place, a yeahr ago last summeh… He run oveh t' see me as soon as Anne come home, buried his head in my lap an' cried—said that, till then, he would of been happy with a night now an' then; but afteh livin' with you, he wanted the days too… He'd been strugglin' against it, almost give up a few times, even packed his bags once, did ye know?; but that was the end of it for him, he was hooked; an' I think it was his fightin' his final surrender that partly kept ye in the dahk as t' his feelin's."

His eager face as he followed my words was almost more than I could take; and I nearly come and set down beside him and took his taut, trembling hand from his knee. But before I could move to get onto my feet he looked up like a bird dog in the field, when it's picked up the air of a foreign scent in the bush; and I seen he'd caught the sound of the wind as it whistled and throbbed away at the eaves. "Is that a west wind?" he asked suddenly, all at once coming back to the present; and I listened a minute for its strength and direction, after plotting in my mind the position of the room.

"West-nor'west, aye," I determined, wondering what on earth he was onto.

"C'mon, let's go!" he suddenly jumped up, for all the world like a boy on the wharf.

"Where in blazes to, man?" I gaped, dumbfounded.

"Why, t' Boston, a' course!"

"Jesus Christ, Ben, have ye taken leave of youhr senses?"

"No, by thundeh— I'm findin' 'em! If I can't know Jim in the future, why, nobody c'n stop me from knowin' him in the past! I've got three whole months with nothin' t' do—an' it's winteh, too, just like it was for him. Let's go find Jim's past!"

"Gawd almighty, man, this is the craziest trek ye've tried t' rope me into yet!"

"You know Ann Street better'n I do… d'ye think ye could find Jim's old boardin' house if y' tried?"

"I… I s'pose… I know about whehre it was, Jim pointed it out that time he was to the doctoh… It's on the corneh of Creek Lane an' Lime Alley, in that mess o' streets b'tween Blackstone an' Union, off Ann…that is, if it ain't been vacated, b'cause Lomond broke up business an' moved on, or the police kept things hustlin'."

"Oh, the p'lice are all in on it, y' just said so youhrself… They must be makin' a pile off that landlord. I'll bet things're all thehre; or the set-up's still thehre with different faces… I could…maybe I could even find Jim's old room… D'ye have any idear how it was situated?"

"It'd be on the top floor," I said doubtfully, "undeh the eaves—he wouldn't of been able t' afford more; an' it'd be lookin' east oveh the harboh—he told me he woke up that last mornin', threw open the shuttehs an' looked out t' sea."

"That's it," he cried, "I'll bet we c'n find it… We'll sail down t' Halifax an' ship int' Boston, on some packet or otheh as common sailohs—the runners 'll pick us up in a minute. We'll lodge whereveh they take us, scout around, an' eventually work ouhr way oveh t' Jim's."

"Have ye thought about how half the ships fast in Boston'll recognize us as soon as we make port?" I asked dryly. "Why, my cousins're there—Tom's lookin' for a freight—an' ain't youhr cousin Jacob due in from Antwerp in the *Malachi Pelham*? Not t' mention all them stevedores that knows us—the harboh masteh, the newsmen, half the hands in the Maine fleet—why, if we c'n make a pahrty of the folks that knows us in Canton, or a two-bit crossroads like Anjier, how're we gon' t' escape it in Boston?"

"We'll just have t' chance it—I'll shave off my beard- we'll leave b'hind ouhr names, ouhr money—not that I've got any anyhow! Nobody'll be lookin' for us t' hop off a packet, in company with a runner an' handcart; an' if we get into a tight spot thehre—if we have a hahrd time passin' ouhrselves off—why, you could always pose as my loveh—we'll get int' places we neveh could othehwise that way—"

"Gawd Almighty," I stared at him, dumbstruck by the direction his thoughts was running, and the speed with which he was adjusting to Jim's past. "Not the wildest imagination on earth could eveh conceive of us as such, man!"

"A' course it could, all ye've got t' do is lean on my shouldeh now an' then, an' look at me like—well, not like that! Look at me like Jim would of, for Christ's sake—I'm not *that* bad a catch, ye just said so youhrself!"

"An' supposin' somebody that knows us catches us up in that act—wouldn't *that* make a pretty piece o' news at Eli's! Can't ye just see us bein' read out of the congregation, turned out by ouhr families—all that rejection Jim faced?"

"Oh, Christ, McCabe, why balk at such an unlikely turn t' events, when you know damn well nobody we know even slums around Pohrtland, much less the back watehs of Ann Street!"

"An' just what is it ye hope t' accomplish with this?" I sighed, watching him industriously bank the fire, for all the world like the hard-driving old Ben.

"I want t' know him, know all thehre is t' know about him—see what he sawr, feel what he felt, taste whateveh made him Jim... I've been cheated out of his body, out of any yeahrs we might of had in the future; I want t' at least touch his past... D'ye understand?"

"I ought to," I smiled, looking back on afternoons gone; "it was what Jim wanted...what he loved, all them times rambling through Cape Damaris, or listenin' t' my stories of you as a boy."

He looked at me wistfully over his shoulder, dusting his hands off there on the hearth.

"We'll have t' be careful not t' get caught up—t' be customehs comin' an' goin' on the outside," I cautioned; "otherwise, we'll be liable for what we know, an' not any betteh off than Jim was."

"That's all I want," he said eagerly; "don't need t' stay long—just need t' get a feel for the place…An' we could turn oveh any useful information we pick up t' John t' use in his cases—or t' pass on t' othehs."

"An' what're ye plannin' on tellin' folks hehre?"

"I'll tell 'em I'm goin' t' Boston on business, lookin' into the insurance an' so on, stoppin' t' see Jackson or t' see off Tom… We'll take *Idris* t' fool folks, run her down t' Halifax, dock her thehre an' hop one o' the packets makin' for Boston from Livehpool… Now, are ye shipmates with me?"

"I s'pose ye'll go it alone if I ain't?" I asked dryly.

"Damn right I will; be off in an oweh."

"Then I'm comin' with ye; ye'll louse up without me… I need a drink first, a real stiff whiskey an' wateh; then I'll be ready for anything."

Having no one to answer to, I could be off with no notice, with my canvas bag slung at my back; but for Ben, who was tied to half the town, it was a more difficult matter; and I never knew for sure how he did it, or how hard Anne hit the roof—just seen him walk briskly up to *Idris* at supper, his old seabag aloft on his shoulder. Aboard for a spell already, I'd cleaned out the cabin, stowing Jim's stray gear away in the cuddy, before Ben should happen to see it; and I was busy overhauling the rigging, and taking inventory of our paltry needs.

Grub for supper, breakfast and noon dinner the next day, with extra stores in case we didn't ship out from Halifax directly; heavy sailing gear and a few changes of clothing, nothing worth keeping, since it'd probably be stole any way; these made up the grand total I'd stashed; and we hung around now only long enough for Ben to shave his beard, and strap his trunk under his berth. With the wind strong and steady out of the northwest, we tripped our anchor and quickly cast off, running before it out of the harbor; then in our seamen's gear—woolen jerseys and peacoats, dreadnaught trowsers and well-greased boots, with our sheath knives fastened at our belts—we stood off for Vinalhaven, and the turbulent mouth of the Bay of Fundy.

Beating down the coast of Nova Scotia next morning—Ben never sailing better, and *Idris* fleet and adept under his hand—we made as good a time as a steamer; and I kept a weather eye on him at the tiller, glorying in his reflexes and timing. I'd only thrown in my lot with him in the first place to support him in the trials ahead—his state of mind as much a worry to me as any hot water he might get hisself into; and I'd already privately made up my mind that, if he showed signs of breaking under the strains of Jim's old life, or under the stress of memories of him he met up with, I'd steer him straight over to Jackson's place on Long Wharf, and care for him there as long as need be.

But now I seen he showed every sign of the old Ben, there at the tiller in the wintry sun: a woolen cap in place of his visor, and the beard he'd worn for years neatly shaved, but his grey eyes as obstinate and bullheaded, and his attitude as straight-ahead and on course as they'd ever been at the peak of the old days, when he'd been hellbent to make a passage. Clamped between his teeth, his clay pipe smoldered and puffed, for all the world like the well-stoked funnel of a steamer; and his eyes was the eyes of a man with a clear head, positive he's on the right track. Far from needing me to care for him, I seen he was back in charge, running my life along with his like in days past; and with a grin I set by and bided my time, awaiting the moment to stick my oar in.

Hauling into Halifax early that evening—running down the stream along the hillside of houses, chapels and shops and modest shipping, then making fast to one of the quays near the town wharf—we paid off the bulk of our spare funds for wharfage, buttoned *Idris* up and treated ourselves to a spree, the last we'd be likely to have in some time; and somewheres along the line between oysters and dessert we turned up the news a packet was due in next day, one of the liners bound from Liverpool to Boston, stopping only long enough to exchange the mails. Getting into character we laid up in a cheap room, bare of anything save a bedstead and washstand, and managed to snatch a few hours' sleep in the cold; and next day we took to helping the stevedores gratis, to keep warm till the packet hove into view.

Hove in she did, pretty much on time—Ben viewing her broad beams and bluff bow with distaste; and turning to me he tried to encourage hisself with, "Afteh all, how bad c'n it be? Even if the masteh's a complete soger, the crew're all drunk an' it blows a blizzard, we couldn't possibly spin out the trek longer'n forty-eight owehs." Giving him a droll look, I grunted in answer; and as soon as she'd made fast and her passengers'd swarmed off, some of them kissing the earth in their frank glee, we steered a straight course for the captain, me struggling to keep up in Ben's wake. Being strong-looking hands, the packet short-handed and the weather making up, we had no trouble shipping ourselves for the brief run, a dollar a head in wages; and giving out the names we'd chosen—keeping our Christian handles, since we couldn't imagine answering to any other, but Ben for his surname using Wood—Jim's mother's maiden name—and me using Lovell, another Rom connection, we signed up and carried our personal gear forward.

With the wind still northwest we commenced our run, me and Ben before the mast for the first time in upwards of ten years; and swarming aloft with a score of others—mostly stolid Dutchmen, Germans and Limejuicers—we cast off our buntlines and overhauled rigging, pitching to and fro in the gathering dark. Though Ben had a battle keeping his station, he managed to do a tolerable job as a grumpy down-easter, and resist giving orders to the whole ship; and I, though as appalled at the state of the rigging, and not any keener on the mate myself, managed, by dint of long practice, to keep my mouth shut. With the wind veering round to the northeast, and a thick squall of snow setting in with it, we raised the distant blurs of Cape Ann and the vague, dark hills of Boston two herculean days later, without running up on George's Island as Ben'd snorted; and getting into the roads early that evening—hearing the bells ring out from the city, as we worked our way in under the pilot—we at last rounded to off the end of Long Wharf, and made her fast to the gloomy pilings.

The usual mob of landsmen swarming aboard and dogging the steps of the immigrants and crew—it being late, and immediate housing needed—we could scarcely wrap up business; and we wrestled to make up bunts in the half-dark. Waving some of the runners off—pretending to have boarded before at a particular place—Ben and me held out for what we wanted; and when an energetic-looking shark missing his front teeth promised us a berth at Nel's on Creek Lane—when we heard the price, which was suitably slovenly, and got wind of the girls said to be waiting—we hoisted our gear, and followed him down to his handcart.

All around us mountains of luggage intermingled with the mounds of cargo, the lot looming about in the snowy dark; while the passengers pouring down the gangway—in a stream of great coats and beaver hats, thick dresses and mantles and quilted hoods—and the immigrants following in their wake, in a mass of threadbare skirts and waistcoats, and linsey cloaks not much better than blankets—all competed for space amongst the chaotic stacks.

Here and there we could pick out a few loafers with no place, not even Creek Lane, to go to, hunkered down in the lee of the hogsheads, their hatbrims turned down against the snow; or a stray dog nosing amongst the offal, or a pig on his way home to some crate. In the dim orbs of the lamps, just being lighted, the long line of wharf buildings marched off toward the street—curio shops, counting houses, warehouses and sail lofts, some still alive with late evening business; while in and out of the snowy lights loomed carousing bands of seamen, on their way into town for a hot mug of flip. But thankfully in all the commotion of landing, unloading and matching of faces and luggage, there was scarcely a chance for anyone to recognize us; and we disappeared behind our runner into the night.

So late did we get in—after a considerable walk, mostly down dark, narrow streets, where lanterns was swinging crazily at doorways, and well-mufflered men was scurrying by us, or dodging down stairways diving off from the street—that there was no time for anything but bed; and we postponed any thoughts of exploring and hobnobbing till the broad, sober light of the morrow. Taking the cheapest room we could get—a dormitory up under the eaves, where a score of men was already bunked down, two or three to a rickety bedstead—we toted our gear up the creaking steps, and dumped it at the foot of our berth; then casting dubious glances at the snoring shadows around us, we paused to take stock of our lodgings. In the dim arc of our candle we leerily eyed the bed, with its ragged counterpane and grey-hued linen, a long time—and numerous inmates—from washday; and warily we met each other's eyes.

"Anything alive in thehre, d'ye think?" Ben asked, as if realizing for the first time what he'd brung on us; and ruefully I turned back the covers.

"Considerable," I answered, "an' soon t' be lunchin' off us"; and wordlessly we eyed the option of the floor. Bare of any covering, it looked oddly stained in the dark, besides being game to the mice, if not rats; and in the end we voted the bed—thinking of placing our spare clothes between us and the sheets, but soon changing our minds, not wanting to infect them too with vermin, and compromising by wearing our pilot coats, as much for warmth as for the illusion of protection.

What with the run down to Halifax with just me and Ben to work *Idris,* then the two-day trek, short on sleep, to Boston, I was feeling pretty beat; and my mind made up, I piled in with my boots on, figuring they was my most valuable property, and guessing that was how the sheets'd got into their present condition. Not long after we'd laid down—tumbled close together for warmth, the temperature in the room at freezing, if that—there was an eruption of noise on the stairs, and two or three choice spirits staggered in to sleep on the floor, too awash to care there was no more spare beds. With some wretched moans and groans, one of them was soon thoroughly sick—on the floor, I supposed, since there was no chamber pots in sight, nor anything that would pass for a wash basin; and between the reek of that, the stale, greasy bedding, and the tobacco juice congealing in the spittoons, I begun to feel unsteady myself—supper that night having been a last-minute scouse, and its mishmash of leftovers sitting none too well now.

"Sure ye don't want t' change youhr mind about this?" I persuasively hissed in Melchett's ear; and in answer he give me a stubborn scowl. Conditioning ourselves to wake at the first creak of a tread, at the first hint of some joker coming to filch our gear, we lay for a long time waiting for sleep, watching the snow drift down through the rafters; then at last in the snoring and wheezing around us, and the droning of wind a few feet away at the eaves, we dropped off into an uneasy slumber.

XXVI

CAPT. BENJAMIN MELCHETT

Boston—New York—Wales, January-March, 1845

By far the hardest part of the first stage of our battle was the hurdle of the filth. Focused as I was on Jim's enigma—on all the fresh vistas of his life round each corner—I was caught off guard by the dirt; and try as I might, I couldn't at first concentrate on anything else. How fastidious Jim'd ever stood it, with his native horror for anything *mukado,* and his instinctive desire to appear at his best, I couldn't begin to conceive; and I found myself looking at his dignity and forbearance in a new and humbled light.

By daybreak we discovered there was one basin for twenty, and no clean water to fill its caked depths—the calcified pitcher being empty, and the handle at the pump in the dooryard frozen; while the public comb and brush, hanging by the small mirror, were in even worse condition—lice, grime, hair and oil being the chief of their house guests. The floor of our dormitory, too, repulsed the eyes at once, there being no covering, and no evidence of mopping; and now we could see—in the plain light of day—that its oddly stained appearance was due to yellow tobacco juice, spat out in streams in all directions.

The chamber pots being nonexistent, and the concept of water closets being limited to innovative hotels like the Tremont—higher up the hill, and as equally elevated in the scale of the pocketbook—all hands used the outhouse in the dooryard, so vile one had to be urgent to visit; while raw sewage and sink waste lay half-curdled in the gutters. Nor was mealtime exempt from the squalor; for breakfast was a matter of buckwheat cakes dotted with weevils, and accompanied by coffee sweetened with diluted molasses; while noon dinner was roast peas laced with chicory and dirt, and an unpalatable slab of beefsteak swimming in a congealed sauce of butter.

By afternoon Eben and I were already at the apothecary, investing some of our slim resources in the pursuit of vermin, soon to make their inhabitance known; and by supper the combined reek of the spittoons, the anthracite stove and the stale, weeks-old cooking had quite taken away the remains of our appetite. But worst of all was the unsavory guise of our fellow-lodgers, mostly down-and-outers on the drift through the city, or sailors squandering their advance notes—their lank, uncombed hair, unshaven stubble, yellowed, decayed teeth and body odors needing all the cut and dash of shore togs to atone; and we could find little comfort in the fact that we ourselves were fast taking on the salient points of their appearance.

Nor was the neighborhood in which we'd taken up lodgings any improvement over our housing. In the thick of the night, the signboards depicting Neptune with his trident—the swinging planks rife with anchors or ship's wheels, full-rigged three-masters or alluring mermaids—had not been without a certain charm; while the lights showing behind tissue-papered windows, or the burst of guffaws ringing through closed doors, had held a peculiar fascination. The store-fronts, too—the slop shops and gin shops and marts selling sea togs, the low groggeries and dance halls and taverns—had radiated, despite their coarse stamp, a certain raw appeal or allure, the same earthy call as salt or wet hemp; and I'd felt drawn to the undisclosed within.

But now—in the harsh light of day—other features commanded attention; and I found myself picking out details with eyes fresh from a night's habitation. The churned-up, grimy snow thick on the cobbled street, or uncleared on the narrow brick footpaths—the glimpses of bleak dooryards behind buildings like ours, dotted with outhouses, criss-crossed with gutters—the refuse-strewn steps leading down from the street, toward cellars where men slept for a nickel: these were what I noticed now; and I wondered how I could have ever failed to consider the obstacles their inhabitants faced.

The passersby too, though of all classes—clerks on their way to counting houses, apprentices hurrying off to the shipyards, servants hiking to market at Faneuil Hall—all somehow partook of the street's burden of neglect, at least so long as they were passing through; and the sailors especially shared its oppression. Hung over still from last night's skylarking, they all looked short of adequate nutrition and rest—beat out from exposure, debauchery and drink; while many exhibited signs of palsy, consumption, rheumatism— the debilitations of their years at sea. On their faces sat a knowledge of their entrapment, fighting yet with an avid hunger; and I could almost pick out how long each man had been in port, by the degree of the one versus the other. In all the fresh weight of my own hardship, my one flame of joy was that I was walking where Jim had walked, treading, perhaps, the very flagstones he'd trodden; and my heart quickened even as I dolefully looked round, trying to imagine it all through his immigrant eyes.

The second part of the battle we faced was the onslaught of the cold. Though we never took off our pilot coats, even in bed, and kept on the move, even in sleep, we were never warm; and I found myself wearing out fast from the strain. Not that we'd never known cold before—never felt the frigidness of Cape Horn, or the frosty chill of our homes; for we'd kept it up for weeks in icy seas, and wakened most every winter's day in port to an unheated, draught-filled room. But there was work at sea to keep one busy—to heat one's limbs with honest exertion, and occupy one's mind with a goal; while the comforts of a gigantic kitchen hearth soon dispelled the shivers of rising at home.

By contrast there was nothing here to pin the mind to, save Jim— about whom we didn't dare speak, except in guarded tones on the street; while there was no work at all for the body—a decided about- face for me, after a lifetime of labor. I would gladly have turned to with a mop and a bucket, and swabbed the decks of our dormitory attic, if such actions wouldn't have pegged me at once as some blueblood, or a foremasthand who'd lost his mind to drink; would have nailed up planks over the gaps in the rafters, through which snow was drifting down on the beds, or aired the straw pallets which passed for our mattresses, and which stank of use and infestation—would have stooped to any job to keep me warm, at least in the beginning.

But gradually I began to feel an indifference to labor, an apathy which formed by degrees, the toll of the very cold I fought; till by the end of even our first day at Nel's, I had ceased to think in terms of action, as if any effort was too much in my state. Evidence of such disinterest I saw in all else around me—in those clustered dumbly round the anthracite stove, thumbing the pages of yellow-backed flash novels, or moving the pegs on homemade cribbage boards, as much as in those trudging wearily down the streets, or huddling wordlessly in dooryards; saw it in the animals as well as in men—in the work horses and stray pigs lowering their heads to the wind, and in even the rodents which came out at night, slipping through the derelict boards of old fences.

Lack of adequate food too was taking its charge—was contributing to our inability to combat the cold, or to concentrate fully on the task at hand. Scraping the surface of the salt—rank with the bites of tobacco-stained teeth—before chipping off a bit for our use, we tried to feel an appetite for anything before us, recognizing that we had to eat; valiantly picked the baked weevils from the bread, then munched away, hoping for the best. At sea—especially before the mast—our diet had been rugged, but never rancid or contaminated as here; and we'd never once shipped poor stores for the men, or been obliged to eat inadequate fare aft. Hard tack, dried peas, salt port, potatoes, even the scouse of our last supper aboard the packet, looked like the cuisine of a dining saloon now, compared to the wretched meals before us; and we found ourselves struggling to restrain the wild impulse to race up to the Tremont to lunch off its menu—to dine in the sane splendor of its gas-lit hall, in company with 200 genteel, well-dressed others—or to dash over to the Exchange Coffeehouse or up Fish Street to Toby's, or even to one of the oyster bars.

Choking down our food we tried not to feel enraged at those who so insulted our persons —at Nel, whoever she was, or her landlord, wherever he dwelt—since no one around us was rebelling: all hands indeed accepting the weevils just as they tolerated the table linen, reversed once a fortnight in lieu of washing, or the dinner napkins, used by others, then re-folded. Dreading each meal, I suffered for the ones who accepted this offense, who took it as it came, expecting no better; suffered for Jim, who'd liked to eat, and who'd had no small frame to fill; suffered even for the stray dogs and cats, at the mercy of the gutters and slop heaps.

Want of privacy, too—though of far less moment than the food, or the cold and filth which eroded our strength, was insidiously wearing us down; and I found myself longing for a quiet recess in which to think, in which to exchanges plans and reactions with Eben. It'd been enough of a shock aboard the packet, to share bed and board and all the functions of life with a score of illiterate, coarse, irreverent onlookers—to find that there was not a curtain to a bunk, not a corner to the ship where we could take shelter. Even worse was it now in our dormitory attic, where the eruption of fights in the middle of the night, the continuous noise of crude conversation, and the degradation of body brought about by the lack of facilities all intruded upon my train of thought, so that I had scarcely a moment to hug to myself my new discoveries of Jim.

Nor were body and mind alone interrupted; for my identity too was broken in on, reshaped and shakily held up to view. No longer Ben Melchett, shipwright, master, father, I was simply Ben Wood, a stolid downeaster from a mythical town in northern Maine, just in via packet from St. Johns, and looking out for a deepwater voyage—blowing my wages meantime like my shipmates. My speech I didn't have to change, since thanks to my father I'd always spoken the dialect of a sailor, in spite of my thorough education; my garb likewise, since I'd never cared to put on the dandy; but I had to be as guarded about letting out my thoughts—my references to genteel life, to seven-course meals and lavender-scented sheets, or to the principles of higher mathematics—as I had to be vigilant about letting in noise. No longer married, in fact or in spirit—the parent of no children that I knew of—stripped of skills beyond the ordinary maritime abilities of an able-bodied seaman: such changes were as much of a strain to endure as the constant presence of others; and I found myself ceaselessly struggling to remember the pretense of my limitations.

How Jim, with his fierce sense of privacy and reserve, his personal pride and independence, had ever withstood such assaults on his person—such attacks of noise and exposure and sham on his dignity and creative spirit, I was at a loss to explain; and I tried to picture him in his days here on Creek Lane, never alone to dress or wash or dream—never alone to play his guitar in a patch of sunlight, or to build the fancies of a master-carver.

Shortage of money was another factor in our struggle, and the one with which I was least conditioned to deal. Never once in my life having had to do without—having always had my needs met, and most of my wants too, as the result of my birthright, or through the course of hard work—it was inconceivable to me that I couldn't provide; that I couldn't simply dip into my pockets to improve our lot. For twenty-nine years my meals, my lodgings, my attire, my travels, my education and business, had been such as I'd chosen— the matter of personal discretion, rather than the consideration of funds; and it was almost beyond my ability to imagine that I couldn't exercise such powers of choice now. Like most of the seamen around us, we were due to be paid off when the packet had broken out her cargo—a matter of ten days or so; and till then we had to live on a prayer and a promise—on almost anything but ready cash, a fact which put most incoming shellbacks at an immediate disadvantage, and handed them to the mercies of the crimps and runners.

To prevent ourselves from falling into such traps, we had a few dollars between us—which at a dollar a week for lodgings, and our apothecary purchase, would go fast; and we needed money for drinks as well—exploration of the taverns and various night dens being our chief purpose. There was the matter, too, of our bags having been locked up in the strong room in the cellar—for safekeeping, as we'd been told, though we knew we'd have to pay to get them out, or forfeit them like so many sailors. The whole scenario was familiar from years of hearsay, and from our exposure to John's accounts; yet to live it was worse than maddening—worse than an intellectual outrage; for it was mortifying to feel oneself falling by degrees into the control of others.

The one safety net Eben and I had was the bank draft at my belt; but this, for Jim's sake, I'd done my best to forget, determined to live without as he had; and temptations swarmed in upon us as a result. Things I'd seen but never wanted—shop windows full of porcelain, madras, sandalwood and silk and japanned ware, the offerings of the East Indies and China—beckoned to me with a new allure now; added themselves to the tantalizations of a clean bed, well-prepared food and a quiet chamber; and staving them off I thought again of Jim, of his love for the mysterious and bright—thought of how these delights must have looked to him, through the hunger of his impoverished eyes.

And finally, to cap off our battle, there was our utter lack of direction—our want of any purpose in life, save to explore Jim's old habits and haunts, and to experience, to some extent, his past in the process; to come to know him by re-tracing his steps, and to put off, at the same time, the void of the future. Jim, at least, with his love of going in circles—his contentment with meandering or following his nose, would have been good at this phase of our struggle; but for the likes of me, whose thoughts traveled in straight lines, with points of embarkation and debarkation, it was like floundering in a morass. On a "spree" without work—imitating others who had a fortnight or so ashore—we lived our days without pattern or plan, simply following one hour into the next; dwelt wholly detached from thoughts of the sea-going or portside routines which had always undergirded my time with order.

Going on 'Change at seven each morning—shooting the sun each seaday at noon—timbering out ships at ice-out each spring—rotating houses for Saturday supper: these unfailing cycles of week, day and hour, like the perennial signals of autumn or spring, had always, like stepping stones, directed my way; and I hardly knew how to proceed without them. Now one hour was pretty much like every other, save for the definitions of sleep or meals, and our job was to chart a course through this barrens—or rather, to unchart someone else's.

One relief from the cold and oppression was to keep moving; and since scouting out Jim's old territory was our primary purpose, we kept on the go most of the time we were awake, scarcely sitting down at all the first day. The narrow lanes, cobbled streets, winding alleys and granite buildings which predominated from here to Ann Street and the shipping, soon became as familiar to me as my own hand; became as well known as the Custom House, or the environs of Dock Square, or the hundred or so wharves which sawtoothed the waterfront, had been to me as shipmaster.

I even found myself getting to know some of the locals: the fat, aproned tar who ran the nearby coffeehouse; the drunks who frequented the steps of the gin shop; the lamplighter who came by each eve at five-thirty; the street cleaners and sweepers who fought over our corner. But it was Jim's old building, on the corner of Creek Lane and Salt, a couple of squares up from where we were staying, that drew my attention again and again. Three stories high, built of granite blocks, the first floor was a combination curio shop—run by an eccentric old salt and a Malay—and a mart selling ready-made sailor's clothing; the second a row of bleared, multi-paned windows, several of them missing their shutters; and the third a line of three or four dormers, jutting out from a steep roof minus several slates, and punctuated by a couple of chimneys.

How to get into the place—which seemed to have no entrance, save for the doors which opened into the stores, and a stairway which led down off the street to a public room, probably a low groggery or tavern; what it was used for now, beyond the obvious purpose of the shops, and the less obvious intent of the underground tavern; and who frequented it, besides the seamen buying clothes, and knickknacks for sweethearts and family back home—these were the puzzles which occupied us; and we stared into the shop fronts and peered down the stairway, or gazed up at the dormers, one of which had been Jim's, without a clue as to how to get closer.

Once, passing by, and exchanging quick glances, we ducked into the clothing mart and browsed through its gear, purchasing a neckerchief for Eben, at a nickel all we could afford; stepped next door and scanned the curiosities there, choosing a piece of coral for me, at a similar price; but though we listened and looked with all our might and main, we spotted no one who could be Slater or Lomond, and overheard no references to assignations or rooms. What the place's secret might be, Jim had never told Eben, nor hinted in any of his few confidences; and stumped for the time we had to turn away, with no more to go on than the stairway leading down, and a door I had glimpsed behind the curio counter.

Our other relief was the chance discovery of an oyster bar, of a character low and coarse enough to admit our purse, yet savory enough to tempt our palate; and since we were ravenously hungry, to say nothing of tired—since the place was just across the street from Jim's, and must have been visited by him—we delightedly stepped in, and chose a booth by a window overlooking the street. With its tables in curtained boxes, most of them meant to seat just two—with its quieter air and beneficent aromas—it was indeed a welcome find; and we took in its warmth, its privacy, its nonchalant comforts, as eagerly as we took in a late supper.

Though it was dark out now, too dark to see anything across the street save the pair of ships' lamps at the shop doors, the dim light down the stairway at the building's left side, and the anonymous forms that flitted past them—this was obviously a key place from which to watch in daylight; a critical spot from which to study the patrons who came and went from the various doorways, and in which to listen in on the low conversations around us; and we quickly saw its merits for the future. But for now its chief beauty was it delicious seclusion; and far into the evening Eben and I sat together, swapping whispered insights and plans for our next move, for all the world like a pair bent on cracking a safe, or a runaway couple plotting an elopement.

Having spent our first night at the oyster bar, and returned to our wretched dormitory as late as we could manage, we decided to spend the second, a Thursday, at our tavern—which, being across from the common room where we ate, and open via a separate entrance to the street, was a fairly frank and public resort. Though other barrooms beckoned to us, especially the one in the cellar of Jim's lodgings, we deemed a visit to ours a wise political move; and we sat on tall stools at the bar counter and drank, not any more than need be for appearance—afraid the whole time that our cheap rum'd been drugged, and that we'd wake up next stripped and dumped on the street, if not on our way to Madagascar. Trying not to show our suspicions, and wondering whether our garb was worth anyone's effort, we put in a couple of apprehensive hours; mumbled to each other about our packet run and northern Maine, and spun out every glass for all it was worth, our ears on the eddies of talk around us.

But though we heard every word near and far in the barroom, thanks in part to the influence of drink, which brought common converse to a shout; though we soaked up our fill of President-elect Polk, and wearied ourselves on the calls for war with Mexico, or the cries for reparations and the annexation of Texas; though we scrutinized every seaman, every German and Welshman, every Laplander and occasional Turk or Malay, most of them making vast inroads into their tankards—we never made any headway with our particular mission; never made any discoveries at all till quite late, when we stumbled upon a stairway leading down to a dance hall, and understood that this was the prime scene of action. Striking up an acquaintance with a couple of our dormitory roommates, a pair of Kanackers who couldn't imagine sharing a border without having in common as well a friendship, we made plans to spend our dollars there Friday night; and awash enough to care less than before about the vermin, we staggered our way up to bed.

Amongst the patrons of a dancing-saloon we might expect to make some progress—if not on the matter of Jim's personal history, at least on the question of his general lifestyle; and with that hope in mind we went to some lengths the next day, getting into character and sprucing ourselves up. This last alone proved a considerable challenge, for we had to pay a fee to get into our own trunks, and fetch from their depths a change of clothes; and already in an ill-humor at that, we ran up against the stumbling block of fresh water—there being no more sign of ablutions in our pitcher now than there had been on our first day.

In the depths of our basin, however, lay several inches of slops, so someone had managed to procure water from somewhere; and at the first opportunity I collared our waiter, a blunt-faced Irishman who served our establishment in some way, though we hadn't as yet discovered how. Lifting him right up off his toes, I demanded water, and summarily handed over the pitcher; but before I could squelch his protests about frozen pump-handles, or propel him on his way with a well-timed shove, Eben was energetically at my elbow.

"Easy, Ben, easy, he might have ten friends... How about a quarteh, mate, for meltin' some snow," he soothed, with a conciliatory look at our waiter; and simmering down the fellow straightened his collar, then yanked away at the hems of his waistcoat. Giving me a leery look, he disappeared with a grudging nod, somewhat softened by the sparkle which'd sprung up in his eye at the sight of Eben's cash; and as soon as he was out of sight, Eben mumbled sagely to me,

"Settle down, Melchett; practise fadin' into the woodwork."

"Fadin' in' the woodwork's not my best act," I grumbled; and

"Time t' learn," he returned dryly.

Sharing the meager returns, about a pint apiece, and a coarse, ragged towel, an old coffee bag—a communion which would certainly have strained a friendship of lesser standing and years than ours; shaving away at our beards in the miserable mirror, then cleaning our teeth in the used water, we considered ourselves as decent as anybody else; then in company with our two roommates—who'd gone through a similar ritual, including paying a similar price for melted snow—we meandered through our barroom and down the well-worn stairs, and thence through a door into the unadvertised hall beyond.

At once we found ourselves in a fairly good-sized room banked on three sides by long wooden benches, and on the fourth by a small raised orchestra, in which sat a couple of hands with their fiddles, and a third with his tambourine. In the center of the room stretched an open floor, a well-sanded, tobacco juice-splattered expanse for dancing; while all about, on the walls, were scattered colored prints for decoration: the usual scenes depicting sailors departing from their lovers, or Neptune astride a toppling billow—the lot presided over by an American bald eagle, and George Washington and Queen Victoria side by side as if wed. In one of the rear corners stood a makeshift bar, at which the girls could drink with their men without exposure to the public in the barroom upstairs; and drinking they were now, some eight or ten of them—most of them indigenous to our house, though just where they stayed we hadn't yet discovered.

Since I'd never seen a woman drink in my life, save for a bit of wine or sherry at dinner, I noticed the glasses in their hands first of all—noticed them even before I took in their looks, which were certainly not comely to the fastidious eye. Coarse, overblown, ill-dressed, they were a far cry from the sedate fashionables I'd pictured in plush houses; but with their vigorous charms and clamorous voices, and the suggestion of strenuous warmth which seemed to cling to them, they were apparently not without attractions for our fellow lodgers. Sitting side-by-side with them some half a dozen shellbacks, already having made their choices, were drinking; while a dozen or so others, idling on the benches, suddenly sent up a call for a dance; and at the cry almost all hands scrambled to their feet, while the orchestra tentatively sawed, plucked and rang.

Feeling utterly idiotic—wondering how anyone of my cumbersome size and clumsy ineptitude could fade into the woodwork—I shuffled with Eben over to the bar for a drink; then trying not to down the whole glass at once, I shrank up against the wall on a bench, while eight or nine hands claimed partners on the floor, including our pair of Kanacker friends. Marshaled by a black, a sort of caller, who could out-dance them all without any effort, they embarked on a vigorous breakdown: shuffling and spinning, cutting and crossing, kicking their heels and snapping their fingers, then meeting hands and down the middle—their zest recalling, with a sharp pang, Jim's dance at the Seven seas almost two years ago now. Hoping no one would notice our cowardly hold-out, I spun out my gin as long as I could, gradually coming to know the candle-lit faces; gradually felt the slow warmth of a liquor even this cheap, vaguely conscious meantime of the drunk a-doze beside me, chin sunk on his breast, arms crossed before him.

"Don't set so close t' him," came Eben's buzz in my ear, just as I was thinking in terms of a refill; and looking up, I gave him a puzzled stare.

"Why the devil not?" I scowled, tossing off the last of my tumbler.

"B'cause them ain't his arms—they're false" he hissed; "his real ones're right about now in youhr pocket."

"Well, I neveh," I marveled, glad for once in my life I was broke. "How on eahrth did'je know?"

"Jim told me once, it's one of theihr old tricks… The runnehs make out like they're common sailors, passed out from too much drink in the bahrs… an' the women doze them all-night packet runs to New York, with their real arms hid inside theihr mantles."

"Well, I'm damned," I muttered, trying to move over a little, and still look unobtrusive about it. "First ye c'n hahrdly sleep two winks youhrself, for fear of somebody robbin' ye blind; now ye can't b'lieve nobody else is asleep neitheh… I think I need anotheh drink."

Just about to get to my feet, I became aware of a large, buxom, broad-faced woman of an impossible to determine age, coming up through the crowd in my direction; and giving a final smooth to her peppery hair, she peremptorily stood before me.

"D'ye dance, sar?" she asked me, not impolitely, nor without an energetic warmth to her voice; and taken aback, I boggled there on the bench. Trying to ignore Eben chuckling beside me, I hastily thought back to the eight-handed reels, the endless waltzes and minuets that'd bored me since I was twelve—but decided she couldn't possibly be making reference to those, based on what I saw going on around me; so laconically I shook my head no.

"No time like the present t' l'arn," she gusted, pulling me industriously out onto the floor; and with a backward dubious glance at Eben—whose face wore an unforgettable expression—I stumbled along in her considerable wake, feeling more utterly imbecilic than if I'd been asked to strip on the spot. Trying to imitate her perambulations, her saunters and swings and fancy footwork with switches and claps and kicks of my own, I shuffled along like a barge overloaded; but so miserable was my initial effort that she stopped the caller and held up the band, and fetched me a generous tumbler of rum—me downing it with brutal disregard for any consequences which might follow, not even caring if I did wake up robbed, or en route to some two bit port.

Commencing anew—the tambourine shaking, the fiddles blithely skipping and bowing—I tried to forget all eyes were on me; but again she stopped short, called off the band, and fetched me another from the bar counter—all hands clapping loudly and cheering her on, with enthusiastic cries of "Nel! Hearty Nel!", till even in my lunatic state I realized I was partners with our landlady. Tossing off her second offer—wondering if it indebted me to her in some way, besides financially of course, which was probably a week's board—I stood at the ready, more or less clay now to her moves; and though I still feared to utterly let go—associating that with Hilo, and the events after San Francisco Bay—I found I could clap and kick with the others, if not with abandon, at least with relish.

Swinging into the dance I found it swung me, as if its very forms had limbs of their own; and spinning, stomping, whirling, I saw things made sense, the same instinctive way they do sailing—the same intuitive way one tack or maneuver leads you inexorably to another. The whole room twirling with me—reeling, surging, wheeling, all hands and Eben's face turning as well, and even George Washington and Queen Victoria spinning by, their eyes a-glint as if they had designs on each other—I kept up some eddy or other for some time; and at last when the fiddlers' bows dropped, Nel pronounced me a passable partner: my spontaneous pleasure at her words so taking possession of my mind that I found it impossible to think of her as someone who was robbing me blind, and serving me prison fare three times a day.

As we were leaving the floor one of the sailors slipped her a couple dollars, and disappeared with Nett or Sal or his arm—where I couldn't imagine, certainly not to our dormitory attic; and glad of an excuse to break free, I made Nel a bow, and threw myself back down on the bench. Shipmates to the end, Eben'd bought me a drink, which he had ready and waiting for me; and joining him in progress we drank together, watching new partners pair up at the bar. By now we knew the names of not only all the girls, but the fiddlers and not a few of the resident sailors; and wondering which of the lot would make the least objectionable bedfellows—as equally unable to imagine ourselves with the lice-ridden women, as with the tobacco juice-spitting men—we put in the better part of an hour.

Having commendably spun out our drinks, we were counting out our spare change, on the verge of making one last visit to the counter, when we were accosted by someone new on the scene, perhaps taking the place of some of the disappearing women, or already back on the floor for an encore: an immense Irishwoman with the height of a lamp post, and the biceps of the best stevedore on the wharves. Surveying the hall, she spied us in our corner, though we tried with all our might to shrink into the woodwork; and approaching us with a glass, she made a move on Eben, sitting down beside him and taking his hand.

Having had fun up till now at my expense, he went an unmistakable seasick hue, dwarfed there on the bench by her bulk; and trying to reclaim his paw, he looked imploringly at me, as if he thought I still had the wits to effect a rescue. Pretty uninhibited by this time—my native forthrightness aided by several drinks, and the invigorating success of my dance—I simply said the first thing that came to my head: got apologetically to my feet, gave this Amazon a bow, and blurted out "Ye'll have t' excuse him, ma'am—y'see, he's the sort that only goes with otheh men."

Completely wiped of all expression, Eben's face simply went blank, taking on the stunned look of a moose; while our Irishwoman—in company with Nel nearby, and several others who'd overheard—immediately broke into uproarious laughter. "Lordy, misteh," guffawed Nel, coming up on Eben from the counter, "ye're in the wrong place—y' need t' visit Houghton's across the way, or Eddie Slater's up the street."

My heart—even in my inebriated state, and my lingering shock at my own words—took a leap at Slater's name; but before I could begin to register our success, she was already promising to introduce us to her cousin, some shark or other for the dance hall across the street. Wondering how much further this indebted us to her, not to mention him, when we met him, we took our leave as soon as we decently could; and noticing our Kanacker friends had quit also, each with a girl victoriously on his arm, we made our way blunderingly to the attic.

Later on the next day, well into the evening, she kept her promise, and showed us across the street to Houghton's: another in an endless line of lodgings which predominated in these backwater alleys, with nothing in its granite blocks or dormers to show it was any different from any of its neighbors. Its tavern, which stood on street level like ours, was already filling up with run-of-the-mill seamen, decked out in ordinary slushed boots and fur collars, pilot coats and striped mufflers; but behind its bar counter, tended by a brisk octogenarian, was a sliding partition which led into a bare hall; and beyond this was another door which opened onto a private room, large, at first glance, and peopled by both men and women. Giving Nel a curt nod, the old codger at the bar pulled a cord and allowed us to slip through the partition; and we were met in the hall at the opened far door by a burly tar with bright tattoos on both hands.

"Here's a couple o' customers, Harry," Nel introduced us with a businesslike vigor; "they've got good manners, an'll clean up your dance floor"; and with a shrewd look at us and a salty retort, tattooed Harry ushered us into his own hall.

At first sight it was as blood-related to Nel's as its owner; was kin from its bar, tucked away in one corner, to its orchestra, consisting of three or four pieces, to its decorative prints adorning the wall, right down to Neptune with his trident, and George Washington and Queen Victoria side by side under crossed swords. Well-sanded like ours, its dance floor was crowded, vigorous with sashaying couples; while its ceiling was spangled with bright tissue paper, cut into ornamental stars and shapes. It was not till we'd sat down at one of the far tables, which, like the benches, banked the walls—not till we'd commenced on our first round of drinks, the perpetual cheap rum, well-watered, that we hit upon the place's chief point of departure. Skipping from one feminine partner to another, I realized, from their shapes—from a certain bulkiness to their shoulders, not to mention, an unmistakable shadow to their faces, noticeable now even in the soft light of the candles—that dresses or no, they were all men; and to get him to decently clamp his mouth shut, I kicked Eben hard under the table.

"Well, which one're *you* goin' t' dance with, hm?" he shot back at me, deadpan; and floundering to adjust the lines of my own face, I returned,

"I'll worry about that when the time comes."

"It's goin' t' come a lot sooneh than the buzz ye'll need t' deaden the shock, considerin' these drinks," he retorted, gazing woefully into his tumbler.

"Well, thehre's one easy way t' solve the problem," I offered, polishing off the whole of my glass.

"Cash that banknote, an' bring in oweh own rum?" he looked up hopefully.

"No, drink what we get, an' dance with each otheh."

"You call that a solution?"

"It's me or one o' them—what d'ye say?"

Glancing deliberately around the floor, he laboriously studied the be-skirted men—took in their ludicrous flounces, their billowing berthas, and the awkward grace with which they handled their partners; then as laboriously he scrutinized me. "Hahrd choice," he pronounced dryly.

"Well, you'hre going t' have t' make it a lot quickeh than ye'd thought: one of these beauties has already got his eye on us," I told him.

"Which one?" he scanned the room, wary.

"The one in green silk who's just left the bahr."

"Too tall for me, he'll have t' take you," he breathed, relieved.

"McCabe, for Christ's sake—"

"You wanted t' do this, remembeh? You wanted t'—what was youhr words, now—experience Jim's past, or—"

"I wanted t' taste it, not wallow in it… Now be a sport, let's be partnehs."

"Where else d'ye see two men dancin' t'getheh who're actually both dressed as men?"

"Oveh thehre by the door, them two sailohs that came in afteh us, *they're* partnehs."

"Oh, all right," he gave in, scowling, his expression anything but romantic. "But I d'clare, Melchett, you'hre goin' t' have t' pay big for this."

Getting out onto the floor just as a breakdown finished, and the fiddlers took up a kind of rude waltz, we clumsily confronted each other, trying to figure out what to do with our hands; and regarding me with irritation, Eben said exasperatedly, "I'll lead."

"I'm the biggeh of the two of us," I protested, as half a dozen sodden voices took up the song, a sentimental version of the old forecastle favorite, "Home, Dearie, Home."

"What in Gawd's name has *that* got t' do with anything," he gusted, about as tenderly as a mate with a monkey's fist.

"It'll look betteh," I insisted, my hands on my hips; while "Oh, Boston's a fine town, with ships in the bay; And I wish in my heart it was there I was t'day," floated mournfully in the air around us.

"Well, if it's *looks* we're talkin' about, we've come t' the wrong place," he proclaimed, thankfully not loud enough to dent the fiddlers' whine; but at length simmering down, he took my hand, and grudgingly allowed my arm round his waist; and we sailed off with an exchange of dark looks, trying not to fall all over each other.

Neither of us expert dancers—my schooling having been mostly wasted, and his tutoring having come from the cleared floors of bait sheds—we would hardly have made commendable partners in the best circumstances; and our doubts now about how to proceed with each other—our gingerly touch and dubious footwork, as he kept forgetting to reverse his moves—didn't improve our performance any. Nor could our expressions have conveyed much amore; for he had the look of some fowl on the meat block, and I kept having to reel him in closer to at least maintain the pretext of interest. But in the full swing of the evening—in the rasp and mourn of rough voices, broken from years of harsh weather and drinking—and in the ludicrous medley of costumes around us, we might have passed more or less unnoticed; might have pulled it off without mishap or comment, if we'd somehow managed to keep our mouths shut.

"I'm afraid we don't look very convincin'," I made the mistake of muttering, just as the fiddlers took up the chorus.

"Damn right we don't," he snorted, "since we ain't lovehs; an' if ye want t' know why we ain't—if ye want t' know one reason amongst hundreds—it's be'cause you'hre too gawddam pushy."

"Pushy, am I?" I scowled, holding him out at arm's length; while "Then it's home, dearie, home, it's home I want t' be; And it's home, dearie, home, across the rolling sea," fetched sighs and sweet looks from the host around us.

"Pushy, that's right, an' controllin', a regulah quarterdeck Napolean—just what always got Jim's dandeh up," he snapped, with a rebellious cloud to his mug I'd never seen there before.

"Dandeh, hell!" I protested; "he liked it!"

"That why he hauled off once an' decked ye?" he bellowed, drawing the attention of several around us, and diminishing the nostalgic effect of "The oak and the ash and the bonny ellum tree."

"Well, he liked it," I insisted; "he just didn't know how t' admit it."

Dropping my hand, he let out a rude hoot. "Well, what was good for him's not necessarily good for me; did 'je eveh once in the last ten yearhs stop an' think o' that?"

By now we'd stopped dead in our tracks, though the fiddlers were still going at it, and the dancers were yet swaying wistfully about us, some cheek to cheek as they took up the next verse; but as our hands came to our hips and our voices rose higher—high enough to combat the sentiments about New York, and the mush of the ensuing chorus—several couples broke off and began to gather round; and hands rubbing together, they urged on a fight. Bent on enforcing my will, or at least wheedling my way, I scarcely heard them or the desperate fiddlers, sawing on now in an impromptu intermission; while Eben, out of choice words, and even running low on scowls, simply all at once gave me a shove—a shove, after all these years of tolerant friendship.

Why he'd had to choose this of all possible moments in the past two decades to balk, I was left feeling too nonplussed to fathom; and I merely stood gaping there at him, witless. Made all at once conscious of ourselves by our ring of onlookers, staring on with varying degrees of sympathy and ill will, we sheepishly slunk back to our table, cries of "Lover's quarrel!" singing in our ears; and as if touched off by our dissension, a tussle commenced near the bar counter, some shellback going at it with his beskirted partner, and the two of them rolling over and over, skirt, pumps, petticoats and all twirling by in a whirl. Their attention diverted, our onlookers regrouped, cheering on one or the other of this pair; while a remaining few danced it out, blithely stepping around them, and dipping to the last whining trill of the fiddles.

Considering ourselves temporarily out of the limelight, we wolfed down a number of drinks in succession, regardless of our purse and the imminent threat of being shanghaied—uneasily eyeing each other meantime, and silently assessing damages done to our masquerade and friendship. The former question was quickly settled by the arrival of free rum, a vote of confidence from the sympathetic bartender—whose spirited support, uncharacteristically pure, was accompanied by amused winks, and a word or two of romantic advice; but the latter was resolved, or at any rate, peaceably shelved, by a series of unspoken stages, mostly revolving around the exchange of sheepish glances. When we'd at last relaxed to the point of recovering our sense of humor, it was considerably later in the evening, and we'd lost the entire purpose of our mission; but I made an effort to get things back on course, speaking up in the midst of a rollicking reel.

"Tell me Jim didn't go in for such dress," I pleaded, my eye on the false curls and furbelows around us.

"No, not that he eveh told me," he returned, tiptoeing, like me, round the issues between us. "He liked handsome togs, no secret t' that; but he always seemed comfortable with bein' a man—with his idear of bein' a man, which was mostly Rom, as y' know; an' he wanted you t' love him as such."

"What d'ye make of what Nel said last night about Slateh?" I asked him, relieved I needn't pursue images of Jim in silk stockings, and as eased in my mind that Eben was at least speaking to me.

"Y'mean, the way she named the place up the street as his instead o' Lomond's?"

"Aye."

"Don't know," he lowered his voice, "unless him an' Lomond finally squared off—or unless Lomond moved on because the turf got too hot for him."

"How're we eveh goin' t' get from hehre t' there?" I put in.

"Not by dancin' with each other," he said sagely, sweeping the rollicking group on the floor. "We've got t' meet folks, an' pick up an invitation some way. The only way t' get int' his place, you c'n bet, is through some door ye need an introduction to open."

Unable to argue with the logic of his words, I took to hanging around the bar counter longer, every time I ordered a fresh round—hoping to pick up a fresh reference I could use; even accepted a couple invitations to dance, extended by skirted beauties obviously hoping to come between Eben and me; but the opening we sought didn't come until late, and again, only through a ludicrous incident.

Trying not to wonder what it would have been like to dance with Jim, I sifted my partners' words for the information we needed; but all I discovered at first was faces, simply the faces behind those fake fringes. Feeling the rivalry and abuse which simmered just beneath the taffeta and curls, I wasn't surprised by the sporadic eruption of strife; understood why Eben and I hadn't been so out of place, after all; for in costume or no, they were taking out their frustrations on each other in dozens of small, intimate frays like ours—and seldom did I dance out a waltz or a reel without witnessing some tiff or skirmish.

It was just such a clash that led us at last to our long sought-after invitation; for seething all evening with small scraps and conflicts, the place at last erupted into a full-scale commotion, with the squaring-off of two seamen over one of the "girls"; and before we knew it Eben and I were caught up in the contest. Whatever the original spark, the pair soon came to hot words, then to a flare-up of angry blows—one of the sailors suddenly leaping up onto the bench, snatching down the sword from above George Washington's picture, and straightaway going after his rival, for all the world like a Minuteman in a charge.

Easily the biggest man in the room—discovering again the advantage of size, which heretofore had always been an awkward burden—I overpowered our zealous swordsman, coming at him from behind and pinning his arms, while Eben and another customer disarmed him; and disgruntled, the fellow was soon out on his ear, vigorously shown to the street by tattooed Harry. Stopping by at our table, his hapless opponent took a minute to thank us for his timely rescue; and seeing an opportunity too good to miss, we invited him to sit down and join us.

"You lodgin' hehre for the night?" we asked him, trying to make conversation.

"Nah," he returned, "up the street at Slater's—know the place?"

"Heard of it, but ain't been by yet," Eben answered, with the barest lift of an eyebrow at me. "Is it any betteh than this?"

"It ain't so rowdy; there ain't no dress-up; an' it's got the best-lookin' boys this side o' the wateh—always did," he informed us with a grin.

"Sounds invitin'," Eben deadpanned, turning up his tumbler to keep from looking at me. "Meet me here t'morrow—no, t'morrow's Sunday—meet me here again Monday night, an' I'll show ye over t' thank ye," he offered; and refraining from a triumphant exchange of glances, we straightaway downed our glasses, and treated him to a round to show our appreciation.

Sniffing the snow in the air the next morning—watching the flakes drift silently down, shrouding the bleak line of warehouses and sail lofts—we turned up our collars and lowered our hat brims, and struck out in an aimless way for the hushed wharves. Somewhere up the hill barely discernible in the flurries, town-folk were wending their way to church, picking their paths through the snow or gliding along in bright sleighs; were preparing for massive dinners at two, marshaling mounds of cooked fowl and hot stewed oysters, and looking ahead to erudite mealtime conversation, to talk of theatres and lectures and news from abroad, of Emerson and Carlyle and Cambridge College.

In the numb consciousness of our own far ruder setting—in the general feeling of let-down after the intense pursuits of the week, and before the high prospects of tomorrow night—we had no idea which way to go; and we came to a halt near the foot of a wharf, as if by an unspoken need to assess. My heart heavy with mute memories of Jim, with a dumb groping for where in this wide world he might be—despairs which only broke on me when I wasn't busy, a situation I seldom allowed—I looked over at Eben, perplexed; and speaking out of my hollowness I asked, "Well, whehre do we go from hehre, mate?"

Huddling deeper in his collar he peered up the street, the visitation of a sudden idea brightening his face; and smiling back at me he suggested, "Y' said you wanted t' hear Fatheh Tayloh whilst we was in pohrt; well, let's go do it while we still can. B'fore long all hands'll recognize us as Wood an' Lovell, considerin' the splash we've already made at Nel's, an' the commotion last night at Houghton's; an' if we leave it for last an' go as ourselves, somebody or other'll be bound t' make the connection."

"You don't think Tom'll be thehre, or some of his men?" I asked, half-interested, half-anxious.

"Far more likely they'll be in t' heahr Jackson, since he's right on the same wharf, an' a friend; but just in case we'll sit well t' the back, an' not hang around any afteh."

Refreshed, I headed up the waterfront with him past chandlers and coopers and manufacturers of gun powder, to Father Taylor's waterside chapel, visible even from a distance with its bright blue flag, flying from its roof like a pennant from a mast; entered in with a host of dog-eared seamen, decked out in the usual drab coats and wool trowsers, and settled down near the door opposite the pulpit, which, raised on its pillars, with its ornamental drapery behind, was plain to be seen over the heads before us. Off to our right, and less ready to view, was the gallery with its simple choir, composed of women and men, a violin and a cello; while on the benches around us sat a congregation of men, sailors to the last, from half a dozen nations, all hushed with respect for Father Taylor's reputation. Many, I supposed, had spent the past nights much like we had, and were here today to cleanse their conscience, or at any rate, improve their credit; none, fortunately, looked familiar; and all huddled deep in their seagoing garb, to keep out the chill of the unheated room.

A former mariner himself, and sympathetic to seamen, Father

Taylor was already present, pouring over some papers on the desk in his pulpit; and though it'd been three years or so since I'd last heard him, I recognized his hard, weathered features, strongly graven with deepwater experience and age. Commencing first with a hymn—violin, cello, and choir chiming in—then following up with an extemporaneous prayer, he went characteristically straight to his text, in preparation for his discourse; and thumping upon the great Bible before him he read from the 77th Psalm: "Thy way was through the sea, thy path through the great waters; yet thy footprints were unseen."

A calm came over me as soon as I heard the words, a stillness that yet stirred me with pangs of alertness; but before I could identify my own reactions he'd already launched forth with his application; already leaned over the pulpit, peered down into our midst, and finger jabbing the air, embarked "The deep!" All hands having sat up the straighter, or shifted into attention on the benches, he sailed on in his usual eccentric manner, now and then taking to pacing to emphasize his point, or the energy of his conviction:

"Think of the deep, with the voice of the Lord upon it—think of the waters themselves, the mighty abysses, quaking with fear at the crash of his thunder! 'When the waters saw thee, O God, when the waters saw thee, they were afraid; yea, the deep trembled,'" he read; then looking up, he again thumped his Bible, and striding back and forth, persevered with his voyage. "Think of the depths, the imponderable fathoms—the impenetrable springs and recesses God spoke to Job about from the whirlwind. Think of the fearsome creatures peopling that dark, the disembodied moans and whistles— then think of the frail scraps that skim above them, the splinters of wood that ply the surface. 'Yonder is the sea, great and wide, which teems with things innumerable, living things both small and great. There go the ships, and Leviathan which thou didst form to sport in it.'

"Think of the clashing heights which torment those scraps, and the shadowy monsters which threaten their passage—then think of the invisible trail across that turmoil, the impalpable marks of footprints. How did they get there? Where are they going? How do we see them? How do we follow? No signposts. No roadway. No innkeeper to guide us. No marks of a boot in the soft sand of the bar. How do we chart the track in that deep—how do we plot our way?"

Peering down at us again and jabbing the air, he victoriously cried "Navigation!"; held up a quadrant, that we might not mistake his meaning; then still waving it aloft, he paced back and forth, as if on a quarterdeck of his own. "Direction-finding—that's the idea. That's how we traverse the tracts of the deep. That's how we follow the print of the Lord. Do any mortals know the meaning of navigation better than we do? Depend on it more for life, limb, bread than us seamen? It's the getting from one place to another—isn't that it? The finding of 'the way through the sea, the path through the great waters'? Simple. Direct. Point to point, port to port, earth to heaven—isn't that it, brethren?"

Pausing for effect he held up the quadrant, as if about to take a reading; peered into one of the shaded lenses; then still perching it at his shoulder he leaned back down towards us, and embarked anew with a throaty quaver. "But wait. There's more. It's not so simple. There's unexpected depths t' plumb here. Unlooked-for trenches in the deep. Here we are, and here's the sea; and here's our quadrant, the centuries-old tool for direction-finding—for measuring our position and place. But we need another object to measure ourselves by— another position and place to determine ours. We need the sun. The moon. A star. An altitude to fix our point on the plane."

Raising his voice a degree he picked up pace: "And we need a chart, a map that can unravel the code—the particular set of coordinates for each point. We can't see that code, anymore than we can see the track of the Lord, the invisible trail in the deep— but it's there, governing our course and position, criss-crossing the globe like an invisible skein. And we need"—lifting his voice another notch, till it wavered and cracked from years of hoarse orders—"the particular features that define each watery intersection. There's tides at each point, currents and trade winds, zephyrs and mistrals for each place and season. There's specific patterns and colors to each depth and ocean—peculiar sands and muds to each shelf and sounding. And there's constellations above, fixed migrations of stars—the coming and going phases of the moon—quite a host of factors that determine direction.

"And finally"—raising his words to sea pitch, and vigorously pointing down at us on our benches, as if relishing some quarterdeck muster—"there's *us* in it all—us, the mariners, brethren. Us and the stars. Us and the winds. Us and the currents. Us and the clockwork of navigation. We're a particular set of coordinates of our own—each of us an individual set meshing with nature's. No one of us navigates like any other, or shapes a course anything like his shipmate's. How do we determine our place in this concourse? How do we interpret our data?"

Picking us out with his fingers almost as if he'd met us, or had shipped us once on some long-ago voyage, he catechized our faces sea fashion: "Do we proceed like some, regular and systematic—shoot the sun each noon, taking two or three sightings, instantly noting the time and recording our figures? Do we compare our computation with other sails we speak? Obtain back-sightings in times of fog? Or do we dead reckon like most through those long cloudy stretches, relying as much on instinct as data? What about chance, the margin of error—the role of the faulty reading or quadrant, the flaw in the chronometer or compass? What is our sun, the star we steer by—and what chart do we use when we've gathered our data, to transmute it into position and place?"

"Well, *here's* our chart, boys," he resounded, holding up his great timeworn Bible, and thumping it with weathered knuckles. "Here's our chart, our map, our almanac, our tables—our tidal graphs and lunar forecasts. And *there's* our sun, our steering-star—the point aloft we plot our place by"—giving a dramatic sweep toward the tapestry behind, where the figure of Christ predominated. "And *yonder's* the wind that propels us on our way, the breath of the Holy Spirit on the deep—throw open that door a moment, son!"

Realizing what was meant, the man nearest the entrance unquestioningly jumped up to do as bidden; and instantly a gust of raw wind swept the room vigorous with the swirl of snow; as instantly fell hushed when the door was shut to, and all eyes returned to the man in the pulpit.

"And where's our quadrant, our direction-finder?" he carried on full force in the quiet. "In here!" he cried, victoriously thumping his chest with triumphant raps of his hardy fist. "It's here, mariners, our quadrant's in here! The device we need to read our position, make sense of it from our tables and charts—it's within! It helms our soul like a man steers a ship. It's our own inner tool of direction— our unique inner pilot, guiding star, compass—our interpreter of signs, charts, the Bible, of our own peculiar correlation with nature. It carries on the navigation of soul even as it works out the navigation of life, the execution of a seaman's duty. It sees the *linkage* between the constellations and the architecture of our migration— the correspondence b'tween God's vast machinations and some instinctive homing within. It's not just a tool but an unseen pilot within, a response just like a bird's to the season. Do the geese know the longitude and latitude of their flight? Pick out the north star from the myriads of others? Yet they know their direction from the same inner quadrant, the same inner timing of creature and nature."

Holding his quadrant aloft once more with a flourish, he thundered home to his conclusion: "It's the interpreter of the partnership of us and nature, us and God, Creator and created. It's the face of our own inner selves, the features within which conduct our voyage. Mariners, learn to trust the quadrant you carry! Learn to navigate with its devices—to make manifest the unseen footprint! This is our rare privilege in creation, the lofty gift given alone to man. To discern paths in the pathless. To find shape in the shapeless. To forge direction from chaos. In partnership with God. In harmony with ourselves. In unity with nature. Amen."

Scooping up his Bible, then clapping his quadrant in its case, he straightaway tumbled down from the pulpit, and spoke his benediction in the midst of his hearers; and immediately besieged by a flood of well-wishers, many of whom had heard him every leave in port for years, he was swiftly swallowed up from view. Stirring on the bench, I emerged from my thoughts—from the cavalcade of remembrances which had convened from all points, and the painful odyssey of the present; and sighing, I looked over at Eben. Though he'd said nothing beside me, and made no sign during worship, he'd turned to share a glance with me now; and his weathered face was kind.

Gone were all the indications of last night's strife, the stresses of our past week's undertakings—indeed, of all the peregrinations of past years; and it was with surprising gentleness that he took my arm, and steered me out ahead of the others, already jesting and laughing in small groups. As if understanding I couldn't find words, he said nothing to me, and expected nothing in return; simply walked aimlessly about with me for awhile, in the cool and feathery hush of the snowflakes. Wandering the backwaters of Ann Street, we passed dark, silent chandlers, liveries and cooperages and smithies, shrouded in snowy Sabbath stillness; passed taverns and grog shops, hushed for the day; then stumbling upon our little oyster bar and finding it unexpectedly open, we came to an attentive halt near the doorway. Looking me over in the dim light, the feeble grey of a winter's noon, Eben wordlessly studied my face; as quietly skipped to the scene thorough the windows, where dishes gleamed on candlelit tables; then abruptly reaching a conclusion, he impulsively nodded me in.

"Can we afford it?" I asked doubtfully, speaking up for the first time—longing to enter, to slip into some warm, private alcove with him, yet dutifully remembering our circumstances.

"We'll have to," he said simply, sounding the change in his trowsers pockets; "you need it."

"Do I look that bad?" I inquired, trying to see my reflection in the window—all at once conscious of my grey-hued features, and the undeniable smell which permeated my garb.

"Worse than I've eveh seen ye, which is sayin' a good deal," he informed dryly.

"You don't look so good youhrself," I told him, scrutinizing his homely features.

"Stands t' reason, considerin' who I've took up with," he returned with a wry look at me; but an unwilling smile welled up swiftly after, and his hand at my elbow was tender and steady.

Entering together, we took our window alcove, snuggling down in its curtained recesses; partook of steamed oysters, hot bread and coffee; and communing as often without as within, we commerced in memories of travels we'd shared, in recollections of waters unfolded— as contented as we two had ever been, as contented as we could be at present, without the one who was missing from us.

The following night found us back at Houghton's, sipping watered rum at our corner table, and wondering if our hapless friend would show up. A couple of hours having passed, and our position having grown once again tenuous, we were about to commence our quest anew with another round of making contacts when we spotted him with tattooed Harry at the door, and gave him a hail from across the room. Joining us straightaway he stayed around long enough to share a drink with us at our table; then pushing back his chair he kept his promise, leading us up the street to the granite building we'd so often scrutinized from without.

Turning onto Salt Lane and scurrying down the dark steps we'd studied from our oyster bar window, he led us into a cellar tavern, an ordinary outer façade, like Houghton's; spoke a word to a man on a corner barstool, who seemed to be soddenly pouring over some newsprint; then forged the way through the door he'd apparently released, which again led into a nondescript hallway, superintended by a well-muscled ouster. My heart hurrying at the thought that this was the same hall down which Jim had three years ago wandered— that I might be about to meet some of the men who'd known him—I looked eagerly around at the cracked stucco walls, the marred wooden doors and stained granite floor; glanced over my shoulder as if he might suddenly appear, or as if Slater or Lomond might be following in our steps.

From behind the many doors came a variety of sounds, shouts of gaming, drunken sport, and at the far end of the hall, music; while in and out of the rooms issued an occasional patron, always with a word and a tip for the ouster. Passing one of these chambers just as the door opened, we glimpsed a cluster of tavern tables, at which coated men were playing at cards; raised an eyebrow at one another, having never witnessed professional gambling; then passed another door from under which escaped steam, and the unmistakable plashings of water. Alert from our lengthy deprivation, we were both about to shout out a question when this door too opened, and we caught a glance of a long rectangular room, divided into small alcoves, each staffed with wash tubs, basins and mirrors, and neighbored by a mighty stove on which a giant kettle was going.

In each of the cubicles the bathing men, in various stages of dress and undress, were performing acts for one another frank enough to color our faces—to force us to turn our heads away, abashed; though so desperate were we both for ablutions by this time that we nearly hurled ourselves in anyway for mercy. Following Pennell to the farthest door, and leaving a coin in the hand of the wary ouster, we entered what we saw at once was a dance hall, a smaller, more intimate room than Houghton's; and going directly to one of the partitioned booths which banked the walls like an English pub, we settled ourselves at a well-scrubbed table, while Pennell went to fetch us hot glasses of flip.

My heart laboring so I could scarcely make conversation, or attend to my glass without quivering fingers, I looked around with quick, avid glances, taking in sights I knew Jim had seen, and trying to orient myself to my surroundings from my previous experiences at Nel's and Houghton's. Like the foregoing halls this one had a dance floor, well-sanded and presently well-attended; a small orchestra of immigrant fiddlers; windowless walls festooned with prints, most of them maritime, a few patriotic; and a bar counter at the far end of the room, its pigeon-holes well stocked with bottles of rum, with here and there plate glass or colored tissue, in a rude attempt at decoration.

But there the similarities between the halls ended; for there was a far different air pervading this place—an atmosphere at once apparent even to one as inexperienced as I was. Perhaps it was the orchestra, which seemed to play mostly waltzes; perhaps the booths, which gave a private aura; perhaps the clientele, which, though in the main nautical, lacked the element of the coarse or bizarre. Whatever the cause there was a climate here almost approaching gentility or refinement—a sensibility that could be seen as much in the deportment of the dancers, even the crudest sailors conducting themselves well, as in the demeanor of those in the booths. Combating the fumes of rank ship's tobacco, and overcoming altogether the noxious reek of chewing plugs, was the aroma of cultivated smoke—a hint of Cavendish or perhaps Havana; while amongst the rude clay pipes of the sailors was an occasional well-made briar. The faces around us too were distinctive—a far cry from the faces we'd encountered on past nights: the seamen's, though rough, somehow more subdued, as if they'd picked up something of the place's refinement; while here and there was an older countenance, or a brow showing unmistakable signs of intellect and breeding.

Indeed in the booth opposite ours sat a couple of men in their forties who, despite modest coats and nondescript trowsers, bore every mark of hailing from Cambridge; every evidence of the professorial and highbrow; and a sudden fear darted through me that nearby, in other booths, there might be an instructor from Bowdoin, or someone accompanying someone from there who might in turn recognize me. Uneasy at this sudden turn to events, I cocked a quick brow at Eben beside me, and gave a slight nod at the booth across; but he gave me an encouraging pat on the knee, and finished off his flip, unconcerned; and giving his attention back to Pennell, he glibly engaged him in a fresh round of small talk, that I might have more liberty to study the room.

But the biggest difference between this place and the others—increasingly clear to me as my wits collected, and I adjusted myself to my surroundings—was in the quality of the establishment's young men, and in the air of intimacy which prevailed. No overblown women here, no furbelowed men, but fresh-faced youths, none of them older than eighteen, and all of them seemingly in the flush of health and beauty; all of them emanating a winsome charm, and a sensuality which made one forget their hard lot. There'd been nothing desirable to me at Nel's or Houghton's—nothing that could enable me to imagine Jim in their midst, even given the news of him Eben had imparted. But here I was suddenly aroused by what I saw, so frequently hot-cheeked that I had to take refuge in my glass; and Jim was everywhere I looked, in the play of the eyes, in the lift of a shoulder, in the cocky assertion of a jest or laugh.

Nor was it just the unpretentiousness of these youths, conscious as they were of their artless coyness, that had so swiftly captured my interest; not just the thought of Jim in their place, and the revelations of him their practices evoked; but the shows of affection going on all around, calling forth my inmost fancies. Here at one booth, an older man and a younger—the latter without a doubt one of Slater's— unreservedly sat side by side, unabashedly sharing the same glass, and an interplay of frank looks and laughter; while out on the floor, a young man danced with a seaman, in a broad clasp of arms and meaningful touches; and in a far corner two men were kissing in a way I'd certainly never kissed Anne before, or ever observed any man kiss any woman.

Filled first with an embarrassed awe, then with an eager, flurried interest, and finally with the rage of envy—the sheer ache of lonely, covetous yearning for the intimacy I'd never had, through my own doing, with Jim—I shuttled from one scene of fascination to another, trying not to openly stare, or give away my millrace of emotions; and again and again I buried myself in my glass, hoping to quell my inner commotion, and steady the clumsy tumult of my fingers.

But above all it was the drawings, tacked up on the wall, which bespoke the place's sensuality and candor. Going once to the bar to fetch us a round, I saw them in a line behind the counter: pen and inks mostly, done by one artist, though some looked as though they'd been scribbled off by an impromptu hand, while sipping flip on a bench or barstool. No studio scenes, these, at a daguerreotype parlor—no velvet hangings or high-backed sofas, on which sat suited gentlemen in black, looking soberly out on the distance: these were ribald views of, I supposed, the young men who'd worked here down the years, some fully nude, others partially clothed, others still engaged with partners, in erotic acts which made those going on around us, or glimpsed in the cubicles of the baths, look tame.

A frank man myself—as forthright a character, I'd once thought, as had ever peopled the coast—I was embarrassed to find that I was timid; that these youths who brazened such practices with one another, much less in front of an artist, bespoke a far greater forthrightness. To see such passions, for years kept decently in my hold, bluntly displayed on the wall before me, was like colliding head-on with my inmost cargo; and uncertain how I felt about it, delighted or nonplussed or appalled, I kept returning on any excuse to the counter, hoping to take in further details—to maybe encounter, amongst the older drawings, one or two that might be of Jim.

On the fourth or fifth trip, not entirely responsible anymore, as much due to the stimulation of the hall as the flip, I thought I spotted a group, somewhat yellowed with age, that portrayed him; thought I detected something in the strong, handsome face, fine form and flair that was unmistakably his; but it was hard to tell for sure in the candlelit dim; and my heart laboring as if it really were he— as if, after all these months, he really were here, in all the honesty and forthrightness of my dreams—I peered as best I could in the commotion around me.

Two or three sketches portrayed him alone, an equal number partnered with others; though all were potently, uncompromisingly suggestive, more powerfully sensual than I'd ever dared imagine him; and I understood why I'd hesitated to match my experience against his. One in particular, the finest of the lot—as much because of what it withheld, as because of what it revealed—especially captivated and moved me; showed him from behind, looking over his shoulder, just dropping his dressing gown from about his waist to his bare legs, with a teasing yet inviting look to his eye, and an unforgettable smile. So like him was it—so like how he must have been—that it was all I could do to keep from rushing behind the counter, and snatching it from the wall when no one was looking.

One thing I knew for certain by the end of the first hour—just from observing what I could from our booth, and from my hasty forays to the bar counter—was that I hadn't ever really known him; that the simple-minded townsfolk who'd gossiped about his romantic past, motivated by the grossest curiosity and interest, and illuminated by the crudest conjecture, had come closer to the erotic quick at his core than I ever had in three years of friendship. Looking around, I could see his true self in the room; could see it in the subterranean allure of the youths, in the appetite of their expressions and glances, in the adventure of the almost disclosed, but not quite, as plainly as if were into his heart, rather than into this old cellar I peered. As I'd studied his trunk that first night a Hannah's, a few squares and a world away from here—as I'd scrutinized its outer signs and carvings, speculating about his origins in Wales, and wondering what lay within—so now I examined the trappings of this hall; looked into its depths as into a coffer, a storehouse in which reposed his essence.

There he was, over there in that warm nook; in the spice of that young lad sidling up to my Cambridge fellow; in the coy gleam of that popinjay taking the dance floor; in the scented beauty of that dandy. The aroma of candle smoke, the incense of the briars, the subtle brush of fingertips, the audacity of a frank touch all bespoke him; inventoried his sensual allure as directly as the room's proclamation of drawings. Even the obvious intellect and refinement which characterized the place's aura played their part in eliciting his nature; for both underscored it, disciplined it, like the blows of a blacksmith's mallet; and it was easy for me to understand the initial appeal of the place to him—his selection of it as a base for business.

So easy was it for me to picture him here, in the smithy of the room's surroundings, that I too slipped in and took my place in its forge; slipped in like one essaying a transfer—like one cautiously, tentatively making himself at home, till I was the frock-coated gentleman seated next to him, the burly seaman just in from a voyage.

Leaving us after an hour in the company of a young man, our cohort Pennell gave us a final thanks; offered us a drink and a chat another evening; and as soon as he was gone we hastily compared notes, Eben sharing bits of the conversation they'd had, me distilling thoughts from my observations. That Pennell himself had never known Jim— that he'd patronized the place only the past couple of years, and couldn't possibly have crossed paths with him—was apparent from the outset; that he knew nothing of Lomond, or at any rate made no allusion to him, was equally clear; but his talk had been full of the establishment's youth—of the subtle contests between them and of their ensnarement by Slater, manifestly not a man to cross; and he'd been generous with details about the baths, the rooms upstairs and their cost and so on. How to get lodgings on the top floor, cheap—

through the old salt who ran the curio shop, a sort of front man for Slater—Eben had learned; and we laid plans to move tomorrow, when our week at Nel's would be conveniently up.

It was while we were swapping thoughts that I spotted a young man, new on the scene or at any rate, near the door, who by the hectic flush on his cheeks and a perpetual cough, appeared to be not at all well; who in consequence seemed to be courting a night with some of the cruder seamen, not likely to be fussy about a partner, or amongst the first chosen themselves; and his haunted face had stopped not only me, for I noticed how Eben, in the midst of our talk, repeatedly stole glances at him.

"What is it?" I asked him, understanding he was onto something, and trying not to stare as I tipped up my glass.

"I ain't sure," he returned, with a sip at his own mug; "Jim only described him once—an' it's been three years; but if I ain't mistaken, I think that's Beckman."

My heart picking up at the thought of encountering this, Jim's only real friend and confidante in Boston, I looked him over harder; saw that he was amongst the oldest of the youths, surely eighteen, perhaps approaching twenty; guessed from his face, with its cap of wavy brown hair and bluish eyes, that he was Flemish. That he must once have been handsome, almost as comely as Jim, though of a lighter, smaller build, came to me forcibly even from a distance; but now he appeared to be ravaged by illness, his fair features set, his shoulders frail through his jacket; and his eyes showed he knew he wouldn't recover. At once I wanted to protect him, not just for Jim's sake, but for his own, out of a compassion which seared me hotly in the chest; wondered cynically whether that was why he was still pandering—whether Slater had kept him for that very value, or whether Slater had some inexplicable hold on him, as Lomond had had on Jim.

So powerful was my urge to safeguard him that I almost marched right up to him; and when an old derelict of a sailor who'd picked up his bait started to give him a rugged time—to take out on him his own years of misuse, the only such venom I'd observed all evening—I impulsively hailed him over to our table: his blue eyes darting from one to the other of us, then instinctively settling on me. Giving me an ill look, the shellback ordered me off, till I stood and he got wind of my size—till he spotted Eben there as well to back me; then giving ground he subsided for the time, sidling over to the bar counter.

Our newcomer, meantime, having sat down beside us, said little in answer to our greetings, making only short responses, and volunteering nothing—partly due to indifference, partly to frequent fits of coughing; and now that he was near, I could see how frail were his fingers, how almost palpably transparent—even more than his face proclaiming his illness. But in spite of his fatigue, and his visibly jaded incuriosity, he made no effort to duck out on his business, at once allowing us the freedom of our addresses, and the unquestioning use of his name; and indeed, this proved Jim's old friend, Jacques Beckman.

Nor was his advent our only windfall; for scarcely had we adjusted ourselves to his presence—scarcely had we begun to anticipate questions, and the wealth of information about Jim he might provide from his store, if once we won his trust and goodwill—than the door opened again to admit another man; and I knew at once—from the sudden crispness in the hall, from the alert look to Eben's face and above all, the dart of fear on Beckman's—that this must be Ed Slater. Rail-thin and tall, sharp-faced and hatchet-beaked, with an indescribable poise of calculation and shrewdness, he was certainly one to strike caution; and it was remarkable how trepidation ran through the hall, all hands suddenly pulling up short as if to overhaul their behavior, and keep a weather eye on future responses. Beckman in particular seemed to flounder about, as if he'd committed some daring indiscretion, instead of offering apathetic rejoinders; and not till Slater's eye had flickered on him, rested awhile, then wordlessly departed, did his finespun fingers stop to quiver, and his cough-ridden answers cease to quake.

As if to impress upon me the need for discretion, Eben's foot came quietly down upon mine, and rested there a warning moment; and reigning in my impetuous feelings—spilling some wind from my instinctive regard for Beckman, and my eagerness for news of Jim—I patterned myself on the restraint of the others, speaking offhandedly of this and that. For an interminable time—though it couldn't have been more than ten or fifteen minutes—we thus tiptoed about with our drinks at the table, skirting all the topics I longed for, and scarcely even daring meet one another's eyes; and I began to wonder if any of the three of us would ever stir, even to fetch a fresh round at the counter.

Not till the old sailor again made a move on Beckman, lurching up to our table and asking him for a dance—not till Beckman rose, there being no concrete reason to refuse, and I caught the flash of something in his eye, a wordless glitter of entrapment—did I begin to think in terms of an act; but suddenly it was all clear to me, clear enough to thaw my limbs, and throw off the paralysis of mind that had stalled me; and I said to Eben, "I'm goin' t' put a stop t' this."

"How?" he gaped, as if convinced that, after gaining ground, I'd suddenly taken leave of my senses.

"I'm goin' t' give him a night off—pay for him myself, an' get him a night's sleep for once. I've got as much right t' try as that bastihd oveh there; an' it'll be him if it's not me. I'll see what it's like upstairs as well."

"Look out, he'll rob ye blind," he cautioned, with a dubious look still at large on his features.

"He won't," I insisted, offended at the idea—at the very thought Beckman might not reciprocate the honest regard I felt.

"He will," he contended, with his usual unemphatic firmness. "Jim did, every single time. He will, or Slateh or someone else will. They'll sneak in at night, or slip through a partition."

"Then I'll give every cent I've got t' you, except the three dollahs or so I need for t'night."

"Look out for youhr boots," he reminded.

"I'll sleep in 'em, for Christ's sake."

"He's goin' t' find this pretty odd, y'know."

"Not afteh he understands I really mean well for him."

"That's the pahrt he's goin' t' find oddest of all," he smiled, with a not unloving shake of the head at me. "An' how're ye goin' t' keep Slateh from gettin' wind?"

"How's he eveh goin' t' find out?" I put it.

"Don't know, but it strikes me thehre ain't much here he can't discoveh."

"Once I close the door it's none o' his gawddam business, unless he's hidin' undeh the bed; an' I can't see that it should matteh t' him anyhow, once he's got his money."

"I just don't want t' see ye land in hot wateh, for homin' in on his private turf—which I've got an idear is what Beckman is."

"I'll keep us out o' trouble; trust me," I promised, as he made ready to go; and arranging with me to meet him at Nel's for noon dinner, so we could wrap up business there and fetch our bags, then giving me an encouraging look over his shoulder, he got up from our table and left.

Marching up to Slater as bold as brass—as if I'd done so every night of my life—I held out three dollars and calmly named Beckman, with a nonchalant jerk of the head toward the dance floor; and looking over first the silver, then me, then Beckman's current partner, the derelict sailor, he finally returned his gaze to me, then pocketed the money, saying nothing. Less than sure of my next move I walked over to Beckman, then tapped him on the shoulder, wondering what on earth to say to him; gave the down-and-out sailor a shove, in answer to his push at me; restrained myself from more hostile action, aware of Slater's scrutiny from afar; took a step or two toward the door, with no clear idea where I was going; then clumsily turning back, I simply danced out the waltz with Beckman, thinking that would at least give me time to muster my thoughts.

It was the right tack to take, for when the fiddlers had ceased, all I had to do was ask "Where to?"; and he unemphatically led me out of the dance hall, down the corridor all the way to the end, and up a dimly lighted stairwell, to a door which opened out onto the third floor. No dormitory room this, like the one at Nel's, but a regular hall with a number of entries, all leading to private chambers; and familiarly selecting a candlestick from the worn bureau, then lighting it at the single lamp, he led the way down to the third door on the right, and opening it, admitted me into his room.

That he obviously lived here—alone, if not with Slater—I could see at once, even in the dim light; could tell from the homely scattering of garb, the jumble of coats and mufflers on pegs, the personal clutter of brushes and razors: not a hefty array, if it was his world's possessions. Against one wall was a rumpled bed; along another, a chest for clothes, and a chair or two with sagging cushions; while above slanted the usual inadequate slates, through the cracks of which drifted the same relentless snow about now settling on Eben at Nel's. Wondering what in blazes I should do or say—feeling far less comfortable than even with Nel on the dance floor—I was about to simply fall into bed, boots, coat, hat and all, before he could make a move; was actually turning back the hectic bedclothes, when I noticed the significant chair near at hand, and the way in which he seemed to be setting an example by laying his own outer gear over its back.

Understanding at once—guessing there must be a partition nearby, or an arrangement by which a quick hand could rifle the clothes without having to search through the whole room every night—I hesitated, in an upheaval of doubt; debated between the possibility of losing my pea coat, the only warm gear I had with me now, and the certainty of getting Beckman into trouble, if I failed to comply with his direction; then remembering Slater's face, tossed my coat and hat on the pile, and stuffing my boots under my pillow, fell into bed.

Uncertain, curious, obviously not used to such an approach, he cautiously followed suit, climbing in beside me still dressed; and feeling utterly idiotic—wondering what on earth had possessed me to try this, and what reasonable move I should make now, whether I should explain my motive, and simply tell him to get some rest, or whether I should keep my mouth shut, fearing I might insult him with pity—I lay there like a duck in a reed bank, hoping to escape further notice. Realizing he must think me a novice, too abashed to initiate any activity of my own, I nonetheless half-pretended to sleep, going back and forth over the issues, Beckman meantime coughing beside me; till at last, after an age, or at any rate, half an hour, I sensed that he was about to make a move, and felt his tentative hand on my hip.

It was the best thing that could have happened, for it cleared the air; and putting his hand back, I simply said gently, "Just have youhself a rest for once, mate." Turning my back, I again pretended to sleep; and coughing for a long time beside me, with wrenching hacks that wracked the bed, then at last propping up the pillows, with a sigh—almost like a child's—of relief, he gradually relaxed by stages, and finally fell deeply asleep.

Perhaps it was the revelations of Jim in the hall, the fascination of the youths and the allure of the drawings; perhaps simply the nearness of one whose memories of him were earlier and more intimate than mine; but after a long time of watching the snow, of taking in the sights and smells of the room, and of wondering about the man beside me, I fell into a deep dream—not about Beckman, but Jim.

In its scenes I was moored somewhere on the waters, not far from Krakatoa, which rose with steam in the distance; not far from Anjier which gleamed like a jewel above the surface of the sea. It being a still, hot afternoon, without a breath of wind to speed us, I was in the bow, fishing; was astride the bowsprit with my feet dangling bare and my hook a few fathoms down in the deep. Though I'd been at it for hours, I'd made little progress, for something kept getting afoul of my line; kept nibbling at it and frolicking with it, and tangling it up with the anchor chain; and feeling increasingly irritated, I decided to dive down and investigate. Clamping my line, I slid down the anchor chain, though I couldn't possibly have done so in life; dove in with a splash of crystal bubbles, searching below the sun-bathed surface; and immediately became aware of something dark and comely, swimming in playful circles about me.

Coming up for air, I saw that something else too had surfaced, sporting and laughing as it took hold of the anchor chain beside me; and behold, it was a merman—a stranger to me and yet not so, for though below shaped like a fish, with silvery green flanks and a well-formed tail, with which it beautifully plied the waters, above it had the strong, brown, contoured chest, the dazzling blue eyes and vivid face of Jim. It was the first time I'd seen him in eight months—the first reminder I'd had of features and shapes that were inescapably beginning to fade; and my whole being wept, irradiated with joy. As soon as he saw that I recognized him, he laughed and cavortingly splashed water at me; dove in and out and all round me, as if he wanted me to follow; looked out at me from the corners of his eyes, with a teasing, winsome allure; and suddenly I realized that he was flirting with me—coquetting with a mischievous frolic; understood that he'd been fishing for me, even as I'd been angling for him.

The next time he swam by, I clung to the anchor chain with one hand, and with the other drew him close to me, till we were face to face on the waters, his red lips but a breath from mine; and I kissed him, a shy kiss, which he sweetly gave to me, with his own half-trembling favors. Even in my dream a shudder ran through me, as if those touches really were his; and I caressed his bare shoulders, his wet eyelashes, and tasted the tangy brine of his curls, as I'd always longed to, but never had in life. Swimming a little ahead of me, he again beckoned, as if he wanted me to follow; and I swam after him to the nearby beach, to the sands of exquisite Anjier, where we'd lain before but done nothing, hungering in the spicy warmth of the noontide, and in the firefly-lighted dark.

But now we lay side by side on the beach, and I stroked the curves of his glistening hips, shapely with their silvery mail; sipped his smooth breast, and kissed him deep; and he relinquished himself to me, allowed me to take him there in the sand. Far into the evening we lay, watching the stars; then back out to the ship we swam under the gathering clouds; and there he disappeared with a splash, and a circle of ever-widening rings; till finally there was nothing left of his presence, only the play of lightning in the sky, and the boom of thunder on the drum of the waves.

Though I woke the next morning in the bleak January daybreak, in a room so cold the water had frozen in the pitcher, and so used it was impossible to distinguish the character of its chief inmate, this great gift yet uplifted my heart and swelled it; carried me to the window where I looked out on the wharves, the same jumble Jim's eyes had three years ago wandered; empowered me to imagine him close beside me, to actually feel the magnetic warmth of his body, and perceive the world with the vitality of his vision.

Below, as far as the sight could reach, lay Boston Harbor, alive with the clutter of winter traffic; in the middle ground, busy with carts, jutted the piers, piled high with the wares of faraway ports; while near at hand, crusted with snow, stretched the profusion of chimneys and gables. Pallid and grey with the early light, grimed with the layers of winter's refuse, they yet spoke of the allure of travel and commerce; suggested the enchantment of mobility, the wanderlust of navigation. No wonder he'd been drawn down out of this room by that beckons, by that come-on of masts and white caps and canvas; no wonder he'd found, in that teeming wharf front, an invitation more enticing in its promise, than the seductiveness of this place in practice; no wonder he'd seen, in the symmetry of those spars, a hope for a partnership in journey.

Though I'd traversed the globe, stopped in ports of call with magical names like Java, Whampoa, Rio; though I'd been roused by what I'd seen here, never disclosed anywhere else, and hoped still to discover more, I too yet felt the draw of that armada; longed to fling myself down out of the dormer and hurry my steps to the end of the wharves, to enlist myself in another migration. Turning away with a sigh, I all but patted his hand, with an understanding too profound for words; drew on my boots, then ran my hand through my hair, meeting my own bleary gaze in the mirror; and thankful he couldn't see the unkempt man I'd become, I searched through the garments on the back of the chair, and found my pilot coat still there. Though it was disarranged as if it had been searched, it was there to the button, with my hat as well; and gladly pulling them on—able to see my breath in the room—I stood for a moment looking down at the bed, at the man who lay consumed on its pillows.

As if aware of my gaze Beckman stirred, then peered up at me, fully waking with a cough; and patting his knee under the covers, I said to him gently, "You haven't seen the last o' me, mate."

Getting up on one elbow he returned hastily, "Not t'night," with a note of fear in his voice, and a look of trepidation in his eyes; then after a pause, as if feeling a need to explain, he lamely added, "Slater won't have it."

Understanding at once—perceiving Eben was right, and

wondering how a man who so jealously guarded his pet could have so neglected his health—I nonetheless insistently offered, "T'morrow night."

"T'morrow night it is, then," he agreed; and respectfully tipping my hat with my hand, I turned away and left the room.

We moved the same day, into a room up the hall—into a chamber that might have been Jim's, as it looked, like Beckman's, out onto the harbor and the wharves. Not that the transfer had been as easy in the doing as it was in the telling; for getting our gear out of Nel's had been about as complex as breaking into the vault of a bank, and almost as expensive as last year's taxes; and paying off the Curio shop man, with our lack of finesse, had proved an awkward enterprise at best. But nonetheless it had its reward; for early afternoon found us exploring our room, feeling the horsehair and lath plaster walls for partitions, and peering out on the view from our dormer window, as eagerly as if we'd finally met up with Jim.

Nor was our immediate environs the full extent of our discovery; for there was the dining hall on the second floor, privy to fare like Nel's; and the privilege of the baths, of which we straightaway availed ourselves, despite the restraints of modesty and apprehension: our passionate need for clean persons and laundry overtopping all other considerations. Taking over a nook we went right to work, zealously scrubbing and sudsing and rinsing—first ourselves, then our clothes, oblivious of all going on around us; barely aware even of the boys coming by for a tip, with their actual clean white linen towels. Even Eben, when accosted by a youth who made a suggestive move as he passed, merely muttered "Lateh"—so caught up in single-mindedly scouring, and rippling garb up and down the washboard, that he never so much as looked up from his business.

Back up in our room later on in our fresh clothes, dried, for a sum, by the cook round the stove—back, once again, in our right minds, having done battle with body lice and grime, and toweled ourselves to a sheen with rough coffee bags—sitting down with a newspaper, authentic print requiring literacy, in our pea coats to ward off the chill wind through the dormer—it was possible to feel we were at least human; and I felt close to Jim, as close as if I'd finally joined paths with him, as if I lived in common the same hard-won delights he'd cheered, cleanliness and privacy and quiet.

Later on that night we made our way back down to the dance hall, even though we knew Beckman was off-limits; and here we at last met up with a man whose memory held tokens of Jim, though once again, our encounter was unexpected. For an hour or so we'd sat drinking in our booth, watching Beckman miserably pander to the same derelict of a seaman who'd tried to make a move on him the night before; and on seeing them depart I'd instinctively got to my feet, half-intent on putting a stop to their exit. Feeling Eben's warning nudge, I'd grudgingly subsided; and clumsily sitting back down, I'd buried my face in my glass, trying not think of the hours that awaited my friend. Looking up once more, I encountered the eyes of a man—in a booth just kitty-corner to ours—whom I hadn't noticed earlier on, in all my flurried concern about Beckman; and an uneasy chill ran down my spine, a chill as of eerie recognition, though I knew I'd never seen him before.

Of all the faces I'd regarded in Creek Lane, his was the most stark—even more so than Beckman's; for though he seemed in full possession—at fifty—of ordinary health and reason, he wore the very look of determent. The set coldness of his face, as if braced against rejection—its fear of denial, and so its distance—and above all its silent unfulfillment, from behind which its eyes peered with undimmed yearning: these all spoke of his attainment of nothing, as eloquently as if with words; and I found myself fumbling with shock at my glass, trying to understand why I'd recognized him. Hastily scanning the haze of the past week—the dance halls, the groggeries, the oyster bars, the bleak streets—I tried in vain to place him in some scene; then with a swift clearness, I understood.

As plainly as I'd known Beckman was Jim, Jim as he would have been, if he hadn't met me, so I perceived this man was myself—myself twenty years from now, if I hadn't met Jim; knew it with a chill of certainty like no other. Pity, and a contrite gratitude of heart—a spontaneous upwelling of thanksgiving that, whatever else lay in store for me, I'd at least escaped this broken aloneness—moved me to get up, to try to shore him up with a word; and leaving Eben with a nod—bringing with me my glass, and a host of reservations—I went and sat down by him for a moment.

I expected no welcome, and it was a good thing, for the man simply said coldly, "You're not what I'm lookin' for," and kept drinking; and unperturbed I as simply returned,

"You'hre not what I'm lookin' for eitheh," blandly helping myself to my tumbler.

For a while we thus sat there, he ignoring me wholly, and I trying to feel natural in our wordless stand-off; slipping in glances now and again at his face, as I fidgeted with my glass or jacket. Seen closer to, his face was no less unpartnered, no less left behind by the fortunes of love; and I couldn't rid myself of the notion that I was in the presence of myself—myself as I would have been after thirty years of marriage to Anne, three decades of the want and void of convention. So long did the silence between us grow, as I guardedly scrutinized him—so long did it extend, emphasized by the lack of music, the orchestra having taken a break—that at last he was obliged to take notice of me; and running over my face with a sharp eye, he unemphatically embarked, "What *are* ye lookin' for, then?"

"Somethin' I had once, that's gone," I managed.

"Ran out on ye, did he?" he gruffed.

"No; he was lost at sea, eight or nine months ago now," I sidestepped; for even now, I couldn't bring myself to announce Jim's death, as if that would in some unearthly way finalize it.

With a sympathy I never would have expected of him, he pronounced, under cover of curtness, "Sorry"; and suddenly unable to meet his gaze, I nodded.

Another long silence stretched between us, but this one less awkward than the first; and at the end of it he declared, as if he'd been mulling me over,

"So you're one o' them rare ones, a one-mate man."

"Must be," I said, marveling that he'd understood, and only now fully seeing he was that way himself; "at any rate, I ain't got heart for any others."

"Well, you're lucky," he averred, with no hint of a sigh; "at least ye had him: no one c'n take that away."

"Take it you ain't found youhrs yet?" I ventured, careful of every word I uttered.

"No; an' gettin' too old t' turn heads my way." The unemphatic statement conveyed no regrets, and invited no compassion; yet it carried to me a world of longing; and watchful of his pride, I had to look down.

"Been lookin' here long?" I queried.

Unexpectedly, he laughed. "Long? Five, six years—I f'rget how many."

With an alertness in my heart, I looked up again. "You must be particulah," I smiled, taking a drink. "I only been hehre a couple o' nights; but if I hadn't lost my heart, I'd of found plenty t' catch my eye."

"Catch the eye? Oh, there is that. Had mine caught a few times in the old days, when I was still somethin' worth lookin' at m'self. But there ain't nothin here t' catch the heart—Slateh mostly shuffles 'em all off, time they figure out there might be somethin' t' matin' for life."

"Seems like a hahrd man," I ventured, cautious—anxious now to steer him back into past years.

Again he laughed, but more hollowly than before, and not without a look over his shoulder, almost as if he checked to see whether Slater lurked there. "Hard? Aye, ye don't know the half of it, Sailohr. Look how he treats Beckman, the young lad that just left, an' you'll have an idear how he rules the rest."

"What is it that ails him, Beckman I mean—consumption, is it?"

"Aye; it's made quick work of him. He won't last t' see spring: sad waste of a young man."

Again a silence fell between us, a respectful quiet, as if both of us instinctively felt it thoughtless to tread too quickly past Beckman to other subjects sure of life; then at last, driven on by my own inner need, I attempted,

"He didn't used t' run this place, did he? Slateh, that is—wasn't thehre someone else in chahge?"

Taking out his pipe, he paused. "Lomond," he nodded, leaning back in the booth, and puffing away at a fresh light from the candle.

"Slateh here was only a runneh, an' Jimmy Lomond run the show for a few years."

"Move on t' make a fresh staht, did he?"

"Who, Lomond? Nay, he's in South Boston, in the asylum, y'see—been in there, locked up like a monkey in a cage for the betteh part of a year now… The French pox, some says," he added, in answer to my wordless glance; "but me, I've got my own idears."

"Went…just up an' went mad, did he?" I got out, struggling to rearrange all my thoughts—having not even been sure, until now, that he'd survived that final fight with Jim.

"Aye; though there's plenty as would swear he'd been off his bean t' b'gin with. He was like Slateh, but hardeh, more jealous… especially with the boys that was his pets. He'd strike 'em or turn 'em out on the street, for merely panderin' like he expected. There was one a year or two ago, that he nearly kilt right here in the bar, for seemin' t' enjoy his companion too much…actually pulled a revolveh on him. An' there was anotheh, I remembeh, one o' the best this place's had, that turned on him an' nearly kilt *him*, one night two or three years back—then disappeared off'n the face o' the earth."

"Made his escape, eh?" I managed, aware of a sudden lurch to my pulse.

"Oh, thorough—Lomond an' Slateh an' all was trying t' pick up his trail for months, but neveh so much as turned up a scent."

"Sounds like an audacious fellow," I flustered, trying to check the eager heat on my cheeks.

"Aye, he had a bit o' the devil in him—more of a kick, anyway, than Lomond calculated. There wasn't many that was sorry the old buzzard'd met his match. Roberts, that was…had a odd first name, not Gilbert but…Gethin," he nodded, as if thumbing through an old directory in thought. "He was a foreign chap, from someplace or otheh across the wateh… That's him, in them half-dozen sketches at the end," he added, gesturing to the drawings I'd earlier spotted.

"Handsome lad," I mustered, offhand, though my heart was racing in my chest.

"Aye, he was the talk of the harboh."

"Knew him, did ye?"

Again he laughed—a crude laugh this time, though not without an element of play. "Couldn't get him t' look my way," he confessed, drawing up to the candle for a fresh light. "There was plenty in line for him b'hind Lomond—a numbeh of women as well as men. He was one of them sorts that attracts both—an' they flocked here, I mean even the women did, if ye c'n imagine." With a look as if into the past, he shrewdly chuckled, puffing away with slow draws at his pipe. "He got pretty full o' himself toward the end—was known for bein' proud, an' bein' the best butt in Boston. I could of given him as good a time as any, but he was hahrd t' get close to—played his cahrds close t' his chest; an' I doubt if he eveh knowed I was here."

To hear him spoken of so baldly was almost more than I could bear; while the cool certainty of the facts, till now relayed kindly by Eben, put me to the test as nothing else had in Boston. Having barely got used to the idea of his relations with other men, I now had to deal again with his affairs with women; and the double sweep made me feel betrayed, swamped with the evidence of his indiscretion.

"Anybody here eveh his…friend?" I attempted, still struggling to absorb the whole picture.

"Friend?" he puzzled, as if unsure of the meaning of the word, or unfamiliar with its workings. "That'd be Beckman, I guess—they was new here t'getheh; an' he looked afteh Jacques—would of been grieved t' see what he's come to… Y' like him, don't ye?"

"Who?" I stumbled, thinking he'd tumbled onto my secret, and was about to pry from me my connection with Jim; but tapping his pipe on the tray he unnoticingly went on,

"Young Jacques… I seen ye go off with him last night, an' nearly deck that sailohr t'night."

"Just wanted t' give him a night off," I shrugged, sheepish.

He smiled at me with a penetrating gaze, a peculiar look that probed my eyes. "You're soft, Jack, too soft t' last long here… I give ye four or five days at the most."

I lasted not even that long, as matters turned out; but on my way up the stairs that night after more talk—listening to the drone of the wind, rising now to the pitch of a blizzard, and thinking of Beckman coughing away under the eaves—my conviction was that I was a man of iron, at least as strong as Jim, who'd made it out here several months; and turning in under my paltry covers, with fresh images of Jim in my mind, I figured I had it in me to persevere.

Due to the effects of a blocking snowstorm there was very little in the way of business the next day, save in the streets, where men were busy breaking out paths, and round the stoves, where customers huddled for warmth; and the bar was unusually quiet that night, subdued enough to make it easy for me to spot Beckman, and go off with him to the dubious warmth of his bed. This time I'd brought with me a bottle of wine, a splurge I was wondering now how I'd pay for, when it came time to reckon up our bill; but I thought it would help break the ice between us, since we'd never shared more than a sentence or two heretofore, and provide him with some rare fun as well.

Sitting up together against the pillows—the bedclothes pulled up under our chins, and the wine nestled in the hollow between us— we talked on well into the small hours: Beckman short-answered at first, fatigued from a difficult day—from another bleeding spell, according to rumor—but gradually warming up, changing by degrees from jaded indifference to curious interest to something like confidence, as I maintained my simple companionship. Much of his talk was inconsequential to me, save to convey the rigors of life, the treacheries and conflicts which too had been Jim's; but in answer to the question, had he ever had a friend here, he hesitated, then spoke of someone; and I knew right away it must have been Jim, though he never referred to him by name.

"Oh, two or three years ago, there was a fellow," he commenced, his serious features even more introspective than usual, and quietly wan in the light of the candle; "and he was pretty much a comfort to me; but he disappeared in the middle of one night; and there really hasn't been anyone since."

"Some chap that worked here, a loveh, or—?" I prodded, trying not to imagine three years here without a friend, or at least some companion who from time to time showed support.

"Oh, not a lover, no—just one of the lads that lived here, like me."

"Come across the wateh with ye, did he?" I asked, since he'd already referred briefly to his early days in Belgium, and to the voyage that had landed him here at sixteen.

"No, he was already here when I came; though he'd come across not long before—from North Wales, I believe."

"Had a lot in common, did ye?"

His smile broke at once, the first to light his face, and, with his accent, a great charm, even in illness. "Don't really recollect as to why we were friends, now that I reflect upon it. We were the only foreign lads here, and the best educated of the lot—though I don't really know as he ever went to school; but he was far handsomer than me, far more reckless and bold—full of a fiery, wandering spirit."

"Must of made quite a splash here," I ventured, finding myself looking back to those days gone, and picturing, with some unexpected gift, these two friends—the one so hearty and vivid and restless, the other so contemplative and quiet.

"Oh, he would have made a splash anywhere," he smiled, fetching the bottle from its depths with frail hands. "But yes, he made quite a name for himself, and for this place, which was new at the time—drew others to him, I guess, just like he did me. There was many that was willing to pay for his favors, women as well as men; and he won quite a reputation as a lover. But he got pretty well full of it towards the end; tired of using folks and being used; and I always guessed, down deep, he was really like me."

"Like you?" I encouraged, puzzled.

"Yes; well," he hesitated, as if trying to find a delicate way to express his thoughts, or doubting whether to reveal anything further of himself. "He was afraid, you know, to let go—the way you do when you're someone's wife. He needed a partner, but was too proud to admit it; so he kept up a show of going it alone. Others found him vain, or high-handed or cocky; but I knew; all along, I knew."

"That why he finally left here, d'ye think—t' find something more permanent, or t' run away from the whole thing?"

His sigh came as much from old regrets, as from thought. "Don't know," he responded, with another spell of coughing, which left him short of breath and rough-voiced. "He had it awful hard here, with Lomond—the fellow that ran the place before Ed. Maybe he drove him off, Lomond did—being so possessive and jealous. Things came to a head, and there was a fight; and next day he was gone, and there was no way to trace him. It was incredibly brave of him to go—considering what would've happened, if he'd been found; and I've wanted ever since to follow—but as you see, I never have."

"Neveh found youhrself a partneh, all this time?" I asked, realizing that he too was looking, and harkening back to his earlier words.

"Yes; but not the one I wanted. I expect he'll carry me off this spring, if not before; and I can tell you, it's hard to let go."

I had thought he meant Slater, and was sympathetic enough—but understood all at once he was referring to Death; and like a specter in some dance more outrageous even than that of the beskirted men at Harry's, masquerading as what they weren't—than that of Slater and Lomond, confusing love and hate in their passion—than that of the lonely man in the bar, doomed to an undeserving rejection—Death's bizarre face rose, unbidden in my mind's eye, his insistent hands encircling Beckman's frail ones. Irresistibly I wanted to weep—but couldn't; nor could I support him with comforting words, shallow gestures coming from one still sure of life. So quietly, I simply took his hand in mine, my big, awkward, strong paw, and sheltered it for a moment; and he said no more, but laid back and rested, closing his eyes as if dreaming an old dream.

While he rested I thought all at once of Jim—of his own last struggle, if it had come; dared imagine his final encounter with Death; imagined them, bite to bite, kick to kick, throw to toss, as Jim and I had been in our absurd contest. Faced with that ultimate surrender, he wouldn't have gone easy—wouldn't have submitted any more gracefully than he ever had with me; and knowing that, whatever the final outcome, Death would have come off the lesser for it, I smiled into the flickering darkness; I smiled.

The following day, though the storm had abated, it remained gloomy and lowering throughout the afternoon; and oppressed by the dark and the insistent cold, Eben and I supped at our oyster bar table, thankful for a semblance of light and warmth. Unhurried we shared our past couple of days' gleanings, me speaking of Beckman and the lonely man I'd sat by, he filling me in on bits of gossip he'd picked up, mostly acrimonious rumblings about Slater; then regretfully we left our snug booth, and stepped back out into the wind. Heads down, collars up, mufflers over our mouths, we wandered the streets for an aimless hour, finding exercise a better antidote for the numbing wintry rawness than the inadequate shelter of our room, or the dubious haven of the dance hall; though the bleak walls we passed, and the dumb forms bent double, more like brutes to a burden than humans, did little to lift our oppression of spirit.

It was while we were crossing the street, heading for the steps leading toward the shop entrance, that we noticed two men, heavily hatted and coated, looming up out of the late afternoon dark toward us; and though something about their abrupt walk and gestures—something about their invisible mien chilled us, there was no particular reason to take notice of them, till unexpectedly a cat crossed before them. She was just a neighborhood stray, on business of her own, head down to the icy bite of the wind; but out of nowhere—out of a bitterness rooted in an unguessable birth, out of a malaise or hostility of will unknown—one of the pair brutally kicked her; kicked her hard enough to send her flying, then walked unconcernedly on, still talking.

From my heart a passionate outrage burst forth, raking me like a tidal surge rips a shore—rage for Beckman, for Jim in his early days, for all those ill-used by the force of another; and racing to him in two steps I swung back my arm, and struck him with all the might I could summon. Down he went in the dark, his companion fleeing in panic; and while I stood there dumbfounded in the dim, heart pounding and rage still pulsing in my ears, Eben swiftly knelt down by the man, a grey shape now in my vague awareness. Quietly looking at him, then getting to his feet, he took my elbow and at once walked me on; then the two of us round the corner he hissed in my ear: "Ben, d'ye know what is is ye've done? Knocked out Ed Slateh—because of a *cat!*"

All the implications of the act tumultuously rushing upon me, I turned witlessly around in the street, dazedly wondering about witnesses, and where the companion had fled to; but the most intelligent response I could muster was, "What...what d'ye think we should do now?"

"The only thing we *can* do, I'd say, since we was seen," he said grimly; "get out!"

Instinctively we walked on a square or so, then took shelter against a building, under the doubtful protection of an awning; and here we continued our hasty parley. "You mean," I struggled, "leave everything... now.... just go? Without stoppin' t' pay or pick up oweh gear? They'll know then, for certain, we did it."

"*You* did it, y' mean," he devilled, huddling into his collar. "Well, they'll know anyway, since thehre was a witness—even if Slateh didn't recognize us as we approached."

"How much time d'ye think we've got?" I floundered, witlessly trying to get a grip on direction—thinking poignantly of Jim in the same situation, the night of his own final confrontation with Lomond.

"Almost none," he said bluntly. "Till someone finds Slateh, carries him in, an' he comes to."

"What time is it?" I pressed, emboldened somehow by Jim, and beginning to think on my feet, as at sea.

"Don't know for certain... around half four, or five."

"The apothecary's still open on Ann Street... take my bank draft there an' cash it. They know me thehre—as Ben Melchett, I mean; cash it, an' hire a sleigh," I persisted.

"Ben, what the devil're ye up to? Let's just leave oweh gear, hike up t' the Tremont, an' have a decent meal an' a bath: nobody here'll think t' search for us *thehre*."

"No," I insisted, clearer and clearer by the instant; "I'm not lightin' out o' here without Beckman."

"Without—oh, Melchett, you'hre—you'hre mad, man! Deck Slateh, then take his—why, he'll be afteh us both for—"

"Thehre's no time t' argue," I kept at it, urgent; "he's comin'; now run for it!"

"What the sam hell're *you* goin' t' do?"

"I'm goin' t' fetch Beckman from oweh place—I'll find him...

We'll meet you an' the sleigh hehre, it's quiet."

"It'll kill him t' get out into this wind," he warned.

"It'll kill him t' stay… Now get movin'—I'll meet ye hehre in half an oweh."

Unquestioningly he walked off quickly, bank draft in pocket, head down to the wind; and as swiftly I fled back to Slater's, steering not for the curio shop entrance, but round the corner for the tavern doorway. As I approached the building I could see in the dim two men half-supporting, half-dragging Slater up the front stairs; and heart pounding I hurried down the steps of the back way, through the commotion of the tavern facade, and toward the corridor that led to the dance hall. Whether Beckman would be there, whether he'd come with me, whether we'd be noticed as we made our exit—what would happen when we turned up missing, and our gear was found abandoned—these questions drummed through me till I felt half-faint; but I managed to speak the password with a cool nod at the doorman, enter the passage and walk down toward the dance hall as on any other night. Glancing swiftly round at the dance floor, then darting my eyes at the booths, I felt my heart sink as I spotted no sign of my friend; and too pressed for time to play down my presence, I spoke to the man behind the bar counter, asking if he knew where Beckman might be.

"Jacques?" he looked up, with a nod of recognition, and a shrug that seemed to warn me not to pursue him so persistently, "I think he's in the baths"; then with a parting glance that I hoped missed my agitation, he hurried off with two steaming mugs. As soon as he was gone I snatched the one thing I still wanted out of the place, more than any gear I had in my trunk—yanked my favorite drawing of Jim right off the wall, and slipped it under the lapels of my coat; then quietly I hastened out—the last thing I saw, as I closed the door, being my lonely friend of the other night, sitting by himself with his ale.

As if that summarized somehow my whole sojourn, the cutting twist of my days and nights here, I leaned for a moment against the wall, in spite of the need for haste and discretion; then leaving him behind I strode hastily to the baths, and stuck my head in the half-open door. Peering anxiously into the steam, I spotted Beckman not far off, ministering to someone but still dressed himself, coughing in the vaporous air; and in response to my urgent gesture, he hesitated, then spoke a word to his sailor, and crossing to the door, stepped out. For a blessing we were alone in the hallway; and without any preamble I simply said to him, "I c'n get you out of here—come with me."

For a moment his face showed a stunned hesitation, as if he weighed in the balance the decay of his life here, against all of the risks that lay ahead—including Slater's vengeance, and his knowing nothing of me; then with a sublime trust he squared his slim shoulders, and followed me silently down the hall. It was a courageous act—the most daring I'd ever known, in a life full of witness at sea and on land; a risk-taking on a par with Jim's, that fateful night after Toby's in Boston; and so moved was I by his faith that I could scarcely get the partition open.

Turning around at the doorway I said, "Ye'll have t' leave everything, an' follow me down the street t' the sleigh: as soon as we get outside I'll give ye my coat."

Again he simply nodded and walked wordlessly through the tavern, even as Slater was probably coming to upstairs; then pausing briefly outside the door he accepted my pilot coat, and hurried with me down the square toward our meeting-place. Eben not having arrived yet, we huddled under the awning, me trying to shield him as best I could, through freezing myself in little more than a wool jersey; then the sleigh pulling up I bundled him up in its lap robe, on the floor so he looked like a package transported. Though it was by now completely dark, and no other sleighs were passing, there was no preventing us from being observed from a window; but heedless of that, we drove swiftly to Nel's, where Eben drew rein in the dark away from a street lamp.

"What now?" Eben called back over his shoulder, as I huddled beside the still-shrouded Beckman, and buried my benumbed hands in his lap robe, "—Jackson?"; and "Aye!" I rang out on the chill of the wind, though I hadn't till now conceived we were bound there.

It was the last word we exchanged all the way to the wharves, past rows upon rows of bars, warehouses and lofts; past wharves, raking bowsprits, the stark forest of masts, and an occasional sleigh out after the storm. As we came closer to our goal without a shout or a halt—as square after square fled by and our sleigh bells brazened, ringing louder and louder on the whistles of wind—our feeling of imminent victory mounted; and pulling up short of Jackson's on Central Wharf's broad planks—tying up our horse, and climbing stiffly out, me helping to unravel Beckman, Eben hurrying on ahead to fetch Jackson—we again felt almost flushed in our glad haste.

Coming out at once to us Jackson beckoned us to a side door, and quietly admitted us to his own apartment—a single room looking out on the wharf; then springing the latch he shut the door on the night, and one or two derelicts still out combing the hogsheads. Drawing the curtains, he tucked Beckman up in front of the fire, a coal warmer at his feet, wool blankets about him; sent one of his aides to return the sleigh, without a word as to its purpose; found us soup and bread and coffee, all piping hot, actual downeast fare: all this without a word or a question, as if understanding the need and haste that drove us. When at last we'd cleaned our plates and warmed our hands, and shaken off some of our initial tension, enough to look ahead to shape a tentative plan, I took Jackson aside and said to him simply, "He needs t' get out of town"; and with a kindly look at Beckman, calm now, but coughing, Jackson returned unperturbed,

"At once?"

"Aye," I responded, grasping ahead for a course—the safest for Beckman, the surest for us.

"He's not well—what is it—consumption?"

"Aye."

Folding his arms, he took a moment's thought, a fine strength and resource of mind on his face; then breaking into a smile, he asked, "Any reason he can't go t' Portland?"

"None that I know of," I admitted.

"There's two sistehs there—widows—friends o' mine—one just lost her only son at sea. They need a boardeh and—I just have a feeling—they need t' take care of someone like him."

A glad light breaking over me, a vision of an easy end to his life, and the sympathetic tending he deserved, I at once offered, "I'll pay his board… Have ye got some kind of a boat?"

"Right here at the wharf," he returned, unperturbed.

Even in my haste I could pause to marvel at his readiness and preparation; could take a second to wonder how many other escapes he'd aided, how many other nights, and for whom—slaves getting away underground, immigrants fleeing harsh lives, apprentices giving the slip on cruel masters; could hesitate to ponder how long before he himself was caught in the act. "Someone t' help Eben sail her?" I asked, leaving unspoken my admiration.

"My aide, as soon as he gets back from deliverin' the sleigh."

Eben and I exchanged a sudden look, a long, understanding look full of parting, as if we both understood, without words, the separate courses opening out before us.

"Then Eben'll steer her," I said, "an' see Beckman into the hands of these sistehs… They betteh be off b'fore the wind takes a drop, or cants any furtheh round t' the north… I'm on m' way t' New York."

Neither of them raised an eyebrow, as if both were in on my private thoughts, and knew exactly where I was headed. "The night steameh leaves at nine o'clock," Jackson offered; "sure ye won't have someone there lookin' for ye?"

"I'll change m' clothes, if ye c'n find me somethin' betteh t' wear… have a shave an' borrow a coat… othehwise, I'll just have t' take a chance."

Things now were happening so fast I could scarcely keep track, though the three of us working together without words all somehow seemed to know our direction. Before I knew it Beckman was into a whole new warm outfit, and stowed away in the cabin of the little ketch; and he was looking up at me with eyes patient and thankful, while the sound of Eben's boots stomped about overhead, and coils of rope thumped the deck in a staccato of leave-taking. Meeting his gaze I realized with an odd awe he'd come to love me; that in the matter of forty-eight hours or so of simple kindness and care I'd shown him, he'd changed from diffident and jaded to trusting and dependent; and touched, I put my arms about him.

Impulsively he nestled against me, not with any of the coy arts of past years, but with the simple confidence of allegiance; and still holding him I slipped into his pocket a gift, the shell in its case Jim had given me—the one treasure I'd risked to take with me to Boston, but which I dared not carry into the uncertainties ahead, preferring instead to leave it in safe hands.

"This hehre's from Gethin Roberts," I said as I transferred it, feeling justified now to speak openly; and his glance as he swept up from my shoulder was startled.

"Then it was you who…" he excitedly began; but I put a soothing hand to his lips, as Eben's bawling "All ready!" rang out; and "Eben will explain," I finished. Smoothing his hair from his forehead I kissed his temple, wondering if I would meet him again in this life; then murmuring comfortingly, "I'll be back," I hurriedly stumbled up the companion.

At the tiller Eben was almost ready to embark, the hawser just bent round the piling by a turn, and the mainsail mightily shaking; while Jackson and his aide were huddled at the bow, dark forms against the scuttling clouds. Snatching the chance for our own hurried exchange, Eben and I put our heads together; and "See him into these women's care, an' stay with him till he feels settled… Let him know I'll be back," I managed to get out over the wind.

"Aye; an' I'll get him int' the hands of an able doctoh," Eben shouted back in my ear.

"See Anne for me, an' the children," I bawled on; "send me lettehs care o' Walsh an' Brown, Livehpool."

"Aye," he rang out, with not a flicker of surprise.

"I'm goin' on t' Wales," I added, though unnecessarily, as he knew it perfectly well.

"Thought ye would," he bellowed calmly.

"The trek across won't be long—it's downhill all the way—an' I won't be but a couple o' weeks in Wales—just—I've got t' see Bala." As soon as I spoke the name there flamed up in me the hope that I might even find Jim's father; that I might come upon patterins or signs by the roadside, that transcribed his passage and direction; that I might see the sheep, and the footbridge and the stream, that had so conveyed Jim's past in my dream. Overcome with panged longing, I almost ran from the deck; and it was all I could do to keep my mind on our business. "It's the trip back that could stretch int' time; but all things considered, look for me in April."

"No longeh than that," he bawled; "don't forget the trial."

"Ain't likely I should… Tell folks I'm t' Livehpool on business; if they think I'm makin' money, so much the betteh."

"Aye," he mustered, with a quick hand to my shoulder.

"I'll miss ye," I got out hollowly, realizing it'd been a decade since I'd sailed without him.

"I'll miss ye too, ye cat-lovin' lug."

A-heel in the wind, the ketch put out, hemp thrown to the deck, canvas snapping; but not till she was safely lost to the night, and the wharf was still empty of pursuit, did I at last take a deep breath, sitting down all of a heap in front of Jackson's fire. For a moment I didn't even realize that he was there too, so intent had I been on seeing off the boat; but suddenly glancing across at the other chair, I saw he was in it, smiling at me; and really looking at him myself for the first time this evening, we exchanged a lengthy gaze, sizing up each other's appearance.

What he thought of my feeble get-up—of my general rugged, unkempt, smelly look—I couldn't begin to hazard a guess; but caught up as I was in his own transformation, my ragtag turn-out was of little consequence to me. Weather-beaten, rough-handed, lean as a belaying-pin, he looked like he'd been out combing the wharves for his last meal; while his garb spoke of an even greater alteration. Gone were the striped pantaloons and black frock coats of a preacher; now I could scarcely tell him from a bricklayer. As if he'd followed my train of thought, he seemed to observe all this with humor; and putting his hands together in that old judicial pose, he said nonchalantly,

"So we're the cream of Bowdoin, '35."

"You were valedictorian, if I remembeh," I fell in with him wryly.

"You carried off high honohs in math."

"You were quite the dandy," I went on; "frock coats, gloves."

"You were going t' be worth six figures by the time you were twenty-five."

With neither regret nor rancor, we laughed; then turning more serious, we exchanged news on into the evening. I felt safe now, harbored from pursuit—Beckman was well out of it, and there was no one to risk but myself; and something about this man, despite his slight build, made me feel secure and protected. Carefully editing my experience, I shared some of what I'd learned, these past couple of weeks at large back of Ann Street; gave out that we'd been compiling data for John, while he caught me up on his progress with his task, a kind of combination seaman's home and immigrant tenement.

As if he understood it all, our evenings' flight, and the departures of the past couple of weeks; as if he foresaw the uncertainty ahead, and destinations beclouded from me, he suddenly paused in the midst of our exchange, and regarded me with an alert eye; and smiling he said, "So ye've cast off."

Meeting his eye and realizing he'd understood—that he'd somehow gauged the unspoken within, from the signposts of the spoken aloud—I simply answered, "Aye."

As if he'd been expecting such news all along, these many months since we'd parted, he knowingly smiled into the fire.

"Did ye think I neveh would?" I asked wryly, looking back myself on the long years required for the tossing off of a single rope.

"Oh, I knew ye'd get round to it; you were a sure bet," he returned, with a look of genuine affection and feeling; "an' now you're on your way, I wish you a safe voyage."

I shrugged and smiled at him a bit wanly. "I neveh felt more uncertain about anything in m' life," I confessed, with a hollow ring to the chords of my voice.

"It's risk-taking that guarantees a rich journey… nobody eveh grew wealthy still tied t' the dock."

Though I'd been going to sea for the better part of thirty years, I knew perfectly well what he meant—knew I was only now setting out for the first time; and doubly glad for the words from one whose wake lay ahead, I smiled as I shook his hand by the door; smiled as I shrugged into the old pea coat he'd found for me, and bereft of any luggage, lacking even a seabag, walked off into the winds of the night.

Though I'd never before in my life set foot aboard a steamer, I did so
now, even as Jim had done three years ago, en route to Boston from
New York; trudged up the gangway with my fare in hand; and trying
to find a place out of the wind, out of the scrutiny of the idle or of
anyone else who might have reason to spot me, I settled down for the
long, cold night's voyage.

My berth was a matter of a plank, or to put it politely, a protruding
shelf—the middle of three tiers which thrust out their rows from
the lengthy walls of the gentlemen's cabin, lodged somewhere in the
depths of the ship. But its cramped quarters were better than the
open air of the promenade two decks above, where the confounded
noise of the boiler, the incessant sawing away of the connecting rod,
and the spewing of sparks and steam from the chimneys fed my
constant suspicion that at any moment we'd all be blown to Kingdom
Come. When at last we raised the misty villas of the narrows and
opened out the waters of the bay—when in due time we hove in
sight of the confused heap of buildings and forest of shipping which
marked, even to unfamiliar eyes, New York, and touched at some
fog-enshrouded wharf, I was bleary still from lack of sleep; and I set
out down the rattle and clang of South Street searching the raking
masts for a packet to Liverpool.

Though my Uncle Jacob, agent for Melchett Bros. in New York,
dwelt serenely in a townhouse near the Battery Gardens, not far
away from where I now trod—though I knew the length and breadth
of Broadway, and all the best hotels within hail of its high life—I
understood the inside of a shipping office was the noblest thing I'd
see this stay; and I certainly wasn't disappointed. By noon I'd located
the Black Ball Line, in the shape of a new packet, the *North Star*—
commanded, to my lasting amazement, by Billy Walker; and seizing
a chance not just to re-trace Jim's path, but to settle a score with one
of his old adversaries, as I hadn't been able to do with Lomond, I
presented myself—forged papers and all—to the Line's shipping
agent in South Street.

Desperate for seamen as they always were, and doubly anxious for one that actually knew a reef knot from a bowline, they were ready to pounce upon me, given my size; and by early afternoon I was Ben Winslow, A.B., in possession of my advance money—seventeen dollars—and a call to present myself to Walker on deck, less than twenty-four hours hence.

Making it the next dawn to South Street, where I encountered the eruption of carts and sleighs, capstan bells, whistles, and creaking masts I knew so well, I fetched the *North Star,* stirring to life; reported to Walker, sober, unlike most of my shipmates, now staggering aboard in drunken stages; and a seaman myself for the first time in ten years, found myself dazedly jumping about to orders. All about reigned the chaos of an imminent departure: barnyard beasts being marshaled into their pens; passengers struggling about under portmanteaux or boxes; well-wishers, brokers and agents hobnobbing with Walker; and in the midst of it all, scrambling to make sense of an unfamiliar ship, and someone else's system of order, my own harried self, stumbling about in the semi-dark.

Used to standing myself on the poop, detached from the flurry, with my eyes on the ropes, it was something different now to stoop to the bidding of someone else, particularly Walker, not the kind of master to lay a hand to a task; something different to haul on a line without the perception of the progress of the rest, or of the fabric of the whole; something different, indeed, to stoop to the valise of some well-to-do, sharp-voiced lady, or heave away at the freezing brass bar of a capstan; and the anchor coming to as the mail at last was thrown aboard, I was belatedly wondering if I really needed to follow Jim, and venture the February North Atlantic.

Within a day or so I'd had my fill of Walker, even though we seldom crossed paths; for though the weather, typically inclement, usually kept him below, he was highly visible in the dispatch of the ship. The wind being a howl of cold out of the west, we'd simply made shift to run before it, in a maniacal drive to win a passage that made me look hard at my own priorities past; and I'd had every chance to study his intentions through the deportment of the tophamper, and through the leadership of the mate.

That he knew how to make sail, but not how to anticipate the ship, or intuit that point beyond which she could not be pushed, was plain at once from our speed—a steady twelve knots —and the unnecessary canvas we carried away; while it was clearer still that he knew nothing about how to manage a crew, a factor I'd hardly have rated important myself until a year or so ago. While wining and dining with what few passengers could still turn out of their berths, and apparently winning their approbation, he had no idea how to speak to a seaman, or even to effect an approach; and his few attempts at intercourse were a hopeless compound of hostile mistrust and condescension.

Through indifference or careless remark he succeeded in alienating the crew of diverse nationals, right down to the stewards and cook; and unlike myself, who'd been blessed with McCabe, he'd no way to rescue his fault through the mate; for Gage was a perfect driver's bully, lacking in either instinct or tact. Through him I saw McCabe in his true light, with an unexpected surge of gratitude for his administrative knack; understood why he'd initially rebelled when I'd added Jim to his watch; marveled that he'd managed, after all. But above all through Gage and Walker I saw myself; saw myself as I must have looked to Jim three years ago aboard *Charis*; and though mindful of the graces given me and not Walker, I blushed for my distance and detachment.

How different our two tasks had been, Jim's and mine—how different our runs with Walker, yet how similar at heart! Jim's job had been to accustom himself to discipline; mine, to gradually undo it. Thrown aboard against his will, fresh from the chaotic backwaters of Liverpool, he'd had to condition himself to the temper of the work, and the harshness of the elements as well; while I had to unravel years of quarterdeck order, and dispense with my passion for control. No longer could I concern myself with latitude and longitude, the level of the glass, or the layout of the sails; but rather had to model myself on my shipmate George, whose success may have had something to do with his secret cache of rum.

Baiting the passengers with their lubberly malaise—offering them hope of relief, for example, in the open air, then watching them careen helplessly back and forth in the waist, with every pendulum swing of the deck—or filching sacks of mail to read round the mess: these became my primary preoccupations on deck; while aloft I had to hide the scientific skill of my brain, and limit my brawn to a kind of bovine speed.

Yet the one thing we had in common, Jim and I, whether building up or breaking down discipline, was our resistance to injustice; and it was a revelation to me what a deep bond this was between us—our common dignity and respect for fairness, even if our concepts of fairness differed. I'd straight off learned how Jim must have felt by my orders, my first hours at sea with Walker—how his pride must have flinched at my bombast, however well meant in the course of events; understood now, two or three days out, his outrage at Walker's, as he illogically inflamed the crew, setting man against man in all hands work. Jim'd refused to haze his shipmates, and been logged repeatedly for disobeying orders; now I found myself in the same dilemma, with identically the same reaction—mutinous at sea for the first time in my life.

Walker's bullying of the two blacks in our crew was bad enough, and immediately apparent; but it was nothing like his abuse of the lone Irishman, whom he and Gage brutalized like a dog in a kennel; and constantly checking my own urge to run things, I found myself at daily deeper odds with those aft. Yet my rebellion worked in the end to my advantage; for the only way to get aft to see Walker, size him up face to face, and seize a chance to even Jim's score, was to get into enough trouble to make it worth his while to go over Gage's head to summon me; and I knew that would be the result if I persevered.

Refusing to do duties that would haze the others, or place them at repeated risk in tasks all should take turns sharing—protesting at over-work and verbal abuse, even hurling out responses in kind—I did battle on behalf of my shipmates, all my instincts in rebellion even without my protective interest in Jim; and it wasn't long before I'd created enough tumult to wrest myself my hard-sought notice.

It was at the end of the first week that Gage bawled me aft and sent me below; and his move came as no surprise, though I hadn't calculated for it—the event that triggered things purely instinctive on my part. We'd been on deck since midnight, in a roaring nor'easter, shortening down all save the topsails, which were chained; and we had a job beyond that with the foresail, which went anyway with a blast before dawn. Frapping down the tatters, then getting up a staysail to keep her up to something like course, and finally sending down the blown sail and bending a new one in the gradually abating wind had, with the cold and sleet, beaten us out; and there was an atmosphere of risk in the air, the peril that steeps when a ship is being driven too hard, and the course of events is out of hand.

At it for eight or nine hours without yet a sign of breakfast, or even so much as a mug of coffee, our hands in some cases split to the bone by the frozen rigging, the order rang out for us to re-set the jib; and as there was still a ferocious head sea, raking at times the entire forecastle, it was not merely a foolhardy but a dangerous command. With his usual dispatch Gage pegged Coyne, our Irishman, to be the man out over the bowsprit; and goaded on by the night and a week's relentless abuse, Coyne turned on him with a snarl of contempt. Snatching up a belaying pin from the nearest rail, Gage made a move to herd him on; but he never struck his man, for before he could swing, I'd grabbed the pin and hurled it into the sea; then pushing Coyne aside, gained the bowsprit myself

It wasn't a job I would ever have done under other circumstances, my life still too precious to me, with even the slim hope of Jim's, to risk out of hand for a cause less extreme; wasn't a job I would ever have commanded anyone else to do; but by dint of sheer strength, which I called up from fury, I set the sail; then timing every inch with the hurl of the sea—submerged twice in the lurch of a cascade—I made my way back on board. He was waiting for me, Gage was, with a blessing out such as I'd never heard in all my days, and a directive to present myself to Walker; and wringing myself out in the lee of the longboat, I marched, grimly satisfied, aft.

Approaching Walker's cabin—opulent trappings passing me by on either side, the plush velvet and brocade of saloon sofas and curtains mingling with ridiculously fragile china—I felt no remorse for my unseamanlike conduct; felt instead a sudden inexplicable upsurge of delight—a fiendish elation at not only the prospect of squaring the yards for Jim, but at the realization I'd stepped, for the first time in my life, totally out of bounds. Amazed at my own hot gush of rebellion, the product of years of mannered suppression, I rapped like a landlord on Walker's door; stepped, as unintimidated as a pit bull by a boot, into his room; and came to a bold, dripping halt by his desk.

Looking up from his papers, he adjusted his spectacles with a maddening air of deliberation—a drawl of hand that matched the dip of his pen, as he set it to rest in its ornate bottle; and I knew by the glint of his gaze as it met mine that he already knew all the details of my exploit. Eyeing my gear, which was dripping on his carpet—some intricate, absurd drawing room stunt from Persia—he bawled without preface: "Sailor, stand abaft there on that oilcloth!"; and letting out something between a snort and a hoot, I rallied with,

"Damned if I will!"

"You will, bastard, or live to regret it!" he snapped back—his force of will no less for the British lisp of his accent.

"It's Ben Winslow t' you, misteh: you've got no call t' address me as bastihd!"

"I'll address you as I will, and repeat my order: your place is abaft there on that oilcloth."

"An' *yours* is on deck in this hell wind!" I blazened, without a move toward his square of decorum. "You ought t' be up there overseein' youhr men, an' preventin' youhr mate from singlin' one out for hazin'!"

"Who in damnation are you to tell me my job!" he met me, summarily on his feet; and now I could see—mounted behind him within reach, but set obscurely in all the scrollwork of rosewood and mahogany—the impressive glint of a knife.

"I'll tell ye who I am!" I bawled, trying to size him up as he stood there, not near my height, but clearly without scruples in combat. "I'm James Robehrtson's shipmate, hehre t' square the yahds with ye for him!"

"Don't recall the man," he clipped coolly, with the assurance of one who's measured his options, and found plenty.

"Then I'll remind ye," I blazed, no longer trying to gauge to what point I could push him, but simply caught up in the heat of my wrath. "He was a lad from Livehpool, seventeen yeahrs old, when you bought him from youhr shippin' agent, who'd drugged an' shanghaied him; an' when he rebelled at that, an' youhr hazin' of his shipmates, you logged him all the way across the Atlantic— stripped down his wages till he was broke, an' dumped him in New York without a dollah."

"Still don't recollect him," he returned curtly.

"B'cause youhr memory is poor—or b'cause he's just one of many?"

"Look, sailor," he snapped, "if he refused to obey orders, whoever he was, he's lucky I didn't throw him in irons—which is what I'll do to *you*, if we cross paths again; so see to it I don't have anything further to do with you!"

"Oh, ye'll have plenty furtheh t' do with me, as long as you'hre grindin' youhr political ax with a lone Irishman, an' breakin' every maritime law in the book for a fast run!"

Cocking a wary eye at me, as if he had but the barest trust for my self-control, and taking up his pen again with that deliberate air, far more maddening than when he'd been my equal in anger, he made a notice in the crew's accounts. "I hereby log you for six dollars, a third of your month's wages, for interfering with orders, and disrupting the course of business in a storm; and mind what I said about bein' thrown in irons—I'm too smart to leave an old sea lawyer like you at large on deck."

Suddenly it was not just anger at him; not just at my father or Lomond, but at all I'd been supposed to do all these years—at all the oughts and shoulds of the past: at my marriage, at convention, at what my family expected of me, and above all, at what I'd always expected of myself; and as suddenly free of their constraints—of even the consequences of their abandon—I sent off a last salvo as they fell away behind me. "An' mind what I say in r'turn, misteh: ye'll wind up in a court of admiralty for youhr abuse of youhr men, an' for jeopardizin' eighty passengers with youhr foolhardy risks:—I won't stand by an' watch ye do it! Jim was just a boy, an' didn't know international law—but *I* do!"

"So many have said, yet here I am; Black Ball's pleased enough; now get out!" He was back on his feet and within easy reach of me; and for a silent moment we contested with our eyes. Yet even in the midst of my conviction that I could easily outmanuever him in a fight came the bitter knowledge that he was right—that in a court of admiralty, pitted one against the other, he would indubitably emerge the winner, so stacked were the cards in favor of masters; and torn between that painstaking legal process, by which I might anyway dent his reputation, and the more efficacious route of tipping him over the rail some dark night, I unhurriedly took my exit.

My one source of delight, in the frigid days to come, was not in anyone living—as my shipmates, fiercely independent, kept their distance in our few moments of socializing, and our passengers, business and literary magnates from the world's capitals, lay doggedly reading in their berths; rather, it was in the one fixed, reliable feature of our lives, the one spot which, like a storm's center, stilled and soothed: the ship's figurehead. In all the gloom and drear of our days—which seldom provided light longer than eight or nine hours, and frequently less, with the darkened caverns of waves—it wasn't easy to see, even when I was forward enough to view it; but at every opportunity of duty at the bow, I slacked in my work long enough to lift my heart in a gaze.

Not that it was handsome, by New England standards; far from it. No fleeting, fetching slip of a lass, this, nor buxom, winsome, capable matron; it portrayed a man, and no good-looking one, either. I couldn't gaze upon it with the thought that it reminded me of Jim; it was an older man, with none of Jim's sensual allure; none of the dash and flair of a young blade, with a countenance that conjured up romance and play. This was a serious face, worn with care and fatigue, aged beyond its years by responsibility, perhaps; but resolute and unwavering, its eyes set on the distance, with a perception that inspired confidence and hope.

Its steadfastness was the more striking for the proof it held in its hands; for at its breast, as if just lowered from a reading, or about to be raised to take the sun, was a quadrant; and as a carpenter holds a plumb line or a surveyor his measure, so he seemed to revere it as the tool of his task. Nothing in all the pathless chaos of dark seas or the lowering, scudding masses above seemed to have the power to daunt or dismay him; and riveted by his carven steadfastness, and the conviction he imparted in his discernment, I never failed to find, in his visage, the coordinates of our way.

One night, not long after my first interview with Walker, and fresh from a twilit visit to the bow, I fell asleep still musing on this face; and as if transfigured by its vision I slipped into a dream that became another source of buoyancy in the sleet-fraught days to come. In my dream I was at sea, but not the winter North Atlantic; rather, in a summer clime that reminded me of Rio, or the latitudes of Anjier. I couldn't see beyond the rail, or I might have confirmed my whereabouts by the color of the water and the cast of the clouds; but the whole of my gaze was filled by the sleeping form of a sailor, curled up in a great bight of rope on the deck.

Though I saw him from behind, I knew with an instantaneous bound of the heart—the first leap of life in me since my dream of Anjier, and my response to that picture in Boston—that this was Jim; and I approached him quietly so as not to disturb him. On a long, lazy swell, the ship rose and fell; and he dozed on the planks, content as a cat in the sun. There were his bare feet, the soles dusty from the deck; his fine hands, one of them curled in sleep on the hemp; the curve of his hips in worn denim trowsers, the swells of his shoulders in a faded shirt. His hair, thick and dark, uncut from a long voyage, spilled in loose tendrils on the coils of rope; and I could see their mahogany glints in the sun.

Like a man who's searched for years without hope, and finally stumbled by chance on his trove, I tenderly knelt on the deck behind him, and gently turned him onto his back; and drowsily opening his eyes—lifting that fine, dark blue gaze—he recognized me, and smiled. Unabashed, I bent my head, and touched his lips in a sweet, slow kiss; found him waiting, unguarded and serene, as one who knows another so soundly no words of greeting are needed.

At his yield I wakened with a pain in my heart—a stab of need the greater and more piercing for the accompanying conviction that he was alive yet in some place—that I had seen him as he was somewhere else, and touched him with the knowledge I loved him. So great was my pain, with its wrench of hope, that I sprang from my berth and paced feverishly on deck, though a night inclement with sleet waited there, and two hours till the bell of my watch; and never in after days was I without it, like a blaze of stinging assurance at my heart.

And I needed it, that blaze, along with the confidence of the figurehead; resorted to them constantly in the hours to come; for the closer to Liverpool we managed to haul, the more demanding the stint of our days. My second encounter with Walker—this time on deck when, in one of his rare appearances, he intervened to reinforce Gage, bent on hazing Jubal, our Dahomey black, till I stepped between them—resulted in my being logged again, another six dollars; but it increased the respect of several of my shipmates. Disunited still, and untrusting, they were yet beginning to turn to me as a source of direction independent of the officers; and I realized I had it in me to lead—and just cause to head—a revolt. Not that they admired or befriended me, or followed me in any way as a spokesman; they were too diverse in background, and too hardened by their past, to come to a coherent support of a shipmate; but I somehow sensed I was imparting to them the right to rebel against the injustice of orders, and the assurance they wouldn't stand without me if they did.

They understood by now, too, that I knew my way about a ship—that in spite of my efforts to conceal my scientific training, and downplay my knowledge of skills, I could dead reckon and renew the most difficult damage; for when a blow to the wheelbox disabled us for some hours, leaving us at the mercy of the sea and wind, it was not Walker or Gage who best knew how to jury rig it, and who came to within a few miles of our position without the sun, but me. Yet it all might have come to naught, tensions and rights and conflicts in leadership alike, close as we now were to Liverpool, and rampaging as we were across the Atlantic; all might have passed off very much like Jim's run, without issue, if it hadn't been for a pig.

It was the night before Ash Wednesday, the commencement of Lent, and the close of the Shrove Tuesday festivals, as in Rio; and inspired perhaps by more sober days to come, or just looking for an excuse to dine finely, Walker called aft the head steward, and demanded he kill the last pig. For some days this fellow, tossed miserably about in his pen, had been a sort of companion at odds of mine; and I was sorry when I learned of his fate, not least because he wasn't doomed for my plate, but for the cabin's, and for the few passengers who could still ingest a meal. I mightn't have given him another thought, if it hadn't been for the sport with him Walker suddenly got up; for appearing on the quarterdeck for the first time in days, in all the absurdity of tophat and cloak, walking cane and varnished boots, he unexpectedly called down to Brock, the second mate, to masthead him.

Throwing back his head in a laugh, Brock fetched a rope, and lassoed him—Gage and the rest of the watch crowding round in the waist, as for the onset of a contest or lark; then reeving the hemp through a handy tackle, Brock raised the pig, bleating in fear, the ninety feet or so to the masthead, swinging him to and fro all the while. Totally and unthinkingly incensed—swept up again by an unreasoning fury, like the rampage that'd been triggered by my first interview with Walker—I summarily stampeded aft; accosted Walker near the break of the poop, down which he'd just climbed to join in the sport; then flung myself infuriatedly at him, for all the world like Jim at me in our fight, and succeeded in knocking him headlong and senseless.

If that had been the full extent of the action, I would have found myself in the next five minutes in irons, with nothing but my solitude to comfort me in the three or four days ahead; but at the instant I decked Walker, as if released from bondage, Coyne attacked Gage, no doubt already on his way to me; and he wasn't alone, several assisting him, and one or two turning on Brock before he could make his way aft and to arms.

Floored by the immensity of what we had done, and by the dilemma of what to do next—finding all hands actually looking to me, the watch below having tumbled up in a panic, and impetuously joined in on the melee—realizing what I was in for, either the burden of illicit leadership, or the consequences of a mutinous act in Liverpool—then perceiving, in the end, it was either the cabin in irons, or us, I chose the former; took over the quarterdeck, ordered master and mates bound up in hemp—the very rope that'd been used to seize the pig, now cut down—then detaining all three in irons, took charge of the keys myself.

Assisted by the fact that all the passengers were in their berths, it being inclement, and that the head steward was on terms with me, and pledged to say nothing without my consent, I tried to organize some sense out of chaos; named Coyne and Jubal my mates, not that they were any better qualified than the rest, but just out of deference to justice; re-set the watches, then cleared away a place for myself in the charthouse, not wanting to have anything to do with the cabin—save for the arms, which I'd confiscated. To the passengers we gave out that Walker and Gage were both sick, confined to their berths with the measles, highly contagious; and terrified themselves of an outbreak, and deluded, anyway, that such an act as a mutiny couldn't happen aboard a civilized packet—seeing that we knew what we were doing, and were supported by their contacts, the stewards—they kept up a polite, aloof distance.

If we had been obliged to be at sea for more than a few more days, it would nonetheless have proved a disaster; for the new ticket was no better qualified to run the ship than the old, and just as dangerous; and with feelings running high on all sides in the aftermath—some reluctantly aware they'd just forfeited their wages, others no fonder of Coyne than of Gage—I felt as uneasy asleep in my berth at night as before, and took to keeping awake almost round the clock. The only time I was ever absent from deck was during my short stints in the hold, when I brought food down to the prisoners—not trusting anyone else to the task; for the bulk of my hours was devoted to overseeing both watches, and preserving the delicate balance of power.

Unpalatable as things were, I had to depend upon my men, as they were all I had; and they upon me, as I was the only one aboard with experience enough to manage the ship. Daily expecting an outbreak in all the tensions, despite our obvious interdependence, I found myself challenged by the slightest maneuvers; but determined to make Liverpool without further trouble—mindful of the trial already waiting me back in Maine, and not overly anxious to face one in England—I bent my whole will on raising land.

Matters being tentative at best, I blessed the least need or consideration which enforced teamwork; blessed tacking or reefing topsails, miserable as were our efforts, and liable as they were to take every stick out of her; blessed above all the onset of a seasonal storm, which threatened to cast us headlong onto the Menai, and which required the cooperation of all hands to weather. When at last we hove into the Mersey, in all the mist and gloom of a February night, I did the one thing I could do—came to anchor, and fired for a pilot; then with Coyne and the others—in the one move we'd all actually agreed upon, and planned out—lowered the boats of a single accord, and rowed for the Liverpool shore in the cold dark.

Abandoning our boats, we cleared out in all directions; and I found myself walking alone, with nothing but the crunch of my boots to cheer me. With daybreak came dense fog which, mingling with the black coal smoke, and the vapors of a melting snow, condensed in a dreary sludge on the whole fume-infested city; but the ringing of buoys on the Mersey harkened me back to Jim's words, that first night at Hannah's; filled me with a sudden gladness and sense of exploration that transcended the dismal gloom about me.

Heading for the waterfront in the early hours—plodding past cabdrivers leading their horses, and truckers their carts, so as not to collide in the fog—I came at last on Exchange Street; and though I was not the best looking specimen of humanity Walsh and Brown had ever seen, I was Ben Melchett to them, respectable at least in my antecedents, with a good story as to how I'd arrived without luggage, and a bona fide right to almost unlimited credit. By noon I'd dashed off a couple of letters, one to Anne and another to Eben, with a gentle enclosure for Beckman; shared in the general astonishment at the news, that the *North Star* had been discovered downriver with all three of her officers in irons, the victims of a mutinous plot; and washed, shaved, and flush with sterling, sat down to a mug of hot coffee and a meal, with a map of Wales before me.

Though Jim had spent some months in Liverpool, and the city intrigued me because of his life here, I felt the urgent draw of his homeland; and mindful of my own critical need to be home before May, I spent but a short time in the city—saw little I didn't already know, save, on a whim, a tattoo parlor. Passing by it as I was shopping—trying to fill a valise with garb that would mark me out as a gentleman tourist to the Welsh and Rom, yet would not overplay the part, and hold up as well to the stresses of journey—I noticed it, a little hole of a place between a gin shop and a pawn shop; and descending its steps on a creative impulse I forked over some shillings, and rolled up my sleeve.

An artist in his own right, my Burmese engraver went right to work and fulfilled my design: an anchor, made up of Jim's initials and mine, the M of my last name broadening out at each end in the blades of the hook; and as smugly satisfied with the result as any adolescent bent on making a sensation—pleased to have Jim's name a permanent part of my body, regardless of any inquiry caused to beholders—I put up with the pain and marched out, head high. Gathering up my valise, a simple carpetbag with a white shirt for Sundays, a waistcoat or two and a spare pair of corduroy breeches—stuffing on top my gift from Walsh and Brown, a small portable secretary, with a stock of paper on which to record my journey—I cleared out next day on a horse loaned by Walsh; and heading west, I took the road to Bangor.

As soon as I crossed the border my heart took a bound, almost as if I were really on my way to meet Jim; and I drank in every detail around me like a boy setting out on a first journey. Indeed, trotting along, great heights to the southwest, an occasional glimpse of the Menai Straits to the north, I realized I'd never really had a boyhood; and I patted my saddle, my horse, my valise—all I needed to sustain me on my journey—with a proprietary pride. After those darksome days in Boston and New York, and the demanding weeks at sea, my clean clothes, good breakfast, and anticipation of nights ahead in Welsh inns filled me with a radiant gladness; so vivified all around me that each valley seemed to blaze in the rain, and the sheep to grow brilliant white against green.

In Bangor I put up at an inn, the White Horse, kept by one Owen Pritchard, a bulky, weatherbeaten chap nearly a head shorter than me, like most of the Welsh I'd so far seen; was shown upstairs by his lady to a room with two beds, and given the one next the window, with a candle, for it was late. Saving the town for the morrow, when I was fresh, I eagerly took in my surroundings; surveyed the cold, clean, spartan room, with its solitary print on the wall; washed up in the basin of hot water, before its steaming depths grew cooler; then descended to the comfortable kitchen, where a fire burned in an immense grate.

In the settle to the left a couple of men lounged, while two others sat in nearby chairs, and yet another claimed the chimney corner, smoking a pipe—all of them dressed pretty much like the landlord, in brown coats, broad-brimmed hats, yellowish corduroy breeches and gaiters. Struggling to make sense of their talk, fraught with colloquialism and accents, and long stretches of incomprehensible Welsh, I soon had to confess myself ignorant of the three main topics of passion, British politics, Methodism, and Welsh poets; but as a saving grace, I shared their understanding of horses, and roused their interest with my background in shipping. Lapsing at whiles into the ale, a first rate brew, I studied their tones and their garb, then the rest of the kitchen, with its clock and its rack of Staffordshire dishes; then gave my attention to the fine hounds on the slate floor, a brindled greyhound asleep on the hearth, and a shepherd's dog, wandering about.

When at last it was time to turn in, I found a strange calm had descended on my spirit, as if I'd stepped back into a time without words; and going upstairs, settled into a bed too short by a foot— interrupted, just as I was dozing off, by a couple of latecomers bearing a rush light, which they stuck in an old blacking bottle while they pulled off their boots. For a few moments I saw their fantastic shadows, twitching like puppetry on the ceiling; then at length heard their snores, and gave a last glance out the window, at the crisp, winking stars in the late February night.

Next morning after a hearty breakfast of mutton I was off on my horse in a carnival spirit; and trotting up and down the narrow streets, past rows of townhouses brightly painted, with bay windows clad in white lace curtains, I took in all the sights of the city, including its venerable cathedral and harbor. Seated on the spurs of high hills near the Menai, with a population of six or seven thousand, it was a much bigger town than Cape Damaris, much more worldly in its own way than any New England village; and I tried to imagine Jim here five or six years ago, ready to set out on his first voyage.

Passing stone churches with square, open towers, their bells bold in the spaces against the grey sky—passing big stucco country houses with avenues of bare trees, then open fields, very green for the season, with new lambs frolicking between the hedgerows—I came at length upon the Menai Bridge, a suspension structure built around 1820. Paying the penny toll for the privilege of its view, I walked my horse to its center, and gazed down at the narrow, congested waters. With Angelsey less than a mile to the north—with Holyhead the guess of a grey rise on the skyline—the Straits were an obvious navigational challenge; but a ship in full sail was passing beneath, in company with lesser coastwise vessels; and I watched it ply its way into the Irish Sea with a hush at its fragile, graceful maneuvers.

Leaning over the palings before their stone cottages, or looking up from their barrows filled with rocks to repair roads, farmers, shoemakers, carters alike eyed me on my return route with a bepuzzlement that had nothing to do with my tourist gear; while women knitting at their open doors, or girls in chintz gowns and modest bonnets, stepped back or aside in dubious regard. Taking in their slouch hats and duffel great coats, rough muddy clogs or snappy highlows as I passed, I practised my meager Welsh; stumbled out *"gwr bonedigg, croesaw,"* wrestling—as I always had—with the incomprehensible consonants; was still musing on them, and Jim's fluid way with them, when I tumbled upon an explosion of folk in the Bangor market, and an outpouring of language quite different.

Till now I'd encountered only the Welsh, short and dark, with an occasional European on his way in or out of port; but clearly this excitable band was not native; and my heart blazed with a fiery fierceness in my chest at the thought I'd already come upon a Rom clan. Barefoot, despite the cold—bareheaded, with wild hair, and coarse features that contradicted my imaginings—they were caught up in loud and dissonant gabbling, the men waving stout sticks and articles of tin, the women in striped gowns soliciting Welsh women; yet despite their soiled gear and vagabond abandon, and the cold shoulder they were obviously receiving from the Welsh, they exhibited a proud and free carriage. Convinced from their fairness of skin they weren't Rom, but having no idea who they might be instead, I appealed as soon as I could to my landlady, settling gratefully down to tea by the turf fire; and pouring for me, she at once understood.

"Oh, the *gwddeliad*, sair—the vagabond Irish; that's who ye've seen; marry, it is. They swarms through the town, selling tin they've put right, and telling fortunes—*dim and celwydd*, nothing but lies; and whilst we're not looking, steal us blind."

"They're gypsies, then, who've come over from Ireland?" I prodded, fascinated to have unearthed another store from Jim's past.

"Come over and settled, aye, things there being poor as they are—settled after a fashion, that is, mostly coming and going. They swarms in, and swarms out, caring not a straw for fair business; but now that spring is upon us, and the Ingrine coming for weekends—from Manchester and Liverpool, those trumpery holes, sair—they'll stay around longer, depend upon it."

"I thought, at first, that they might be Rom—the Welsh gypsies I've been hearing about," I said carefully, blessing the opening I'd looked for all last night.

"Oh, bless ye, sair, no; the *gypsiaid*, they're far handsomer and darker, and come through in vans and carts, mostly buying and selling horses. They tinkers, too, and tell fortunes—but never at the same time as the *gwyddelaid*—they're mortal enemies, sair."

"The *gypsiaid*," I ventured, struggling clumsily over the word; "have they passed through the town lately?"

"Not this year, sair; not as I recollect. They winters mostly about Bala and Betwys-y-coed, or maybe Langollen—they favors the heights; then in summers they comes down to the coast, to the horse fairs, ye know, where there's plenty chance for tinkering, and fortunetelling and other such tripe."

Savoring my new knowledge gustily, as a thirsty man savors ale, I wrote it all out in detail in my log; spent upwards of an hour there by the turf fire, before things began to bustle with the to-do of the evening. Then having polled the night's guests about the road to Betwys-y-coed, and their recommendations about the inn there, I turned in again into my midget bed; and despite a restless night's sleep, in which a commotion of dreams figured, I was the first one abroad next morning, another cool, cloudy day with scarfs of mist in the mountains. Laying out half a crown for my couple nights' lodging—feeling almost like I was departing kin, I took leave of the Pritchards; found my horse, saddled and fed, and tipped the boots; then taking the road they'd pointed out, set out for the high pass, up to Betws-y-coed and, at last, Bala.

As soon as I headed inland a compelling feeling that I was heading into Jim's heartland came urgently upon me—a conviction that I was steering into the core of his being, even as he guided in the core of mine; and I stopped now and again to gaze, deeply moved, at the steep, rocky heights of the magnificent pass above, and at Angelsey, to the Welsh "Mona," and the Menai falling away below. In the coziness of his nearness I spoke to him often, sometimes just out of a yearning to hear his name; sat murmuring "Jamie," as if I'd just met him; or sometimes more lengthily, "Oh, Jim…I had no idear… no idear it would be this rugged, this wild… how could you eveh bear t' leave it?"; while my horse, now dubbed Dee, bent her head to the new grass.

In the late morning air the mists had lifted, and the gorge up which I travelled swept bold, deeply scoured, as if by some ancient, masterly sculptor, with a carving tool the span of a mountain; sheered upward on both sides of me, and ran dramatically seaward behind, rocky-walled, smooth-valed, still reddish with last year's vegetation, and studded with rare, gnarled, stumpy trees. Now and then came gravel lanes, veering off at spare intervals, or stone cottages, bleak and bare in the dramatic landscape; while along the way fieldstone walls, broken and bony like the land, partitioned the valley of the river

Ogwen, or criss-crossed the heights all the way up to the snowline.

That such a land could only give birth to a man of passions—to a nature like Jim's, sired by contrasts, by the heights and depths of vivid thought, yet the subtleties of tone and temper—I understood at once plainly, gazing about; understood the hardihood, yet the sensitivity that were his heritage; and as much to him as to the land about me, I murmured phrases from one of the old bards they'd managed to drum into my head last night, with a belonging as if they were my own birthright:

"*Av i dir Mon, cr dwr Menai,*
Tros y draeth, ond a ros trai..."
"I will go to the land of Mona, notwithstanding the Menai, across the sand, without waiting for the ebb."

It was brisk and damp and there was a wind, whistling down the wide canyon toward the sea—a deep breath as it were from out of the heartland, not forbidding, but bracing and vivid; and I went on with short rests till I reached Capel Curig, a small village not far from Betws-y-coed. Here I picked up another river, the Llugwy, and the woods for which I'd been looking—the forests so predominant in the region of Betwys-y-coed, and so beloved as a reunion site by the Rom; and my heart even higher, I stopped for a late luncheon, then rode on, gazing all the more intently about me.

About five miles or so from Betwys-y-coed, I came upon a sturdy footbridge which crossed the Llugwy—now rocky and racing—close by on my right; and on impulse I picketed Dee, then wandered across the wooden planks of the span, staring up at the steep ridges on either side of the road, and wondering if Jim had once been here—trying to remember what I could from long back, as if my memory bridged his in the past. Feeling my way I began scaling upward toward the ridge, possessed with the need to touch the earth with my bare hands—to walk upon it and so somehow claim it, this common ground I shared with him; but I found it hard going, the earth tussocky and clumped, and the trees gnarled and humpy about the roots.

Often using my hands, due as much to the steepness of the incline as to my need to touch, I found myself bent close to the grasses and the vegetation of the forest floor; and soon I was studying them in the minutest detail—the mosses dark green, spiked like miniature firs, and mixed with lighter green patches of velvet, even on all the rocks, which abounded everywhere. Moved by our kinship, because Jim too must have once trod them, barefoot as a boy or with the fleet step of a young man, I impulsively bent to stroke them, then caressed all the nearby rocks, in the gladness of our belated reunion; and into the wind at the top of the ridge, looking down on all sides into ravines and dingles, I declared simply "I'm hehre, Jim… I'm home."

That there was no answer save the raw, wintry gusts and the plashing of the river below mattered nothing; it was enough to look down the steep sides of the dell, or gaze out toward the heights of Carned-Moel-Siabod, majestic in its company of thickly wooded peaks, with the certainty I shared his presence. Not till the sheets of sudden rain came, driving me off the exposed face of the high ridge, did I stumble my way back down to the footbridge, back to the roadside where I'd picketed Dee; and then I went laughing, as if chased by an old friend—went laughing on the last lap, toward Betwys-y-coed.

Yet the footbridge proved to be not my last stop of the day; for just a couple miles further on, hard by the road, this time on my left, I came with surprise on the Swallow Falls; and I dismounted again with swiftness and joy, for I knew this place—knew it from Jim, and knew it for myself without guide maps or signs. There on the right, across the road, was the inn, a rambling, grey-fieldstone, white-windowed resort, closed for the season and silent for now—the inn where, in summer, the Rom would tell fortunes, and fiddle for the clientele; and here through this gate and down this path was the rock from which one could view the falls, divided into upper and lower.

The rapidity with which the waters rushed and skipped, like a swallow which flits and darts in its flight, had given the place its fanciful name, Rhaiadr y Wennol; and I sat for a long time regardless of the wind, musing upon the watery courses—watching their brisk and erratic capers in living strands down the face of the hillside, divergent above, yet fusing below in a pool. As I sat there it became summer; green spanned the trees; gorse and whin banked the roadside above; and women in long skirts beside men in dustcoats, fresh from their escape from the factories of Liverpool, promenaded in the midst of the road, or helped one another, laughing, down the perils of the steep path; while up in the gardens of the inn, Rom men fiddled in bright shirts and neckerchiefs—fiddled and clapped as their ladies danced, a twirl of color before their rapt onlookers.

It was with some surprise that I found myself back in late winter, surrounded by the bare limbs and brush of a grey day; but the falls were a degree brighter, with the sun peaking through; and I bent my face to the pool before leaving its side, anointing myself with the bracing waters; then climbing back up the path, swung into Dee's saddle, and continued thoughtfully on my way.

Betwys-y-coed proved to be an age-old village, the most picturesque I'd so far seen—splendid with rows of fieldstone houses, mellowed with time, dark grey, deep-windowed; a village surrounded by wooded heights on all sides, up which ran, here and there, green meadows. Over the Llugwy, noisy and rocky, spanned a stone bridge, antiquated like the houses—indeed Roman-looking, of a single arch; while in the narrow vale on either side of the town ran stretches of open field and lawn, dotted here and there by a stray cottage, or flocks of lazily grazing sheep. The place was old, very old; and I realized as I rode up and down the main street that I'd never dwelt in the midst of such age in Maine—in the heart of such an atmosphere of the medieval; and a hush fell upon me at the recognition that the ground common to Jim and me was ancient—far older than the shared years of our acquaintance, or even the communal ties of memory.

On the north side of town, where I'd first entered, stood one of the oldest dwellings of all, the Crossed Keys Inn, which surely hearkened back to the days of Shakespeare; and returning to it, I tossed Dee's reigns over the hitching post, and surveyed it closely as I went in. Of whitewashed stone, long and low, with walls two feet thick, and green awnings at the windows, it welcomed me like a familiar chair, or a pair of slippers long worn and known; and foreigner though I was, I felt at home, hanging up my hat on the rack in the hall, where a magnificent grandfather clock ticked out the hours as it probably had for a hundred years.

Greeted at once by the landlord, Hugh Jenkins—who beckoned me into the public room on my right, and set me up with a brandy and water—I settled by one of the narrow windows, alternately looking out over the deep stone sill at the glow of the evening light on the hilltops, and at the coal fire on the broad hearth; and though I knew Jim had probably never been inside here, unless he'd scampered in as a boy, I drank of his invisible presence, with the certainty I had him beside me.

Indeed so close to him did I feel, yet so full of yearning for the confirmation of his touch, that I found myself instinctively writing to him; found myself here by the coal fire, no longer making notes in my log, but penning him something like a letter, since we couldn't talk as I longed. Never handy with words, at least not face to face, it wasn't much of an art to begin with; but left without choice by my need, and by the discoveries of the day, it was at least a start.

> "Jamie," I wrote, and paused for a long time, lingering over the name, and the personal warmth of it—the intimacy of its lover's belonging; "I found us a place earlier today, a place up in the hills near the Swallow Falls, above a little footbridge, a place I've been now, like you; a spot like the ledge we sat on together above Rio, when already I wanted to take your hand, and didn't... a ridge that's ours for all time, where we'll never be parted...And when I'm gone, and you're gone"—determinedly I wrote the words for the future—"we'll be there still, at our place in the heights, in the wind, in the rainfall... Now sit a spell by me... Your hand is in mine, where it belongs; and the fire is warm; and the moon's bright in the trees."

The next couple days—thin and pale, with an occasional glimmer of sunlight—found me spinning tales with the landlord by the fire early and late, and the rest of the time exploring the side roads round about, winding stretches in the valley or up on the ridge where here and there a lone cottage broke through the trees, or dotted a pasture of grazing sheep. Pausing at a bend in the road on a slope above town, I gazed for a long time at a simple homestead whose archaic form seemed to have sprung from the ground. From the chimney of the house, pale smoke was curling; while on either arm of the road—above and below, lined with tumbling stretches of rockwall— an unencumbered rooster was hurrying, the only spots of color in the grey day. For a long time I gazed, wondering who dwelt within— picturing an old crone by the hearth, knitting and tending the turf, or children, long grown, a-dash in the firs; imagined Jim passing by, in company with kin, a rumble of carts in the gathering dusk; then tipping my hat with a murmured "*nos da*," I rode back to the Inn, and made ready my bag.

The road to Bala wound southeast up over a moor, and so along its plateau for miles upon miles; and having never seen moorland before, I felt a-churn with excitement—with almost as much eagerness at its prospect as Bala's. Climbing up out of Betwys-y-coed in a series of hills, whose wooded heights gradually thinned and fell behind me, I found myself on a lofty highland, unbroken except for the dips and swells of the land's roll, and the suggestion of peaks all around the horizon; and indeed it was like nothing I'd ever experienced before, except at sea: a barren vista under leaden grey skies, void of all save heather as far as the eye could scan. The vegetation was still yellow and reddish brown from last year—there being no hint of new green up this high, and no remnant of winter's snow either; no sign of detail, not so much as a stepping stone or a shed, or a crumbling wall or a spine of rock terrace—nothing but a ceaseless wind to wear one.

For the better part of the day, forty miles or more, I rode, wondering at what point I'd crossed into Merioneth, the shire of Jim's birth; till at last a peak stack, then a stone cottage and crooked paling, warned me I must be getting close. Cresting like a wave which tumbles, rolls and re-forms, the land beneath my feet billowed down, as toward a shore; then over the curve of its brow, twisting down in its descent, I saw the lake, Lynn Tegid. Long and narrow, steel grey beneath the pearl grey skies, it filled the valley between rounded heights; and at its northeast end, in a medley of slate and tile, still glistening as from a recent rain, shone the dark grey peaks and roofs of Bala.

Too moved to go on, I sat poised for a long time, till Dee, sensing freedom, began to tug at the new grass, evident once again lower down; and I let her graze, simply staring at this grand place, as if stunned by its advent—by my attainment of it after a hardship of waiting. Three years ago, I'd sat thumbing my atlas, pouring over the half-guessed contours of the land—chanting the music of new names, Merioneth, Bala, as if their charm might unleash the vistas of Jim's birth; now they lay before me, revealed at a glance, ready for exploration and knowing; and I sat atop Dee feeling graced, yet unworthy, like a man on the brink of an incantation.

Bala Lake, six miles long, filled the narrow, oblong valley, surrounded on all sides by hills and moels, those at the southern end tallest, actually mountains; while the town, at the northern end, lay scattered beneath my feet, home of three of four thousand Welsh—a couple long main streets threading a jumble of buildings, mostly townhouses and shop fronts, with here and there an ivy-grown church. Built of stone with slate dormers and roofs, they gave off the air of places hardy, indeed solid, yet not without the grace of music; emanated the underlying spirit of the land, of the fieldstone and hands which had wrought them.

In their midst rose a moel, perhaps thirty or forty feet high, with a circumference as great, and a lofty vantage of the lake—Tomen Bala, the heart and soul of Jim's past; and off to their left, flowing out of Lynn Tegid, past outlying cottages to a green vale to the east, ran the river Dee, still and silver in its course. So unconscious was I of all save their splendor that I discovered only at length they were blurring before me; and trying to clear my sight, I took out my log, and quickly made another rude sketch with fingers that quaked at my bit of pencil. Then descending at last, I rode into town, feeling less a stranger with each passing gate; found the White Lion Inn, recommended by all as the best inn in Wales, with no difficulty—so central was it, indeed the heart of the market square, and so big, three-storied, many-gabled, Tudor-style. Hitching Dee I stepped in, finding my way through the confusion of red-carpeted halls and low-ceilinged drawing rooms as if I'd been born here, or stopped by for tea every day of my life.

In the public room I ran abreast of the waiter, another Jenkins, the local brewer of ale; and presenting himself with a low bow, he seated me with a flourish, and produced a welcome brandy and water. Drinking it, and thinking hungrily of the goose dinner even now materializing in the kitchen, I eagerly looked round the room— long and low, with a massive walk-in fireplace, and deep windows overlooking the main square; studied the rather mixed clientele, my companions for dinner and the night—a draper from London, a Bangor clogmaker, an Italian of unknown calling and purpose, and a couple of locals, farmers by their frocks, who essayed, in fair English, guesses at my home state.

Adjourning to a drawing room, we were served a feast, the goose being but one course of many; then feeling refreshed, and yearning to walk the town—to savor its details slowly on foot, despite sore legs—I fetched my hat, and strolled out onto the lamplit streets. Finding them nearly deserted now, and silent except for an occasional clatter of wheels, I walked out the cobbled way to the edge of town, but a stone's throw from the lake; stepped right up to the shore, still and placid in the night, my boots crunching on the pebbled beach.

Kneeling, I touched the stones, small and brown, so unlike sand; dabbled my fingers in the cold water, then tasted it, with its hint of peat; wet my face, wet with tears, and washed it fresh; then stood again, looking south, toward the dark heights of Arran, and the slopes of coastal fields in the dusk. Not a stir, not a sound, not even a ripple sullied this, the still center of Merioneth; and I listened to the hush, hearing from afar the remembrances of Rom laughter, and the tapestried stories of harps. The lake, so legend went, was fed by two fountains, Dwy Fawr and Dwy Fach—Great and Little Day, whose waters, springing from somewhere high up in Merionethshire, passed through those of the lake without mingling with them, and joined at last to form the head waters of the Dee; and I heard their

Druid story, and the chanted songs of the mist, moving in formless sheets on the mountains, in the textured memories of Rom strings.

"Well, Gethin," I said hoarsely, kneeling again in the pebbles, "well... I'm hehre at last...drink with me"; and scooping the waters in my hands, I drank deeply, without words, in a soundless confession of homing and return. Then rising, I bowed in inexpressible homage, and quietly sought my room at the Inn.

Perhaps it was the feeling of coming home, and the upsurge of contentment which sprang from it; perhaps simply the eager warmth which always gushed from my nearness to Jim; but whatever the cause, I found myself, in the dark hours of the night, in the midst of an inexplicable moment. I was deeply asleep in my clean, airy room, my bedstead—next to the window overlooking Bala Lake—too short as always, and my legs still dimly aching from rider's cramp; and I roused enough to know I needed to turn, and seek a more comfortable position for my limbs, if that were possible in a bed a foot too short.

As I wakened I became aware that I wasn't alone—that I couldn't move myself without moving another; for someone weighed me down, his shoulders clasped in my arms, and his touseled head slumbering on my chest; and suddenly I knew it was Jim. The crisp feel of his hair, the sweet curl of his hand, the familiar curve of his hips, and the confiding warmth of his feet intertwined in sleep with mine, all told me that it was he; and instinctively, as if I'd wakened for years thus, I cuddled him.

Roused a little by my movement, he nestled even closer to me, with such a mute confession of comfort that my heart burned like a brand in my chest; and yearning again to speak my claim, I simply murmured, "Jamie." His response was a sigh, the vaguely conscious acknowledgement of sleep, and another nestling movement, tucking his head under my chin; and as before off the Horn, in the extremity of that night, when the perils of storm had stripped our defenses, I cradled him in my embrace—enfolded his arms, sheltered his feet, housed his body close to my chest, never knowing the moment passing from waking to sleep.

Then confused, I found I'd slept into waking—into an awareness of myself half-sitting up in the bed, with my pillow damp in my hands and myself unable to breathe, as if I'd been weeping in my sleep; found myself alone, touching off in my limbs such a famine for him that they ached with a tangible regret. In my need I stumbled dumbly to the window; and here I stood for a long time looking out on the lake, with its dim, trailing scarves of dew and mist, till its tranquil, half-inwardly lit moon glade stilled me.

As if we'd communed in the night I woke strengthened, refreshed— my memory wiped clean of all save his presence; and after a hearty breakfast of bread and mutton, eggs, fried trout, pickled salmon and shrimp, the half of which would have kept a man a week, I re-immersed myself in the life of the streets. Powdered with snow during the night, they were criss-crossed with cartwheels, or ground into a thin film of slush at the doorways; while overhead a crystalline mist still hung in the clean air, or glinted now and again on slate roofs. Poking into the old, ivy-covered church, or hanging about the market with its crowds of woolen shirts, heavily-knitted shawls and greatcoats—with its cries of bargaining in incomprehensible Welsh, and its slabs of mutton, fresh trout and bread, all producing a steam in the cold air—I saved for last Tomen Bala; skirted around it, in the northern center of town, like one who savors some final advent.

In the pale warmth of the afternoon I at last ascended, jumping its lower wall from the street, then scaling steeply up its green slope, encountering banks of holly which tore at my trowsers; till at the foot of the *gwern* or alder tree—which had surely crowned the hill even in Jim's father's boyhood—I cast myself down, and surveyed the north end of town and the lake. A little below me now, the dormers and slate roofs were still touched with snow, a jumble of dark angles above fieldstone and brick; while off to the south, encircling the grey lake, the green hillsides too were dusted with white.

For a while I dwelt on the myths of the mound's building—by the *Tylwyth Teg*, the fairies, some said, or by a people who'd raised it over their dead king, others had it; then I simply drank in its storied presence, as if drawing strength from its roots. Here, Jim had come

alone as a boy, to look out on Bala lake from its height; here too he'd
come with Djemail, to relish the first flush of youth; and here Idris
had stumbled upon them—memories so deeply imprinted on him
that the words "Tomen Bala" spilled first from his tongue, that night
I'd bent over him at Hannah's.

Not till suppertime did I stir, in spite of the cold which cramped
my limbs; then at last I rose and took out my penknife, carving my
initials and Jim's in the alder bark; paused to admire the effect, J.J.R.,
B.G.M., united for all to see, midst the hieroglyphics of others; and
content with the marks, as if they cast a memorial for all time, I
climbed back down and made my way to the Inn.

For the next several days I rode out in all directions, trying to get a
feel for the lay of the land; explored both the east and west sides of
the lake, and headed Dee up into the heights above—finding, to the
west, bleak pasture and moorland, with scarcely more than a peat
stack to break the wild; and, to the east, the lush valley of the Dee,
which I was saving for a sunny day. On one of my first jaunts I rode
the east shore, a stretch of six or seven miles; encountered lofty hills
on my left, with wandering dingles and ravines, in which sheep with
dark faces and long tails tended lambs; and on the right, Bala lake, a
little lower than the road, which seemed to follow a natural bank. A
stone farmhouse here and there, a wagoneer's cart, or now and again
a narrow church, with a square, open steeple and lavender trim, and
a burying ground off to one side, passed me by; and at the sight of
the latter I remembered Jim's mother, who'd been laid to rest not far
from Bala.

Here, near one of these austere churchyards, was her grave,
outside the confines of the paling—she having been denied, like
all Rom, a Christian consecration; and on impulse dismounting
at one spot near a church, I walked through the unmarked stones
in the weeds. If Jim's mother lay here, outside the iron fence, there
was no sign to demonstrate it; but other signs abounded, which
at first startled, then amused me: jugs of ale boldly set out beside
graves, some sporting straws leading down into the earth; and other
jumbled items of comfort, ranging from bread to colored beads, even

shillings. None had been touched by the Christian gadje, evidently out of the same superstitious terror that had prompted the Rom to provide ease for their loved ones, lest in their discomfort they revisit their kin amongst the living; and out of respect I disturbed nothing, saying only as I left, "Narilla Wood, you had a fine son; I wish y' could have lived to see him grown."

At her name her image sprang fresh to my mind, dark-eyed, dark-haired, with a beaver bonnet, and a costume vivid with gold loops and beads, and the red cloak common to Romany women; then wondering if I should have named her out loud—remembering Jim never would, and feeling I'd called her out of some repose, with vague consequences still to come—I hurried away, on the winds of the same superstition as others.

On my fourth or fifth day—each one a banquet, a rich sustenance for the spirit as well as the stomach, with explorations sandwiched between meals of ten or twelve courses—the sun came out strong, though the air remained cool; and at last, after noon dinner, I followed my heart, setting out into the valley of the Dee on foot. Somewhere ahead in the low, winding hills, green valley floors and wandering streams lay the footbridge where Jim had played as a boy, in the midst of his task of tending sheep; and with the certainty that I could find the place—the same certainty that had directed me in my dream, that fateful night on the Pacific before our last day—I felt my way along the Dee. There had been flowers then, in the fields of my dream—a living skein of blue, white and yellow; now there was nothing but the sweep of green, and the still bare trees of early March to steer by; but no matter; I knew this vale utterly, with total abandon of reason—knew if from its feel, its call, its inarticulate draw of memory.

Wandering amongst the knolls in a basin not too broad, deeply blue already beneath an azure spring sky, the Dee carved its way in an unhurried manner; and turning in its vistas as to a quadrant, or any other instrument of science—homing in on a sheltered stream-fed dale, just over a hill from the main branch of the river, like a bird which responds to the earth map below—I found it, the wooden footbridge I'd seen in my dream. That it existed I'd known—apart from my dream—from Jim's rapt, incredulous reaction, that last afternoon we ever talked together; but where exactly it was located he hadn't said, apart from remarks that it was near Bala; and I beheld it now without words, without drama, with the simple celebration of vision.

Here, unaware of me and probably of the whole of America, he'd dallied as a boy, barefoot in the summer flowers; here he'd played on the bridge, conducting a stage, or a ship, while the sheep strayed in search of their favorite grasses; here, for sure, we'd already dwelt together, in or out of dreams—he in his straw hat and worn blue trowsers, me in some bodiless form of knowing, brought home by the power of his presence. Here I'd claimed him with his secret name, as he'd walked up the hill with his file of sheep; here he'd answered me with a smile, and a jaunty wave of the hand as he'd disappeared over the crest; and I made no secret of him now, speaking in a loud, firm voice:

"Taliesin, I'm hehre… it's me, Ben… thehre are no flowehs, it's early spring… I couldn't bring you some, I… would have liked t' have made a wreath for youhr hair…but I brought you this, from Tomen Bala… I… miss you…" Voice breaking, I laid a sprig of holly by the post, with its image of a carved swan in the dark wood; then for a long time I sat leaning against it, suddenly old and bereft in the noontide, my face palely warmed by the rays of the new light.

So far, in all these days, I'd caught not a sight or sound of anyone Rom, save for the signs left in the churchyard by the lake; and the disappointment that I hadn't found them wintering in Bala, in some nook or dingle by the Dee, had been deepened by Jenkins, who said they hadn't been seen since mid-winter. The recollection that they travelled in huge circles around North Wales, even crossing the border sometimes into England, was little help to me in my search; for unless we happened almost by chance upon one another, I might go on following them in circles forever; and it was frustrating to be no closer to seeing them than in Boston.

But now, unexpectedly, I came upon that which I had sought, as

I climbed up out of the vale of the footbridge in the late afternoon, and began to follow the road back to Bala: a collection of innocuous leaves and branches, arranged near a milepost by the roadside—fresh, and pointed not into Bala, but out of it. Sitting down on a stepping stone, I wept, wept and laughed, like one overtaken by some in-breaking of fortune—like one who for years has attempted to wrest his own grace, then suddenly been gifted it by another. There was trepidation, too, not unlike that set off by Narilla Wood in the graveyard, now that I'd disturbed her rest—anxiety at being on the threshold of the unfamiliar, even dangerous; and I swayed to and fro, uncertain what to do next.

What exactly the patterin meant, I had no idea, save that it pointed northeast, back toward Betwys-y-coed, and that it was fresh, not more than a day or so old, lightly crumbled by the frost; and as I got to my feet I began searching my brain for every small remark that Jim—a man of few words—had ever chanced about such signs, cursing myself for not having made him say more. Hurrying along in the gathering dusk back toward Bala—pondering what I should do, and springing ahead now and again in hopeful spurts, then slowing down in painful be-puzzlement, I all at once became aware of a sound on the road ahead; heard a distant rumor, then a rumble, drawing nearer; and like one stunned by an unlooked-for invasion, I barely had time to get under cover behind a hedgerow, where I waited, heart pounding, for events to unfold.

Gradually the noise grew louder—the unmistakable clatter of carts and vans, accompanied by the crisp clap of hooves, and now or then a piercing shout or laugh, and the busy chatter of children in words unknown, exactly as in my guess of vision. Witless at first, I simply watched them pass by, wild-haired folk at the reins in cart boxes, or high atop embellished saddles, excited silhouettes in the dusk; then realizing all at once I had to stop them—that on foot I couldn't hope to follow, and that, unable to read the patterins, I'd never be able to trace them with Dee—I desperately gathered up what was left of my nerve. Leaping out into the dusk—raising my left hand with its little finger pointed aloft, and accosting the last cart by that signal—I cried out, with a ludicrous mixture of Welsh, English and Rom:

"*Nos da, chai*; where may you be jawing to?"

At once drawing rein at the sound of Rom words, or at my sign, with its familiar command of greeting, the man—decked out in brown topboots and corduroy breeches, with a jockey coat and cap with visor—spoke hurriedly to the lady at his side, then sharply to his children, whose heads darted obediently back into the van; then at last he addressed me, half-suspicious, half on the look-out for a bonanza,

"*Savo shon tu?* Are you from across?"

"*Avali*," I affirmed, with a wonder at his perception, and a quick thanks to God that I did not look the part of a bill collector, nor a constable nor a Methodist preacher—with a swift sense of relief that, apart from the fact there were almost as many Rom deported to the States as to Australia, there was no reason for them to fear an American. "My name is Ben Melchett," I went on, blessing my accent, "and I'm a *pani-engro*, a *sher-engro*, a ship's captain."

"Well, I'll be jiggered if I wasn't thinking so, and if I wasn't penning so to my *juwa* just now," he gusted, with a thick, lilting accent which rang out like Jim's. "'There's an American cove, a *pani-engro*, by his walk,' I penned; 'now, *so se tute's kairing tuley the bor*?"

I understood, from the *kairing* and the *bor*, that he questioned my hiding behind the hedge—that he entertained doubts as to my motive, and had probably pegged me as a *boro-drom-engro*, a highwayman, or some other equally unpalatable fellow; but unable to explain my impulse of fear, I simply went straight to the point: "I've been on the road all day, searching for the Rom, and trying to read the patterin yondeh, for I need to find John Roberts—I've news from across."

"And what news for John Roberts comes from across?" he asked, his suspicion muted by a neighbor's eagerness for gossip.

"News of a death," I met him, thinking swiftly on my feet—which fortunately I could do, after years of sparring with Jim; sorting out in an instant what he'd be most likely to believe, and what might allow me the gift of further information.

At once there was a flurry of looks between man and wife, and I knew I'd gotten right in amongst them, though it cut me to the quick to speak of Jim's loss; though it triggered in me a swift superstition, as if my words were the agent of danger.

"A death, *prala*?" he queried, and I thought it a good sign that the word "brother" had crept in, however formally.

"*Avali,* the passing of a near kindred, and a friend of mine: I came in person to tell, since my ship lies in Liverpool." So dignified was I they had to believe me, however inclined to disregard *gadje*; and before they could get at me for a name—if by chance they dared hear it, and risk being harassed by one nearly passed—I pressed on: "*Tatchipen si*—it's the truth; please, tell me how to find him."

His laugh rang out frank and clear in the night air. "The truth to a gadje is seldom the truth to a Rom; a rum thing, truth! But John Roberts may believe ye or serve ye out, as need be. It happens he's jawing to the same place as we, to a wedding in Betwys-y-coed."

"Congratulations; one of youhr kin, perhaps?"

"No, *meero Duvel*, no kin of ours would stoop to marry a trumpery Lee! Only her as is daughter to John Roberts' brother would take up with such a *sap-engro*!"—at which a quick sound of concern from his wife, the only sound she'd so far made, shushed him: not, I presumed, on account of the slur to the young lady's character, but out of regard for the threat of her superior powers—a well-founded fear, if this niece indeed be Idris.

"I'll follow you on my horse, if I may," I put in, in a fresh flurry at the thought I might see Idris' wedding, and with a wild cast of my thoughts round Jim's other relations; "but I can't read youhr patterins. How can I find you at Betwys-y-coed?"

"How can you find us, *prala*! Why, look for the south ridge, *dui mear* from town—that which has the finest sight of Eyrie, and the finest music, harp and strings!"

"*Para crow tute*—thank you, *prala*."

"Whether ye thanks me remains to be seen, *pani-mengro*."

"*Koshti sarla, prala*."

"*Koshti divous*, Mr. Melchett."

No sooner had he disappeared into the night, hurrying off with a crack of his whip and a clatter to catch up with the caravan of the others, than I was on my way post haste to Bala; and there I packed up in such a hurry, saying farewell to Tom Jenkins, the Inn, my shore by the lake and Tomen Bala, that there was time neither for pain nor regret. The only thing I lingered over was my appearance, and this I took some pains with, before the mirror; for I figured if I was to hope to win the notice of John Roberts, him of the gold buttons, I'd damn well better dress the part. Saving my best white shirt front and collar for just outside Betwys-y-coed, and filching a fresh linen towel for a quick wash-up at dawn in some river, I donned freshly blacked topboots, woolen trowsers and waistcoat, a beaver hat, riding coat, gold-topped whip and all; then tipping like mad as I went out the door—boots, waiter, ostler, on down the line—I jumped atop Dee, and hurried off into the night.

It was a dark ride, long and cold, with no moon to steer by, or to cheer the bleak valleys and broad, rolling moors; but at least the road was impossible to miss; and dawn found me outside Betwys-y-coed, washing as planned in a branch of the Llugwy, and pondering which south ridge had the best view of Snowdon. So far as I could tell, they all looked north alike, with none having features to recommend it over the others; and I wasted a good deal of time on the south roads, craning my neck at the wooded heights above, and eating a quick round of bread as I searched, my stomach too churned up to accept more. At length, however, coming round a bend, I stumbled upon that which I sought—not the ripple of harps, but the rise of wood smoke, the puffs of a multitude of campfires in the cold air; and pausing to still my heart—adjusting my collar, with its confounded stiffness, and running a hand through my unruly hair—I started Dee up a narrow, winding lane toward the smoke.

It was by a wood fence at the edge of a thicket, set like a border at the mouth of the dingle, that I came upon the first of them, as on a herald: not a man or a look-out, but a child of three, strayed from the heart of the camps in play. In short breeches and leggings, with worn clogs on his feet, and a woolen frock for a coat—with cheeks ruddy from the crisp air, his hair dark and curling, and his eyes deeply blue, the sapphire of a June sea—he might have been

Jim, eighteen years ago; and thinking at first he might be a vision— part and parcel of Narilla Wood's spell on my life, ever since that afternoon at the graveyard—I hardly dared at first speak to him, for fear of what might happen to me. Drawing rein at the sight of him, I actually had to catch a breath before I could talk; and as I did he climbed tentatively atop the fence, looking none too certain of me either. Wondering if he spoke English, Welsh, Romany or what— longing to touch him, as I'd longed to touch Jim, a yearling in the drawing I still kept—I simply courteously lifted my hat; then gently, hoping I sounded friendly, ventured,

"*Sar shin*, my lad; can you *rokkru Romanes*?"

A broad smile lighted his face, a smile far more forthcoming than any response on the face of his compatriot of last night; and he gave me a ringing, "*Avali*."

"*Angitrako* as well?" I prodded, hoping I could intersperse plenty of my own tongue.

"Oh, yes, *meero rye*; aye, aye!" he rang out, almost comic in his proud display.

"*Sossi youhr nav*?" I asked then, thinking that, if I could determine his clan, I might find by process the Roberts; but his answer simplified matters.

"Sacki Roberts," he declared proudly.

"I thought so," I said gently, my heart awed at his words. "I jinned it by your blue *yackor*. Is John Roberts your *kukkodus*?" I queried, hardly daring hope for so near a relationship, and trying to imagine how he fit in with Idris.

"*Meero dad*," he proclaimed, catching me totally by surprise; and I realized only slowly that Jim's father must have remarried— realized, in a daze, that this was Jim's young half-brother.

"Youhr dad," I smiled, in the midst of wonder. "Do you think that you could take me to him? I have important news from *pawdel*."

In answer he slipped from the fence with a wave, then darted on his way down the grassy lane, beaten by wagons and banked by gray trees; and soon they were passing me by on either side, vans, carts, and tents, the latter covered with brown cloth, their flaps pinned aside to reveal dark recesses. Before them burned cook fires, over which great black kettles were suspended, the steam of their contents mingling with wood smoke; while dogs, mostly lurchers, and bareheaded children cavorted with puffs of breath round the tent stakes, and red-becloaked women and haïted men paused in their business to gaze silently at me. Raising my hat to each, with a polite "*kosko divvus*," I said as little as could be, simply following my ambassador Sacki; and as if each already knew of my coming, via some arcane underground channel, they neither hindered me nor welcomed—one or two nodding the way toward John Roberts' encampment, now but a hundred yards of so distant.

If they had a reaction toward me, it was reserved for my horse, all hands swiftly moving from silent assessment of my person to a suddenly animated inventory of Dee's points; and heartened a little by her impression—not pausing to think what I would say to John Roberts, or he to me, if he stopped to talk—I simply boldly walked up to his camp, still following my miniature pilot. Pitched near a wagon and a horse and pony, oval in shape, and bent like the others, his tent too was covered with a rough brown cloth, its flap pegged open to reveal childish faces—the brother and sister, apparently, of my youthful guide; and while the young ones dashed out with cries of "*ake, ake!*", their mother kept wordlessly stirring her kettle, suspended over the nearby fire—her face unreadable between two wild, black tails of hair, and her dark eyes signifying no reaction either.

Near her side, kneading dough, then rolling it on sticks, sat an older woman, much older, maybe Taw—grey-haired, bent, with wonderful quick, gnarled hands, and ropes of beads round her fragile neck; though she too said nothing, merely darting swift glances which peaked like beak-thrusts at my soul. In the midst of their silence a man stepped forward, coming all at once from behind the wagon; and at his approach all the others scattered, except the child and Taw, who went on working her bread; and I found myself face to face with John Roberts.

In that first moment I realized I was scared to death of him—ten times more afraid than I ever had been of my own father, years ago, when he still towered over me; and taken aback all at once by the idiocy of my mission, it was all I could do to find my voice.

"*Sar shin, meero rye,*" I at last managed to greet him, holding out my hand, which he disregarded; and trying not to mind, I let it fall. "A fine *tikno,* your son," I bowed politely, hoping to show I meant him no harm; and the boy, far friendlier than the father, bowed in return, flashing a dazzling smile I knew at once as Jim's.

The man's chin came up, in a kind of aggressive pride—in a spontaneous jerk not without a hint of guard; and again, so like Jim's was the gesture, I nearly wept as I tried to look him in the eye. He was tall—as tall as Jim, if a couple inches shorter than me; more slender, with less of the bulk and build of a sailor; but gentlemanly, indescribably genteel, even in the worn garb of winter. Away from public, dressed not in Newmarket skirts and gold buttons, but stovepipe breeches and a leather waistcoat; bareheaded, his dark hair long to the collar and waved like Jim's, framing eyes the same dark blue of a deep sea, he was nothing if not unwavering and unspoiled, yet diamond-hard in the purity of his gaze; and it was all I could do to keep up my glance.

In return he took his wordless measure of me, and I wondered what on earth he was seeing—whether my fear, or my hope, or my love for Jim blazed from my face; but whatever he saw, it was nothing of harm, nor anything which activated his contempt; for after his search he gestured to the fire, to the stump of wood left vacant by his wife in the haste of her flight with her children into the tent, and seated himself on a similar perch nearby.

Following his lead, I sat myself down, wondering how in the world to proceed—realizing I still knew essentially nothing about the Rom, even after all those years of probing Jim. What in blazes was the proper procedure? Should I expect us to take tea first, then talk? Or should I launch into my mission at once? Could I take any notice of Taw; and could I speak to John Roberts' wife, at least to thank her if she served me? Would I be staying to breakfast, which apparently—judging from Taw's bread, which she was only now baking—they hadn't yet partaken? And if they tolerated me that long, could I look in on the wedding? Or would they be packing me off at once, as soon as they heard my news of Jim, whom, after all, they had ostracized long ago?

My uncertainty was not alleviated by the fact that John Roberts was none too easy either —-his natural suspicion compounded by an air of expectation, as if he guessed already the subject of my visit; and so self-conscious did I become in those unending first minutes, that I wondered even about the propriety of my crossing my legs, and the potential volumes spoken by the posture of my hands.

While I was still pondering my next move, his wife came out with a cup—a gadje cup, I was sure, since it showed no sign of matching the others, set half-filled here and there round the fire; and she poured me tea from a blackened kettle, which I accepted with what I hoped was a smile, and a polite *"para crow tute."* For a while I simply gratefully drank, watching Sacki stoke the fire for Taw, and his brother and sister come out to fetch wood; then turning my attention to John Roberts, I awkwardly took the plunge, explaining how I'd met his kin on the road last night outside Bala, who I was and where I was from. At least I could speak wholly in English—his being better than mine, with his perfect diction, and his utter lack of slang or contractions; and never once mixing in Welsh or Rom words like the others, he answered me briefly at whiles, his responses courteous but cool.

Skirting the real purpose of my visit, we spoke of preparations for the afternoon wedding, which indeed proved to be Idris', and which was already generating preparations around us; then overriding my polite protests, they included me as they broke their fast, the children with their mother and Taw near the fire, and John Roberts and I a little apart, quietly munching warm bread and cheese.

As we ate I added bits and pieces to my understanding of the family—learning the name of his second wife, Reyna, a Lovell; the older children's handles, Lasho and Shuri; and the fact that sharp-eyed Taw was indeed Jim's grandmother, the indefatigable mistress of their finances and fortunes. As the children capered about, shouting *"bavalyako bero,"* "sailing ship," and pointing at me—as I studied their horse, their wagon, their tent, into which I could obliquely peer, catching sight of bright quilts and colorful boxes, as one catches sight of attic treasures in the swift moment before the stairway door closes—I drank in details of Jim's jettisoned boyhood, confirming details I'd so far only imagined.

But above all, with an ache, I looked into his future; saw now, in his father's face, how he would have looked in his forties, even as in Boston I'd had the chance to gaze into his teens; and I travelled the years with pangs of bereftness. Though there were no grey hairs in John Roberts' dark mane, there was a maturity, amounting to worldliness, about the lines of his brow, and a dignity to the set of his jaw; an austerity in the ripeness of his gaze—not the seasoned warmth Jim would have attained, under the influence of a love such as mine, but the self-disciplined force he'd already possessed at twenty, brought to fruition in a harsher clime. Reserve, strength of mind, a fine creativity, especially about the hands—all these were present, as I would expect them to be in Jim at forty; but missing were the spontaneous outburst of feeling, and the sensuality which were uniquely Jim's; and I could only guess what they would have come to, under a tutelage such as mine.

As if he'd understood the direction of my thought, John Roberts had fallen silent, looking down as though to shield his mind; and I realized all the others had left us—had scampered off, or cleared our dishes—leaving us alone by the fire. It was their intimation that we could now talk, though I had no doubt they were listening nearby; and seeing no reason to delay further, I all at once gently said,

"I'm sure you'hre wondering the real purpose of my visit, *meero rye*; and I won't keep it from you any longeh."

His chin came up, and his blue gaze sharpened; but in response, he said nothing.

"The fact is," I went on, as carefully as I could, "three yeahrs ago, I met youhr oldest son." Something told me not to name Jim— Narilla Wood, perhaps, still haunting me for my last indiscretion; but he knew perfectly well of whom I spoke, for nothing in his eyes contested my reference. "My ship was made fast for a spell in Boston, taking on cahgo for a run to Rio; and he signed on as a sailohr at the last minute. He proved a good hand, one of the best I eveh had. Oveh the yeahrs I got t' know him…came to understand where he was from, and who his people were. Being a man who was private, he didn't share his heritage with many; but he was proud of it, and spoke often with me; and I came to admire you through his description, though I neveh thought to meet you."

Goaded on by his silence I floundered round, searching old memories for subtle proofs, for unarguable witnesses to the ties of father and son; for evidence of far less pain than their final parting, or Narilla Wood's death and funeral blaze. "He said it was you who taught him to cipher, and t' read Welsh and English as well as he did, which was first-rate… that thehre was always volumes of Shakespeare and Taliesin lying about in youhr *vardo*. And he said," I went on, remembering, as from a flash, words spoken in delirium at Hannah's, and carved into reality later on for my own young, "that you once made him a wooden top… a large, wooden top with colorful stripes, that he used to spin as a lad on the moor."

Something deepened in his eyes—a faraway glimpse, perhaps, of the top as it spun, or a soundless warning at the name Taliesin; but still he sat in utter silence, a complete and final, ghastly hush: the muteness of pain, or loss, or regret, or even—as they surfaced— denial. Torn between his old love and a resurgence of his principles— the forces which had led him to bow to his son's ostracism, and which even now flashed forth to search me, as if to question how much I knew, and where I stood—he probed my gaze in the awfulness of his hush; and the awkwardness widened between us.

Scrambling about, I sought a conclusive moment, some unshakeable testimony to our mutual bond—to the history of the three of us; and so slowly I drew out my necklace—the locket his wife had worn, and youthful Jim had snatched from the fire. "He kept this for years after she died, and gave it to me one Christmas t' wear," I said, my voice shaking; and as he looked at it a spasm of pain passed over his face, an undeniable recognition, though he made no move to claim it.

"About a year ago," I went on, my voice less and less steady, "we were sailing back from China; a sudden gale sprang up, and one of oweh young sailohrs fell from aloft as he was taking in canvas. Youhr son…went ovehboard himself t' try to' save him; but neitheh of them was eveh recovered." I made the story far simpler than it was, that he might have no doubt of Jim's death, nor any doubt of the urgency of my visit; and his face—though still, though disciplined—showed his loss. "I know you'd come t' a parting of ways," I pressed on, deciding I could impart that much without risking a disclosure of the reason why; "but I'm here t' say he was a man of honohr… If I'd been his fatheh, I'd have wanted someone t' come say the same t' me, at the end."

His face had now changed, his growing emotion, still checked, mingling with a sense of respect—respect for the son long missing, unclaimed; respect for me; and, I guessed, respect for the words I'd left unsaid; and it showed in the chill that slowly left his eyes—in their steady regard, and their softness. I closed my fingers over the locket and prepared to slip it back inside my collar; but suddenly he stopped me, catching my hand; and I realized he wanted to touch it. Instinctively I took it off—undoing, with difficulty, the little clasp, and handing it over with sudden reluctance, this being the first time I'd been without it since Jim had given it to me, that crisp winter morning three Christmases ago.

Taking the locket in his hand, John Roberts smoothed his thumb over the surface, then familiarly opened the catch; then after a final caress he closed it, wordless in his careful restraint, though there was a quiver in his fingers. Without regret, he handed the locket back to me; and brushing off his knees, stood up.

I realized by that signal that our conversation had come to an end; that there was no more to be said; and I bowed my farewell to Taw and Reyna Lovell, washing dishes by the wagon—my cup, no doubt, being scoured in separate waters, by a dishcloth kept solely for that purpose. But as I spoke a kind word or two to the children, lined up in a wriggling row by the woodpile, John Roberts suddenly disappeared into the tent; and when he came back out, he held something wrapped in a cloth: something of awkward shape, which he handed to me, with a bow that brought the swift rush of tears to my eyes.

Taking the package with wonder, I drew back the cloth; and there before me was a little harp, such as a child might practice on in the beginning; a harp beautifully carved, no doubt by John Roberts himself, and embellished with painted symbols.

"It was his," he said simply, the only words he'd spoken since breakfast; and I realized he'd saved it in spite of the threat of contamination which probably sprang from it—the same taboo that, no doubt, had caused him to destroy all the other childhood property of Jim's.

Delicately touching the strings, I caressed their surface; and a music sprang forth—a gush of life such as had issued from small, fine brown hands long ago; a rush of sound which hung in the still air, and tapestried the bare trees with the sudden verdure of spring. Gone were John Roberts, Taw and the children; the flaps of the tent were flung back, as in summer; and there, shaking out worn, red satin quilts and bright comforters none the better for wear, in the smoky shafts of early morning sunlight, was a slim young woman dressed for the warmth of the season. Bare-necked, bare-armed, in colorful gingham, her hair drawn into two thick, untamed tails, she stood up to face me; and all at once I knew she was Narilla Wood.

For a fleeting moment I looked into her eyes—fine, black, piercing eyes so unlike Jim's, save in candor; travelled her face, fragile-boned, dignified, with its evidence of a Romany pure line; dwelt on her expression, with its transfigurative power—with its transmutation of the ordinary into the sublime. Subtle, strong-willed, it was yet a face of youth, with a vulnerability about the brow—a tenderness about the lips; and under her influence I was carried back to days gone, to a time when her awareness elevated my own, when her fingers conjured together rich moments. Then she was gone, the tent flaps lowered, and the trees stripped back again to bare grey; and stilling the strings because my hurt was so great—my hurt and John Roberts', as his face vividly showed—I simply quickly re-wrapped the harp, and bowed my thanks, speechless.

As if recognizing that his services might again be required, Sacki darted forward to show me the way back to the fence; and leading my horse without a backward glance, with the harp tucked under my arm, I followed.

Two days later I was back in Liverpool, reading a letter from McCabe—a characteristically brief scrawl which held no news of Jim, no word from any of the foreign consuls to whom we had written; and suddenly homesick for the old fisherman—suddenly yearning to lay the past weeks before him, to feel his homely hand on my shoulder, and to look upon my own children in a chance to re-claim them, I immediately prepared to sail home, buying a ticket as a passenger for only the second time in my life, aboard a damnable Cunarder. My last evening at the docks, strolling alone from one of the waterfront pubs, I came upon a couple of sailors—German, I guessed, from their Aryan features—just setting forth from their ship for a night on the town; and as they were arm in arm, I looked curiously at them.

Oblivious of me, they passed only a few yards away, fully visible under the street light; and as they swept through its arc they looked at one another with obvious partnership and affection, the one fondling the neck and hair of the other. That they dared be so bold I was astonished, in view of how their acts might affect others—might provoke, from chance observers, vigorous reprisals; but they looked perfectly able to defend themselves, burly men both, and worldly besides; and so they strode off into the night, till their footfalls were just a dull clatter on the damp wharves. For a long time I listened with unspeakable longing; then I too turned, alone, into the night.

XXVII

JAMES ROBERTSON
Rio de Janeiro, March, 1845

I called her Sarah, because she looked like Ben's mother: not her face so much, for she was older, being considerably past middle age; nor her hair, which was straight and white, long to her shoulders, always with a dark veil; but her expression, with its outflash of a godly spirit. Indeed she looked hallowed, with a compassion that beamed out from within, illumining her work-worn features, and bathing me in the throes of my illness—inviting me to bask in her kindness, as a child basks itself in the grace of its mother.

In the heat, she brought cloths, cool cloths for my forehead, and washed my feet in the flow of cool water—not hastily, but slowly, as one devoted to her work; in the evening, she sat beside me, reading words I could not understand, her face wavering in the glow of the rushlight; and in the dark, interrupting my fear and confusion, she spoke near at hand with a voice of assurance. I understood nothing she said, but I knew her tone: the tone of a caregiver, a healer, a servant; of one sainted in the crucible of the mundane. I tried to say to her once, "Holy," and couldn't; but later, sometime later, when I could swallow without fire, I managed my first words to her, "You have the face of God"; and I was rewarded with a gush of laughter, rich and throaty, despite her old age—laughter which was echoed later, when she said to others coming upon me: "Here he is, the man who thinks God has the face of a woman!"

She called me Ben, not because I so named myself to her, but because I summoned him over and over: not with the expectation that he would answer, but for the assurance his very name called up of him—solid, concrete, hardy, a sure haven in the wilderness of my roaming. In the heat, in my thirst, in the labyrinth of my memories, with their competing snatches of disjointed locale—now a boat, now a beach, now a fiery cascade, or a hammock swung in a sweltering t'ween decks; in the nautilus of their unwinding landscapes, shot through with shimmering glimpses of mountains; in this maze of swift, horizonless vistas, his name was quadrant, wheel and compass: the landfall I made day after day in my roving.

Once, to explain it—this potency of his name, and the reason for my repeated petitions—I tried to show her my wooden carving, my hand fretting over the bedclothes to find it: searching here, searching there, because it had never been far from me, not since I'd first shaped it from a bit of block in the boat. In its rendering of him rising up out of a billow, with me borne up in the brace of his arms—in his mettle, his might, the massive calm of his face, I knew she would find the explanation for my call; but I couldn't make her comprehend, even though I knew it was nearby, where it had always been, a reassurance to my touch.

In the end, thinking of another wandering I knew she would understand, and another wilderness I knew she would remember, I simply said to her "Succoth" and "Etham," and pointed to the rush light on the pillar; and a glow of comprehension came over her face. "Ah," she said, her voice splendid with knowing; and every time after that, with each naming of Ben, came a lighting of the wick, even in the waste of broad day.

It was then I began to understand her reading, for the words, suddenly familiar, came to me with a clearness, the same words I had read in the boat when I cut the carving of Ben: "He took not away the pillar of the cloud by day, not the pillar of fire by night, from before the people." Knowing that she understood, and eager to enlarge our common ground—yearning to share the sustenance of his name, not just wheel and rudder, but rain, life-fed rain, I said to her, "Massah" and "Meribeh"; and I took her hand to beat on the rock.

"Yes," she answered, and brought me a dipper of water, cool water with a mineral taste; then taking out her book again she read to me further, saying "Behold, I will stand before thee there upon the rock in Horeb; and thou shalt smite the rock, and there shall come water out of it, that the people may drink."

"Water," I nodded, satisfied, "Ben"; then thinking of another journey, and of altars built to mark a safe passage—finding comfort and continuance in those names as well, I named them for her, Shechem, Bethel, Hebron; and smiling, she read the familiar story. Able to attend longer, I listened, encouraged, tapping out the stages of the migration on the coverlet; and this time when she closed the book, she asked me something I was able to understand:

"When did you first begin to read it, child?"

"In the boat," I managed to answer, the first time I'd been able to hook question and response together.

"Yes," she said; "you came here in the boat."

I knew I hadn't, not in that boat; but it was too much to explain; and in the scorch of the day, I fell asleep.

For a long time, we progressed no further—me sleeping long stretches in the heat, always the heat, which numbers of times became the fire; she bathing my feet or bringing me water, and, in English or no, reading to me from her book. That she was able to help and could relieve me for short spells was enough, since I needed simply her presence; yet that she wanted to know more about me herself, and strove to fathom me as she served me, came clear sometimes even in my confusion; for I could tell, as she tended me, she was trying to ask questions. Making an effort, I would strive to respond—not always with such success as with Abram and Sarai; and there was humor in our exchanges, though perhaps she didn't see it. Once, when I thought she had asked me where I was from, I proudly managed to answer, "Wales"; but in response she only read me a long passage, which I recognized part way through:

> "Now the Lord had prepared a great fish to swallow up Jonah; and Jonah was in the belly of the fish three days and three nights. Then Jonah prayed to the Lord out of the fish's belly, saying,

I cried by reason of my affliction unto the Lord,
and he heard me; out of the belly of hell cried I,
and thou heardest my voice.'"

"Not that Whales," I explained to her then, rippling with humor;
but I could tell from her face she never knew why I smiled.

But there came a day when, opening my eyes—though all nearby
was still hazy, and wandering as it had been—the mountains in the
distance were clear; and in their sudden blaze of clarity, which lasted
but a moment, I recognized one and cried out with conviction: "Rio."
With an eagerness that lighted her voice, and maybe her face, though
I couldn't see her, she responded at once, "Yes, senor, Rio Janeiro;
and you are safe here, in Misericordia." I knew nothing of what that
was, but I needed no more, even though she tried to tell me; for at the
name of the city I was off on horseback, down a road beside Ben on
an early afternoon; and my heart was high within me. On our right
were forests, dense stands of tree ferns, sago palms, jacarindas, all
intertwined with thick vines; whilst off to our left, in the vast space of
our height, were the fantastic shapes of the Rio summits, great peaks
and loaves in the upsweep of the bay.

For a long time we followed a conduit, the water carrier for the
city, as into the course of a distant wellspring; stopped for a spell to
worship the rich growth, pausing before a coral bower; then climbing
the last ridge sat down on a ledge, just we two alone, side by side on
our loft. So near was he that our shoulders were touching; and his
thigh beside mine was warm in the sun. It was the first time I'd known
his body, save when he'd picked me up half-conscious at Hannah's;
and I drank in his touch as though it were nurture, nourishment for
a stubborn hunger within.

As if he were a near friend, a watchmate, and not any more the
aloof master of a ship, he pointed out the landmarks of Guanabara
Bay, naming for me the Portuguese names of the summits: Leme, the
Rudder; Arpoador, Harpooner; Gavea, Topsail; Dois Irmaos, Two
Sailors—landfalls for a generation of mariners on the move. A-blaze
in the newness of our experience together, the whole mapland

below bedazzled and shone, as if just spied through the glass of men yearning for shore; and for an untold time we celebrated on high, this pristine landfall, his and mine.

When next I woke I knew I was in Rio; and then came the landmarks one by one from my journey, like altars laid out to commemorate safe passes, or like wells re-dug after years of dis-use. Though sluggish and slow, my first thoughts were for shipmates; and since they were French, I said to Sarah: "Ou est Vernet...ou est Dijon, Ricard?" Though she responded in French as alertly as English, it was clear she knew nothing of what I was speaking; and trying again, I petitioned our ship. This time she answered, "Ah, *Mistral*, monsieur; she lies in the harbor, next the British bark that helped her; but all aboard her are ill." Uncertain of her meaning, I puzzled it out; realized only slowly I myself was unwell; and in my silence she prodded, "They are here, like yourself, some in nearby beds; how did you ever bring her round the Horn when you were so few?"

I couldn't answer her then, but her words triggered old scenes— the cold, raw seas, ludicrous contrasts to fever; the shipmates lost, including my friend Gigot, though how he had become my friend, I couldn't recall; the sheer effort to make headway though wasted with illness. Like wells of memory re-claimed from sand and wind, the intervening forces of confusion and time, I saw glimpses of passages forgotten—saw Dijon running up the distress signal when both master and mate fell ill; saw myself at the charts, torturing over their French; saw sightless days of sleet and fog; saw faces, mostly illiterate, far less experienced than I, turned to me for course and direction. Sometimes there was confusion, and Gigot's burial at sea became Abby's; and there was Ben reading the service, his face strained and set in the sting of the wind.

I understood it then, the weight he'd carried—discerned it not anymore just in his face, harsh with the ceaseless drive of decision, but in the demand of the faces turned toward me; and I thought of words spoken long ago in the desert: "Have I conceived all this people? Have I begotten them, that thou shouldst say unto me, 'Carry them in thy bosom, as a nursing father beareth the suckling child, unto the land which I sworest unto their fathers'?" As a father I was, the bearer of many, beset by human frailty and nature's frenzy; and I thrashed to defend that which I cradled. Then I was the suckling child, and Ben the nursing father; and we were a-bed together in his cabin, that night, that sweetest of nights; and my head it was that was close against his chest, muffled from the wail of the night and the wind; and his arms were those close and sturdy about me.

Sleep came to me then, as always when he held me; and as if fed by his touch while I was in slumber, I woke with the strength to remember further:—the passage round the Horn, without a single sail in company, not a ship running down her easting with us; the first outbreak of fever, then its rapid spread, and my battle to remain on my feet even when ill; the rescue two weeks out from Rio, by a northbound bark which gradually overtook us, and put a mate and five hands on deck to relieve us—me slipping into a swoon as soon as they cleared the rail. But the puzzle of Gigot, and of how I'd come to be aboard a French ship, frustrated me for long, as I knew I was not French, but Welsh; and to prove it to myself I harkened back to Ab Gwilym, reciting verses long ago read by my father— recollections clearer now than anything that had happened since.

"*Gwr wyf yn rhodio ger allt Dan goedydd, mwynwydd manwallt,*" I wandered, transported in time to a fireside in early spring; "*Rhod a geidw, rhydeg adail, Rhodiais wydd, dolydd a dail.*" Overwhelmed by my feverish rambling of Welsh—one of the few languages that didn't figure into her competent mix of Portuguese, English and French— Sarah sat quietly listening beside me, every now and then tapping her book, obviously supposing I was quoting scripture; and at last, to disabuse her, I managed to render—though without their music— the words in English: "I am a man who wanders by the hillside, beneath the woods, fine hair of gentle trees…" So great must have been the longing in my voice that she touched my hand, when I had finished, asking "Are you he, then… the man the poem speaks of?"; and smiling, I answered,

"Not anymore… I'm Isaac."

"Isaac?" she puzzled, for she still called me Ben.

"Aye," I responded, "re-digging old wells."

To cool myself, and her, one torrid spell in the heat, I recalled other lines, lines of dews, vapors, mists; lines that carried me back to a heath in raw spring, till I floated above it, a peregrine on the wing: "But there came a mist, resembling night, across the expanse of the moor, a parchment-roll, making a backdrop for the rain..." Half-wandering in sleep I recited the words, like a child who repeats old hymns vaguely grasped, till my father's voice overtook mine; till I could see the mist, the mist on the green, which gradually became the mist on the sea. There was something now I remembered about it, some secret in its opaqueness, which explained all else; but like many other thoughts it eluded my grasp, and I could only search its still hush.

Then as with a shifting of winds, or with a movement forward which altered the scene, the mists seemed to flow, some to the right, some off to the left; curtain after curtain was lifted before me, till I saw a great ship, its spars dark in the grey; saw it gliding along through the pearl of the dawn mist, slipping its way through the shrouds that had half-cleared, like some grand Behemoth in the fog. Somehow with a bound I knew Ben was at the helm, and that I was about to meet him—that our courses at last were about to unite; and so great was the gush of joy in my heart—so profound the expectation he was about to embrace me, to snatch me up at last in his arms, and bury me like a child in his bosom—that the thought slipped through me, "There lies the Beyond... I'm dying... and Ben must be dead, waiting to take me to the other side." But before I could join him I wakened once more, not to heaven, but to Rio's heat; and long-lasting this time were my throes of confusion.

When next my mind cleared, the puzzle of Gigot—and of my presence aboard a French ship—was still waiting; but every time I strove to resolve it, a fire burned in my heart and body, so vividly I often cried "Fire"; after which Sarah always fetched me cool cloths. But abruptly one night as she lighted the rush, and its flame sprang up quick and bright in the dusk, I saw the lurid masts of a brig—saw the blaze that surged up through the rigging and spars, fueled on by explosions of sap and tar; and I realized my ship was on fire—not *Mistral,* but some other, on whose deck I stood; understood in swift succession—and with inexplicable precision—exactly where we lay, a hundred miles south east of the Galapagos Islands, and what steps for survival we had to take.

As if unleashed by my recollection I felt the hot rage that'd swept through my frame then, the same passionate drive to survive to return home that had later kept me on my feet, even in fever; then saw all the swift scenes leading up to our lowering away. I saw me ordering my shipmates not in French, but in Spanish, to fill the deck boats not just with the obvious—casks of fresh water and tins of sea biscuit—but with supplies I would not have expected I'd think of, hooks for fishing and tarpaulins for awnings; saw my perfect control and command of the others as though I were master, though I knew I wasn't, and their instinctive response, all hands looking to me for leadership. As the night blazed like noontime and the livestock yammered, careening maddened and abandoned on deck, I saw us successfully lower away, then take to the oars in the gentle swell, oddly tender and soft in contrast with the brig, now a spectacular skeletal display; saw, for some ludicrous reason—with absolute clarity and perfect detachment—Ben's ceaseless fire drills on the Line aboard *Charis;* then watched dumbly with the others as with a final explosion, probably of powder, the brig burst asunder and sank, brightly hissing.

Recalled to our predicament by a thump under our hull, I comforted the others as I sat in the sheets; heard myself saying, in my inadequate Spanish, "*Tios,* that was a turtle, there'll be plenty of fresh food… and anyway, this being a sea lane, surely the fire has been seen—a ship will investigate, and maybe spot us by daylight." At daylight there was nothing save the broad back of the sea, not even a sight of the other boat; and realizing I should have bound us together, I wept—on my head the soft hand of Sarah.

"'Comfort, comfort my people, says your God,'" came her voice, after a while in the midst of my weeping; and at the words of Isaiah on the gentleness of her tongue, I calmed, finding my head now in her lap.

"What happened, senor... was there a fire?" she asked then, when I was hushed.

"We were separated....separated," was all I could explain, for the pain of it still filled my whole being.

"Separated...at sea?"

"Aye"; and as if it had just happened, I wept again.

"After a fire?" she prodded, as though piecing things together, her hand still tender in the tangles of my hair.

"Aye," I answered again, though it seemed to me now that there was something more than the fire, some hurt more sweeping than our separation, some anguish far greater which had happened before this, and of which this pain was but a rough echo; some inexplicable torment which lay hid in the fog, though like the ship in the mist it eluded me, all save its pain. Yet her calm, sane, gentle hands had their soothing effect; and in my grieving I actually managed to tell her, "It was a Spanish brig...I don't know why I was aboard her...a hundred miles or so off the Galapagos Islands. We were bound for Lima," I now remembered, memory growing bolder, "when smoke poured from the hold... It must have been...the cargo."

"And you all got off safely?"

"Aye... in the quarterboat and long boat... but...we were separated... I don't know what became of the others."

"How long were you adrift?"

"Twenty-nine days," I answered, amazed at my own precision. "We tried to reach one of the Islands...jury-rigged a sail, even rowed by turns, though it dehydrated us... but... the current was wrong."

"And how did you survive?"

"We had water and sea biscuit, at first...but...rations went fast... there were ten of us in the boat."

"Ten," she marveled, as if she understood what it meant, ten volatile men so long in so small a space, with so little.

"Aye...they fought the whole time," I told her; and now came other memories, swift and hard—memories of me imposing order in the midst of chaos, me of all people, as though I were fitted. "Twice they overturned the boat...two drowned that way, before we could reach them…To keep them in line, I…I struck them, I made them follow my orders… I…I had armed myself… I made them listen."

"What, senor, did you eat?"

"Turtles…there were many…green turtles…" Quick and hard came the memory of killing the first—the teeming of waters as we drained the blood, the trigger fish actually trying to suck our fingers as we dipped them in the water to rinse them; the sickly-sweet liver, the more delectable heart, and the dry-tasting eggs with their golden membranes, and their peculiar burst of yolk in my mouth. "And fish…mostly trigger fish, though we caught milk fish, sometimes."

"You ate them raw?"

"Aye"; but now again came that curious sense that there was more to the story, much more that was unremembered and hidden—not about this time, but about some time earlier, of which this recollection was but a thin echo; and once again, I grew restless.

As if she understood, she didn't press me, though I could see the light of interest on her face. "How, finally, were you rescued?" she asked.

"A French bark….*Mistral*…she that lies now in the harbor…We had rigged a small signal out of yellow oilskins…and she spied us." Out of the confusion of past days came a ladder, a bosun's ladder; down it scrambled a nimble lad, whose chipper hand was held out to me; I clasped it, looked up, and at last understood, for there was the smiling face of Gigot.

"So that was how you came to be aboard her."

"Aye. But I'm not French," I insisted.

"Perhaps not, monsieur; but you speak it perfectly."

"I'm Welsh," I kept on; and raising her hand as if to fend off another spate of Ab Gwilym, she smiled.

"I understand."

My brows came together in the silence that fell between us; for now loomed the puzzle of how I had come to be aboard a Spanish brig, to which I knew I belonged no more than the French; and reaching back into my memory, I struggled for clues.

Seeing my restlessness, she interposed, "Enough for now, senor; it is time to sleep again. You are doing so much better than yesterday, when you recognized the mountains."

Dumbfounded that it had only been a day since I first realized I was in Rio, instead of the weeks that seemed to have passed, I became even more agitated; and seeing my look—perhaps fearing another reaction—she again picked up her book, and changed the direction of my thoughts. "Would you like to hear something more from Isaiah?" she offered.

I nodded, perfectly at home, though I felt as amazed at my knowledge as I earlier had at my precision.

"What chapter and verse, then, senor?"

Deeply moved by what I wanted to hear, though I couldn't remember how I had come to love it, I hesitated a moment, seeking words; then knowing she would understand, I simply touched the palms of my hands.

"Oh, I have no need to look up that part, senor; I, too, have memorized it." Closing her eyes—a sublime calm on her face, as it flickered in the shine of the rush light—she began with the tenderness that was her art, and that resonated in every chord of her voice: "'...Can a woman forget her sucking child, that she should have no compassion on the son of her womb? Even these may forget, yet I will not forget you. Behold, I have graven you on the palms of my hands...'" And so saying she bent forward and swept the hair from my face, kissing me lightly on the brow; and less troubled than before, I slept.

Yet even into my dreams crept the Spanish brig; and in sleep now I searched back through the haze of afternoons, through hot Pacific middays to my hammock between decks; saw myself slung to rest in the equatorial heat, half numb to the lifting and sway of the swell. Like hypnosis the rolling and heat blurred my mind; though every now and again when I opened my eyes, I registered a sight which stirred my thoughts, or some discomfort which prodded my memory into motion. Once it was my hand as I raised it to my eyes—not my hand at all, emaciated, white, with sores that ran freely about the nails; another time it was pain, unlocalized pain, with neither throbbing nor pang to indicate source; and yet again it was thirst, the thirst not of fever, but of sweltering heat and long deprivation. Neither hand nor vague pain was ever attended, at least not in the torrid blur of my stupor; but thirst was assuaged in spells regular and generous, not just with water, but with the juices of limes, which I sucked like a babe in the short spans I was awake.

Gradually I understood I was not shipmate but guest, to judge by the expectations of those around me, which were nil; or to guess by the curious courtesy with which I was served, my Spanish-speaking steward almost servant-like in his acts. How I had come to be a guest or what was so curious about me, beyond my inadequate Spanish or emaciated hand, I couldn't, in the sultry haze of my thoughts, begin to fathom; but the slow advance of the days with their windless wallow and their confusion of babbled, disputed orders was all too clear; and I chafed in my hammock for strength, purpose, progress.

The humor of my thoughts instinctively struck me, even in the vague haze of my dream; for words like chafe, order, progress chimed in so like Ben, and made me break into a slumbering smile; tugged at the corners of my mouth even as they filled me with a longing, a fresh wave of yearning for his blunt mind and voice. The crispness and strength with which he'd run *Charis* and every ship we'd been aboard after contrasted sharply with our lazy wallow, and the chaotic jumble that passed for day's business; and I ached for his direction and dispatch even as I wondered at my transformation—at my slow transition from a gypsy-footed shiphand to a sure-sighted mariner with an aim.

As if to underscore my alteration there flashed into my dream a scene not from my hammock, but from somewhere before, when I sat in the sheets of what must have been a quarterboat, and stared up at the script of a fathomable heaven—at a star field from whose depths I deftly sounded my course; then another scene, the boat's floor, neatly laid out with fish parts—fillets, eyes, membranes, bait junk, and nearby, hooks, all set for every stage from eating to trawling, and ready to be replaced again with the next catch. Where this boat might have been I was unable to remember, for like the ghost ship it had come earlier, hidden in a great shroud of pain; but I was moved to murmur even in my sleep, "Ben, you'd be proud, it's a regular assembly," glad to show off my maritime factory. As if it had been eavesdropping nearby while I slept, a voice—some shipmate's—broke in in Spanish, "What assembly do you speak of, *tio*?"; and I answered, half-dozing,

"The fish parts in our boat, for eating and trawling; no factory could ever do better."

Hearing my response, he wanted to know if I spoke of the boat from which I had been rescued; and quite clear this was an earlier boat, not the one from which we'd been picked up together, his shipmates and I, by *Mistral,* I told him, "Aye; we had a regular business."

"But there was no *we* when we rescued you, *tio*; only you," he said gently, half cautious in wonder; "you were *a solas*, alone."

At the word *alone* there swept over me a vivid tidal surge of pain, far sharper than the ache of my body or hand—a surge like the one which overtook me when I spoke to Sarah of the separation of our two boats, after the brig had gone down to fire; but before I could understand where this new flood had come, my dream was torn in another direction, shifting altogether away from the sea. Suddenly I was a child and I could see myself clearly, as though I stood just behind me; saw my dark hair, my peasant-like clothes—breeches, leggings, jerkin, garb I'd long forgotten—and before me a blaze: a vast conflagration which shimmered against the blackened night sky. For a moment, confused, I thought it was again the Spanish brig, in the final throes of her fire at sea; but no skeletal outline of spars etched this blaze; rather what looked to be a caravan or wagon, with heaps of belongings scattered all about.

In their midst, close to me, lay a wooden top, my favorite toy, made by my father; and as if released from my terror by its sight, I sprang for it before it could be consumed. At once hands rushed to restrain me, trying to tear it from me, and throw it back into the midst of the fire; but I screamed so they ceased, and tightly held me: it was Father. I could hear his heart pounding under my ear, and feel his gold buttons press into my face; and for a moment the holocaust faded around us. Then came other swift scenes from the same evening: the smashing of dishes, kettles, ladles, and their burial; the shooting of our dog—like our gear, part of our family; the hurling of quilts, books, garb into the fire, and lastly a red cloak which crumbled in dark ash.

When I saw it I understood and I screamed "Mother! Mother!"; for in my childhood madness at her unspeakable loss and at the conflagration of all she'd touched before her death, I thought they had thrown her too into the fire. Only now, slowly, in my swinging hammock did I recollect she had been buried, prior to this destruction of all her belongings, in accordance with our longstanding custom; and in the starkness of my fresh desolation— in the midst of my mourning for the one who'd first shown me the snowdrop, fragile and white on the forest floor in the springtime—I saw myself standing by her makeshift grave, outside the paling of a Welsh churchyard. It was winter, and the old snow crunched under my feet; crunched loudly in the silence of the crisp morning, as I laid my top beside her marker. For a moment I lingered, still hoping to catch the elusive scent of her cologne—the benediction of the brush of her hand; then turning away, I consigned myself to the poverty I faced with my father.

When I woke from my dream not in my swinging hammock, a-gyre with the rolls of the Spanish brig, but in my severe wooden bed in Rio, I found Sarah sitting in consternation beside me; and through my fears I said simply, "I'm not Welsh, but Rom...my mother was a gypsy...but she's dead now... I'm alone."

"No one is alone in the bosom of the Father," returned Sarah with her serene, calm smile; and looking up at her, I at last saw her clearly; for her dark veil and long white hair came into focus as her headgear; and I understood who she was.

"You are a sister," I marveled, my tears ceasing all at once in my wonder.

"Yes, a *religieuse,* like all the attendants here at Misericordia, senor; I am Sister Leonore, though you may still call me Sarah." And she held to my lips a creamy spoonful of plantain, the first solid food I had tasted on land.

As I ate I tried to tell her what I had understood from my dream.

"I was a long time aboard the Spanish brig, lying in a hammock between decks. Someone, a steward, tended me off and on... The days dragged by—there was no wind, we must have been on the Line..."

"Someone tended you; then you were ill, senor?"

"Aye...I don't know, I...my hand was hurt, and I was thirsty... But not like now; I don't think it was fever."

"This was the same Spanish brig that later burned, senor?"

"Aye... the *Estrella,*" I remembered.

"Do you recollect how you came to be aboard her?"

"Not because I had shipped in her... I was ill when they found me... They picked me up," I understood.

"From another ship, do you mean?"

"No, no," I told her, remembering the fish on the bare planks; "from a quarterboat."

"You were again, senor, at sea in a small boat?"

"Aye."

"You are sure this wasn't the same as the one the *Mistral* rescued?"

"I know it... I was... I was much sicker... I had been much longer in this boat."

She was silent, as if contemplating the tragic strangeness of my journeys.

"103 days," I broke in on her thoughts; and she looked disbelievingly at me. "I know; I notched them into the gunnels of the boat."

"Senor, it is a miracle you are alive."

"Aye."

"It is no wonder they tended you... you must have been close to starvation."

I understood it then, my emaciated hand, with the sores about its nails; and I remembered the sea boils about my hips and thighs— recalled the open wounds in my mouth with a distant distaste, as though they had happened to someone else. "I had fish," I explained, "and rain water, by spells."

"You had scurvy, senor, and dehydration, at best."

Her plain words were harsh in the afternoon sun; and I turned away from the baldness of their candor.

"How did you come to be in the boat?" she pressed, not to be rebuffed by my silence.

"I don't know," I responded, distressed.

"It was a whaleboat, perhaps?"

"No…there was no iron, no line, no….I have never been aboard a whaler." Like a gift from the past came Ben's blunt assessment of whalers, only a shade or two less damned than steamers; and to her mystification, I smiled.

"And you were alone in this boat?" she prodded.

A wave of desolation swept me as she spoke, wiping the fleeting smile from my lips. "Only at the end," I explained; for they could not be denied, the three or four faces that rose up from the shadows at her words, then fled.

As if understanding what she had conjured up, and knowing she had to leave me with it, she gently patted my nearest hand, then collected her bowl and spoon; and I was aware of her moving down the line, murmuring in Spanish to others in beds. It was late afternoon, and I lifted my eyes to the upsweep of mountains beyond the verandah; remembered again my journey with Ben, on horseback that second liberty day in Rio. As soon as I closed my eyes, he was there just ahead, the dense shadows a-flicker on his worn checkered shirt; but this time in memory we weren't alone, for all of my watchmates were horsed beside us.

In the equatorial light, shafts of which pierced the trees, Paul reached out a hand and clapped my right shoulder, in a gesture of friendship all the more welcome because I was new; and then at last I understood. Directly in tears I saw the others, Ephie and Roan laughing amongst them; saw them gathered around whilst I played the guitar, or laboring beside me up the last slopes of Corcovado. Then we were together in the quarterboat, the four of us, dividing up tasks as calmly as if we were in the bay, instead of adrift in the middle of the Pacific; saw Ephie rigging an awning, Roan a sea anchor, and Paul and me the necessities for trawling.

Other scenes came too: our crowded attempts at sleeping, two by two in watches of six hours; our efforts at timekeeping, date counting, course charting; our fruitless endeavors at rowing and sailing, toward the shores of one of the Marianas Islands. In the end we had given up, and taken to situating ourselves as best we could in the heart of the sea lane, hoping to raise an east- or west-bound vessel; and in fact we raised five, though none of them spied us, despite flares and oilslicks hoisted as signals. In the tedious heat of the days we kept up our spirits through the doing of tasks, yarn-swapping and reading—Ben of course having supplied a Bible along with every other need: Paul reading the entire gospel of John, me reading Luke, Ben's favorite, and Ephie and Roan reading Matthew and Mark.

After reading we planned or remembered days back in Maine, all the details of life we'd never shared on other lookouts, off Cape Hatteras in fog or in the desolation of Cape Horn; but they hurt so much to recall, the sun-warmed smell of pink granite, the olive strands of rockweed and the wind sprays of salt, that I shut them out then as now.

But nothing stayed shut out now for long. Whether it was my dwindling fever, or the diminishing doses of laudanum which no longer shielded me, my defenses against the past were weakening, as if the walls erected in illness were breached in health; and every time I closed my eyes, I was overflooded with fresh scenes, no matter how fiercely I fought the tide. When I could no longer bear them I opened my eyes, in an effort to beat back the past with the present; and each time my gaze fell first upon Sarah, sitting beside me in consternation, as if she knew the perils of memory I faced. Too numbed to speak I simply looked at her, drawing strength and assurance from the calm of her face; and understanding my silence she never forced words, quietly reading instead, or maybe drifting in prayer.

That there were dozens of others who needed her care—that it was scarlet fever I battled, along with my shipmates, the whole vessel having been swept since we'd rounded the Horn—I'd by degrees managed to grasp, seeing the telltale flush on my arms, or overhearing snatches and phrases muttered low by the servants; but no matter the demands on her, the whole hall around me surely quarantined, she was always nearby, close enough to touch. All the threats of the fever's final inroads on us—dropsy, inflamed hearts, the unspeakable debilities which had yielded our deaths at sea—stood at bay, like my memories, with her presence; and to keep them off I would clutch at her skirt, the stuffy, hot broadcloth of her dark costume, as if there were healing or power in its folds. My whole body shedding its rash—shrugging its skin as a lobster jettisons its shell, then hides, vulnerable, in some ledge close in shore—I crouched, protected, in the shelter of that cloth; carried it like a talisman when I closed my eyes—armed, come what might, against the memories I faced.

The first phase of our time adrift had been marked with calm—the uncluttered directives of simple survival. Convinced that we'd be picked up at any minute, the four of us had entertained few fears at first, the more so since the boat was well-stocked—characteristic of Ben, no one lowering away without what he considered the essentials, even for so small a matter as a row to another vessel in plain view. From time immemorial he'd had the quarterboat ready for just such an emergency as this; and closing my eyes I could still see everything stashed in the cuddy in the bow, or under the seat in the stern: tins of biscuit, preserves, hooks and line for fishing; 2 kegs of fresh water, replaced every day; tin platters and cups; medicinal powders and ointment; lengths of canvas for a sail or awning; friction matches in an airtight; a spare knife, marlinspike and mallet; flares, pencils, twine, rudimentary charts and tables.

Together with the spare chronometer and sextant handed aboard at the last moment, they represented the last word in pragmatic need—everything aboard, as Paul joked, but the sitting room sofa. It was inconceivable that we couldn't survive till we were discovered, even if we failed to make land; and we dispassionately set about doing what all four of us had been schooled to do, all these years under Ben's hand. When the hard tack was gone, we began on the tins; when the tins began to dwindle, we started to trawl; when we brought fish aboard, we set aside bait for more, then ate the fillets raw—smaller amounts at first, then, as we hardened to it, greater. Trigger fish there were in plenty, at least in the beginning, when the weather was fairer; silver fish too, and more delectable, less hard on our hands to clean and handle; even milk fish, a great find, since they were large and delicious. At the height of our efficiency and strength it took from fifty to a hundred fish a day to feed the four of us; and we learned as we went to waste nothing—even the eyes full of a satisfying liquid.

It was the same with options in direction: the Marianas, obviously, our first choice; but when the North Equatorial current outmatched our ability to row—when it became clear we couldn't stay our course, such as it was, calculations coming hard with so little horizon to work with, and our chip of a boat incessantly moving—we allowed our drift into the broad lanes to the west, thinking to raise a ship bound in or out from the Orient. With each failure—with southing unachieved, with sightings blocked by noon clouds, with dead reckoning more and more a matter of guesswork, and our flares unnoticed by the vessels we did spot—there was no time to mourn; for there were always new options to explore, and work constantly to be done.

In fact fatigue, not despair, was from the start our chief problem; for the physical labor of fishing, with its assembly morning and night, and the mental wear which sprang from our lack of space, or the ceaseless conversation of those on watch, rendering thought difficult and sleep nigh impossible for the rest, eroded us all like rain on a rock. The monotony of our diet and the relentlessness of the sun made inroads on our resources as well; but nothing wore us down like lack of privacy—especially me, raised to a stringent physical ethic. Never in my days—neither at sea, in that gutter of a forecastle which fetched me Gibraltar, nor on shore, in those prisons which passed for boarding houses or sailors' rooms—had my bodily functions been so completely on display; and I struggled with the broad light of day of our boat. Neither bathing, which left a salty scum, nor laundering, which wore our few garments to rags, nor calls of nature were ever out of sight of another; and the latter grew more irksome as we succumbed to dysentery.

Almost as wearing was my lack of mental privacy; for in the ceaseless shifting around, and the anxious need to talk, and the perpetual searching for anecdotes not already shared, I seldom felt

free from the prying of others. Having always drawn nourishment
from my thoughts—having prized especially my memories of Ben,
or dreams of encounters yet to be—having now, more than ever,
need for silence, in my cherishing of his caress at Anjier, or that last
brush of his lips on my hand at the rail—I found I couldn't so much
as raise an image; and I eroded in mind as well as in body.

To keep up our spirits or ease our fatigue we tried to vary our routine—
our watches and watchmates, our patterns of sleeping, our times all
together for work or amusement; our hours for meals or trawling or
washing, and our recording of each day's events, which we notched
with a penknife into the gunnels of the boat. Our reckoned position,
the date, the number of fish caught, our sightings of unusual marine
life or birds, all these we etched in hieroglyphics in the planks; and
we took turns at being scribe as faithfully as we did filleting the fish
or handing a line. To manage the vast, unwieldy blankness of the
sea as well as the plotless void of our days—to demonstrate we were
in an exact location, moving inexorably to another, in spite of all
evidence to the contrary—became our prevailing occupation, as key
to our survival as food and rest; and as I tried to marshal our hours
into something like progress, I understood Ben as never before; saw
it was I who was leading the others.
    Though we called Ephie "Captain"—though all three of them had
been schooled far longer than I with the view to becoming master—
it was I who laid out the day's routine; I who rationed the pints of
water; I who imposed periods of quiet; I who, in an effort to keep
up our spirits after each failed sighting or southing, led the chanteys
while we worked. It was as inconceivable to me that I wouldn't live
to see Ben again as it was that I couldn't survive—the two being one
and the same, anyway; and I used my conviction to lift up the others.
It was I who made them notch each day in the gunnels, and as they
did so, recall anniversaries past, as well as celebrations to come; and
as they charted theirs I silently marked off my own: June 3, 1842,
the day we'd climbed Corcovado; July 5, 1842, the eve we'd supped
in Havana, and Ben had shown me his prize, the shell; July 10, 1842,
the day I'd fallen ill, and he'd carried me into the sick bay; July 15,

1842, the night I'd cried, and he'd held me; July 31, 1842, the day I'd first hauled into Cape Damaris. In tidy order they rose and docketed themselves in my mind—lined themselves up with their kindred just a year later, or with their unrealized brethren of the future; and I ate and drank from them as from a platter.

In the same vein I encouraged them to share hopes—not merely events past but anticipations, in an effort to keep their thoughts pinned on the future; encouraged them to maintain some connection with their dreams, in an effort to take their minds off their bodies. Our time together after supper, in what would have been the dog watch, became set aside for such confidences; and at first they took the form of confessions—yearnings not shared those hundreds of lookouts off Cape Horn. Accustomed as we were becoming to nakedness of body, this bareness of spirit came easier than it might have, any ordinary dog watch in times past; fit in somehow with the bald blaze of the sun, and the elemental strokes of sea and sky.

His face gaunt and bearded, no longer guarded by station and wealth, Ephie shared not just his dream to become a master, which we'd all known was his primary goal, but his need to prove himself to his family—doomed as he was to be always on the fringe of Melchett Bros., neither a brother nor a son but a half-bastard cousin, tarred with his father's brush before he'd ever been born. Roan, who'd been as good as engaged to Louisa, shared memories of her he never, under other circumstances, would have; confided hopes, his slight shoulders hunched and wracked with his cough, to break away altogether from the family, and establish the two of them outside its confines. In their unbosomings of family I caught glimpses of Ben—his craving to detach himself, as with his unconventional dress, and his striving to succeed on their terms and to please, as with the building of *Abigail* and the boat race; and though moved by their disclosures I wasn't wholly surprised, these being the tensions I'd come to look for with the Melchetts.

But Paul struck us amidships, one eve as the sun westered, with his suddenly confessed love for Damaris—which none of us had remotely suspected—and the revelation of his resentment toward me: a keenness of rivalry which, now that he expressed it, created a wall

between us, the first sign of edginess and aggression to come. That I
cared nothing for her, beyond as a friend, and had done nothing to
invite her affection—even had labored to keep her at bay—seemed
to matter little to him; and as the evenings crept by I began to host
the suspicion that he saw in our plight a chance to win her one day—
saw, in the possibility I might not survive, a fresh opportunity for
her heart. Wrongheaded as it may have been, the wariness put me
on edge; and my unease was not helped by the expectations of the
others, who seemed to be looking to *me* for confessions—not merely
hopes and dreams, but revelations.

Frustrated I didn't have the common ground of their
experiences—just as I'd been frustrated by my lack of credentials
at Ben's sickbed—I stalled, my heart the one thing in our talk off
bounds; but they never ceased in odd moments to try to catch me
off guard; and it was surprising how quickly such prying put me in
an ill humor—the more so since, as the days passed, I longed more
and more to talk about Ben, to name him out loud, to reminisce, as
they did.

When our first fight came it was not between me and Ephie over
who called the shots in our little vessel—he seeming not to have
noticed who really was in charge, in the kind haze of fantasy and
expectation—but between me and Paul, over Damaris; and it was I
who struck out in the upflash of frustration, knocking him over with
the sudden force of my blow. On land the event would have passed
in a day, as even my explosive fight with Ben had, leaving scarcely a
ripple of consequence in our lives; but here at sea it spelled disaster,
re-ordering the whole of our fragile existence. The waters having
been calm in this stretch of early summer, and the boat fairly stable,
if always in motion, we'd taken to leaving our gear lying about; and
now as we capsized, Paul's fall knocking us off balance, many goods
spilled with us, and were lost. All of us being trained swimmers
and the swells low, we soon righted our craft, and hauled ourselves
back aboard—madly grabbing tins, bowls, and other flotsam as we
clambered in, then rowing to snatch up anything still floating; but a
hasty inventory revealed many things missing, or ruined for all time

by the water.

The sextant, in its case in the cuddy, was wet, and the chronometer gone, marking the end of our primitive efforts at direction-finding, and leaving us to the mercy of sun and stars; and the last flare and friction matches were damp, throwing us back on the expediency of signals. More important was the loss of several hooks, goading us to guard the few remaining with our lives; and most crucial of all was the condition of our water—one of our two kegs, though lashed, now brackish, leaving us only the other, which was unbroached. Bitterly blaming myself for my impetuous act, I reined myself in with the staunchest discipline I'd ever known—a self-command far more unyielding than any physical mettle I'd shown; and I swore—as if Ben were watching me—never again to act merely for myself, but only for the good of the whole.

Our loss of water was all the more critical as we were suffering from dysentery—Roan especially, the slightest and smallest amongst us; and we struggled daily to replace the body fluids we lost. The sun, too, advanced our dehydration; and as we prayed persistently for rain we crafted our stretch of canvas into a sort of fabric funnel, the spare tin bucket at the ready to set beneath it, should the wet season ever commence. When the rains did begin, enabling us to replenish our keg, my sense of guilt lifted a little from me; but now came consequences of a new kind in the discomfort of our continual wet. The awning being barely large enough for us all to fit under, especially with the bucket in our midst, and the rains continuing day and night, there was no space to move about—neither by day, when we ached to exercise, nor by night, when we longed to stretch out; and our cramped position only added to our exhaustion.

Nor did the wet help our bodily health; for our skin, already blistered from the constant fishing, now erupted in sea boils from the drenching; and our sopping clothes rubbed and chafed us to new sores. So torn were we between wishing to discard them—the cloth rotted anyway with last month's sun and salt—and wanting to wear them due to the cold, that we changed our minds about them by the hour; and we took to simply draping them upon us, in a kind of compromise between pain and need.

Our bodies weakening from want of exercise, and the crowded position under the awning—or fatiguing from the opposite problem, the constant labor of bailing, the seas rising now to add their spray to the rain—we fell to sleeping more and more, our heads in one another's laps: the pair sitting up supposedly on watch, but truth to tell, more frequently drifting, waking up in swift intervals not to search the horizon, but to ease the sores on legs and haunches.

By the 40th day we'd each lost considerable body weight—a condition we could gauge not so much in ourselves as in others, each man's body becoming another man's mirror; while our faces had become gaunt and bearded, even Roan's, though he was sandy and smooth-skinned. With the inroads of lesions and sores on our limbs, and the ignominious drapery of cloth round our frames, we had the disreputable look of highwaymen on the hunt, long without a profitable haul; and our eyes spoke of a corresponding inner dissipation. Plagued by dysentery and coughing, and weakened by bailing, we were the manifestations of lassitude and loss of will; and as I looked on myself in the guise of the others I felt the rise of an inward panic—an uncontrollable battle between resignation and pride.

Never in my life had I not been handsome—had I not, even in illness, had something comely about me; and as I gazed on us now I realized my looks were gone—the looks I'd especially come to cherish as the one ultimate appeal I had in my arsenal to attract Ben. In the bald glare of the present I could see how openly shameless I had been in my reliance on them—how I had used them to work my will upon many, not just Ben, though he was last and chief; and beyond my thankfulness that he couldn't see me—a gratitude beyond measure he was nowhere near me—came the eerie sense that I was dying; that I was losing my old self, my appearance, my body.

My self-erosion might have troubled me even more than it did, had it not been for the decline of the others—their obviously greater needs placing demands on my attention which frequently turned me away from myself. As I had once comforted Ben's children, in days long ago on the beach, so now I succored my shipmates at sea, as if

I were their maritime father; placed Roan on my knee or even laid him upon me to spare his thin frame the hard planks of our boat. With his additional weight my own lesions deepened; but he seemed to take such comfort from me, his sandy head inclined on my breast, that I encouraged him to indulge his need.

When it rose within me, the inevitable sense of burden of giving over myself to nurture another—when it began to wear me, holding him over the gunnels, or cleaning him up when he could no long control his bodily urges—I listened in my mind to evocative words from the desert, "Have I conceived all this people?... Have I begotten them, that thou shouldst say unto me, 'Carry them in thy bosom, as a nursing father beareth the sucking child'...?"; for these were the verses we had read aloud to each other before the boat had capsized and our Bible become wet; and they had stayed with me, like all the words of wilderness.

The others, too, seemed to find solace in such lines, passages of trial and doubt, exile and hope; and it was often all we talked about now—not our physical discomfort or our future aims, but the stages of journey which recalled our own. Listening to them recite from the Psalms or recount experiences of their life in the spirit—listening to Ephie describe, for the first time, his encounter with Jesus in the shrouds of a blizzard—I learned many things about the scriptures, things which had been closed to me, in my haphazad Rom way; but I learned above all things about my shipmates—about even Roan, when he could talk—which I hadn't, in all these years, held a clue to.

That they all knew Christ more or less as Ben did—as the one who called men and women to justice, and as a self-sacrificing giver of life—I'd always understood; but now I could see, in their reliance on him as sustainer, something more—the sheer intimacy and allure of relationship. With this I began to feel on common ground, for it was the simplest part of the whole Bible for me to grasp: all that wooing and winning between God and people, man and man, so vividly portrayed in Hosea. In fact the more physical and concrete the relationship the better—beyond gates, water, bread, to the touch of a hand; and Christ was not so alien now as he had been, when I'd first, as a Rom lad, heard Methodist preachers on horseback prattle

on about self-loss and finding; or even when I'd stood in Jackson's
sitting room a year ago, in an effort to encounter the Lord Ben knew,
and heard him speak of the Guest in his house.

Instead he was eerily familiar now, in the drama of my burden,
as uncanny as the sense of my dying; and as they dried the pages of
the Bible in the wind, Paul and Ephie, so they could read what they
had forgotten—or failed to memorize—all those Sabbath Schools
long ago, I struggled with the threat of his presence. At times I was
outraged with all the vigor of will, all the force of survival against
surrender; but at other times capitulation was sweet, as sweet as
Roan a-drowse on my chest; and I began to dream about it, myself
asleep on Jesus' breast, and his arms about me in a haven of rest.

What they understood about God was still far beyond me—all
those abstractions about the Trinity, in the letters of Paul, or those
treatises on justification and atonement, displaying the maddening
bent of all gadje to compromise Power with words; and it was
seldom their explanations left me other than cold. How Ben had
ever navigated it all as a boy in that wooden pew, triced up in a
neckcloth between Galen and Sarah, or survived into manhood with
an untarnished grasp of the holy, was a wonder to me still; and I
could only put it down to some dead reckoning of the heart. But the
Holy Spirit was another matter, that part of the Godhead being easy
to comprehend—far easier for me than for my shipmates; for here at
last was something like O Meero Duvel, which blazed at the heart of
every living thing. When I looked out over the gunnels at the flesh of
the world, it was still a-flash with that empowering force, beyond me
and my body forevermore: as a-fire as it had been that day above Rio
when, in the crucible of health and hope, we'd stood at the bower to
worship, Ben and I.

On the 64th day for the first time there was no morning catch, it
being too rough, and the fish having gone deep; and we ate the fillets
left from the night before, thinking to tide us over to supper with
meat set aside for bait. They had little effect on Paul, Ephie and I,
those fillets, beyond the inevitable cramps one would expect from
old meat; and so accustomed were we to digestive discomfort that

we accepted it as preferable to hunger. But for Roan the result was dire, in the onset of severe dysentery and pain; and we could see he was weakening by the hour. In an effort to stave off dehydration we spared him all our rations of water and a precious biscuit, stale and soggy, but still wholesome, from the tin; and I laid him out atop me that night with my shirt over him, that his aching muscles might be eased.

But toward dawn I half-wakened with a strange sense not of his presence, but absence; and rousing directly, I realized he was gone. In the instants that followed it was not he who was missing but Djemail, who never landed atop his circus horse after taking the hoop; and the first I understood it was the cry of the audience as I gained my own landing, and saw his riderless horse beside me. In the swift terror of loss and confusion that came next—he being my one friend in the world, and my first love—I wakened, not to the sea and my shipmates, but to Sarah; and under the softness of her hand I wept long and freely for this lad, for whom I'd never mourned, in the fierce self-reliance of youth; settled only after a slow, sickening time to sobs, which faded at last to the calm of my low voice, awakening my shipmates to our loss.

As Ben had for Abby, I read a service over Roan, doing my best to recall words heard long ago off Cape Horn, or on the North Sea when I'd first lost a watchmate; haltingly brought in bits and pieces from the Psalms that Roan liked, or that Jackson had once marked for me. There was no question afterward of dividing up his belongings, as custom always had it at sea, since he had nothing to his name—his sheaf knife weeks ago transferred from his side to the cuddy, like the rest of ours, as they wore our skin; and his calfskin boots long since discarded. But I took his ring to give to Louisa, should I ever chance to see her again; then together Paul and I put him over the gunnels, surrendering his frail form to the deep.

In the days that followed we missed him keenly, not just for his own sake, but for his place in our crew life; and we struggled to know what to do with all the hours we'd served him, and with the odd number of us that remained in the boat. In the aftermath of his loss someone was always alone now, not paired off, waking and sleeping, as we had been; and though the activity of fishing and drying the Bible helped take up the slack of our extra time, nothing seemed to ease our sense of bereftness. Being left alone became nearly fearsome, as fearsome as the abandonment I'd felt as a child, seeing my mother's red cloak in the fire—as frightful as the separation I'd known as a lad, left behind by the riderlessness of Djemail's horse; and we fought over who'd be the odd man out—finally settling matters by using the dog watch to shift the third man onto a different team, instead of simply onto a different track, as at sea.

Thus one day we watched and slept alone, the next, with the felicity of a partner; and long would have been that twenty-four hours, had it not been for the companionship of the Bible. So many questions would I save up in my time alone—pondering them while fishing or cleaning the first catch, dead reckoning or making the day's notch—that when we were all together in the dog watch, or what we supposed was the dog watch, gauging it by the sun shadows or deepening shade of the sea—they began to call me the Ethiopian, and play Phillip to my plaintive inquiries. At pains not to speak of Roan or their deepening sense of our vulnerability, they were only too glad to help me with my scriptural tangles; and now with scurvy making its first appearance on Ephie about the 70th day—with all our tins gone, and the relentless rain and cold still wearing upon us—we found that our reading was the one thing that could lift us.

On the 71st day we caught sight of a vessel, only the fourth that we'd raised since we'd taken to our boat; and though we hailed the best we could with our broken voices, and waved the yellow oilskins we'd attached to the gaff; though we even made ineffective efforts to row toward her, she never saw us on the choppy surface of the sea, and soon stood off to the distant east. Where we were ourselves had long been uncertain, despite my endeavors to calculate—from the direction of our drift, and from my estimation of the speed of the current—something like a set of coordinates each noon; but my best reckoning had us well to the northwest of where we'd lowered away, though still in the broad shipping lanes to the Orient—in fact as likely now to be picked up by a ship in or outbound from Japan, as one from Singapore or Whampoa.

Still struggling to exert some control over our options—to exercise some influence over what happened to us, especially now that scurvy had made its appearance, and our days were effectively numbered—I refused to relent, even after the defeat of our futile sighting; refused to resign, as frequently did the others, from that office which distinguished us from the seawrack; but in fact I too found myself more and more often giving myself up to the will of the sea, to the direction and pace it chose for us.

The first sign of scurvy was the loosening of our teeth—which we could soon detect with our tongues—and the bleeding of our gums, which we couldn't discern for ourselves with our little remaining sense of taste, but which we could perceive in one another. Like all seamen we knew the sequence of stages—the lassitude, which was already upon us, the bleeding under the skin and the trenches in our mouths; and these we tried to stave off as if it were a matter of will—as if we could control our decline with our minds. Processing our fish, we tried eating parts we'd discarded, in case they possessed the vitamins lacking in our diet; even attempted at whiles to sample the gulfweed, though its saltiness, even after washing in our precious water, proved too great a risk of dehydration.

The cold damp was having its effect on our health as well—all of us, but especially Ephie, having been coughing for weeks; and now as I notched the 80th day, this posed as great a concern as the scurvy. That our malady was not lung fever was at least apparent, for we suffered none of the other symptoms I remembered so well from Ben's illness; but the coughing and pleurisy-like pain in our chests impaired us almost as severely as if we were fevered. Ephie the night before had coughed up blood, and today complained of such discomfort he was unable to help us clean our catch; and as Paul and I knelt, leaning athwart the seats—this being less painful than sitting on the sores of our haunches, and one of the ways we tried to alter positions—we exchanged worried glances. With my anxiety there now rose something else as well, the dawning of a persistent anger—a fury that at times shook my frame, and filled me with a sense of desertion; and it was all I could do to keep it under command as I endeavored to mother Ephie.

What exacerbated my anger was Ephie's—his reaction to his decline not submissive like Roan's, but wrath-filled and irate at all the unresolved issues behind him. Though he made no comment about his state—indeed seemed not to notice the speed with which he was failing—he spoke bitterly of the Melchetts: ruminating on the history of their cutting his father out of the shipyard, and venting his resentment at being relegated to the sidelines, though he'd tried harder than many to support the business, and earn the kind of notice that had come easily to others. As he spoke his words evoked subtle resonances in my own heart, old memories too formless and vague to recount; and the more he rankled at his unfinished missions—his dream of winning the kind of acclaim that Ben had, and matching his performance at sea with a creditable role at the yard; the more he railed at his double losses—at the past which had cheated him, and the future which seemed likely to—the closer my own fury rose to the surface.

It wasn't my anger on behalf of Ben's similar family challenges I felt, but my own; and like Ephie's rancor, it affected us all—my tensions with Paul too returning to the fore. Now for whole afternoons I sat staring off into the distance, not at the sea or the guess of a sail, or the flight of a frigate bird on the hem of the sky, but at scenes from my past long resisted or denied: scenes of the kris meeting while Djemail and I stood outside, awaiting the inevitable verdict from their tent; scenes of harsh faces and the inhospitable moor, to which we were irrevocably condemned, for no greater offense than an unconventional love; and bitter were the hours I revisited them in my heart.

When at last, near the end, Ephie fell into a kind of coma without ever once discussing the dispensation of his property, or leaving so much as a sentence for his kin—when at last he sank into a hoarse calm, his breathing the only sound of a still night, and audible the next day even over windspray and rain—when at last, with broken breaths, he was silent, my own rage rose at last; and as I beat the planks of the boat with my first, it was my father I pummeled, my father who'd failed to stand by me; and it was rage I wakened to vent on Sarah; it was rage.

In the exhausted hush after Ephie's death—in the aftermath of his muted service, when Paul had removed his shirt for our spare, and I had taken his Cape Horn earring, to wear home for him if I was able—I wandered through many uncharted hours; roused for little more than our reckoning at noon, and the minimal demands of fishing. Though we handlined together and slept side by side, too lonely to stand the interminable watches alone, and too fatigued to keep up a lookout at night, even for the rare chance of a ship's light; though we conversed at times, exchanging remarks as we fished, neither of us really attended the other, or answered one another's words, simply carrying on two wholly separate conversations; and I drifted in mind for long spells on times past.

At whiles it was the circus tent, quiet at last for the night, which came into focus instead of the sea; and I was a-drowse on the mound of hay on which I slept, with Enrico my trainer beside me. Nearby were the horses, their breaths short bursts in the cold; while frost hung in mists in the reaches above. A-stir on the straw Enrico turned, startling me with his unexpected alertness; and I felt his hand settle warm on my thigh. Then my throat was bare and his breath at my breast; and my open lips were upturned to his kisses. Then it was Boston, my old lodgings on Creek Lane, and it was Jacques who was saying good night; Jacques taking the lamp as he went down the hall, with a backward look at me and a grin; and I answered him with a ready smile, and a receptive lift of the shoulders. Then again it was night, with the clattering of cups and conversation somewhere below; and now it was Lill who came into my room, strong with the gliding hush of her skirt, and sat down on the bed beside me. Half-awake at her step, I roused to her touch, warm and firm at the drawstring at my waist; yielded myself to the hand which slid down under the cloth, and parted my thighs to the press of her will.

Then it was late autumn, in the clearing beside Ben's house; and I was alone beside his bare garden. Though the air was cool, full of the thoughtful nearness of winter, the sun was warm, undimmed by either cloud or wind rush; and the little knoll was bathed in a late afternoon stillness. Off in the distance, lining the far shore, the birches were still pale gold and sere, the fallow hue of trees in the last stages of fall; but they were the only notes of color lingering in the dark green of the spruce, for the shouts of red and orange of the maples and other ornamental trees in town were already silenced for the season.

Now and then the patter of a falling birch leaf, wafting past its kin with the plink of a raindrop, or the whir of a locust broke the hush; but otherwise there was absolute stillness—the shuttered peace of the sheds with their boarded-up windows. Attending the earth, my gaze came to rest on the garden, what seemed to be the center of the stillness; and I dwelt upon the upturned furrows. About them the blades of grass, now fallow, bent to and fro in the sun; and their clumps of soil, sewn with the gravelly sand of the shore, lay open to the ways of the weather.

In their tranquility they spoke not of the finish of a productive season, nor even the promise of the season to come, but simply of a quiet acceptance; indeed, if I had not known the hour, I would not have been able to tell whether it was late autumn or early spring. In them was no hint of the harshness of winds to come, anymore than of the enlivening sun; just a receptivity, a preparation, a hush. Over my head there beat the rush of wings, marking the passage of some great heron on its annual migration; but all about the still garden was neither coming nor going, simply openness to the here; and I wakened with a calm that both blanked my past anger and relinquished any hold on the future.

Now the Sarah I saw when I opened my eyes was not just Sarah, but someone more—the one I knew in the boat for her gentle hand; knew for her Godly face, full of compassion and feeling, and the knowledge of suffering in her gaze; and I allowed her to stroke my fever-wet hair—allowed her to braid it, for it was long, and bathe the most private parts of me with the relinquishment of one newly made, unable to attend yet to life. Or perhaps it was with the resignation of one about to depart, about to be laid out, clean and arrayed, upon a makeshift bier with candles; for there was as much surrender in the one as in the other. Indeed I tried to tell her —to make her understand I was clay to her hand, without will; but all I could explain was "I'm Adam," and accept the ministrations of her hand; just as at times I could only say "I'm Abram," and seek the final release of my cave.

Earth and cave, clay and bone, they grew as intertwined as old wineskins made into new, or wells reclaimed from the sifting of sand; and I abandoned all sense of their bounds and order. Then it was healing she brought, the healing I'd sought in the boat, when I'd tried to find a position in which to sleep; when I'd understood why it was they'd all wanted to touch his robe, or have Peter's shadow fall upon them. It was always high noon now, there was never any shadow—but I sought it still with a hunger that would not abate; and again came that Divine hand on my forehead, stroking with pity her child; and again came the strength to meet a new day.

Once I thought I caught sight of her, walking away from me on the water, an aged crone bent over her basket; but before I could call her she was gone to the next swell, which flowed from the crest above and its valley. Then she was Paul, Paul sitting across from me; and we were tired, he and I, too tired to fish; and the seas all around us were rugged. No longer between us, Damaris was gone; and he was again the man I might have loved, if I hadn't known a better. "Paul," I said, "notch the 96th day"; and he did, carving it into the gunnels while the seas tossed recklessly all around. Though it had been rough by spells all summer, and the times we were unable to fish more frequent, I'd never been afraid of a capsize; had been able to maintain our seat in the water with the bucket dragging as a sea anchor.

But now, summoning our strength to attend to each other—first daubing the blood from one another's gums, that we might eat, then cutting one another portions of last night's bait—we cast a weather eye over the bowline; and it was not wholly unexpected, the rogue wave which rose just off to our narrow horizon. For a moment, benumbed, we simply watched, as with a massive wall, it stood up from the deep; then I knew as we began to rise to it that we would not be able to top it; and a thrill of energy raced through me. "Paul,"

I cried, "cling to the bow seat!"—for he was there, putting away his sheath knife; and I threw my arms about the stern seat with just enough time to draw in my breath.

With an awful grandeur the blue green curl hovered perfect above us, poised ready to break; then came the cascading masses of white foam bearing us down with their thunderous weight; and it was Maine again, winter, and Ben was in the boat with me, guiding it with strong strokes toward the shore. Then we were buried, the hurtling torrents tearing at our arms and legs; but he was holding me, cradling me in my torment of lungs; and we burst to the surface gasping for air, still clinging to the intact seat; and Paul was gone, gone without a trace, in the rough seas writhing and boiling all around.

In my shock I called him over and over, like a child that's lost the grasp of its mother; hailed, wept, even rowed, the strapped oars miraculously spared, though my hands were so broken I could scarcely make headway. With sea after sea confusing the near ground, and the foam hissing white in thick trails all around, I labored to make out where he might appear; struggled against the spindrift sting in the air, and the tearless burn which afflicted my eyes. Then suddenly there was fog and it was the first time we'd lost him, falling abruptly from *Abigail's* yardarm; and Ephie and Roan were in the boat with me, searching the swells for his form in the mist.

Any moment I expected his head to surface, or his voice to hail us from the next sea; but they didn't, only the fog closed in deeper; and all at once I understood what was lost—what was gone with finality in the shrouds. It was Ben who was torn irretrievably from me, Ben who was wrested, cut off in the fog; we were rent apart, bereft of each other; and I screamed at his loss as a shipmate had once shrieked for his limb, with such a stark wrench of bodily anguish that my skin felt torn from me, and my cries echoed pointlessly on the deep.

In the finality of my aloneness I had time, nothing but time to realize my need, and the enormity of my loss; and in the unalterable silence I was engulfed by both. The kegs were gone now, the gaff and awning also, so that there was no way to obtain fresh water save to lick the planks of bilge in a rainfall; and I set my one remaining hook in the sea when the swells relented enough to permit fishing. Besides oars and hook, only the spare shirt and oilslick remained—articles we'd stashed when the weather turned threatening—and Paul's sheath knife, still in the bow cuddy where he'd stowed it. Bible, spare hooks and line, marlinspike, bowls, waterlogged sextant—all were swept away when the stern cuddy was forced; and with them went not only the means of survival, but every form of activity with which we'd kept busy.

But their departure was as nothing compared to my loss of Ben—the realization of which I'd kept at bay till Paul's death had struck down my last defenses; and stunned, I sat bare and bereft in the boat. Craving his nearness, I paged every one of my physically close memories of him, from the night he'd carried me back to the sickbay off Cuba to his caress at Anjier; from the night he'd picked me up at Hannah's to his final kiss of my hand at the rail off the Marianas. Even our fight, full not just of anger or the clash of wills, but the solid reassurance of him, fed my need; while his insistent force in the cold—on his beach in the blizzard, in the extremity of Cape Horn—surged now in the naked chill of the rain. But no memory long abated my desolation and hunger; and never, waking or sleeping, was I without their raw ache.

In the unbreakable silence there was time too to repent—time to realize the consequences of my pride, the irrevocable results of my self-reliance: not just the haughtiness with which I'd gone over the rail, to lower away for Paul when others might have, but my unwillingness to confess my need for him, ever. Why hadn't I made him tell me what had happened, to interrupt our closeness after Anjier; why hadn't I just gone in and laid down beside him, one of those balmy nights in Whampoa, as I had more than a year ago off Cape Horn? Why hadn't I surrendered, sometime when I wasn't too ill to dissemble—why hadn't I let him have the upper hand, which was what I'd wanted all along for him to have, anyway? What was I afraid of—that he would never touch me again, if I forced matters to a head before they were ripened?—or was that just an excuse for my fear of his power?

Like damnations they swept down and picked at my flesh, these demands which posed themselves over and over; and bitterly I reproached myself in the silence.

Then out of my craving I made a companion, a kind of embodiment of presence; took the oar from its strap, and the spare shirt which had been Ephie's, and dressing the pole, set it across from me in Paul's place. For a while I tried talking to it while I fished; tried calculating our position with it out loud each noon; tried counting off the watches or planning my next move or sharing with it my meager catch—though its features as the days passed seemed unaccountably to change.

It was hotter now, for the weather was abating; and in the boldness of the sun, the face of the blade grew unfriendly; and I could begin to feel its hostility toward me. It had sentient eyes now, eyes which ceaselessly watched me, even when I turned my back to sleep; eyes which looked on my deteriorating frame, and regarded me not with pity, but disgust. As time passed I even felt that it might make a move on me—that it might attack with a precipitous strike; and I was able to sleep even less than before. In my anxiety I tried covering its face with the oilslick, or turning its back on me in the stern; but its hostility and anger increased all the more, to the point where I couldn't endure; and when I relented and uncovered its face and turned it around, there was almost a smirk now to its grimace.

That I had to discard it, I understood—but it comprehended, as well; and every time I plotted what I might do—simply jettison it, when it wasn't looking, or dismember it, returning the oar to its strap, and donning the shirt, since my own was a rag, and I was wearing nothing else due to my sores—it seemed to read me off, and be prepared to thwart me. No longer could I talk out loud or reason with it, as I had in the beginning; certainly not share a meal with it, as I had in hospitality at the start; yet I hadn't the courage to combat it either—to confront its mettle or will with my own.

As if my separation from Ben had stripped my resources, I had fewer reserves than ever before; had even less strength of mind than of body; and I knew my diminution was not merely the result of my failing health. But at last with what little was left of my voice, I tried praying; and with the naming of Christ came a feeling of fullness, a floodtide of Presence that partnered my shorn self—a sense of confidence, an inner buoyancy that invigorated me almost like power. In the midst of that buoyancy, I made a move; and without considering the consequences I simply snatched my foe from its place, and threw it, oar and shirt, into the sea.

Then never looking back—for fear I'd see its face, as it sank beneath the barrier of the waves—I sat alone once again; and in my aloneness, I looked at the oarlock, a substantial block of wood at the gunnels; and suddenly, I had an idea. Taking Paul's sheath knife, I gradually pried it from its plank; and though my hands were near useless, and the weatherbeaten oak still hard, I began to painstakingly carve. This time when I created it was two men I fashioned, two men interlocked into one; and they were Ben and I, Ben rising up out of the sea like Neptune, the brine still dripping from his unruly locks, and myself borne up in his arms—myself as I had been, handsome and hale, but surrendered to his hardy care. As I carved for endless hours my concentration tamed my sores, tamed even my unforgettable thirst; and I dwelt on many things beyond the cradle of arms that bore me, beyond the bosom, matted and firm, that soothed me.

From out of the haze of the heat and the sun came words from one of St. Paul's letters, almost the only part of them that made any sense: one new man made out of two—Gentile and Jew, heathen and Christian, shaped inclusively into a whole, yet neither losing his integrity in the forging; and I pondered the thought as I turned my creation in my hands—as I traced the tender gaze that looked down on my humble eyes. As Dwy Fawr and Dwy Fach, Great and Little Day, had slipped spring-like through Lake Bala to birth the headwaters of the Dee, without either one of them losing the purity of its character, so it was with these two in their making of one; and I bowed in my heart to the authority of their new face.

Then it was gone, my last hook, gone with a fish I couldn't bring in, and I ate the little bait that remained; and the water was gone too, for there was no rain. In the distance the sea shimmered coppery and flat, and I sought the bit of shade in the lee of the boat, shrinking down into its dwindling shadow. So thirsty was I, and so swollen my tongue, that I could scarcely open my mouth; but with harsh croaks I petitioned again and again for Another, though I understood I was not worthy.

Flitting in and out of my vision there came images to soothe me; and I reached out as if to catch them to me. Once it was Peter, bold Peter's shadow, flickering along the hot cobbles of the street; and swiftly I bowed that it might fall upon me, rippling across my back in the heat. And once it was the old woman again with her basket; and when I called out to her "Lord, come," she came walking to me on the water, and allowed me to see what was in her hamper. It was a tent, all folded up, and ready to pitch, with even its stakes in a neat bundle; and when I touched the cloth I knew it was goat's hair. Then it was night and she was gone, and I sobbed like a child, dry, tearless sobs on the wooden planks of my berth; and as if she were not far off she hastened to soothe me, hushing my sobs in an age-old manner; for she was rocking my boat like a cradle.

Then it was day again, and there was no water; no bits of bait or algae to salvage; no memories left to recall; and no ahead to stake my mind to—no beyond to insure the present. There was only now, and I was forceless; for there was no way to rely anymore on myself. No more armed with resources, no more fitted with strength, I just knelt, crouched down in the shade of the seat in the waist; and with my spent voice I prayed, "Oh, Lord, you who blew into my life that day in Boston, when I threw open the shutters and looked down on the wharves…blow into my life once again."

Then there was a stirring, not in the air, but the sea; and all at once, abruptly, there flung itself into the boat, athwart the waist, a young porpoise. It had taken a leap and fallen short, and now could not disengage; yet in its entrapment, it didn't struggle. In my distress I threw myself upon it, trying to dislodge it, for I couldn't kill it; yet I hadn't the strength to move it. When I realized that I couldn't free it, that in spite of my reluctance I would be able to eat from it, that it was full of the juices I needed to survive, I couldn't kill it even then in my pity; and I waited for it to expire, thrown sobbing across its failing body, before I raised my knife at last, and drank.

Then there came climbing down a ladder, with bights of rope thrown over their shoulders, two Spanish sailors, and the broadside of a brig rose up like a wave out of the water beside me; and they put me into a sling, since I couldn't stand, and swung me up onto the deck from above; and I opened my eyes and proclaimed to Sarah,

"My name is James Robertson, and I must write to Ben Melchett."

XXVIII

McCabe, Melchett & Robertson

Cape Damaris—New York, Spring 1845

Ben hadn't been back from Britain a week, but already he'd thrashed through a mountain of mail: in fact, his correspondence'd been one of my main jobs whilst he was to Wales, and now that he was home, I had my work cut out for me, bringing him up to date on a month's worth or more. Most of it was business letters, everything from the harbormaster in Valparaiso trying to track down information about freights two years ago, to Baring Bros. in London barking about Joe's transactions. And if this'd been a normal season in his life, that would of been the bulk of the backlog; for no one ever troubled to write him personally, knowing he'd never bother to respond; and certainly nobody would of sent out invitations. But this wasn't a normal season, to say the least; and nothing told the tale plainer than all the personal missives he'd insisted I open as well, desperate as he was for word of Jim.

First there was a number of letters from Jacques Beckman in Portland, established now with his old lady caregivers, and gaining a little ground in his battle—ground he was sure to lose in the end, but just the same, worth celebrating; and intimate letters they was, full of confidences —the kind of letters you might write to another knowing you was second in line to his heart. Then there was hate mail, scribbles pouring out anguish about money lost on the run from Whampoa, and lawsuit mail, piles of documents about his trial coming up in May. And there was still directives about Jared's death and final affairs in Havana, Ben being the executor of his estate; whilst finally there was a handful of letters from American consuls all over the Pacific, in answer to his inquiries about Jim—polite responses with no fresh information or hints of news to follow up on.

We went over it all together, there by the fire at night in my cabin, or sometimes in his office at noon; for I'd got in the habit of picking up the overland mail from the Portland stage at the livery around dinner time; and I'd bring it to the yard, where we'd sort it out together, then walk over to the Seven Seas for a bite. It was all I really knew of what was going on in his life; for though we'd had some talk, fairly intimate talk, about this or that as we opened his letters, it wasn't as frank as I would of expected, considering we'd been dancing partners.

His journal of his journey he'd handed me freely, and I'd already read every line of it; but he hadn't yet spoke to me about it, letting me draw my own conclusions about his state of mind; and true to form, I hadn't pressed him. About his family he hadn't spilt much either, though I knew he'd been overjoyed at meeting up with his children, and nearly been eaten alive by them in return. But already he'd spent a couple nights at my place, in Jim's old room, and one at the Inn; and I suspected, from words the children had let slip, that he was sleeping at home in the library, as he had for months, even before our trip to Boston. That he must be struck all of a heap, facing up to life without Jim, and yet with all the old burdens of his trial and home, I could fathom without a word; but he wouldn't lean on me for support, or even so much as a sympathetic ear; and so I carried on as his secretary, thinking to at least help lighten the load.

With such a hurrah's nest of mail showing up every day, it come as little surprise that there should be a missive from Rio; and when I picked it up one noon at the end of the first week of April, I thought very little of it, save to take note of the handwriting. It was a very feminine hand, sort of flowery and fine, unlike what you would expect from all them dealers in coffee; but that curiosity aside, it hadn't much to recommend it; and I set it without thinking on top of the stack in my satchel. It being noon now, I headed down Water Street to the shipyard, where Ben, like his brothers, had his own office; and since I was expected, after a quick knock, I walked in.

It was a fairly small room, almost like a lawyer's, with a rail between the visitor's chair and his desk, and a wall of leather-bound books, mostly treatises in international law and charts, just beyond the brush of his elbow. Today he was holding forth in his shirtsleeves—there being a goodly blast from his stove—and his spectacles was perched on the bridge of his nose; and his stack of papers having already been wrestled down to size, he looked at my satchel with only mild dismay. Adjusting the lamp, he accepted the grubby collection I dug out; and he tackled the Rio letter first, just as I handed it over, noting with a curious glance the fine, ornate hand—me meanwhile lounging back in the chair with my boots firmly planted on the railing.

At the first choking gasp from him I was back on my feet and instantaneously at his side, whilst he, hunched as if in pain over his knees, clutched at his chest and at the edge of his desk with shuddering, fumbling hands; and my first thought was that his heart had at last give way. But glancing aghast at the now open letter I seen, along with several pages of the same fine, delicate script that'd adorned the outside of the envelope, one sheet in a hand which, despite signs of strain, was familiar and flowing, graceful and strong; and I knew in a flash what'd forced his reaction, for the writing was unmistakably Jim's.

Being unable to speak, still clutching his chest with one great, stumbling hand, he reached out for the pages with the other—fumbled at them—tried to pat them smooth—set them one beside another—then patted them again, in helpless, ecstatic, stabbing motions that was half caresses, half attempts to flatten the folded paper. Determinedly gathering my wits, I tried for the sake of his heart to calm him—took hold of his agitated hands and tamed them in the sane grip of my own; and speaking for the first time—nodding his head at the longer, more delicate letter—he mumbled as if through suddenly numb lips: "You read it—I can't."

Letting his hands go—seeing one of them flutter forward again and land, like a homing pigeon, on Jim's page—I reached out for the other letter, my fingers so froze up with hope and fear that I could scarcely pick up the pages. Smoothing them out and unconsciously sitting down on the desk—seeing the dateline Misericordia hospital, and feeling an even greater fear that this was not the herald of joy but, in fact, a final farewell—I leaped on to skim the closely written lines in silence, till Ben's hoarse cry "Out loud! Out loud!" recalled me to my senses; and simultaneously I cried out with the news: "He's all right! He's all right! He's in Misericordia—he's recovering!"

At the first sound of his outburst I flung down the letter—I'd still only read the first two or three lines—and threw my arms around him, wordless; ran for the Scotch and back to him again with the decanter, slopping most of its contents over his wrist; then dropping the container down on the desk, threw my arms about him again, whilst he rocked back and forth with his head bent over his knees. Forcing a glass at length to his lips, I at last succeeded in calming him down enough to proceed with the reading of the letter; and fishing in my pocket, I handed him my handkerchief. Still shuddering, but the color now returning to his face, Ben blew his nose with great, forceful honks; then fumbling for his spectacles, which'd been knocked to the desk, he hooked them shakily over his ears, and dropped his hands back to Jim's letter, where they hovered quivering, like the wings of birds.

Nodding at me to commence, he sat at attention, his hands still fluttering atop Jim's letter; but I got no further than "Misericordia Hospital, Rio Janeiro," when he interrupted again, "The date! The date!" Looking at the corner, I read: "25 February, 1845"; and "More than a month ago!" he cried, "Go on!"

"'Dear Capt. Melchett,'" I began, then proceeded:

I, a sister of the order of Franciscan nuns who staff the Misericordia Sanitorium here in the city of Rio Janeiro, take my pen to inform you that I have for the past three weeks had in my care a naturalized American seaman named Mr. James Robertson, who has only today become well enough to make me understand that you are his nearest relative.

Mr. Robertson was taken off the French brig Mistral, *bound for Rio from Lima, along with fourteen other sailors on the 3rd inst. when the health officials who met them in the harbor for clearance found they were suffering from scarlet fever. That they reached the harbor mouth at all in their condition was only due to the intervention of a party of seamen, including the second officer, from the British barkentine* Anna Ross, *who answered their signal of distress off the La Plata, boarded the* Mistral *and escorted her to the city.*

Several of Mr. Robertson's shipmates have since passed away, but he himself has, I am pleased to inform you, prospered to the point where he can sit up for short spells against his pillow, and take a little solid nourishment. Aside from one brief relapse which is not unusual in such a disorder, the course of his illness has run as expected, without any signs of rheumatic fever, and we will soon allow him to sit in one of the wheeled chairs, and take the sun for a while on the verandah. I will permit him to write you a few lines when he is stronger, and enclose them with this letter, which I intend to send with the British steamer Isle of Wight *when she embarks for New York in three days.*

As for Mr. Robertson's remarkable history, which he will not be strong enough to write in great detail to you, I will summarize briefly what I have been able to understand. I have learned that, after becoming separated from your ship off the Marianas, he was at sea with his companions for 103 days, a remarkable total which he kept very careful track of on the gunwales of his boat, along with the ciphering he did to calculate their position. When he at last was picked up by the Spanish brig Estrella, *bound from Tokyo to Valparaiso, he was in an emaciated condition; but his calculations proved his position to be only a few minutes off, and the Spanish captain hauled the boat aboard and gave it a place of honor. It was well that he did, for it was in this same boat that Mr. Robertson and 9 shipmates lowered away some weeks later, off the Galapagos Islands, when the brig took fire—there being not enough deck boats otherwise available to allow the large crew to escape to safety.*

After being at sea for another 29 days, and losing two of his shipmates to drowning, Mr. Robertson and his fellow survivors were rescued by the French brig Mistral; *and again their boat was taken aboard with them. It was this brig which was swept with scarlet fever as she rounded the Horn; and Mr. Robertson took charge after the master and chief officer took ill. He himself succumbed as the ship reached the latitude of La Plata; and as I have described, his signal of distress was answered by the British bark* Anna Ross, *which escorted* Mistral *here to the city.*

Through the American consul here in Rio Janeiro we are attempting to secure Mr. Robertson a passage to New York—probably not aboard an American vessel, due to the troubles with Mexico. Mr. Robertson states he can ship as steward, a berth for which he assures me he is qualified, and which I hope will not be outside his strength.

We will be sending with him his remarkable quarterboat, if at all possible—the hieroglyphics of this little vessel telling a tale of heroism and endurance which ought to be preserved. It is hoped that Mr. Robertson, on meeting your relative Mr. Jacob Melchett in New York, will be able to take charge of it himself, and after a rest make his way on to Maine.

It has been my privilege to serve this humble, modest Christian man; and I commend him to your care with a light heart, knowing how highly he thinks of you.

Respectfully,
Sister Leonore.'"

So overcome was we both by all of this news—the astounding fact that Jim was still alive crowding in and out of the amazing details of the past year, and colliding again and again in our minds—that for a moment neither one of us could say a word: me setting the pages down again with a dumbstruck awe, and Ben still sitting exactly as I'd left him, but hunched forward now with his arms tight over his chest, as if he clutched an invisible Jim to him.

In our staggered hush the noon bell rang out, signaling the yard's break for dinner; and as if released by its peal we at last stirred to action, me pacing back and forth with a fresh Scotch, and Ben wringing his hands feverishly in his lap, working first one, then the other, as if he was molding a new heap of clay. Shakily sipping his drink, he found his voice to beg again for the letter; and obliging, I read it to him more slowly, pausing this time to exclaim with him over the details of Jim's voyage, and to commiserate with his suffering. Not till I'd concluded the pages a second time had we collected our wits enough to ask questions—Ben drilling me first about the threat of rheumatic fever, me warily wondering about Ephie, Roan and Paul, no mention having been made of their rescue—then Ben leaping ahead to speculate about when Jim might arrive in New York, and scrambling to his feet to exclaim: "If he sailed at the end of the first week of Mahch—if he was aboard even so lubberly a boat as brought this letteh—he could raise New York in five or six weeks—less, if he was aboard a steameh—Christ, he could almost be thehre now!"

Catching up Jim's letter in one hand, he grabbed for his coat with the other, nearly knocking down the hat tree as he snatched at its collar, and struggling hurriedly with its sleeves as he headed for the door: "My Gawd, we've got t' go! We've got t' get aboard the first boat! He could already be at my uncle's! We'll go first t' Jacob's townhouse—we'll meet every vessel —we'll get a list from Lloyd's, from Customs—"

Wrestling feverishly with his sleeves, he flapped his arms like an albatross, trying to take off from too short a deck; and catching him by the collar, I forced him back into my chair, where I tried to calm him back to his senses: "Whoa, slow down! We've got t' think—we've got t' plan! You ain't even read Jim's letteh yet—maybe there's some more news in there."

Looking down at the page still clutched in his fingers, he begun to tremble stem-to-stern once again, overcome as much with Jim's presence in hand as with his imminent arrival; and patting his sleeve, I said, "I'll step out for a bit."

"No, don't," he stopped me, "no secrets b'tween us"; and hunching over his page, still bunched in his coat, with his spectacles awry on his nose, he read Jim's few words with a silent hunger, then handed them without a sound over to me.

Receiving the page as wordless as it was given, I read the short lines which rang so like Jim: brief, labored, self-restrained—written, I knew, from the point of view of a man uncertain how he really stands with another, and determined to be disciplined:

28 February 1845
Rio Janeiro

Dear Ben,

Sister Leonore says I may only write ten lines so I must be brief.

I am here at Misericordia Hospital in Rio Janeiro recovering from scarlet fever. I came here roundabout, by way of the Horn, on a French brig (the Mistral*) which picked me up, along with seven Spanish shipmates, about a hundred miles SE of the Galapagos Islands. We were the survivors of the Spanish brig* Estrella*, bound from Tokyo to Valparaiso, which went down in flames and which in turn had picked me up, after 103 days in the quarterboat, NE of the Marianas.*

Sister Leonore has written you a more detailed account of my journey. But she has left it to me to report the unfortunate news that Paul, Ephie and Roan did not survive our ordeal. You must tell their families how courageous they were, and that I was able to save something from each of them to bring home.

It is expected that I will fully recover and that I will be able to ship for New York in a week or ten days. There are a number of vessels in the harbor due to clear for the States at that time, none for Boston.

Please write to Jacob to inform him that I will be stopping by his place, if he is willing, till I can sign on for some berth to Boston or Portland.

Give Eben and the children my love, and a share to yourself from

Jim

P.S. Though Misericordia is a charity hospital, I feel as though I should pay for my care here. Can my 20 cents per month hospital money somehow be transferred?

It was the simple statement of an honorable, indeed heroic sailor—the bald note of a man who suspects, moreover, that others besides the one addressed will read it; and there was nothing in the few words, except the way he'd signed off, that give away the depth of his feeling for Ben. But whether Ben seen all that too, or felt any lack for Jim's want of confession, it was impossible to judge; for on his face was simply the intolerable pain of joy as he accepted the letter from me, kissed it, and—slipping the page gently into his breast pocket—stood up to galvanize me to action.

I knew that he was about to crack the whip, for I'd seen that look on many a quarterdeck in the past; and getting to my feet from the rail where I'd been sitting, I made shift to head him off: "Now, Ben, we ain't flying off this time like we did the last—"

"He ain't got a dime, Eben, he won't have his wages till he's been a week in New Yohrk —an' he may arrive ill, I won't have him thehre for an oweh without me, an' that's flat—"

"Now, I know what you're sayin', but I'm tellin' you, we've got t' take care of—"

"Does he really seriously imagine that I'd just write Jacob a letteh, an' not go there at once myself?" he marveled, paying no attention whatever to me.

"Remembeh, Ben, he ain't an assuming man…an' the last he knew, you knew nothin' for sure about his feelin's toward you, an' nothin' at all about his past." His face told me he seen I was right; and as he begun to harken back to where he'd left off with Jim—at the rail of *Abigail,* and not in Boston or Wales or any of the territory he'd covered since—he set down all of a heap; and I had my chance to reason with him.

"Now as I was sayin'," I went on, "we can't just blow out o' hehre without thinkin'. B'sides packin' his gear, since he don't have none, an' packin' ours for what you know damn well's goin' t' be a lengthy stay—b'sides all that, you've got t' wrap things up hehre, well enough t' permit you t' walk right back into your trial; an' more important than any o' that, we've got t' do as Jim asked, an' visit every one o' these families hehre."

Seeing the truth of what I was saying, he reined hisself in long enough to let me fetch a bite from Eli's, and set it out for us to eat at his desk; and there we struggled to find words for the grieving, and for Anne as we framed yet another departure.

The news hit the town like an explosion—as though some charge destined for the quarry had detonated instead in Ship Street; and by the time we'd done the sad duty of breaking their loss to the last family, Ephie's, word was already racing from door to door, making it wholly unnecessary for us to spread the news further. Everything else going on near and far—the timbers just being laid on the ways, the war brewing with Mexico and its impact on shipping—all was left astern by this; and so swallowed up was we by the commotion that there was no way to slip out of town like last time, and no way to keep Ben on an even keel for a minute.

From his agitation at the homes of the lost men—this being another double loss for his family, and a terrible blow to the Talbots as well, Paul having been the cream of his generation—to his elation in Jim's old room at the Inn, where he joyously petted the furniture as if it was alive—he was like a sail that's busted its bolts; and every time I nearly got him lashed down, some newshound would pop in from the *Recorder*, looking to print word of Jim's 103-day stint in an open boat, or some acquaintance new-arrived in town would drop by, and the whole tale would whip him up all over again.

Nor was it just the story's impact I dealt with; for something else was happening too, something I'd already foreseen, though I doubted Ben had reasoned it through: the town's invasion of his privacy with Jim. It'd started at the Talbots, where they'd demanded to see Jim's letter, as they was bound to do, and as Jim'd surely expected they would; then it'd continued at the Melchetts' where the letter was called for again, everyone craving to see the news in black and white, and passing Jim's page from hand to hand till it was crumpled from use; and it went on with even the reporter—me hardly daring so much a glance at Ben's face by that time, so robbed did he look, or worse.

Nor was it just the town's moving in on his letter that was the issue; for his private feelings as well was at risk—his unbridled joy whenever anyone spoke of the upcoming reunion with Jim a dead giveaway of his affection. The outburst of action which'd been building for more than a year and which exploded from him now was something of a distraction or cover; but the hot color to his cheeks and the hectic light to his eyes would of been read in a flash, if the object of all his activity had been a woman; and I felt poised on the brink of his exposure all day. When at last it'd been decided that the service for the lost men would be delayed till our return, that Jim might be part of it, and bring what news he could to it, I headed gratefully back to my cabin; and I was thankful for a night's sleep when we set out aboard *Idris* next morning, a-sail with the dawn, to meet the Portland steamer for New York.

*   *   *   *   *

It took us three days to raise Block Island, for though the steamer made time, our run to Portland was slow; and alone as we were the first twenty-four hours of the journey, we had plenty of time to talk there at *Idris*' stern sheets, scarcely ever needing to adjust the canvas. By now my excitement was such that I could hardly control the tiller; and Eben stood that trick the whole time he was awake, barely trusting me to send over the boom when we tacked. Nearly crazy from inaction, I compensated with my frenetic thoughts, my preoccupations coming again and again in waves—whether Jim would already be in New York, what he would look like, how soon he would understand my feelings, whether he still felt the same toward me; and every moment I wasn't talking I was racing ahead with such whirlwinds of mind.

How well Eben kept pace with my thoughts was always a matter for conjecture; but he fell silent respectfully when I did, and listened, his eyes patient and steady, when I talked; and when I gave him the chance he had a thing or two to venture himself, things he'd saved up, as usual, for the right moment. Once, in a lull, when I'd gusted on like a gale for the better part of an hour over what we'd do when we made port, he looked over at me with a cocked brow; and I could tell he was about to deliver himself.

"Now, Ben," he began in that cautious way of his, "when we get thehre…I know ye'll go at it hammer an' tongs. An' it's natural that we as Jim's best friends be excited. But…what I'm tryin' t' say is," he fumbled, putting matters as considerately as he could, "ye've got t' contain youhrself a little."

Mulling his words, I listened, silent.

"Jim could do it t' perfection—he'd had t' learn; now ye'll have to."

"B'fore the Lord, Eben, I know, but—even if I could control it, which I can't—I'm proud that I love him—I want the world t' know—"

"Well, it can't," he said flatly, "only I can; I'll be the world."

Full of mute pain, I simply looked at him, old gratitude welling up for his friendship.

"It's eitheh that, Ben, or you won't be on trial just for wrongful prosecution of voyage; it'll be for sodomizing a minoh, an' you know what the penalty for that is: ten yeahrs in the cellah at Thomaston."

Stunned by the harshness of his directness, I kept silence.

"You know what happened t' Jim in Wales. D'ye want t' put him at risk again?"

"For Gawd's sake, Eben, you know I don't—"

"Then don't. Ye'll have t' be alone with him b'fore ye c'n be honest with him; an' you'hre goin' t' be alone with him rarely at Jacob's: the gawddam place is crawlin' with people." His hand came down kindly on my knee. "I don't mean t' take the joy of it from ye. Just...be careful."

"I will," I promised him, earnest.

"I'm tellin' ye this b'cause I know he'll be tired...too tired an' overwhelmed t' look out for things the way he usually does. Somebody's got t' be payin' attention; an' at least in the beginnin', it's goin' t' be you."

"Aye... I understand."

"You know I'll help."

"Aye...thanks, Eben." Our eyes met with the wordlessness of old friends; then hesitating, I ventured, "D'ye... D'ye think he still feels the same, afteh all this?"

He smiled. "A' course."

Arriving at last at Jacob's Bowery townhouse—battling the carts on South Street and the carriages on Broadway, then sweeping into the entry as unannounced as a gale—we found no sign of Jim, but every evidence of family: the entire place from third floor to cellar simply swarming with aunts and cousins and servants. Hauled in to noon dinner, which thankfully was bereft of other guests, we brought everybody on board with our news—Jim becoming an immediate celebrity even in absence, and everyone from Jacob on down unable to get enough of the details of his voyage. Caught up in his story, and commiserating with his trials, all hands leapt into action, as galvanized as if preparing for a visit from the governor: even the servants picking up the excitement, and getting ready for him as if he were kin of their own.

The townhouse being well-equipped and roomy—the sort of residence you would expect of a New York overseer of shipping, complete with the obligatory drawing rooms and ballroom— Eben and I took over a couple of chambers, with Eliza readying a sitting room, off mine, for Jim; and stashing our satchels as soon as it was decently polite, we dashed off for the Customs House and Lloyd's, buying up every paper to be had on the way. Drawing up a list of all the vessels that had recently entered or were imminently expected to enter from Rio, we began making the rounds of the wharves, not forgetting to check quarantine or the sailors' hospital: commandeering even my gadfly cousins, Rowan and Stephen, for wharf duty, and so firing up my uncle Jacob with our zeal that he himself lent a hand, as well as his considerable influence, to the hunt.

As our stay lengthened into a couple of weeks, our days began to take on a pattern: rising to an early breakfast; driving the carriage to the wharves to wait for ships in the roads, or to interrogate any master who had recently entered from Rio; badgering the decoders at the signal towers; haunting the Customs House, Lloyd's, and the offices of news agents to continuously update our lists; and combing the hospitals for any new admittances. Despite our daily lack of success, my spirits kept relentlessly climbing, each dawn deepening my conviction that Jim was drawing nearer—that I was on the brink of the moment when I would spot him hauling away at a capstan, or stepping down from a gangplank or hailing me from a rail, the sun on his hair and a light on his face, and his neckerchief blowing in the harbor wind.

Now and again I paused in the midst of the rush to sit down on my bed, and take stock of my thoughts—to try to imagine what Jim would look like, what he'd feel like in my arms, what he'd say when he first came upon me; but straightaway I became so excited that I could only rise and start pacing again. Sometimes it was my own appearance I thought of; and I crossed the ornate room to the mirror, trying to see myself through his eyes—trying to trim my beard and train my hair and garb myself in decent attire, as if, at any moment, he might step in the door; but inevitably I became so agitated that my stubborn-minded thatch, my wrinkle-prone clothes reasserted themselves in a kind of explosion, as if they'd been unaccountably pent-up; and I looked like a waterdog all over again.

At last giving up all my attempts to order my thoughts or plan my words or make myself presentable, I simply gave way to anticipation, hurtling myself through each new day, refusing to be disappointed or frustrated, my elated expectations so coloring my impressions that everything around me took on an almost palpable aura. I was particularly attracted to the cranberry lamp at my bedstead, which one of the servants always had lighted when I turned in; and long after the rest of the household was asleep, I sat watching its lustrous glow in the dark room, its warm flush on the crisp, white linen beneath it.

*   *   *   *   *

Once we'd raised the latitude of the Bermudas it was impossible for me to eat a bite; and I paced in the dog watch long after the boys had knocked off at the spun yarn winch, and ducked below for supper; paced long after my carpenter's bench had been cleared away for the day, and the red and green running lamps set aglow for the night. Standing in the waist, anxious at every lull in the wind at the topsails, I watched the red and green globes cast their luminous glades on the waters; felt the waft of the wind in my hair, and counted the days we might expect to take to raise all the old waymarks—the Gulf Stream, Cape Hatteras, Block Island.

Shipped as a carpenter aboard the *Cliffs of Dover*, busy with the pace of a craft coming into port and wanting to make a good show on arrival, I was exhausted; but in the midst of my fatigue pulsed a hectic hope, and an even more hectic confusion. At times I was convinced that Ben would be there in New York, waiting impatiently for me at Jacob's; at others that my letter had miscarried, obliging me to find the strength to carry on to Maine to see him; and at others still that he'd shipped out some months since for Havana or Havre or Valparaiso, leaving me to reach Maine wholly spent, only to wait for him indefinitely there. On days when my strength was barely sufficient for the carpenter's berth I'd been fortunate enough to obtain, I longed simply for him to take over, to meet me in New York and carry on for me there; but there were spells when I felt ready to take on any obstacle, possessed of the vigor of a man rested and well; and at such moments I was set to walk, head high, into Jacob's, and all the way on to Maine if I had to.

As we hauled into the Gulf Stream, slipping into the bank of clouds and warm, brackish waters as into a veritable hillside on land, I was sick, sicker than I ever had been at sea, even those first miserable days aboard Redmond's brig to Denmark; and I gave up trying to eat, since I lost every meal—not due to a relapse as my shipmates feared, but to the sheer turbulence of nerves. Twice now as I shaped tackle for our ceaseless overhaul of tophamper I passed out; and to keep going I focused relentlessly on my bench, on each successive task which paralleled the ship's progress or, in my spare time, on my land gear—anything to pin my mind to the concrete hope of arrival.

Having shipped with little more than the shirt on my back, I'd been obliged to spend the whole of my advance note on clothes; and though there was little enough due me now in the way of wages when we made port, I dipped into my earnings further, outfitting myself in fits and starts from the slop chest. No matter how spent I might be upon our arrival, I wasn't about to set foot in Jacob's townhouse, with even the slimmest hope of Ben's being there to meet me, looking anything less than my best; and to that end I put in the daylight hours of the dogwatch sewing a shirt that could set me off to advantage, though I hadn't a clue he would notice now any more than he ever had before. With the navy round jacket I'd found in the slop chest, and the duck trowsers I'd made up those first days under the Line, it completed a decent outfit of going-ashore togs; and the hours I poured into their planning and execution not only sped the time, but took my mind off my ill state.

As I sewed—rejoicing in the spray at the bow, and leaping ahead to Ben's expectations of me—I sometimes wondered whether, in the past year of silence, Eben had broken my confidence and told him frankly how I'd felt, the way a man wraps up another's business after he's been presumed dead; or whether the shock of our parting had brought into wordless focus what was already coming to pass between us. How he'd react to a frank confession or a quiet epiphany, either one—whether he'd retreat behind his downeast diffidence or become distant or awkward or, as I sometimes had reason to hope, finally meet me halfway—I had no idea; and I found myself making up as many responses to his prospective variations in greeting as a playwright concocts endings to a play.

But even more than by doubts I was gnawed by excitement at the expectation of seeing him again; and our progress up the American coast, marked by soundings as we approached New York, paralleled the progress of my dual hope and panic. As the boys hove the lead line and hauled up their samples of sand, mud, gravel and shells from two or three score of fathoms, I could read them as well as a printed chart; remembered Ben, our first voyage, hauling up those same samples, and drumming their meaning into the heads of the boys— his agitation over the faintest gradations in texture or color for all the world like a madman's to me then. Now I smiled at these arcane bits of news from the depths, for my excitement was his equal; and when they brought up the black mud which signaled Block Island I bowed, the quiet inner recognition of homecoming.

By the third of May we were hauling in toward Long Island, all the landmarks so plain we had no further need of our charts; but the wind having fallen off, or worse veered from the westward, our progress was marked by repeated anchoring and waiting, or hoving to to ride out conditions. These halts being more maddening than any delays I'd ever experienced, I was as wild as ever Ben had been on the Line after two or three days of a flat calm; and I carved and re-carved unneeded fittings by day, and packed and re-packed my meager gear in the dogwatch, unable to invent work enough to pass time.

But at last our relentless wait was cut short when, still off Long Island and well before the city's signals, a tugboat puffed up in the early afternoon, obviously steering a course straight for us; and so preoccupied was I by visions of Ben, and so strikingly like him did the craft look, from its determined mug to its pipe puffs of smoke, that I fully expected to find him aboard her. Instead our owner, who'd been on holiday on Long Island, and who'd intercepted the signals there from his camp, came scrambling up our Jacob's ladder, having commandeered a local tug as a ferry; and after a brief time of pomp with the captain in the cabin, he reappeared on the quarterdeck, and hailed me.

He was off for the city at once with the captain, leaving the mate to bring her in; but having heard my story from the old man, and knowing some of the Melchetts, particularly Jacob, he was ready with the master's permission to take me ashore too. This bit of news sent me scrambling for my seabag, so long ready and waiting I only needed to snatch it, and scurrying into my shore togs, all but tripping me with their pant legs—my shipmates hurrahing me or ribbing me about my sweetheart, whom they supposed must be the object of all my preparations; and hastily bidding farewell to their comradely concerns I was off over the rail and onto the tugboat for a record passage to the city, at least a full day ahead of the ship.

Arriving at the company wharf in the late afternoon, and—excepting Rio, when I'd been too ill to care—finding my feet on solid turf for the first time in well over a year, I gazed around at the teeming environs of South Street, at the crowded facades of sea chandlers and import and export houses; then I stood, heart lurching, ears ringing with the noise, trying to confer with my hosts. Unsure whether to accept their kind invitation to tea—feeling manifestly out of place at the thought of our owner's townhouse, and wondering whether I hadn't better humbly hike the distance to Jacob's Bowery place—I was hunting about for a reply when my dilemma was cut short by a sudden hail from across the street; and after a jump of the heart I recognized the man who was gesturing me as Stephen, Jacob's son, whom I'd met once at *Abigail's* launching.

This meant at the least that my letter had been received—that word of Ben, if not Ben himself, waited me in the city; and my heart lashing now like a sail in a blast, I bowed my apologies to owner and captain, with Jacob's compliments for their service to me, and dodged the darting traffic toward Stephen and his carriage. Throwing his arms about me, shouting "You look well, man!—just look at your hair!", then snatching my seabag, he led me jubilantly to the carriage, all the while bragging about how he'd heard the *Cliffs of Dover* was soon due, tracked rumors about her owner's being out on Long Island, and putting two and two together, posted himself at the company dock; and wild for news of Ben, I unceremoniously interrupted,

"I take it Ben received my letter, then—Is he here?"

"Aye, him an' Eben both—they've been kickin' up their heels for the past couple o' weeks, combing the wharves an' badgering Lloyd's—won't it just dash them when I bring you in!"

"Is he well, then?" I kept at it, barely able to hear over my ears' pounding.

"Aye, he's fine—though he's had quite a yeahr. They all have, down there in Cape Damaris. They looked all oveh the Pacific for you, man—all the way t' the Sandwich Islands an' San Francisco— and the tea was a total loss. Ben's up for trial lateh this month for wrongful prosecution of voyage—doubt he'll come out of it with a cent."

Struck dumb by this unexpected news—one of the few developments I hadn't over the past year imagined—and aching for Ben as I climbed into the carriage, I barely managed to press him again, "Is he all right?"

"A' course he's all right, you know the man: doubt he'd crack if the ship was on her way down beneath him...though they say he was completely off his rockeh when they first hauled home—why, he thought the ice bergs off the Horn was you boys, an' was all set t' loweh away for you! Then his brotheh an' wife—Jared an' Kate—that's right, you'd know nothing of it—died o' feveh in Havana, leaving Becky t' him an' Anne; so he had his hands full there for while." Then seeing my numb expression and halting, as if looking back on all that he'd said, he hastened on apologetically, "I shouldn't ramble on, you must be dog tired, an' needin' t' hear the news in spells. Ben'll have my head for talkin' too much—an' b'sides, we want t' hear all about *you,* mate."

"I'm all right—just tell me—how is Eben—an' Ben's children?"

"The children sound fine, an' Eben, he's right here—see for yourself in a matteh o' minutes."

At his "minutes" I sat back green to the gills, the floor having completely dropped out from under my stomach; and though he rattled on, oblivious of my state, shouting questions over the hectic creak of the carriage and the commotion of wheels on the cobbles, I barely heard him, only managing the briefest of answers and finding, in the flurry of scenes out the window, a reflection of the tumult within me.

*   *   *   *   *

We'd just returned, Eben and I, in the late afternoon—not for tea but a drink, the pace of the day having flustered even the even-keeled McCabe; and Eliza was in the drawing room setting out a plate of those absurd miniature sandwiches I knew I'd never be able to choke down. Rowan had just hauled in from his rounds as well, checking one or two of the wharves on his way home from Jacob's counting house; but it was Stephen we were waiting for—not that we expected much of him, his methods having been erratic. Hearing the clatter of the carriage wheels in the quieting street below, Eben strolled over to the window, drink in hand, poked his head through the festoons of brocade and announced, "Here's Stephen—an' by thundeh, if there ain't somebody with him."

Racing to the window I was in time to see Stephen step down from the carriage, go round to the opposite door, and help someone out; and as they came round the horses to wait for the traffic, Eben sang out, "There he is!" with a sudden jubilant whistle. At the same instant I saw Jim, clad in a dark blue jacket, striding confidently into the street beside Stephen, his step as jaunty and poised as ever; and gripping the ledge of the window I looked on as he struck out ahead of Stephen, and nearly walked into the path of an omnibus: Stephen jerking him back just in time by the elbow, and Eben bursting into a roar of laughter. As Rowan dashed out ahead of us to the stairs, calling out for Eliza along the way, Eben turned to me with a grin, and a jab of his thumb down toward Jim. "He's in love," he laughed, still delighting at his fluster; then grasping me by the elbow he made off for the stairs.

Coming to a halt at the top of the stairwell, we could see Jim in the hallway below, framed by the daylight of the street door behind him, and engulfed by the excited circle of Eliza, Rowan and Stephen—one hand sweeping off his hat while the other pumped Rowan's, and his head stooping down to Eliza's embrace as he gently answered her barrage of concerned questions. With Stephen's high tenor stridently announcing just how and where he'd found Jim, his remarks not failing to assess his own genius—with Rowan's deeper tones half-drowning him out, and Eliza's motherly inquiries piping insistently on—we watched, Eben and I, still halted at the top of the staircase, barely able to make out Jim's fine, resonant voice, reassuring Eliza, thanking Stephen and answering Rowan. But his face spoke more loudly than any of their voices, his features so a-flood with the light of homecoming that I, half-frozen, caught my breath.

Then as the voices around him dropped to a quieter tumult, I heard him ask Eliza gently, "Is Ben here?"—his hand anxiously at her shoulder. Giving a quick side nod to the stairwell, Eliza answered, "He's waiting for you upstairs, lad"—and Jim's gaze, darting up, fell on me, all expression fleeing his face save for a dazed disbelief. In the brief flash our eyes met he stood as motionless as I; then I was on my way down to the landing and he on his way up with a cry to my arms.

Catching him fiercely to me I crushed him in my hold, my hands claiming him again and again, and Jim shielding his eyes at my face; then Eben was upon us breaking us apart, grasping Jim by the shoulders and laughingly shouting, "Give me a chance a minute thehre, mate!"; and his embrace too was round Jim with glad cries. Then we were surrounded by noise and exclamations as Rowan, Eliza and Stephen, swarming up from below, and Claire and the servants, sweeping down from above, engulfed us together on the landing—

Claire pulling at Jim's jacket and grasping for attention, the servants hovering close by at his elbow, and the whole lot of them erupting into competing questions.

Mastering himself—gamely squaring his shoulders, and bracing himself for the onrush around him—Jim gave himself up to Claire and the others, sharing embraces and trying to sort out questions, his shining face marked with the strain of exhaustion. Looking him over with a wary eye—exchanging quick glances with me full of caution and warning, aimed as much at censoring me as at guarding Jim—Eben abruptly broke in with the insistence that Jim be given the chance to sit down; and recalled to their senses they all adjourned to the parlor, the servants sweeping on ahead to set things ready, Eliza and Claire coming up just behind them, and Rowan dashing down to fetch Jim's seabag where he'd dropped it. Succumbing for an instant to the strain of his reaction, Jim instinctively leaned toward me, in a gesture that nearly turned my knees to water; and with a fierce protectiveness I clasped my arm round his shoulder, and helped him climb up after the others.

*   *   *   *   *

Feeling Ben's arm hard and sure on my shoulders, I mounted the stairs and crossed into the parlor; then gratefully collapsing into a chair, I tried to steady my wits in their swirl, making an effort to hear the others—their words even now flashing in and out like the crash and flow of a sea. Gazing dazedly around, I saw we were in a large room, spacious and formal, and filled with a darting number of people; but starved for the sight of Ben, I had eyes only for him, taking in snatches of him—big, blunt, weathered as ever—in between the dashing of the others.

Leaning over me in my chair while the others flew round us, fetching my seabag or delivering my hat or throwing together the makings of tea, he was asking whether I felt well enough for a drink, and offering to bring whatever I'd like; and avoiding his eyes, for fear I'd give away my heart to all hands, I stumbled out with a fumbling answer: "Ben, I… I ain't had a drink in over a year, and—not much

in the way of food lately... I think I'd better pass for t'day." Offering
to bring me something, anything else, he kept insistently at it; and
I asked simply, "May I have some tea?" Coming up at that moment
Eliza heard me, exclaiming "Bless the boy, of course he may have
tea!"; and scurrying off for the sugar and creamer, she beckoned
Claire to pour me a cup.

How I managed to drink even the few sips I partook I couldn't
have said, since I couldn't swallow; couldn't swallow any more than
I could get a deep breath, or answer questions in a voice that didn't
quaver. With everyone settling down now, a cup of tea in hand, or
a ceremonious glass of champagne—with food enough before us to
make a meal, and all of the servants invited to listen—the grilling
really began; and I found myself jumping back and forth from the
Pacific to Rio to the *Cliffs of Dover,* trying to pin my mind on what
was being asked, to hear my own voice above the pound of my heart,
or still my wild urge to seek refuge in Ben.

At one point reaching over with a comradely hand, Eben
inquired about my health; and reassuring him that my carpenter's
berth on the run to New York had not been too demanding, I praised
Sister Leonore's care of me in Rio; but outside that question he and
Ben remained silent, as if they understood the pain of the past was
still near me. No such consideration came from the others, who
simply couldn't hear enough survival stories; and growing anxious
that they would ask me point blank about Ephie, Roan, and worst of
all, Paul—wondering how on earth I could bear even naming their
names—I began to fear I would break down before them. To steady
myself and keep my composure I looked at Ben's hands—strong,
earthy, blunt, as solid as the granite shore that bred them—since I
didn't dare meet his eyes; and as harbored by them as if they held
me, I kept on.

*   *   *   *   *

Though he carried on with his customary restraint, a valiant mix of
discipline and poise; though he was turned out with his usual flair,
his long, thick dark hair—over which the others had exclaimed—

brushed to its wonted gloss, and his blue jacket set off with a jaunty neckerchief, his long ordeal was clear in the tense lines round his mouth and the brace of his shoulders; and I ached to shelter him in my arms.

Responding to inquiries with brief, guarded answers—volunteering very little about himself—playing down his obvious suffering, and concentrating instead on the help or heroics of others—he re-traced his journey across the Pacific, round Cape Horn and up to Rio, keeping to no clear order due to the chaotic rush of questions, but giving us a fair outline of events. Rowan and Stephen in particular drilled him for details of his voyage from the time of his parting with us in the Marianas to his meeting with the Spanish brig—the part of the journey which, I could plainly see, was most painful of all for him to remember; and fearing they'd be callous enough to press him about the deaths of his shipmates—seeing he feared it too, and perhaps other things as well, his restraint marking him with a visible fatigue—I was about to bawl a halt to the questions when the door popped open and Jacob burst in, having just returned from the counting house.

Amazed to find Jim here in his parlor—unprepared by any hint from the servants, since they were all gathered listening—he started the interrogation all over again, Jim rising to meet him with poise and faithfully responding to his exclamations; while Eben watched, perched on the edge of his chair for the first chance to break up the session, and I looked fiercely on, almost ready to fight the others, beads of perspiration gathering on my brow in sympathy with Jim's efforts.

Just as it became evident his poise was at last breaking, the bell rang out to announce supper; and rising to his feet with the rest of us, Jim made it about half-way to the door before dropping down in a faint without warning. Swarming around him, all hands engulfed him in chaos: Eliza, Claire and the servants falling to their knees in consternation, Rowan and Stephen throwing open a window or hurrying up with a decanter of water, stately Jacob hovering above him in concern, and me—finally losing my temper—ordering everyone back, while Eben worked to bring him around.

Dazedly coming back to consciousness—opening his eyes, then instinctively searching with his gaze for me—flushing with embarrassment at his sudden weakness, and mumbling an apology to us—he tried to get up on one elbow; but Eben and I both pressed him back down, keeping him quiet with a cool cloth on his forehead, while Jacob swiftly diluted a glass of whiskey. Holding it to his lips, I helped him drink it; then surrendering at last to exhaustion, he lay back with his head in my hands, and the spill of his crisp, smooth hair in my fingers. Understanding at once I took charge, announcing I was carrying Jim straight to his room; and offering to bring him soup and tea on a tray, enough to tide him over till breakfast, Eliza and Claire made off for the kitchen, while Eben helped me get Jim up in my arms.

Ferrying him to the chamber which opened out beyond mine, I eased him down on the roomy bed, Eben helping me with his jacket and pumps, while two servants swept in with water and a tray; then setting them near at hand Eben sped everyone out, assuring the need for quiet and rest. Triumphantly closing the door on their backs, I noiselessly turned the lock, then determinedly walked over to the bed—Jim's eyes following my every move, and his waiting expression expectant, suffused with a yearning almost like pain.

Sitting down on the bed beside him, I bent my head to his face—slowly, victoriously kissed his forehead, his cheeks and the tears which sprang to his eyes; then openly crying he offered more, his fingers insistently gripping my hair; and torn to the heart I met him at once, taking his mouth in a kiss so long that he broke away, sobbing.

Dazedly thinking of fetching some water, or a handkerchief for his face, I wandered witlessly around the room, picking up his jacket and searching its pockets before I realized I'd mistaken it for mine; hunted for my own coat, cast aside earlier on my return from the wharves, before remembering my handkerchief was in my pants pocket; and fishing it out, I sat back down by the bed, and tenderly wiped his tears. Closing his eyes, he rested a moment, as if reveling in my touch; then looking up, he met my gaze, so warm and knowing that he flushed, and shyly averted his eyes again.

"Marry me," I said then gently, nudging him softly to catch his gaze.

His face a-flash, he nodded unhesitatingly, saying hoarsely, "Aye."

"Stay by my side for the rest o' my life," I pressed on, lest he have any doubt about my commitment; and unable to find his voice to respond, he simply nodded again, urgently, sweetly. "I don't know how we're goin' t' do it," I told him fairly. "I have so many responsibilities I don't know what t' do with 'em all. But I know I want you by me till the end; and whateveh happens, you'll always come first."

Breaking down afresh, he covered his eyes with his hands; and cradling him in my arms I struggled to soothe him, saying fiercely, "Oh, Gawd, baby, hush… If you cry again, it'll tear the heart right out o' me." Rocking him, caressing his long dark hair and his shoulders, I gradually quieted him; till at last, loosening his grip on me—sliding his hands to rest on mine—he quavered, "When can we be alone t'gether?"

Frustrated myself—bewildered already by the problem of carving out space for us, and railing within against Jacob, Eliza, and everybody else in the whole house—I looked askance at Jim's room which, though protected by the buffer of mine, still afforded no real security; and looking at him squarely, I promised: "As soon as you feel strong enough, we'll take the cahrs down t' Maine; an' I'll sail you straight out t' the island with no one around… Now eat youhr soup an' get some rest, an' do what you can t' get well for me."

Burying himself once more in my arms—resting his head against my face, his wet lashes brushing the curve of my cheek—he immersed himself in my hold, as if, like me, he drew strength from our touch; then at last he drew himself apart, and allowed me to ease him against the pillows.

The soup was cold and so was the tea, but neither of us gave the matter any thought, Jim shakily holding the cup in his hand and drinking a little now and then, and obediently swallowing the soup I spooned him. As he ate—quivering till I put my jacket around him— he asked, "How c'n we be married?"

"Eben c'n do it," I said simply, offering him another spoonful.

"He's got his masteh's papers now—he c'n perform the ceremony for us at sea."

His face a mixture of elation and ever-gathering fatigue, he digested this for a moment, then delicately requested, "When he's done, can we… may we jump the broomstick?"

Breaking into a jubilant grin, I patted his arm and encouraged, "You bet. We'll get Eben t' tie oweh wrists, an' do whateveh else in propeh Romany fashion."

His grateful response plain on his face—our festivity an almost tangible force in the room, as it had been the night he'd cried after Havana, then shared a meal with me on his sickbed—he finished his soup in silence, not stopping till I'd nearly emptied the bowl; then lying back against the pillows, he closed his eyes, scarcely able to keep awake any longer. Seeing his wet lashes at rest on his cheeks, I bent to kiss them softly, smoothing the covers about his shoulders; then picking up the tray, carried it to the door. Whispering, barely audible, he murmured after me: "Ben…ask you something?"

Coming back to the bed, I leaned over him. "You name it," I encouraged.

"When we get married…may I wear your ring?"

"I'd be honohred," I told him, a proud leap in my heart.

"People'll wonder," he murmured.

"We'll find a way t' get around it," I assured him, already beginning to concoct an idea.

"… Somethin' else?"

"A' course, matey."

"When I'm sleepin'…stay nearby me." A twinge almost like pain passed over his face, and stroking his hair, I assured him,

"I promise."

"Don't leave the buildin'," he insisted, softly.

"Honey, I ain't plannin' on leavin' these rooms, much less the buildin'," I pledged; and seeing the pleased twitch at the corners of his lips, I bent to lightly kiss his smile—Jim already asleep by the time I sat up, and rose to carry the tray to the hall.

Opening the door of my room I found Eben in the hall, sitting on one of those stiff-backed brocade chairs that Eliza'd marched along either wall, looking for all the world like a Minuteman keeping guard; and realizing he'd given us our first moments of privacy I broke down as soon as I saw him. Taking the tray from me before I could drop it, he calmly ushered me back into my room, firmly closing the door behind us; and sitting down on my bed he accepted my face in his lap while I sobbed away the pain of my joy, the anxiety of weeks of waiting, the fortitude and despair of the past year. Trying to keep my weeping hushed—mindful even now there could be servants at the door, and not wanting to waken Jim either—I poured out the cargo load of my feelings; then emptied at last I fell to quiet sobs in Eben's lap, aware that he was patiently stroking my hair.

"I asked Jim t' marry me," I managed to tell him at length, a catch to my voice as I confided.

"An' I take it he accepted?" he drawled, not the least surprised—if he ever was—by what I'd done.

"Aye," I told him, my voice breaking anew at the thought; then getting hold of myself, I burst into a hollow laugh: "I guess that makes me a bigamist, don't it?"

"Amongst a lot of otheh things," he said dryly, still quietly patting my hair.

"Oh, Eben," I pledged, "I'll work it out somehow...I'll...come t' terms somehow with Anne...an' the children, I'll find a way t' still be their fatheh... Just...tell me you'll sail us both out t' sea, an' read the ceremony oveh us... I know we're already married in heart...but I want t' heahr it said out loud."

"I'll read it," he promised, "if you'll find a fair way to' deal with Anne... Now set up a minute an' have a drink; I've got a bottle stowed in my case."

He got to his feet as I lifted my head; and fetching his black bag from his chair in the hall, he poured a generous dose of brandy from his kit.

"Now drink this down, an' get some rest yourself; don't set here the whole night, he's goin' t' sleep hard," he said gently, handing me the glass and giving me a pat on the shoulder; and nodding, I took two or three hasty swallows. "I'll go feed Eliza an' the rest a story about how Jim is sleepin' with you settin' by him, an' is not t' be disturbed; an' I won't turn in till they do. Now keep Jim's door locked an' the door t' youhr room closed, an' watch youhr expression when you'hre round the othehs: you look like a loveh if I eveh sawr one."

*   *   *   *   *

Looming above it was poised, ready to break, a great, dark green mass of mountainous sea; then all was foam and I was clinging to the boat, borne down by the pressure and the trap of my seat, battling the weight till I thought my lungs would burst, as I strained and struggled to surface and breathe. Then with a gasp I found I was sitting up in bed, a soft, roomy bed with a curtain stirring nearby me, and the sultry damp of a lowering storm in the air; while an open door stood not far away, with a darkened room just beyond. For a moment, confused, I had no idea where I was, and a quick stab of fear invaded my heart, still pounding from the aftermath of the wave; then I knew with a glad rush in the midst of my fright, and I cried out: "Ben!"

His feet hit the floor as soon as I called his name, bare feet thumping firmly on the bare wood; and he was through the door before I could draw another breath, hurrying to me with long strides in the dim, wearing nothing but drawers in the oppressive heat. Without a halt he scooped me up in his arms, murmuring sounds of comfort in my ear; and stricken anew by the walls that were gone between us, I buried my face in the bulk of him at my cheek. "Close," was all I could say, pressing harder against him; and "Oh, Gawd, baby, I can't get you close enough," he murmured, his arms tightening all the fiercer about me.

Incredulous that he held me, that I'd wakened to him—burrowing deeper, my hands sliding up his broad back and along the hardy curves of his shoulders—I breathed in the smells of sweat and the outdoors; while his hands crushed me to him with command and sureness. "Kiss me," I begged, and he responded at once, his lips coming down on the bridge of my nose, on my lips, on the bare expanse of my throat—hard, fast kisses rough with beard and need;

then his crooning voice and big, tender hands were soothing me as I found I was crying.

"Hush, darling, hush; y' need t' rest," he murmured, his lips in my tumbled hair as I wept; and my fingers digging at his back I clung to him, waves of joy at the sweet names no one had ever called me sweeping over. Rocking me as if he knew he needed to calm me, his arms trembling as though with his own self-control, he simply held me for a quiet time, till my sobbing ceased, and I drew a deep breath; then letting me go a little he reached for the glass of water, set by my bed earlier in the evening; and as he helped me drink it, I realized I hadn't the strength to sit up without his support.

"Bad dream, matey?" he asked then, his voice so loving I caught my breath.

"Aye," I answered, marveling that he knew. "Paul…the wave that took Paul…"

His arms tightening, his voice steady, he said, "When you've rested more, you c'n tell me about it…but not now, Jamie; just rest."

For a moment, in the sweet afterglow of that nickname, I hushed; but realizing slowly other things I needed to tell him—word of Ephie and Roan, his cousins, that I should not have delayed, and the story of my dolphin, its memory even now knifing me with its pain—I stirred; and again I tried to speak.

"Lateh," he stilled me, as if he knew what I meant to say; then bracing me so he could see my face, he asked, "Thirsty?", and I nodded against him. "Want the wateh closet?" he went on, and I nodded again—though wherever it was, it seemed a league off or more. "No, don't you stand up," he warned, as I made an effort to swing my legs to the edge of the bed. "Eben says you'hre not t' put two feet on the floor for two weeks. Let me find your wrappeh an' I'll carry you, honey."

Going to the lamp, he turned up the gas; and in its warm, rosy light I could see his bare back, broad with hard work and native strength. Then something about his arm caught my attention, and I saw what it was as he came toward me—a tattoo which marked the swell of his shoulder; and like a child up late at night, surprising the secrets of his elders, I reached up to touch it, fascinated. "Lateh, matey, I'll tell ye about it," he said gently, in answer to the question on my lips; but I was too busy exploring it to hear him, tracing its design with quick fingertips.

"Ben," I said suddenly, "my intials're here with yours…plain as day."

"A' course, matey; who else's initials d'ye think would be there, h'm?"

Completely taken aback, I gasped, "What'll people think?"—so dumbfounded I sat up on my own.

"Well, it wasn't so remarkable when you was dead, an' everybody knew you were my best friend; but now that you're alive, I s'pose it could be hardeh t' explain," he drawled. "Now, don't try t' sit up; I'll be right back."

Going into the other room, he rummaged around in a trunk, then came back wearing his wrapper, and carrying one for me; and as I looked at it more closely I saw it was my blue one, his gift to me when I was recovering in Whampoa; and I buried my face in it gratefully before I let him help me don it. Then picking me up with ease, he carried me to the water closet, a fine, big room across the hall, and set me down on a chair while I gazed around at the carpet, the brass tub, the commode with its water tank and pull chain, and other wonders of luxury. Turning up the gas, he said, "I'm goin' t' fetch the lemonade Eliza squeezed for ye earlieh; don't try t' walk back t' that room without me."

I was sitting obediently on a chair in the hall when he came into sight with a tray, which he carried first into his room, then mine; and I watched him till he disappeared, my eyes on the sunbleached thatch of his hair, and the unconscious aura of strength in his walk. Into my thoughts darted again the hints of his life this past year—the tattoo on his arm, Jared's death, and Stephen's reference to his trial; and curiosity strove with my anxiety for him. But his face as he came back was steady and calm, his eyes clear and grey; and he ferried me back to my bed with a sureness, untroubled by anything past or to come as he braced me, and held a cool glass to my lips.

No taste on earth could have surpassed the sweet tartness of that drink, one of the few delectable treats I'd had this past year or more;

and he encouraged me to the last drop, promising me all manner of foods as fast as I was able. Then feeling the sudden drain of my efforts, I curled up on my side, nestling in the luxury of the thick ticking; and setting aside the glass, he turned down the lamp, leaving enough light to soothe me in case I wakened again.

*   *   *   *   *

Jacob's doctor, Jarius Windham, a specialist in fevers, arrived in the parlor late in the afternoon—his appearance timed with Jim's brief awakening a few minutes before; and while he looked in on Jim, Eben and I waited on the balcony nearby, Eben steady and calm, me anxious. At length appearing in the doorway, Windham took a seat by the railing, accepting Eben's offer of a smoke as he joined us; and immediately we assailed him with questions.

"Well, his heart seems sound," he declared at once, in answer to our concerns. "I don't hear any of the morbid distractions I've come to look for in rheumatic cases—none of the peculiar to and fro rubbing or bellows sounds one can detect even over a heartbeat. He's fortunate to have escaped all the complications of scarlet fever, especially dropsy; seems not to have suffered any loss of hearing, or sight—though I didn't test him for reading; and I don't at this point look for him to slip into a rheumatic condition.

" Having said that," he went on before we could get in a word, or even an exclamation of relief, "I want to caution you he's exhausted: he never should have left Rio Janeiro as soon as he did, given the severity of his case there and the deprivations he'd faced the year before that. He shouldn't have worked his passage here, but instead shipped as a passenger, even in the steerage, with the American consul's help. But now that he's here he needs a month's rest before you can think of moving him on to Maine; and whatever he's got planned after, he'll need to resume his workload gradually, over an extended period of time: I don't want t' hear of him shipping as an able seaman in July."

Relieved—looking over at Eben, who'd already warned me he thought it would be months before Jim was up to his full strength—I nodded; and as Eben asked questions about his findings, I searched ahead with my thoughts into the future. That we'd find a way somehow to blend his period of recovery into our new life I never doubted; and as we adjourned to the kitchen—tiptoeing past his bed, where he already slept deeply—I breathed thanks again that he'd made it this far in safety. On hearing Windham give instructions about his diet—especially the introduction of strength-builders like meat, and variants like fruit he'd scarcely tasted in a year—the kitchen crew broke into action, commencing work at once on a beef stew; and jealous of anyone else's intrusions into my personal care of him, I went back to his side, where I kept watch the next two or three days, trying to keep him quiet.

Unaware of all our activity on his behalf, he slept for the most part, only opening his eyes briefly to search for me, or to allow me to prop up him up for mealtimes: luxuriating quietly in my touch, or now and then trying to ask me about myself, and about what had happened to me since our separation. Concerned about the impact of my news on his strength, I put him off, passing on word instead from his *Cliffs of Dover* captain, who'd called while he slept, having personally escorted his old quarterboat to Jacob's courtyard; or relaying bits of news about Cape Damaris and the children. As hungry for word of home as he was for the trays I brought him, he devoured every scrap I could tell him; and I only stopped when he grew drowsy from all the detail, or when tears of longing gathered under his lashes.

*   *   *   *   *

The first few days at Jacob's I spent mostly drowning in contentment—in the luxury of a real bed and fresh linen, and the quiet of a room well-guarded by Ben; in the assurance of an arduous journey ended, and the promise of a marriage I'd scarcely dared dream of beginning. When I woke it was to the sound of Ben's voice—his accent, thick with the burr of the coast, never failing to start the hot sting to my eyes—or to his invitation to close my eyes and open my mouth, into which he would place a meltingly sweet strawberry, or some other delicacy I hadn't tasted in a year. Once I wakened enough to find him reading nearby, and apologized drowsily, "I ain't been a very exciting guest so far, have I?"; to which he tenderly replied, "Honey, you've been the most exciting thing that's eveh happened t' me; just rest."

But as I gradually began to gather strength—as I found myself more and more often able to sit up in bed, and take notice of the room and the doings around me, I began to know unexpected frustrations: the interruptions and dilemmas I'd been protected from at first. That Eliza and Claire would want to look in on me for short times—reading me small pieces of nonsense from the newspaper, or selected bits from the shipping columns—was to be expected; as were visits from Stephen and Rowan, always punctiliously brief, and dotted with exclamations over the hieroglyphics of my newly arrived quarterboat, which I scarcely had the stomach to think of myself. But their intrusions broke in on my time with Ben—visitors appearing without warning at his door; and I noticed he was beginning to leave the door between our rooms scrupulously ajar, to avoid the temptations and dangers of an interrupted word or touch.

At a time when I craved—more and more keenly with my returning strength—the intimacy of our guarded moments, these interruptions were hard enough; but they were made harder still by my awakening worries over what had happened to him in my absence, and by our unmet need to talk. By now I was lucid enough to wonder what, if anything, Eben had told Ben about my past; and I began to fear his reaction. Did he know anything about my life in Boston? Shouldn't I have told him about my pursuits there, before I'd told him I would marry him?

That he and Eben had talked about our future I knew, from Eben's response the first time I'd had a private moment with him, and joyously confessed, "Ben asked me t' marry him." But had they talked about Ann Street, Creek Lane, Liverpool—all the ways in which I so wished I'd never compromised myself? There was nothing in Ben's face which gave away anything of what he knew, or of what we still needed to say to each other; but I could feel the tension in his arms as he helped me to sit up against the pillows; and I knew that he labored, like me, under the frustration of our lack of privacy, and the stress of the unspoken between us.

At last, a week or so into my New York stay, I woke up to find him reading nearby, with no one else at hand and the rest of the house quiet; and seeing he was unaware that I'd wakened, I dwelt lovingly on his face, pondering what I might say to bring things to a head. He was sitting in the chair by my bed, one leg crossed over the knee of the other, and the newspaper spread out in his lap; and his big, blunt hands holding the edges of the paper—open no doubt to the shipping columns—made the pages look fragile by contrast.

Looking closely at his face, I could see it had changed—could see it was softer, more tender, suffused with a fortitude almost like patience; and humbled, I knew its transformation had come because of me. Suddenly feeling my stare or perhaps my yearning, he looked up all at once and met my eyes; and as if reading my gaze, he rose to close the door and lock it—something he hadn't done since our first hour together. Then coming to sit beside me on the bed, he looked down at me expectantly and asked, "What is it, matey?"

I had no idea where to begin but cast swiftly about, deciding in the end that before he cut me off and told me to rest, I at least had to know about him; so I said simply, "About your trial."

His brows came together at once—not with anger but concern, as if he was anxious about the effect such a worry would have on me; and he answered protectively, "Who told you about that?"

Looking into his eyes—determined to read there whatever he wouldn't tell me—I responded, "Stephen…in the carriage."

His scowl deepening, he said, "Well, damn him, I would've preferred t' do it myself… Now, I won't have you worryin' about it."

"When is it?" I pressed him.

"At the end o' next week, in Pohrtland."

"Then we c'n leave here by then?"

His face tense, but his voice calm, he said firmly, "Honey, I'm goin' alone—it won't be but a few days—then I'll be back; an' a week or so afteh that, we c'n pack up for home." Understanding my gaze he added, "It ain't what I want, but it's the best thing for you… Not just Eben but Dr. Windham says you need a month o' rest; so a month it'll be."

I knew better than to argue, especially since I could not yet sit up for long spells, much less walk without assistance; and I swallowed a swift, sharp longing for home along with my fear of our separation, trying to still the lurch of my stomach at the thought of him without me at sea.

With his uncanny ability to read me off, he broke in on my thoughts before I could say a word: "Jamie, I'll take the cahrs... I won't have t' sail; the line runs all the way t' Pohrtland now."

So grateful to him for his understanding that I couldn't trust myself to speak, I struggled to control my reaction, feeling my face work with the force of the effort; then at last I managed, "What will happen...in court?"

He said simply, "They'll settle the suit Hull n' Lombard filed against me, it bein' representative of the othehs; it won't take long."

But I held him to it: "Stephen said he doubted you'd win—that you'd come out of it without a cent."

Now his brow furrowed into the thunderous quarterdeck scowl I knew so well—a splendid glower which made me glad I wasn't Stephen; but determined to know the truth I waited for him to answer. "Well, Gawd damn Stephen anyhow; I guess he ain't the Admiralty, an' can't know their mind," he said then, half rankling at Stephen, half trying to protect me. "If John can't carry the day for us in court, I won't waste no time frettin' about it; an' I don't want you to, eitheh."

I looked down at the covers, not wanting him to see my eyes. "Why did they sue?" I asked him.

"The tea failed, matey."

"Then the voyage went on too long."

"Aye."

"Stephen said...the suits were filed for wrongful prosecution of voyage," I pressed; and turmoil filled me again, for I was beginning to understand.

His face spoke volumes of what he thought of Stephen; but again he said simply, "Aye."

"Then...after we...you deviated from course," I kept at it.

"Of course." His face was so full of the pain of that time that I scarcely had the heart to look at him; but his voice held the same steady, everyday calm.

"B'cause of me," I spelled out, the realization knifing me with distress.

"A' course," he said again, though his voice was now hoarse; then impulsive confession breaking through his need to protect me, he went on, "D'ye think there was a corneh of the Pacific we didn't search?"

"Would you…if it hadn't been me in the boat…would you have done the same?" I struggled, looking straight up into his eyes.

His face wholly honest, he said simply, "No."

"Ben…then I…you…you've lost everything, on account of me."

He smiled. "No. I've gained everything, on account of you."

Filled with distress for what he might have suffered, and determined to get round his protective silence, I began to concoct ways to pry his story from Eben; and I'd already made up my mind by the time that Ben left. Getting Eben alone presented a challenge, not just because my visitors were now frequent, but because there was no way to hear them in my inner chamber until the moment they knocked at the outer; then if they were men, they walked right in, making private meetings short-lived at best. My conversation with Ben had been kept low; and now, as Eben stepped in after dinner—looking very much the same as always—I asked him to close the door; and he did so, automatically softening his voice.

If he had an inkling as to what was on my mind, he didn't show it, sitting down beside me and beginning conversationally to speak of this and that, until I raised a hand to stop him.

"Eben, please—I have t' know what's happened t' Ben… everything from the hour we parted till the day that he received my letter… I can't rest until you tell me."

Setting aside his pipe and taking a hard look at me, as if to assess my progress and strength and weigh them against the distress and stimulation that his answer was likely to cause, he paused; and to encourage him to understand I was already aware, I prodded,

"I know that he—wasn't well, that he wasn't...himself; what happened?"

"Who's been talkin' t' you?" he countered, every inch the mate in the rise of his brows.

Hesitating, I confided: "Stephen...on the ride from the wharf."

"Damn good thing Ben don't know—he's already given him hell for spillin' the beans about the trial—if he knew you'd been worryin' about this since you got here—"

"Eben, I'm goin' t' marry him—I need t' be able t' take care of him—I can't do it, if I don't know how he's been," I interrupted, stubborn in my protective appeal.

His face—always wonderfully blended with humor and plain honesty—softened with affection and something almost like awe; and crossing his legs he drew a sigh, gazing out on the room as if looking back over a cast-off span of time. Then forthrightly as a doctor performing some necessary work, he baldly told me, "Jim, it was me who sailed him home...do you undehstand?"

Frankly searching his eyes, I listened; and he met my gaze with a knowing flicker. The image of Ben being captained by anyone else, even Eben, unnerved me—assaulted me with a stab of cold in my middle; but I waited, chin up, for him to continue; and as if satisfied I was equal to the tale, he told it.

"At first, he was hopeful...we searched the wateh in narrowing circles...then we criss-crossed the arear till we'd covered a wide swath. Then we shaped a course for the Marianas...then the Sandwich Islands, where thehre was rumoh three or four men'd been picked up by a ship bound for San Francisco. He didn't give up all o' that time, hahdly seemed t' lay down t' rest... I warned him about the tea when he squared off for San Francisco; an' the othehs, who'd been willin' till then t' break course, stahted t' worry. But he wouldn't hear o' endin' the search as long as there was a chance you was alive; an' he didn't care a tuppence about deviatin'. A' course there was no trace of you in San Francisco; an' that was that...we'd run out o' ocean."

For a moment or two he quietly puffed, as if calling up memories or censoring them for my ears; and I waited, sweat gathering at the edges of my hair in my pain for Ben's ordeal.

"We set sail for home with him b'low," Eben went on, carefully picking his words. "I could almost neveh get him on deck... First it was his mind that was muddled, then it was pain in all o' his limbs... I tried t' carry on as the mate so the othehs wouldn't know, an' I managed all right, till we was off the Horn, an' too far south, beset by ice. He come up on deck then, b'cause I absolutely insisted, but— when he seen the first cake, he thought it was you boys, an' hollehed out t' the men t' loweh away for you... I got him b'low, but the secret was out; an' the rest o' the run I stood in his place."

More agitated by the moment not just for what he had suffered but by the numbing ebb of his mind, I sat up away from the pillows; and not missing my turmoil he hurried on to a finish with a skeleton sketch of the next weeks.

"Things finally come to a head off La Plata, when he ordered Haggai t' fetch him straw; an' bustin' in on his cabin, t' see what was goin' on, I seen he'd made a man out o' straw, fashioned afteh you, with your clothes... From b'hind it was so good it made me catch my breath. He was tryin' t' feed it wateh...about eight glasses full set on a tray. 'He's thirsty,' he kept sayin' oveh an' oveh; an' I knew I had t' act, or risk losin' him foreveh. When I told him the truth—when I made him undestand your battle was oveh, whateveh the outcome— he cried; we both did. That was the turnin' point; the fever broke afteh that."

Stunned by his description of Ben's unbalance—so much worse than I'd imagined—I actually tried to get out of bed, and set off in search of him in the house; and it took Eben's grip on my shoulders— the bully force of a seasoned mate—to settle me down to hear out the story.

"The otheh breakthrough come when we was home, afteh we'd hauled into Cape Damaris," he said, digging anew in his pipe in a way that told me he had something more to say; and still trying to shake off the eeriness of La Plata, I listened to him, hands working. "I found him alone one night in youhr room at the Inn...an' suddenly, he was ready t' talk. He told me then that he'd loved you...not just as a friend, as he put it; that he blamed hisself for neveh lettin' you know. I couldn't see any point in keepin' your confidence any longeh, since there seemed t' be no hope you was alive; so I told him you'd loved him, which gave him new life; an' I shared what I knew of your past."

"You told him….*everything*?" I gasped, dumfounded.

"Aye," he said steadily.

"You told him—about Liverpool, about Boston?" I anguished—understanding in shocked waves that he knew all, from my expulsion in Wales to my prostitution in Boston; that I was as transparent to him as an unshielded lobster.

Hastening to reassure me, he said, "He wanted t' know what'd happened t' you, Jim, the way you just now needed t' know about him…he wanted t' understand you for what you was. You said you was ready t' take care of him—does that include lettin' him know you, an' bein' ready t' hear that he does?"

Feeling my cheeks burn, and casting wildly back over all I'd confided, I floundered, "He —what did he say, Eben, was he—was he angry or disgusted, did he—"

"He wants t' marry you, Jim; ain't that enough of an answer? He's already got the ceremony planned, an' taken out a bond."

"He has?" I gaped, almost as floored as I was moved.

"Aye; paid me the five dollahs for it, an' had me make it out propeh, even if we can't eveh file it."

Overtaken by my reactions—first to Ben's experiences, then his knowledge of mine—I implored Eben to send him back in.

"That's about enough for you t'day, mate," he shook his head, bully again.

"Either you bring him here, or I'll get out o' this bed an' find him myself; an' I won't be responsible for what I'll do when I see him," I insisted, fervent; and with unconcealed reservations, he rose to fetch Ben.

*   *   *   *   *

As soon as I came into the room he was up out of bed and halfway across the floor to meet me; and I barely had time to shut the door before he was in my arms crushing me to him, and I was lifting him off his feet against me. Clasping one another for a long time in silence, we simply leaned on one another, Jim speechless with a hand braced over his eyes, me comforting him with touches and words; till at last, pulling apart a little, we gazed at each other—the first time we'd ever looked on one another in full honesty.

Still tense under my hands but protective of me, Jim spoke first, gripping my shoulders: "Ben, you…are you sure you're all right?"; and smiling into his eyes I reassured him,

"Matey, I'm fine"—adding, "I would've kept it from you—I knew the whole story would upset you—but you was bound t' catch wind of it sooneh or lateh."

Burying himself again in my arms he held me; and compassionately I stroked his hair, feeling the strength of returning health in his shoulders. That I would soon have my hands full with the obstinate willfulness of his old vigor, I already knew from Eben's brief remarks to me; and cherishing his need now, I slipped my arm under his knees, and ferried him gently back to the bed.

Speaking close to my ear as I held him against the pillows, he managed to go on: "Eben's told you…all about Boston"—flushing as I frankly met his eyes.

"Aye," I said, my voice growing husky. "He sawr that…the only way I could go on, was if I could still find ways t' know you. Since we'd given up hope of you in my future, he opened up the door t' youhr past… He didn't mean t' speak out o' turn."

"You've been t'…Creek Lane," he said quietly, looking me carefully in the eye; and I, who had not intended a confession of my journey nearly so soon, nodded calmly.

"A' course." Smiling gently I added, "D'ye imagine I could finally have Eben tell me where you had been before I met you—an' not go an' see the place for myself? As soon as he was done talking, I packed my bags."

"When did you… how long did you stay?" he managed.

"Nigh onto a fortnight, this winteh…long enough t' get the pictuh."

A smile half-wry at the aptness of my assessment, half-awed at the revelation of this new side of me, quivered at the corners of his mouth. "Where…did you stay?"

"At Nel's at first, since it was on Creek Lane, an' I didn't know how t' get into Lomond's… But I put in the second week at youhr old building… Slateh runs it now."

His amazement at hearing me name the familiar names almost overcoming the pain of their memory, he cast his eyes down and murmured, "Oh, God, Ben, I never…wanted anybody I loved t' know what it was like there."

"I didn't suffeh as you did, honey… Eben was thehre with me…I didn't have t' go it alone."

"Was…Lomond still there?" he asked me, not without fear.

"No," I answered frankly. "He'd moved on, probably several times, since you was there."

"You didn't…mention anything about me t' anyone?"

"Of course not, matey: think I'd jeopardize youhr safety, as long as there was a chance in a million you was still alive? I found out what I wanted t' know by boardin' around, drinkin' in the bars an' listenin' t' othehs…encouragin' them t' talk now an' then… an' since I'd left my name an' money b'hind, it wasn't hahd t' fall in with the scene."

"Ben, you…slept in those beds, you…got into Lomond's dance hall?"

"A' course."

"You…"—he paused delicately—"you danced with…"—words failed him.

"With lots o' people…even Eben."

Overcome with all this new information he fell silent, while I guardedly sorted out what I would say from what I wouldn't; then grasping around he ventured, "While you were there… did you ever hear or see…one of the boys at Slater's named Beckman?"

"Aye," I answered kindly. "But that story's got t' wait for a bit, mate."

"Was he…all right?"

Picking my words I said, "When I first came acrosst him… it was plain he hadn't an easy .life. But I found a way t' get him out o' Boston; an' he's livin' now in a place much betteh for him."

His face a study as he sorted out questions—no doubt about how I'd done it, and whether I'd confronted Slater—he fell silent again for a moment; but too exhausted now to put them into words, he asked simply, "D'ye think…later on, I could write or see him?"

"A' course." Giving his hand an encouraging squeeze, I settled him back against the pillows; and trying once again to get him to rest, I told him, "That'll do for now, matey…we'll lose all the ground you've gained, if you don't get some sleep."

Almost too weary to shake his head, he resisted me, saying: "No…something else."

His voice was so determined in spite of his exhaustion, and held such a note of anticipation, that reluctantly I relented: "What is it?"

He cast his eyes down again, almost as if afraid to meet mine, in case what he looked to find there was missing; but a flush almost of hope spread across his cheeks as he asked, his voice even lower: "After Boston…where did you go?"

Looking at his face, I knew that he guessed; and when he raised his eyes, I saw in their depths such expectant longing that I couldn't find my voice to answer.

"You went to Wales," he whispered.

Overcome for him I nodded gently; and his eyes came fluttering down again, moisture gathering at the corners. "You found my people," he went on, hoarsely.

"Aye," I told him, my voice—like his—unsteady.

Pausing, as if he scarcely dared ask the question, he murmured, "My father?"

"Aye," I nodded again, catching him to me to ease him in my arms.

"Was he…kind…t' you?"

I smiled into his hair at the recollection; and the tumult in my middle subsided a little with his easing breaths. "He was a bit suspicious at first," I answered, seeing the tall, austere form of John Roberts by the fire; "but once we'd got through tea an' breakfast, an' I explained the reason for my visit, he began t' warm up a little; and by the time we pahted, an oweh or so later, there as a grudgin' respect in his eye."

"Did you…talk about me?"

"A' course," I said gently. "You was virtually all we talked about—the only earthly topic of conversation I could come up with that would even get me access t' him. I didn't try t' hide from him who I was, or how I had known you; an' because I came on the pretext of announcing youhr death—as a hero, tryin' t' rescue a shipmate—he couldn't hide his longing for news, or his pride in what I had t' say about you."

Feeling his shudder of joy I kissed his hair, and held him while he digested my words; then sensing that he was growing calmer, I added apologetically,

"I'm sorry, matey, that I let him think you was dead; it was the only way I could invent t' get my foot in the door."

"It's all right," he responded, head tucked under my chin. "Better for him t' think I'm honorably dead than dishonorably alive." As I tightened my arms in sympathy with him, he nestled closer, turning his face; and I could feel the soft, wet brush of his lashes on the bare skin of my throat. "Did you…see any of the others?" he added, tensing again under my hands despite his fatigue.

"Aye; several. Youhr cousin Idris was gettin' married; an' the clans of both families was gathered t'getheh," I answered, deliberately withholding word of his father's re-marriage, and of his younger brothers and sister.

"Taw?"

"Aye, she was baking bread by the fire," I acknowledged, and felt his smile against my throat.

"An' my father… How did he look?"

"The second most beautiful man I eveh met," I said warmly; and his smile pressed my throat as his clasp loosened with sleep.

Easing his hands, I lowered him against the pillows; and turning on his side, he slept at once, the sleep of a man overpowered with events. Fanned on his cheeks, his thick, dark lashes, wet and starred with earlier tears, made me want to weep myself; and I sat beside him for a long while, looking at him and stroking his hair; then, when I was sure he was sleeping soundly, I rose, and tiptoed to the door.

It was when I turned the knob that I realized it wasn't locked—

that it had been unlatched the entire hour, so that anyone could have walked in on us at any point, while I held and soothed and kissed him; and wave after wave of nausea attacked me as I understood what I could have brought on us. Groping my way across my room to my door—my nervous reaction to Jim's response and my anxiety for his health compounding the upheaval of my discovery—I found myself urgently seeking the water closet; but when I opened my door there was Eben sitting in a chair by it, calmly reading a book in the hallway; and seeing my face he helped me to the commode, then firmly but kindly saw me to bed.

Now that my departure for Portland loomed closer we shared such confidences daily, trading tales of our journeys this past year, asking questions or making plans before we were again separated; and my chief concern—besides the ever-present anxiety of being overheard or discovered—was how to parcel out my news or invite disclosures of his in a way that wouldn't tax his strength. Sometimes it was my stories we spoke of, and I would lay them out like the strands of a rope; at others it was his, which he twined with mine; but together we wove a many-layered cable, saying what we could, saving painful details for later.

"Tell me about Idris' wedding," he begged, early one warm night with the tang of rain in the air, and the rest of the household in the midst of a dinner party.

"Honey, I only wish I could: I wasn't invited t' attend," I said dryly.

There was a light to his smile which spoke of his old wit and humor; and the flush on his cheeks was of returning wellness. "Can you tell me who she was going to marry?"

"I only know it was one of the Lees."

He wrinkled his nose, though he said only, "Beneath her."

"So I gathered from whoeveh it was I met on the road near Bala," I grinned.

"Did you see her?" he asked me, wistful.

"No. Round the fire that morning was only youhr fatheh an' Taw, an' othehs I haven't told you about yet."

His eyes sharpened alertly, though he said nothing, watching my face.

"Thehre was a woman, young an' pretty, who didn't speak much t' me," I said gently, watching him carefully in turn; "but I undehstood she an' youhr fatheh was married."

Still he said nothing, absorbing the news; and to give him time, I went on, "She looked t' be ten yeahrs or so youngeh than youhr fatheh; an' he introduced her as one of the Lovells… Reyna Lovell."

Still reflecting some tension, his face relaxed a degree; and reading his expression, I asked him,

"A good match?"

"Aye," he responded, folding his arms across his chest, and gazing out on the room for a moment. "It's a little…difficult…t' imagine anyone in my mother's place; but if I had had t' pick, I couldn't have chosen better."

"Perhaps with you gone, an' youhr motheh too, he needed someone t' fill the void," I offered, careful not to name Narilla out loud.

"Aye," he assented, still looking out on the room as if he saw John Roberts alone by the fire.

"They had had children," I went on carefully, "two boys and a girl; so I would say, they had been married several yeahrs…probably eveh since the time that you left."

His face was a mixture of pain, memory and awe. "Then I have brothers, a sister," he marveled.

"Aye."

"You met them?"

"Aye," I smiled, warming at the recollection. "The oldest, Lasho and Shuri, were the whole time in the tent, except when they gathered sticks for the fire; but I spoke with them when I arrived, an' when I said goodbye… They were a lot like Reyna, dark-haired, dark-eyed, shy."

"And the youngest?"

"The youngest," I began, my voice suddenly thick in my throat, and my eyes blurring with the unexpected hot sting of tears, "was a boy of three or so…"—I had to stop to clear my sight of the lad on the fence top—"curly dark hair, dark blue eyes, just like youhrs… Sacki."

At once his hands were tight on my shoulders; and as if released by my words or by his quick show of feeling, wave after wave of longing swept through me—surges of yearning to see Sacki again, to see Jim as he had been, a rare sight on that long-ago moor. Other reactions rose unbidden as well; and in their midst I understood that this was our child, Jim's and mine—ours, if we could have had children; and the pang of regret stung me into a wordless loss. So overswept was I that I couldn't even cry—could do nothing more than to accept Jim's hand at my eyes, to hold it in place with my own; could only hear, in the dark of its shelter, the gentle words of his instinctive understanding: "Just as I've always felt about Nat."

"Jim," I said thickly, still hiding behind his hand, "you…"

"I knew, you know, three years ago, that I'd never have a son…so he's mine, mine an' yours," he told me.

His words were calm and if it hadn't been for his hand, tight with pain across my eyes, I wouldn't have known that he too fought this battle—was still fighting it, despite his acceptance; that like me he knew the unattainable by name. Stroking his hand with my own, I pulled it away, and held his palm for a long time at my lips; then with a gentle squeeze, I let it go; and sliding it down my shoulder to my arm, he moored it there.

"Youhr fatheh gave me something…something of youhrs, when I left," I took up my story again, cautiously—wondering how, if I'd scarcely made it through Sacki, I'd ever make it through his harp without breaking down.

"He'd kept something?" he was surprised into asking, wonder overcoming both worry for me and his own pain.

"Aye."

His face working with the implications of the news—with its testimony that his father's love had been greater than either the condemnation of exile, or the threat of contamination—he said nothing.

"I'd shown him yourh locket," I began, fingering it at my collar, "t' sort of… lay claim t' knowing you, since it…it was so hard t' reach him, he was so distant…and I'd talked about youhr top, how you'd mentioned he'd made if for you, and how you'd played with it on the moor… His eyes seemed t' stir, as if he wanted t' offeh me something in return, something t' thank me for finding him…for sharing my pride in you, an' the honohr of my final news. He went into the tent, an' came out with something wrapped in a cloth…then he bowed, an' handed it to me."

Struggling to master my voice I went into my room, then returned with his harp, still wrapped; and tenderly I removed the cloth, and set the instrument in his lap.

At once his eyes filled and his fingers, trembling, plucked at the strings—hesitantly at first, as if they scarcely dared believe they beheld his old toy; then more confidently, as if recovering a gift long lost, played out since only on borrowed guitars and fiddles; then finally with graceful abandon, a wondrous weave of rippling rhythms. Straightaway rich melodies filled the air, haunting tunes harking back to springs by the campfire, when boyish hands first sought to echo the earth's stir, or tapestry the bare limbs in verdure.

"I can't b'lieve he gave it t' you," he quavered at last, settling back against the pillows with the harp at his side. "He made it himself, a long time ago, for me… He must have valued you…your visit…far more than you knew."

"He neveh…certainly neveh showed it, not till the end," I smiled.

"He wouldn't have, we… seldom showed feelings, certainly not to gadje. I only wish… you could have heard him play."

"Could he play as well as you?"

He laughed, the ring I loved returning to his voice. "Better, far better…. He was the best of the Rom. People used t' come from far and wide, all kinds of gadje, t' hear John Roberts play each year at Bala…We'd have a festival, every fall, and he'd bring his harp, a great harp all carved and painted, which *his* father'd made… There was lots of fine music, but his was the best."

A flame rose up in me, a fierce desire to set sail at once and hear him myself; and with them flashed a swift understanding that my life, and our marriage, would not be complete until we'd performed certain rites together, Jim and I—until, just as we'd interwoven our stories, we'd intertwined the moments that had shaped us; and as if he understood, he murmured,

"We'll go...one fall...you an' I."

Then picking up his harp, as if to call up those days gone, or hasten ahead to an autumn to come, he rippled nimbly over the strings—his melodies conjuring together the crowds, the evening waters of the lake, and the dark, brooding hulk of Tomen Bala; and I sat there close by him, chin in hand, seeing in the chords John Roberts' stern face, transfigured with the flush of his art; and beyond him, like a guess in the dim, Narilla, her eyes astir with the early moon on the lake, and her cloak with the gusts which scattered the leaves.

*   *   *   *   *

Close as we were now drawing to Ben's trial, his impending departure seemed to speed events along, almost as swiftly as he would have allowed if I'd been well; so that, in addition to the news he shared, he came in more and more often with preparations that would pave the way for our wedding. Once it was simply to measure my finger, and I knew he hadn't forgotten my ring; another time it was to show me the bond he'd taken out, so that I could see our names together, and his receipt, in Eben's hand, for $5; another still it was to hand me a sheaf of legal papers, and to request that, in the month or two before I came of age, I allow him to adopt me.

"But Ben," I began, confused as I looked over the papers, close-written with the lawyerly twists and turns of John's script, "what'll this mean?"

"It'll make us as legally connected as we can be, since Eben can't officially file the bond...it'll make us legally b'long t'getheh," he explained, grey eyes knowing above spectacles perched, as usual, well down his nose, and shirt-sleeves rolled up with business-like fervor.

"You mean," I struggled, "it'll make me your son?"

"It'll make you a membeh of my family," he said, careful as always about how he described our relations; "it'll give you all the rights an' privileges of my kinship, an' me yours... It'll mean that when I'm ill or dyin', nobody can eveh keep you away from my room, not even Anne."

Vivid before me came the recollection of what had happened when he had lung fever; and without needing to consider further I told him directly, "I'll sign."

"Jim, I want you t' be sure you undehstand," he cautioned.

"I understand that no power on earth's ever keepin' me away from you again when you need me; an' if this paper protects that, I'm for it."

He smiled, pleasure as always lighting his face at any implication of my allegiance. "That's what I had in mind when I asked John t' drawr this up, not long afteh I had lung feveh... I meant t' talk t' ye about it all the way t' the Pacific—but I neveh got up the nerve."

"Ben, you mean—'way back then, did you—?"

"Eveh since that day I got youhr letteh in Portland, just b'fore you dumped my derrick int' the harboh, I've known I loved you; aye," he said dryly.

Looking down, I struggled to conceal a grin at his reference. "Then it wasn't...that night at the inn you—"

Smiling, he shook his head. "It was in a dream, the day youhr letteh came...We was takin' the cars t'getheh, you an' me, an' you was dressed t' the nines in a light blue suit... Though the cahr was crowded, an' everyone was lookin' at us, such a longing built up b'tween us that finally, you just laid youhr head on my shouldeh... an' when I woke up, I knew."

As an unadorned sea breaks into facets of glittering light when the sun emerges, so his weathered face was transformed by the memory; and my throat taut with swift feeling, I could make no answer. Looking down at John's script, waiting for his small, upright ciphers—so like Ben's—to clear, I finally managed to press on, "How's..."—I paused delicately, rattling the pages —"how's your family goin' t' feel about all this?"

"It won't change anything that already is; just make things more secure...You're already in my will; you're already at the centeh of my household; there ain't nobody back home that don't think of you as comin' t' rejoin the family, especially now, afteh we've lost anotheh brotheh… An' frankly, afteh next week, nobody'll be able t' point t' this an' accuse you of fortune huntin.'"

I looked at him squarely, for it was the one consideration that would have prevented my signing, and he knew it; knew it as shrewdly as he knew all the other motives that moved me. Almost as if he looked forward to bankruptcy as a release, a boon which put us on equal footing, he grinned; and bested by him again, I looked down, lips twitching. "I don't want this t' make things harder with Anne," I went on when I could, raising another issue about which we had said nothing; and now his face tautened as if I had struck a tension far greater than that of his trial, though he tried at once to skip by it.

"Matey, thehre's just some things we need t' do no matteh what her reaction, an' this is one," he answered, refusing to say more. "If we don't do this now, while you'hre still a minoh, we'll foreveh lose oweh chance; an' I'm goin' t' stahrt this marriage with everything in place, done right; I'm not makin' the same mistakes I did the last time."

Searching his face, I saw all the stress of the complications which awaited him with regard to his family; saw them with a hurt that he wouldn't allow me to help shoulder his burdens. Determinedly refusing to meet my eyes, he simply dug out his pen instead; dipped it in the inkwell on the stand by my bed; and letting the moment go, I took it with a smile, signing the document in the space John had provided.

As soon as the pen touched the paper an odd sense of completeness—of having doubled myself the way a backstay is strengthened, once the turns of a seizing have reinforced it—swept over all the strands of my life; and at last finding his eyes, I saw he felt the same—felt a fresh bond in place as he picked up the papers, and carried them to John, who'd arrived earlier this morning.

If he had changed by the events of the past year, I knew that I had as well—in ways he hadn't been able to see yet; knew I needed to tell him, before he departed for Portland; but telling him meant sharing parts of the past year too painful to divulge—not just the deaths of

Paul and the others, of which I'd said nothing, but those final days alone in the boat, when God had rocked me to sleep like a crone, and my porpoise had died that last day in my hands. Behind those events loomed a tidal wave of feeling I'd successfully walled even from Sister Leonore; and I didn't know how I could find the words to release it. Worried about the strains beginning to show on Ben's face, I couldn't see how I could add to their weight; and torn between my yearning to protect him and my selfish longing to pour out the whole tale, I went back and forth in my mind.

Exacerbating my tension was the arrival of agents from Lloyd's and the city newsheets—alerted no doubt by slack-jawed Stephen—clamoring for the story of my 103-day survival, and the very details I meant to tell only Ben; and appalled at the thought of speaking such intimate moments before strangers, or seeing my name in the papers—the same name I'd used three years ago here, among the brothels and dens of Five Points—I was overjoyed when Ben sent them packing. Yet their invasion served to sharpen my need to finally share my experience with him—a need which grew keener as I became stronger with rest; till at last, one restless morning shy but one of his departure, when another sleepless night had worn me, I managed to find him alone.

"I need t' tell you about Paul an' the others…but I c'n only do it once, need you t' tell Eben an' the rest…an' I don't know where in the world t' begin," I struggled.

"Matey, you don't need t' say much," he murmured, big hands on my back drawing me to him in comfort. "Don't you know I've gone out every day an' sat in that boat, an' read the whole story for myself? I've got so I c'n tell Paul's marks from Ephie's, Ephie's from Roan's, Roan's from yours…an' I c'n name every day you caught fish, an' how often it rained, an' when you went hungry. I even know what ordeh they died in…so tell me simply, what happened t' Roan?"

His plain forthrightness strengthening me—and with it, his unnerving vision, almost as if he'd been at my side all along—I began, telling enough of the last days of Roan and Ephie that he would have moments to share with their families; then tensing, I stumbled, "…an' then it was just me an' Paul."

Braced for what was coming, I clutched at his shoulder, as if I could find strength in its burly firmness; and his lips brushing my hair in quiet comfort, he encouraged me, "Say what you can, mate."

"At first things looked hopeful," I attempted, my voice catching with a rasp despite my efforts. "The tension between us...over Damaris...because he loved her, an' blamed me for her coolness... seemed t' have passed, an' the weather was turning milder. But on the 96th day...the seas were very rough...I'd just asked him t' notch the date, when...a rogue wave rose all at once t' starboard..."

As it towered nausea sickened my middle, and I ducked involuntarily against him; felt him clasp me hard, and found I was clutching his shirtsleeve in a desperate wad in my hand. "I screamed t' Paul t' hold onto the seat...then it broke over us, and I held my breath...till my lungs were burning like fire...and when I emerged, he...he was gone...and *you*...you were gone, and I was without you... and everything I'd done t' stave off our separation came crashing on me, an' I was alone."

My breath coming in gasps, I clung still tighter while he crushed me against him, his mouth at my ear: "It'll neveh happen again matey, neveh, neveh...I sweahr it," he repeated again and again, stroking my shoulders and damp hair with his big hands; and gradually growing calmer, I burrowed against him, relaxing my hold on his sleeve by degrees. As my breathing settled to a quieter rhythm, he loosened his clasp enough to face us apart; and taking my chin in his hand, he insisted, "Jamie, I've got t' know this... Look at me... If I'd ordered you not t' get into that boat, would you have stayed behind an' let someone else go?"

In the early light I met his eyes, understanding at once the burden of guilt he'd carried for having had the power to stop me, and failed to use it; and truthfully I shook my head, for I knew myself too well. "I would still have gone," I said wearily, acknowledging once more my pride; then my voice catching I blurted out, "I'd have disobeyed you, if f'r nothing else, than t' prove t' you...I was independent; that I was free of anybody, gadje or Rom... But I swear Ben, if you spoke now, I'd listen... I'd stay."

His hands twining deep in the strands of my hair, he kissed me, then held me close for a long time in silence, though the servants were now delivering hot water for the morning close by, and due to knock on Ben's door after Eliza's.

"I've got t' tell you the rest," I pressed on in the quiet, anxious that we would have to part soon. "Ben, I... I don't know how t' say it...you'll...think I was delirious or sick, after Paul went...but things happened I can't explain. I was so lonely, I made...a companion, out of Ephie's shirt and the oar... He...became hateful, I could see it in his face...and I had t' throw him into the sea... But into his absence, God came... I'd...we'd read most of the Bible, b'fore the wave broke, and I understood... I'd already understood from Jackson, what God's presence felt like...only...she was an old woman, rocking my boat like a cradle... And when it had been days, an' I'd had no water, and I knew I was about finished, I prayed...and a porpoise came... It landed athwart the boat...an' when I couldn't kill it, it died there anyway...an' then I took Paul's knife, and I drank."

Holding me now not just with protective tightness but with something gentle and awed like wonder, he listened; and in a hush I finished, "The next I knew, the brig was there, an' they were lowering away for me...an' the porpoise, it was still there under my hands... So now you'll understand when I say, I want t' be baptized."

Though the breath went out of him for a moment in the completeness of his surprise, he said at once, "Of course, matey, I'll...Jackson is in Pohrtland this month, we c'n see him when we see Jacques...he'd be honored."

"I'm...not any kind of ordinary Christian," I warned, lest he jump to conclusions unfounded; and with a glad, lusty laugh, he answered,

"It's a damn good thing, mate, b'cause I ain't eitheh."

"D'ye think that's going t' be all right with Jackson?"

"I haven't got any doubt about it... Jackson ain't in the business of dealin' with ordinary Christians."

"There's words in the Bible against us bein' t'gether," I reminded him, hesitant.

"There's verses too that permit slaves, an' allow women t' be owned like cattle...but that don't mean our relations should be modeled on theirs. Those rules was made by a society far different from ours, one that didn't understand how people was s'posed t' treat each otheh; an' I neveh did believe they came from God. That's why Christ came, t' give a new law…t' teach love and acceptance, equality an' fairness… It's just taken a while for it t' sink in."

My face beside his, I smiled at his last; then hearing the sounds of retreat in the hallway, and knowing the servants had withdrawn for more water, I took advantage of our reprieve to venture, "Ben?"

He drew a little away from me so he could see me better in the half-light, his eyes smiling on my face.

"After Anjier, why…why did you pull away?"

His brows came together as if he understood the bewildered hurt I tried to keep from my voice; and a sheepish look half of guilt claimed his face. "It was something one of the crew said, that I happened t' hear…askin' in jest for you t' marry him, after gettin' a taste o' one o' youhr pies. I'd guessed, a' course, that you'd…had affairs; but suddenly I…it occurred t' me, that maybe you hadn't gone only with women. I was jealous an' angry an'…more than anything else, had doubts about myself…afraid I wouldn't measure up t' them."

The wind went out of me at the idea that this, the only man I'd craved for three years, could have had such a low estimate of his powers; and I laughed aloud, laughed contentedly against his chest. Then growing more serious I confided, "You pleased me more with your first look at Toby's than all the rest ever did t'gether… I wouldn't cross the street t' see a one of them now…"—I struggled haltingly for the words, which rose with a sudden stab in my chest—"but I'd cross the Pacific…again…t' see you."

Gathering me close to him in his arms, he buried his lips in my tangles of hair, as if waiting for the sweet pain of my words to subside. "Honey," he said then, "I'm just a plain watehdog, an' a broke one at that…but you'll neveh want for *this*," he pledged, giving me a mighty hug. "Now get some rest for me, I bet you ain't slept a wink; the time's comin' soon when I won't have t' leave."

I slept a long, healing sleep, a sleep so long that I never wakened till afternoon, when the sound of John's voice conferring with Ben stirred my slumber—a sleep so healing that, when I finally came to, I found myself more refreshed than at any time in the past year. Sitting up in my bed, and realizing it was past dinner, I listened to the deliberation in the next room, which seemed to be going on while Ben packed; picked out, midst the low, burly tones kept quiet for my sake, the points of John's concern for the upcoming trial, and Ben's bald, understated expectations. Becoming more aware by the minute not just of the financial hazards of Ben's case, but the hurts of business and family desertions likely to assail him in the next few days, I began to formulate a plan; and though I said nothing when they later found me awake, and fetched me enough staples to tide me over till supper, I was ready next morning to carry things through.

Rising early to give myself plenty of time, I tiptoed to my nearby trunk; and going through its contents, I found trowsers and shirt, decent enough for a journey since they'd been recently pressed, no doubt by Eliza in her thorough supervision of my care. My hat, it proved, was nowhere to hand; but I found every other amenity of travel, including a neckerchief and my jacket; and I navigated their arrangements with success, though my hands shook with the maddening requirements of the buttonhook, and I had to sit down more than once for a rest. Standing at last by his door, waiting to catch my breath, I listened to his final preparations, as he latched his trunk and readied himself for the carriage; then giving a soft knock, I stepped in to confront him.

Taking in everything at a glance—my readiness to travel and, no doubt, my determination —he drew in his breath, preparatory to launching a speech; but before he could say a word I insisted, "That sleep put me over the top, Ben; all I need is a couple of dollars for my ticket."

Expecting to see a magnificent display of his best quarterdeck scowl, and hear myself castigated in no uncertain terms for defying Eben's medical orders, I was surprised by the tenderness which softened his expression; was mystified as well till I saw he was looking at my hands, which trembled still with the fatigue of my efforts. Forcing them to be still, I instinctively clenched them, then stuffed them nonchalantly in my pockets; and checking a smile he simply set down his valise, and ushered me gently back to my room.

"Jamie," he said, sitting me down on the bed, "we can't do this yet; y' know we can't; you'hre not rested enough t' leave now."

"I've done the hard part, all you have t' do is get me t' the cars; I c'n sleep till we get to Portland."

The corners of his mouth twitching at the thought of anyone sleeping in the infernal racket of train travel, he responded, "Honey, a drunken seaman couldn't sleep in them cahrs, an' you know it; an' that's just the beginning of the stresses waitin' in Pohrtland."

"The stresses waitin' are waitin' for *you*… I want t' be at your side t' help you," I countered.

"It'll help me most if I know you'hre resting… I c'n bear anyting that happens if I know that you'hre well."

"How can I rest if I know what you're going through, an' I'm not there at the end of the day t' ease you?" I struggled.

"Jamie," he said, taking me by the hand, "you told me just yestehday that if I asked you now t' stay, you'd listen…you'd stay. Am I going t' find out already that when things come t' the test, we'hre going t' fail just like we did out on the Pacific?"

There was tenderness in his eyes, compassion and understanding—but back of their misty greyness, the steely discipline of direction; and caught in my own words, I painfully bowed to the course.

"It won't feel like last time," he went on, seeing me relent; and I knew from his hollow voice he too dreaded separation. "You'll know whehre I am…an' I, you; an' I'll be back in a week—this won't take long, mate."

"I know it," I answered, grasping full well what he meant; and determinedly I squared my jaw, that at least I might send him off with the hardihood of forbearance.

Reading my face he went to his room for a moment, then came back with something in his hand; and giving it to me, he said, "I'll be right hehre with you," clasping my hands about a book. It proved to be his journal, the record of his journey to Wales he'd promised to give me to read; and showing me how to unlock it, he gave me the key for safekeeping. "Journey with me this way," he said hoarsely, tightening my grip around the book; then hearing John's call he kissed me swiftly, hard and deep and rough with need. Feeling my response he quickly picked up his valise—John, appearing at the door, shouldering his small trunk; and without looking back he fled the room, his footsteps echoing in the hall.

In those first dismal days, his journal was my companion; and I turned to it in the beginning with little hope it could sustain me, despite my curiosity about its contents. But so vivid were its words, and so amazing its revelations of him, that soon I was reading it, transfixed; and the room was once again filled with his presence. Now allowed by Eben to sit on the sofa, or even on my balcony of a warm afternoon, I took it with me wherever I went, and read hungrily whenever I was alone: revisiting with him my bitter lodgings on Creek Lane, then re-living his voyage with Walker and his pilgrimage through Wales, as if I too were at his side on the road.

Having never before had any written communication from him more substantial than an occasional scrawl inviting me to meet him for dinner, or damning me for refusing my wages or some other fluke of misbehavior; having never seen any other sample of his adult writing, save the bald, terse entries he made in ship's logs, I was astounded by the majesty and beauty of his words, and the depth of his love and devotion. In his hopelessness at my loss and his homesickness for my past, he had filled his pages with frank confessions, and the artless excitement of a lad first journeying; and even more moving than their confirmation of his feelings were their revelations of his nature, and their testimony to our shared journey, each stop along his way kin to some halt in mine.

So much did I discover about him, especially in the lines he'd penned directly to me, or written the night he'd wakened in Bala to the sensation of me in his arms; so much did I understand about him, not just how keenly he missed me and felt the conviction of our belonging, but how temperamentally like me he was, in the crisis of mutiny or the lure of wanderlust—that I couldn't prevent myself from writing responses, weaving them between his lines like rope yarns. At all hours of the day and night I poured over the pages, his stories intertwining with mine—mingling and yet not mixing with my life, as the springs of Great and Little Day pass unmerged through Bala Lake, or the strands of separate ropes twist unmeshed through a cable; and when I emerged some two or three nights later from my reading, I sat up determined to ready myself for his return, that on his arrival he might find me strong and hearty, a worthy shipmate for his travels.

Looking in the mirror, I assessed the situation; requested a barber, which Jacob readily supplied, sending his own personal valet to my room; and though Eben cautioned me that Ben loved my long locks, not just for their looks but for their testimony to my year's journey, I knew they had to come off at some point, and they did. Giving two or three strands to Eben, I set aside several for Ben; then looking considerably more trim, I ventured into my trunk.

Though much lay in its depths—Ben and Eben having packed not only the practical but the more fashionable as well, such as waistcoats and trowsers suitable for travel—there was nothing formal enough to meet the requirements of the household's night life, since I'd never even owned a suit of clothes; and there was little that reminded me of my Rom past. With Eben's help I began to dress every day, mostly in trowsers and shirts topped off by my blue Cantonese dressing gown; but I longed for the fabrics so typical of Eliza and Claire, and even Stephen, something of a dandy: the satins and poplins, textures and colors which captured the flair of my own people.

As if he understood, Eben one day brought to me a length of cloth—a summery, almost sheer white satin embossed with a design of white stripes; and at once I began to make up a shirt on the festive Rom pattern—full of sleeve, cuffed at wrist, open at collar. Seeing my reaction he bestowed, after his next outing, yards of a textured black sateen, sturdy enough to be made into trowsers; and thinking of a wedding to come, I constructed them on the Rom model, snug at the hips, with stovepipe legs. Last came another length of black satin, interlaced with threads of blue and gold and salmon, as if embroidered with them; and this I made up into a waistcoat, topped off with four or five gold buttons.

When I wasn't sewing or re-reading Ben's journal, I was playing on my boyhood harp—experimenting with long-stowed memories, not just recollections of my past, but of the many men who were me; and I began to release them as I once had for Ben, dressing in my father's costume, or dancing at Jimmy McCabe's on my birthday. Overhearing me late one warm afternoon, Jacob brought me, after some reconnoitering, a larger harp, borrowed from a musician; and gathering around my sofa as I ventured its chords, the entire household begged me to play, requesting familiar songs or improvisations. Delighted with the music, Eliza fetched down from the attic a dusty case, within which dwelt her grandmother's violin; and lifting it out, she laid it on my lap. Having not touched anything finer than a fiddle for years, I was almost too awed to take it; but after tuning it, I found its strings leapt to life; and I played for them upon it as well.

Struck by the romance of a gypsy harpist who happened to have survived a seaman's trials in the bargain—fanning the fancy, perhaps, with the charm of my emerging costume, which she'd chanced to glimpse on occasion—Eliza began to campaign for my performance at a supper dance to be held in her ballroom the night of our anticipated departure, on Friday a couple weeks hence; and she pestered Eben for the postponement of our journey till at least the following morning, that I might play the harp for them, even if I wasn't strong enough to dance.

Though I knew Ben would hate it, as he did all formal occasions, I yearned within for the excuse to play for him—to put on a show that would pleasure him with music, as his words had pleasured me in his journal. Leaving the final decision for him, Eben said neither yea nor nay—how much the old waterdog suspected of my wiles being, as always, a mystery; and letting matters take their course, I sewed and fiddled and counted the days.

By the sixth day or so it was apparent that the trial was going slower than expected, due to the inevitable delays of testimony and depositions; but accounts began to appear in the New York newsheets, since as an Admiralty case it had bearing on all shipping; and we gathered around on the sunny balcony to post ourselves up on events in the papers.

By now I was walking with the aid of a cane that had belonged to Jacob's father—Dr. Windham having looked me over again, and pronounced me fit to try; and since I was still not allowed to use the stairs, an informal dining room had been set up near the ballroom on the other side of the townhouse's third floor, and the balcony there turned into an impromptu gathering room. Exchanging papers in the sun, we followed events as best we could—well enough to see matters were moving as anticipated, with the six simultaneous lawsuits all likely to be settled against Ben's interests, and his career blackened with a judgment of wrongful prosecution of voyage.

Seeing the plaintiffs in print—not just Hull and Lombard, for whom I cared nothing, but family and citizens of Cape Damaris who'd posed as friends and business associates, and who now took advantage of the situation to raid Ben's pockets, or to rate him for decisions made in crisis—I raged for his hurt; and I could scarcely sit still to read. Letting Eben fill in the details for me, I skimmed over all save the riveting account of Ben taking the stand himself, telling off the Admiralty for its lax governance of seamen's lives, and taking on the lot of his plaintiffs for mercenary gain.

Though he never mentioned me by name—John, too, thankfully referring to me only as a "Welsh seaman" in company with Paul, Ephie and Roan—his defense of me and the value of our lives was the center of his contest; and he blasted not only his prosecutors but the whole merchant marine for their failure to put human life first, and insurance mongers for "making money off the possibility of disaster by never leaving the safety of their desks." So compelling were his arguments and the obvious authenticity of his feeling that even staid, stodgy Jacob was moved to respect; and we looked for his return with the anticipation due a merited, if uncredited, hero.

*   *   *   *   *

The first night after the trial, when I'd had the chance to grasp it was finally over—when I'd had the time to register that I'd have to sacrifice not only my half-interests in *Charis* and *Abigail*, as expected, but my house as well, to cover my debts—when I'd set in motion those very acts, in my final conversation with John before parting—I went out onto the porch at Elkanah's to smoke a pipe; and alone at last, I drew in a deep breath of sea air. Standing there, I realized it was raining; and listening to its patter, I suddenly felt strangely light, as if I'd been struck by some buoyant reminder. It wasn't the thought of Jim, for he hadn't been out of my mind for a moment; nor was it the fact I'd be on my way to see him at daybreak, and have him in my arms come this time tomorrow; no, it had something to do with my past.

Breathing in the salt tang, then hearing the bell buoys clang out on the harbor, the rigging clack and bang at the mastheads, or the wagon wheels swish on the wet street cobbles; seeing the greens fade into the greys of dusk, I felt younger—not older from the trial but younger, as if I were twenty instead of thirty; felt I was just starting out for the first time, instead of the second. Deeply stirred, I realized I felt like a youth, first beholding the sweet, earthy rain from my old porch; and as if called by a voice from a long-ago mist, I all at once leapt down the steps with a bound, and began to run in the darkened street.

As I dashed in the rain I turned and danced, with a liberty I hadn't known since I'd been too young to feel awkward; turned and danced with a carefree abandon, while the rain drenched my hair and showered my beard, and played upon my face and shoulders. Making sure to splash in the puddles, I ran till I reached the last house on the street, where a lilac bush in full bloom banked a porch; and there I stopped at last to catch my breath, drawing in the sweet perfume of the bower. As I had with my rosebush a year ago near the harbor, I captured one of the boughs and kissed it, burying my face in the rich scent; then bathed in its jasmine I stood in the arbor, while the rain pattered rhythmically on the eaves, and settled with hushed, steady taps on my shoulders.

By the time I'd reached New York the next day, I was afire to see Jim and discover how he'd been doing; and the press of events weighed even less upon me. Arriving at Jacob's townhouse in the full sun of late afternoon—letting myself in so as not to disturb the servants, and taking the stairs two at a time—I was on my way down to Jim's room on the third floor when one of the maids, with a broad, welcoming smile, nodded me off to the balcony near the ballroom; and heart pounding I slackened my pace, that I might savor my anticipation. As I drew near the supper room I could hear voices—quiet voices of discussion, Jim's amongst them, punctuated once by his ringing laugh; and not knowing quite what to expect, I crept up upon them, hoping to snatch a look at him before anyone caught sight of me.

From my angle in the hallway I could glimpse them sitting in an informal circle, sharing news sheets in the sunshine—the whole lot of them there, including Eliza and Claire, Jacob and Eben; and ignoring all the rest I dwelt lovingly on Jim, as he sat near the rail with a paper propped on his knee. His dark hair cut short, crisp and curling as of old, with a strand or two astray on his forehead—his clothes briskly simple, a white shirt and blue trowsers, with Turkish slippers upon his bare feet—he looked fresh and at ease, almost as hearty as ever; and I drew in my breath at the clear handsomeness of his face, all the more heightened by the thoughtfulness of his expression.

At the catch of my breath he instinctively looked up—the rest of them simultaneously following suit, and jumping to their feet to greet me; and confused by the honor—even Jacob rising from his seat—I realized they must have followed the trial, and stumbled upon my bit of a speech in the papers. My thoughts anxiously on Jim I clapped my hands on his shoulders, to keep him seated and at rest; rubbed my thumb gently on the short hairs at the back of his neck, the only show of affection I dared make; then meeting Jacob's hand and the others' in course, I took the seat offered me a couple places away from Jim, amidst a commotion of questions and scraping chairs.

"Well, Skippeh, that was quite a speech—did it carry the day?" and "What happened t' the boat, did they bring it into the courtroom?" and "What was decided in the end, we're two days behind!" came at my ears from every direction; and trying to sort out demands I gazed obliquely at Jim, who simply met my eyes with solicitous glances. At our first hurried exchange I broke away, flustered; for ripe now with health, his steady regard caused a leap in my throat; and convinced we'd reveal the whole show to the rest, I tried thereafter to keep my eyes off him.

"So what was the bottom line?" Jacob was asking—in his usual abrupt, businesslike manner—once I'd broken news of the decision; and not looking at Jim I said briefly,

"Ninety thousand"—hearing Eliza gasp at the sum.

"Can you get any of it from Melchett Bros.?"

"No; I wouldn't take it if offered," I said firmly.

"Where *are* you going t' get it?" Stephen jumped in, undeterred by the others' censoring glances.

"I already put up *Charis* and *Abigail* for sale," I admitted—again refusing to meet Jim's eyes.

"Will that coveh it?" Stephen pressed, looking from me to Eben for confirmation.

"For the most pahrt," I said vaguely—not wanting anyone but Jim to know about the house till I'd had the chance to prepare Anne.

"I'm good for a loan, y'know; afteh that speech, you d'serve it," Jacob offered.

"Thanks, Jacob," I got out, surprised—in fact, astonished, not at the financial offer, since I knew he had extensive private holdings, but at the unaccustomed business generosity. "I'll have a cleareh idear what's what afteh I get home an' talk again with John."

Though I tried to show with my voice I'd said as much as I intended, a whole host of queries—from what Melchett Bros. thought of me now to whether they'd pack me off on a long voyage to make money—was bandied about, mostly by the irrepressible Stephen; and I would have been exhausted by the effort of fending them off if it hadn't been for Jim: our quick searching glances happening in spite of my best intentions, and buoying me up even as they caused me consternation. When at last the servants rang for supper, I heaved an inward sigh of relief; and I got to my feet faster than anyone else, my thoughts intent on helping Jim. Rising with the rest, he prepared to walk, picking up a cane I now saw by his chair; and immediately I took his free arm, slowing my step to match his.

Not till the servants had cleared the table and Eben had reminded Jim it was time to retire did we have the chance to separate ourselves from the others, me to unpack and Jim to rest in his room; and staying behind only long enough to get a quick report on Jim's health from Eben, I followed him down the hall to our suite, shutting both doors to cut down on intrusions. Though it was too early to lock, I felt a measure of safety; and alone with him at last I stepped into his room, and found him waiting for me out on the balcony. It was the perfect place to be since, when sitting down, no one across the street could see us; and like our perch above Rio it looked out over a vista, the Bowery and forest of masts in the distance, giving us the feel of a private loft.

Entering I found him on the wicker sofa, legs casually crossed, collar open in the warm night; while on the low table before him stood a miniature lamp, the sort lovers use on a chaperoned porch, and a bottle of fine Madeira, already poured into two glasses. Catching sight of the latter and the mischievous gleam in his eye, I immediately chastised,

"James Robehrtson, whehre did you get *that*?"—speaking not without a grin; and looking up with his old roguish air of confession, he handed me my glass as I took a seat by him.

"Nicked it from the pantry off the ballroom—I doubt they'll ever miss it—they have lots," he admitted, picking up his own with a long look of invitation; and wordlessly meeting eyes, we touched rims.

Holding out our glasses for one another—me offering him mine, Jim presenting his—we sipped together, exchanging looks in the flickering lamplight.

"Tell me more about the trial," he prodded, while the warm wind played in the strands of his hair, or stirred at the edges of his collar.

Struck again by how vulnerable short hair made his face look, I managed, "Not much t' add t' what the papehs reported, mate... T' tell you the truth, I could barely keep my mind on it."

Trading grins we confessed our preoccupation, his eyes plainly searching out my week's stresses, and smoothing them away with their glance.

"It all fell out about as I expected," I summed for him, "...though it was a stroke of genius on John's pahrt t' display the quartehboat... Seein' the record of them hundred days in plain carvin' gave the

Admiralty a shot across the bow…an' Percival at least dropped his suit…couldn't press it in the face o' that."

Again we held glasses for one another, taking slow, unhurried sips while the wind breathed about us, and rustled below in the boughs of the trees. In the flickering lamplight his lips, moist with wine, and the curves of his bare throat invited my eyes; and I lingered on the sweet hollow at the base of this throat.

Wandering me in return, his glances drifted, sliding along my face and shoulders; then coming back to my eyes, he said simply, "What do we do now?"

"Wait for *Abigail* an' *Charis* t' sell, an' pay oweh debts."

"Isn't there any way b'sides *Charis*?" he tensed.

"No… my half-interest'll fetch $35,000… I'm sorry, matey."

"It's just…we met there… I…if I hadn't seen her there at the wharf, I'd…probably never have…"

"Jamie, I know it," I murmured, my mind swiftly filling with memories aboard her: the sight of him taking the helm in the tropics, vivid in blue dungarees and a red shirt; the glimpse of him crossing the Line for the first time, festive in the costume of Neptune; the feel of him breaking my cascade in the hurricane, or sobbing in my arms in the sick bay.

"*Abigail*, too…your finest work," he struggled.

"I can't recall a time when one or the otheh of us wasn't suffering aboard her," I returned without regret.

"Except Anjier," he smiled, almost with reverence.

"Except Anjier," I admitted; and now at his long look I saw that this evening we'd been picking up from where we'd left off, that faraway red dawn, and he knew it—saw that at last we were simply courting, enjoying the flirtation of lovers: a time of play we'd never had before, and that I'd certainly never experienced with Anne, our brief courtship looking to me from here about as bald as a business arrangement. Letting go of all save this moment, the flickering lamp on the table, the curve of Jim's hip as he sat, smiling on me with the wind in his collar; jettisoning all save this eve, I became a youth, as I had last night in the rain—a youth adventuring with his first love; and instinctively I touched him, caressing his wrist as I had at Anjier.

Understanding at once he caught my hand to him, his dark blue eyes flashing with wet; and suddenly shy as well he looked down, cheeks flushed. That this man who had enjoyed I still did not know how many lovers could be so abashed by my artless touch moved me with an unspeakable power; and my heart singing in my ears—mingling with the ring of the wine—it was all I could do to keep my mind on our words.

"What about…the balance?" he managed, recovering his poise as he repeated Stephen's question.

"Well, I already directed John t' put up the house for sale as soon as I've had the chance t' talk t' Anne," I told him, watching the stir of the wind in his hair.

"Ben, you…we can't sell *Idris,* or the cottage?" he asked, his gaze catching mine in distress.

"I wouldn't touch eitheh, they b'long t' all three of us, and wouldn't fetch as much as the house in any case. Let me worry about the house, mate… I have an idear Anne won't be sorry about it, she's always wanted t' live in town; an' maybe there'll be a way t' bring that about now. Anyhow, we've got a weddin' t' celebrate first; just give me that, an' I'll be ready t' plan."

As if in a toast we again shared glasses; met each other's eyes over the rims, my gaze searching, his expectant; then reaching out a hand, I touched his lips. Flushing, he looked down, his lashes trembling; flashed an intimate graze on my shoulders, so warmly I could feel his glances; and putting down first my glass, then his, I took his chin in my hand. Leaning over with all the time in the world, I kissed him, so lightly I scarcely brushed his lips; met them softly, again and again, then savored their presses, till generously he gave me his mouth; drew him closer, cradling his shoulders, and felt him yield against me, his unchecked pleasures and sighs rippling through me.

Exploring him as if we had never touched before, as if we had only just now met at Toby's, or on the scented sands of Anjier, I tasted his cheek, danced the curve of his ear; heard the catch of his breath as it echoed my travels, the soft, yielding moans that met my journeys; felt the press of his back hot beneath his shirt as he leaned against the brace of my arms, surrendering the sweet base of his throat.

Into the midst of his sounds and pressing touches came a distant staccato of thumping, an unrecognizable salvo that slowly resolved itself into a nearby knocking; and suddenly realizing with a lurch that someone was at the inner door—that someone, indeed Stephen, was calling our names—we instantaneously sprang apart, Jim with a swift "dinilo" under his breath—busying himself with the wine, though it advertised his theft, and me calling out as naturally as I could, "Come in!"

Oblivious of what he'd just interrupted, Stephen joined us on our balcony; and heart pounding—almost sick at my stomach at the realization that I'd never locked either door, that he might have burst in on us, Stephen who of all people would have shown us no mercy—I offered him a chair. Having come simply to share an idea for a buyer, he sat down nearby us, accepting a glass of the wine we'd so obviously filched; and so grateful to him for having had the courtesy to knock, even if he had stepped into the outer room without asking, and might, in a moment, have stepped into the inner—still sick at what I'd almost done to Jim, to us both in my carelessness, and waiting for my middle to settle—I did not pack him off as swiftly as I might have. When at last he was gone, leaving the door ajar, I made no move to close it; simply looked at Jim—a long look full of anguish, apology, yearning; and his gaze wistful and loving, he offered me a fresh glass.

For a long time we sat drinking, in fact emptied the bottle, not at all sorry to settle our nerves; and far into the evening with its wafts of lilac, its gradually quieting streets down below, we shared what no one could interrupt, the memories of a common journey: recollections of Creek Lane, of dance halls and ribald music, of defended cats, mutiny at sea, and the high roads of Wales, bordered by rolling moors brown with heather. Keeping our voices low, we swapped yarns like old seamen, intertwining stories with one another's; and becoming tipsy—Jim not having drunk in over a year, and me far beyond my allotted limit—we laughed: tipped back our heads at the thought of me dancing with Eben, of Eben trying to bolt from the fat lady at Nell's, of me blowing down Slater over a cat.

Wandering back over my journal, Jim picked up passage after

passage in which I appeared like a ne'er-do-well or a rebel; and coming back at him, I reminded him I'd done little more than walk in his steps, patterning his every move since Wales; reminded him of what a hellion he'd been even that first voyage aboard *Charis*, fighting with his watchmates, disobeying orders. "As a matteh o' fact," I muttered, "have ye *eveh* obeyed ordehs?"; and comfortably listing to starboard by now, leaning back against the sofa with his feet on the table, he smiled, letting me have my fun.

"At least I never led a mutiny," he drawled, thinking back over the pages of my journal. "Over a pig, too. Really, Melchett."

Since I didn't dare trust myself near him at night, I'd already arranged with Eben to switch rooms after the others were in bed; and taking my journal and a fresh cup of coffee, I moved across the hall after Jim had turned in, and read the responses he'd twined with my lines. Throughout the Boston pages there was not a word, as if they called up remembrances too painful to pen; but beginning with the Welsh stage of my journey, he'd mingled many memories with mine, confiding childhood ventures in his strong, graceful script; and sweetest of all was the confession he'd written beside my experience, still haunting and vivid, of waking up with him in my arms in Bala. As if his need for my embrace matched my own need to enfold him, he'd penned simply "Hold me, hold me, hold me"; and the words blurred at once as I read their pleading.

So searing were these words that I threw back the covers and went at once to him, tiptoeing past the gently snoring Eben; stood looking down at him asleep on the bed, one bare arm thrown above his head, the husky swell of his breast tender in the moonlight; and for a long time I lingered on him, dwelling not just on his unguarded beauty, but on the troubling question of where I could hold him, and where in the world a safe berth waited for us.

*   *   *   *   *

The two of them was by now almost driving me crazy; and considering I'd been at Jacob's almost a month, keeping them women at bay in their moonstruck fancy for Jim, and trying to prevent the whole clan—servants included—from overhearing or figuring out the real romance, the job of pushing me over the edge was no hard one. If Claire wasn't pestering me for news about Jim, or even Eliza, at her age—if Eliza wasn't hounding me about that damnable dance, or Stephen and Rowan about Ben's plans—then there was Ben and Jim at the dining room table, eyeing each other with signals plain enough to be read ten miles out to sea, or flirting with their code of gestures, Jim a master at looking out the corner of his eye or giving a comely lift of his shoulder; and I needed all the wits I'd ever developed at sea to keep the whole crew in something like order.

But what was really driving me now to distraction was the complete confusion over when the wedding actually happened—a point not unimportant to me, since I was the one supposed to perform it. Though I knew how different they still was, the gadje skipper and the Rom sailor, in spite of how they'd grown together—though I knew they had volumes yet to talk out, before they was of one mind on even such basics as where they was going to live and work—I was nonetheless floored to discover they didn't even share the same notion about when the wedding begun and ended, or what it was supposed to be like.

Insisting to me, flushing, that the wedding bed came first, and as far as he was concerned, the sooner, the better, Jim found our switching rooms at night to be the last straw; while Ben just as stubbornly held onto the idea that the vows came first, especially since he didn't want there to be any doubt in Jim's mind that he was like other lovers who'd come and gone, out for pleasure without commitment. That Jim had no idea what the Christian vows was like, and had never heard them complicated matters; while Ben, for his part, had no idea about what couples did at Rom weddings, besides jumping the broomstick and exchanging salted bread, the sort of picture you'd get from flash novels.

To try to bring them both to their senses I urged Ben to ask Jim to sketch a Rom wedding, so that we could weave parts important to him into our plans; and taking Jim aside, I showed him the Church of England wedding service, which I was entitled to perform at sea, and encouraged him to read it. To orient him to Ben's wedding night perspective I even shared the story I was sure no one else knew, of how Ben and Tom had gone to some high class Portland brothel, a week or so before their marriages to Anne and Rachel, just to get some schooling, but had given up on the absurdity of the mission and so was chaste as babes when they married. Though Jim'd always suspected that was the case, and guessed Ben'd never had relations with anybody but Anne—though he knew better than anyone Ben's passion for doing things shipshape and in order, and saw how, if he'd taken his vows seriously with Anne, for whom he had so little real feeling, then he'd be sure to put them front and center with Jim—though all of that was bald as an egg to him, he was as determined as ever to have things the Rom way.

Not the sort for many words, he told me plainly he'd prevail in the end—this man, who was still too weak to go up and down stairs without Ben beside him, to catch him if his knees buckled; and though I said nothing in return, I smiled, for I knew who I had my money on.

*   *   *   *   *

It being just two days till the dinner dance, three till our departure, I'd picked up Jim's ring from the goldsmith in the morning; had gone on my mission even before Jim awakened, since he was still sleeping late, as per orders; and I'd kept it a secret through the quiet of the forenoon, drinking coffee with him, and helping him practice the stairs. With the townhouse unaccustomedly silent—with Eliza and Claire out returning calls to all the visitors who'd recently left cards, and Jacob and my cousins all on South Street for business—we were alone on the sunny loft of Jim's balcony, enjoying an unhurried luncheon; and though the doors were open, for propriety's sake, we had as much privacy as we could expect.

Liking the role of bearing a secret, I saved the news of his ring for last; exchanged small talk with him about the dance, watching the wind stir the neckerchief at his collar; then remembering Eben's request, I began to talk to him about the wedding. Knowing little enough about the Rom ceremony, and longing to hear him talk—as he seldom had—about his people, I encouraged, "Tell me what gypsy weddings are like"; and looking up from his plate, he smiled.

"Well, for one thing," he said, sapphire eyes sparkling, "they go on for several days."

"You mean, with dancing and—?"

"Aye."

"Then when I met up with your family and Idris—they weren't about t' have the ceremony?" I asked.

"No," he shook his head; and leaning back against the balcony rail, his hair dark and lustrous against the blue sky, he looked down as if musing on festivities past. "They'd gone through all the initial stages, somewhere along the road, already…and they were just beginning the real celebration."

"What'd happened before I got there?" I pressed.

"The Lees had visited the Roberts an' asked for Idris in marriage, and they'd exchanged a symbolic amount of money… She'd received a gold coin t' wear around her neck, t' show her as engaged, and she and her intended—I assume it was Kusko—had gone into hiding from each other. Then the word'd spread out, all around Wales, for everybody from both clans t' gather; and they came together at Betwys-y-Coed, where we always assemble for weddings and funerals. When you met up with them, they were just getting started—probably building up to the first big feast, and dancing; but there were days yet to come."

"An' what on earth would they do all that time?" I asked blankly.

The wind was so brisk we could almost hear the ring of the rigging at the masts, down the length of the Bowery from South Street; and it whipped up his neckerchief and open collar, the sleeves of his shirt and cuffs of his trowsers as he sat, legs crossed, hips curved in the sun. "Lots of things," he smiled, "mostly symbolic… The groom's family goes in a party t' the bride's tent, an' dyes her hands with henna, t' show her piety…She cries at having t' leave her family, and her past, though it's all an act, of course… Another day, the women of both families take her to a private bath…an' before an' after all this, there's food and dancing. At last the groom's family goes to her tent, or vardo, and takes her t' the one he's made; and that comes at the height of the feasting and dancing. The party goes on till almost dawn; then they disappear into the tent t'gether."

"Then where," I asked, bewildered, "in the midst of all this is the ceremony?"

"The whole thing is the ceremony," he explained patiently, "or maybe you might say the whole thing is the ceremony, but the wedding night is the culmination of it."

"Then what *we* call the ceremony—the exchanging of vows, and rings, and so forth—there isn't anything like that?" I kept on.

"What *you* call a ceremony, we think of as just a validation of the whole event afterward," he said dryly.

"And what is your validation pahrt like?"

"Well," he smiled, his red lips even clearer-cut in the June sun, "sometime the next morning, someone from the groom's family, maybe a brother, goes to the tent, and fetches her *diklo*—her neckerchief, all dappled with blood, an' shows it around, t' prove that she's honest...though for all anyone knows, it's chicken blood; the important thing is the symbol... Then preparations begin for another feast; and one of the elders calls the final gathering t'gether. The bride an' groom exchange salted bread, tokens of their bliss...break a jug, t' symbolize their break from the past...jump a branch of flowering broom, t' show their crossing into the future...and that's it."

Fascinated, I was nonetheless dumbfounded. "No 'till death do us pahrt,' no vows of faithfulness, no—?"

"Not unless the couple is adopting the ceremony of the country they live in—having a civil and not just a tribal celebration. Then they go through the Church of England service, through I've never heard it."

"You mean," it finally dawned on me in amazement, "you've neveh been to what I know of as a wedding?"

"No," he smiled; "have you eveh been t' a Rom one?"

His aping my accent was—as usual—a fairly broad hint of his opinion of me; but caught up in the issue, I kept on its pursuit. "No... though not for lack of tryin'," I said dryly, noting his lips twitched to escape his checked smile. "I just don't see how you c'n embark on a marriage without vows," I struggled.

"The vows are understood… Gypsies are strict about faithfulness, stricter than gadje, so there's little need t' state the obvious…an' the marriage isn't words, anyway; it's action."

"Jim, then…when Eben reads the service oveh us, even if he adds the symbolic pahrts you do at the end…it'll still be just a small piece of all that you'hre used to," I wrestled.

"Aye," he acknowledged, eyes smiling.

"D'ye want t' do things different—with more of the celebrations the Rom have?"

"I… I want us t' be as legally married as we can be, according t' your custom…Yours is the host country, an' if we were man an' woman, we'd be able t' file our marriage after your service, not mine. But…I want t' have some of the Rom parts in with your ceremony, somehow…and"—here he met my eyes with unexpected directness, and a candor that brought a flush to his cheeks—:"I want you t' know that to me, the wedding's already begun, we're already moving through its stages…an' the wedding night's the moment of our true ceremony, not any other."

This was all so new to me that I had to digest it; and standing up to look out over the rail —gazing down on the busy street, with its midday clatter of wharf-bound traffic, and its attending whirl of sea gulls—I stuck my hands absent-mindedly in my pockets, and came upon his ring, almost forgotten in the press of our talk. Seeing my face, he asked alertly, "What is it?"; and smiling, I said, "It'd nearly slipped my mind… B'fore I went t' Pohrtland, I stopped by the goldsmith, an' asked him t' design you a ring…gave him a sketch of what I had in mind…an' this mornin', I picked it up. D'ye…d'ye want t' see it, or do we keep it a secret?" I hesitated, all the familiar rules being uncertain now.

"I want t' see it," he asserted, voice husky.

Reaching into my pocket, I drew it out and laid it in his palm; and as soon as he saw it—a broad golden circle, make up of a great fish swimming nose to tail, a sparkling sapphire for its eye—he knew it was his porpoise; and he broke down without warning as he clutched it in his hand. Wholly caught off guard, I rushed to embrace him; remembered, for a mercy, the open door, and hurried instead to close and lock it; then taking him in my arms I cradled him to me, alternately kissing him and the ring he held to my lips. After a sweet interlude I showed him the inside, where it had been inscribed— "To Jamie, Mande kamro tute," the "I love you" in Romany in case it ever fell into other hands; and I placed it experimentally on his third finger.

"I wanted it t' look like a wedding ring, yet different, so as not t' create any gossip," I told him, satisfied it fit him snugly; "as it is, we'hre goin' t' have t' tell folks I fetched it home from youhr fatheh, along with the harp, as a family heirloom of some kind—othehwise, they'll neveh stop talkin'."

"I know it," he said, reluctantly giving the ring back into my safekeeping with a final, longing look. "Ben, you...we can't afford this," he added, his expression suddenly worried.

"We c'n afford it *now*," I said dryly, "there's still money in the bank; an' I won't have oweh uncertainty oveh finances stahrt us out without doin' things propeh—although...for Christ's sake, Jim, do the Rom even exchange rings?"

Smiling, he shook his head; and in relief from the tension and our sudden emotion, we laughed—laughed as we realized how different we still were, how uninformed about each other, even after three years.

"What *do* the Rom do t' show that they're married?" I asked him.

Still smiling, he touched his neckerchief. "We knot our diklos in a marriage knot."

"Show me."

Untying his neckerchief, he demonstrated the new knot proudly; and taking a hand, I again untied it, and endeavored to imitate him— the wind blowing our hair and the tails of his scarf as we practiced our new privilege solemnly in the sun.

"Will I be a gypsy when I marry a gypsy?" I asked then, as he restored his neckerchief to its old knot.

With a pleased grin at the question, he shook his head. "No; you'll be a *prala*, a brother... Even my grandfather never was more than that, though he married a Rom woman."

"Tell me about him," I urged, for I'd only heard him allude once to his English forefather, the source of his blue eyes and the only slice of his heritage which wasn't Rom.

Wearying now of the conversation—tired, as always, by the direct exchange of questions and answers, and worn out as well by emotion—he nestled his head on the pillow of my lap, for since I'd shown him his ring, we'd been sitting on the balcony rug; and making himself comfortable, he spun yarns about James Robertson the elder—the father of his father, John Roberts, and of Idris' father Arturo, and apparently of numerous others. Though I longed to hear the story in order, I let him unravel events his way; and he wandered in circles as he was wont to do when left to his own devices—his recollections springing up now in England, now in Wales, now in early boyhood, now toward the end of his tenure with the Rom.

Through his eyes I saw Taw as a young woman; learned that her name was Tereina; appreciated that there were other marriages, besides ours, which had aroused controversy and dissension, but which had withstood the trial of differences; and feeling close to this unknown man, long dead—looking down on the striking face of his namesake, on the clear, dark blue eyes and fine, strong features inherited from a marriage which had endured the tests of culture and race—I kissed Jim.

Gladly ending all the talk, he yielded at once; and taking advantage of the locked door, I tasted freely, till at last I warned him we needed to be on the lookout, and regretfully prepared to open his room. "From now on till July especially, while you'hre still a minoh, we have t' be careful as hell," I reminded him; and looking up into my eyes, he searched my face, brow puckered.

"Why does it matter so much that I'm a minor?" he asked me, lips still moist and red from our kisses.

Understanding all at once that he knew nothing of civil law—that even if, in the morass of his life in Boston, he'd appreciated the risks of his standing in the Commonwealth of Massachusetts, he certainly knew nothing of our perils in the State of Maine—I grinned. "B'cause afteh you come of age in July, I c'n only get ten yeahrs in the state pen in Thomaston for havin' relations with you as a consentin' adult, instead o' the twenty I'd get if we was caught now," I said dryly; and directly I saw, from the alarm which sprang into his eyes, that he was overtaken with fear. The old anxiety of separation at sea strong on his face—the old memory, too, of his own culture's penalty, a lifetime of banishment—he immediately got up, and took his seat on the sofa; and though I did my best to reassure him as I unlocked the door, he kept his distance for the rest of the day, a model of propriety and restraint.

*   *   *   *   *

Still alarmed by his words even as late in the day as supper, which at Eliza's was likely to be half-nine or ten—revisited in mind again and again by the image of the prison in Thomaston, which I'd driven past many times, since it was situated on the post road—picturing Ben within, down at the cellar level, where the long-termers were locked except for their brief exercise in daylight—I felt ill; felt sicker by far at this penalty than at my own exile, which at least had left me free to roam; and it was all I could do to navigate my meal.

When I wasn't anxiety-ridden about Ben and the perils that would never really leave us, I was thinking of my ring—awed not just at its beauty but at Ben's clarity in capturing, from all that had happened, the one gift that had made it possible for me to be here, my porpoise; and between the two, the prison and my ring, I was on a seesaw of emotion. It didn't help that most of the talk round the table was about the dance the day after tomorrow—the seating of the orchestra, the advance baking for dinner, and the expectations of all hands for my performance at the harp; for I kept picking up the turmoil and excitement of the whole household; and that contributed as well to the churning of my stomach.

But the final upheaval came when—in the midst of Eliza's elaborate visions for waltzing music and tempting dishes, hothouse plants and hanging lanterns—I suddenly realized the import of all the feasting and dancing; for I saw all at once it was not *their* celebration, but Ben's and mine; and abruptly leaving the room I sought the balcony nearby, where I could get some cool evening air on my forehead. Looking down on the courtyard, shielded by trees and screens of jasmine from the ballroom windows across the way, I felt my nausea not lessen, but worsen; and assailed, I leaned over the balcony rail. As I recovered I found Eben beside me, Eben whom I could permit to see me this way, since he was my doctor; and doubly relieved for his help I allowed him to care for me, then walk me gently back to my room.

By night I was resting comfortably against my pillows, the arc of golden light from my yellow-globed lampshade surrounding me like a warm embrace, as I sat, propped up, with a book on my lap. Calmed by the aromas of night, sea and whale oil, the latter competing with lavender-scented candles, I stared unseeing at my page, dreaming back on the interludes of the last several days; though whenever I thought of the dance to come, there came the familiar lurch of my heart. Too restless to sleep, I searched for something to read that would hold my attention; then remembering the Church of England service that Eben had urged me to look at before the wedding, I pulled out the Book of Common Prayer he had lent me, and turned with curiosity to the earmarked pages.

As soon as I commenced them the majesty of the words carried me back to the streets of Bala—to wintry mornings outside stained glass windows, where the solemn roll of Welsh hymns echoed down stony walls; while the weighty might of the vows, with their unswerving commitment, stung me with a humble awe. As I read them, these vows, they brought home to me more forcefully than ever our differences, Ben's and mine: his disciplined faithfulness, even through a decade of marriage with an unsuited partner like Anne, and my own betrayals by contrast, traitorous from the start with Lomond. How could he trust me to speak these words to him in the face of my perfidy in the past? I wondered, shamed by the prospect of his clear eyes before me; how could I have failed to know the importance of pledging them to him myself? So moved was I that I whispered them to him, practicing my parts in the still of the room; and far into the night I was vesting with power what I knew to be in my heart.

*   *   *   *   *

The day of the dance brought bedlam right from the start, in spite of my best efforts to create something approaching order in the midst of it; commenced not unlike the departure day of a newly-launched vessel, with a green crew and a mob of news agents all tripping over lines strewn about the deck. While I was manfully packing together my trunk, with a view to getting it out the door by mid-morning and onto a Cape-Damaris-bound schooner by noon; while Eben, even more eager to clear out than I was, was already sitting on top of his chest, energetically strapping it shut; while we'd both set aside small valises for the Portland journey tomorrow, and laid out our evening clothes, borrowed from friends of the ever-resourceful Jacob, the rest of the household was coming apart at the seams; and the two of us met frequently in the hall, commiserating.

Orchestra pieces coming up the dumbwaiter—now a French horn, now a base violin—then marching around the corner to the ballroom; potted plants and carved ice ditto—ferns, swans, sailing ships all parading after the horns; streams of deliverymen pouring up the stairs to command them, ordering them this way and that into the ballroom—all added their notes to the rising crescendo; and no embarkation could have topped the confusion. If I'd thought, with their end, there might be some semblance of peace, I was brought up short by the facts; for next came the cargo of eatables for dinner, up from the first floor kitchen and servant's quarters—cakes, pastries, sherries and wines, everything which could be prepared ahead, now herded along to the butler's pantry off the ballroom; while the clanking and clanging of cutlery and silver rattled our ears all the way down the hall in our corner.

And where was Jim in the midst of all this?—holding forth in the middle of his room, not an article packed in his open trunk, and the chaos around him what might be expected after his being a month in residence anywhere: his accumulated belongings scattered hither and yon, atop sofas, chairs, bed, everywhere but the floor, which the servants had determinedly kept clear. The first time I looked in on him, he was still in his bare feet, dressed in nothing more than drawers and a white overshirt, wandering aimlessly about drinking tea; and he looked so distractingly fetching, what with the guess of bare curves beneath filmy cambric, that I couldn't stay around longer than to remind him about his trunk.

The second time I set out to hound him, I'd had the chance to discover, laid out on my bed in my absence, a pair of silk hose from Eliza—she apparently having had doubts about the likelihood of my possessing anything finer than cotton, and fearing to risk the appearance of a guest in such; and I detoured into Eben's room long enough to make sure he'd received the same treatment, which he had—the silk hose being hard enough to take, but the garters to hold them up, the last straw

"What about oweh drawehrs—d'ye think she'll check those, an' should we be tradin' in oweh linen for silk?" he drawled.

"I doubt linen'll do—mine ain't even trimmed; but I c'n tell you, Jim's're embroidered in hamburg, as I've just seen for myself; so maybe he'll carry the day for all three of us," I said dryly.

Looking in on him together, we found Eliza'd bypassed him, at least with respect to the hose, as I'd anticipated when I entered the room; for despite his limited means, she knew he could dress, and trusted him to put on a show. What she had given him, as a parting gift from the family, and no doubt with some conniving from Eben, was hanging before us in his wardrobe: a new grey-blue sack suit, lightweight for summer, the first complete suit of clothes he'd ever owned; and he was admiring it and thanking her, dressed now in trowsers and Turkish slippers; and predictably, my entreaty to pack fell on deaf ears.

By my third visit the weather had become oppressive, the grandfather of all thunderstorms breaking as I entered his room; and what with the crashing of thunder, Eliza's frantic crying from down the hall about the ice, even now being unloaded from the delivery wagon, and the commotion of traffic in the street below, I could barely make myself heard with a holler. "We'hre leavin' first thing in the mornin', you know, an' there's a cahrt in the roahd waitin' for youhr trunk right now," I shouted at him; and yelling back at me to be heard above the storm—a hectic glimmer in his eyes and on his cheeks, and his hand waving indulgently at the disarray—he aped my accent, "A cot in the rod, you say?"

Eyeing him in exasperation—perceiving he was as gone to the excitement as all the rest—I despairingly cocked my hands to my hips; and since I couldn't take revenge by aping *his* accent—the trilled r's beyond me, the soft v's impossible to get a grip on, and my teeth in the way of his French t's and d's—I threatened instead, "James Robehrtson, I sweahr t' Gawd, if you don't get that trunk packed, I'll give you a lickin'!"

"Promise?" he grinned invitingly over one shoulder, as he set off down the hall to help Eliza; and sitting nearby, Eben dissolved into laughter.

"Melchett, you've got youhr work cut out for you," he drawled, looking after Jim's departing swagger; and immediately I groaned in answer, for I knew he wasn't referring to merely the trunk.

The fourth time I marched in on him he was gone altogether, off to the ballroom to help Eliza and Claire with decisions about plant screens and seating, since Jacob, Rowan and Stephen had all gone on 'Change at seven in the morning, and were due to spend the rest of the day in the counting house on South Street: a plan of action I'd certainly have been keeping, if I'd been a member of the household. Standing there watching Jim from the doorway, I could see him nodding heads not just with Claire and Eliza, but one or two of the maids and the butler, and some harried individual who looked to be a deliveryman; and trying to catch Jim's eye—gesturing futilely to get his attention, and succeeding only in thrashing blank air—I lapsed into an impatient vigil.

Waiting for a break in the conversation, I was suddenly struck by how theatrical he looked, straight and tall in his full-cut shirt, his dark hair glossy in the light of the chandelier, and his features animated with feeling; saw all at once how his trowsers, flowing from their snug fit at his hips, seemed as much a dancer's as a sailor's; and I was carried back to Betyws-y-Coed, to the springtime encampment of Roberts and Lees, and the concert of men in their stovepipe pantaloons, strolling about in preparation for Idris' wedding.

There had been about them, as there was about Jim, a sensuality which eclipsed anything I'd seen on this side of the water, a manliness somehow both Rom and European; and I dwelt on him with unself-conscious admiration, my impatience temporarily tamed by my awe. As if all at once feeling my eyes upon him, he turned abruptly and caught me looking at him, his eyes colliding with mine in a quick flash; and feeling my cheeks color I turned hastily away, and hiked back to his room to tackle the inevitable.

*   *   *   *   *

That there was plenty more brewing besides the weather was plain as a fog bank to me; and you could feel it in the air at our noon meal, as if a squall was gathering indoors. Though to all appearances we was simply a calm group, munching on seafood salad and listening to Eliza give marching orders, the mood was as sticky and damp as the napkins clinging to our elbows; and there was that looming sensation you get in the lull before a big blow. When Jim's eyes wasn't loaded with some festive secret—his long exchanges with Ben full of promise and meaning, and signals I feared to God all could read—then Claire was making a fresh play for Jim, about as discreetly as a thunderclap; and since she had no earthly reason to bait him—since he was nowheres near her class, and it wasn't likely she'd ever see him again, much less land a proposal—her angling smacked of coy sport and conquest.

If he hadn't been such a handsome devil, so appealing as a gypsy sailor, she would never of taken up the hunt; but since he was the household celebrity she could indulge in his looks, and use him to lord it over her friends—taking his good spirits, no doubt, as evidence of his fondness for her. Eliza, I suspected, was the one that secretly cared about him, and had even less chance to show it, or expect any token of attention in return; and sharp as Jim was, I wasn't sure he'd even noticed, what with his preoccupation with Ben.

To head off some of the impending disasters I'd let it be known we'd be turning in at midnight, before the supper and the german after; and though it wasn't necessary, since they could all see he still labored at the stairs, I ruled out dancing as well. Hobnobbing with the guests—no less than the Crowninshields and Astors, ilk I knew Ben would rather of died than talk to, especially after the trial last week—and playing the harp or the violin was as much as they had any reason to expect of Jim; but even so I could already sense Claire was plotting some staircase flirtation, and Ben, God only knows what in the closed dim of the pantry.

If the backstairs romances wasn't looming large enough, there was the lowering gloom of Ben's shipping orders, still secret to everybody but me and Ben: Melchett Bros. having sprung on him, in the aftermath of the trial, that he'd been posted for the August run to the East Indies. Though the yard was keeping the news close for business reasons, it was almost sure to surface tonight, in that pack of merchants and shipwrights and skippers; and once Stephen caught wind of it, even if Jim didn't, it'd round the hall from chandelier to chandelier. Already worried about the effect of the orders on Ben— since he almost had to perform, after last year's failures, or risk losing his career altogether—I was even more on edge about the impact on Jim; and I didn't want to see it come up tonight, so close to the stresses of Portland and home.

What Ben planned to do about the job in the end, I was even less sure than him, since he'd pushed any future decision onto the back burner till after the wedding; but I guessed he imagined Jim'd make the trek with him, as steward since his strength wasn't up to a mate's berth, and they'd deal with their need for privacy somehow. But Jim had the face of a man who's all done with the sea, and if Ben couldn't see it, I could—having read that look plain on many a sailor even younger, all used up by the extremities he'd faced; and what it would come to when they locked horns on that one, I couldn't imagine. Pressed down by such worries, and others like in the offing, I was relieved when Eliza stood up, allowing us to clear the table; and it was with no small joy I seen Jim off to rest, and the others break up in different directions.

*   *   *   *   *

Back in my room I took out my costume, too nervous to rest or take afternoon tea; set out black sateen trowsers, cut like my father's, white satin shirt and black brocade waistcoat with embroidered blue, gold and salmon; then laid beside them black pumps and silk stockings, and the gold neckerchief Eben'd bought at a Turkish mart, with a pride in my past I hadn't felt since I'd been sent away. As I touched them with a new owner's wonder, I seemed to re-claim not just days gone but my family, long locked in my mind till Ben released them; began to feel them materialize beside me, as if spun from the fabric of their customs: my father, whose hands could tapestry the strings of a harp; Taw, bent frame swathed in skirts of yellow and red; Idris, black eyes framed by a figured scarf; Djemail, jacketed in blue and gold as he rode; and mother, gathering last, scarcely more than a guess of perfume wafting from her red cloak.

Sweepingly homesick—with the swift yearning which Ben'd set off with his visit, or accounts from afar of rattling carts on a hill's brow—I all at once realized they should be here, to see me dress and send me off into marriage; wished for them fiercely, even knowing they'd condemn me, as they had once before for my choice; and keenly lonely, not wanting to dress without fanfare, I gently knocked on Eben's door, and quaveringly asked for his help. As soon as he saw my face he understood—his plain looks lighting up with fellow feeling, and his earthy eyes with wordless knowing, as if my expression had lighted a lamp in his mind; and stepping in at once this kindly man, who'd from the start been my brother, father and friend, began to help rig me in festive fashion, even slipping out at one point to filch us a glass of wine, and toasting me for all the world like a bride.

Touching rims, we laughed, looking back over the years, to times when I'd been a step ahead of Ben, and to times—rare so far—when Ben'd outstripped me; and the long trick nearly over, I shrugged off old hurts, even the anguish of separation at sea. Down below carriages were clattering up to the curb, full of early arrivals— probably women friends of Claire's and Eliza's, come to help them receive; and while servants numbered their vehicles with cards and escorted them into the townhouse, Claire and Eliza emerged from the water closet, which the men folk'd turned over to them—the laughter from the street and the hall making my own dressing all the more festive.

Putting on my neckerchief last, I tied it in its bachelor's knot—I dared hope for the last time; accepted Eben's final ministrations, including a touch of cologne at the tails of my scarf, and a hasty benediction, "Watch out for the champagne." Then adjourning to his chamber, I helped him in turn, buttoning and fastening cuff studs and cravat, in preparation for the moment when the bell would ring out, and we'd step out, arm in arm, in the hall.

∗　∗　∗　∗　∗

Alone in my room—in the confounded heat—I wrestled with all the infernal stages of formal evening dress: the black broadcloth trowsers, far too hot for summer, the product of no rational mind; the silk hose—which I donned after much debate, and an irresistible impulse to box Eliza's ears—held up by the nuisance of garters; the patent leathers tight, no kin to the informal thump of sea boots; the shirt front a challenge, fastened by no less than three studs; the collar an invention of the devil, stiff as a board, not easy to adjust with the white tie; and the white vest and black coat, tails and all, adding twenty degrees to the heat.

Wishing I had a cane to lean on, if for no other reason than to keep my hands busy—looking down at their ungainly size, always apparent when they had no task to perform—I remembered with an inward groan the gloves, pearl grey and, of course, buttoned; and I put in another half hour tugging them on, and fastening them with a button hook—no small feat with one hand already gloved.

Ready at last—reminding myself, to keep my sanity, that twelve hours hence I'd be on my way out of town with Jim—I cast a last-minute glance at the mirror, with an eye to making sure I looked not as idiotic as I felt; then I stopped, brought up short, and gazed again in disbelief; for this man, this reflection—this captainly shipwright—was I he?

Dead in my tracks, I turned up the gas; stood back from the

dresser for a more critical survey; and my inspection confirmed, I gaped at the mirror. From out of the past came the recollection of the figurehead Jim had made for my birthday, our first year together—the carving of me that still hung over the fireplace mantel in our room at the cottage; for the image I now saw recalled its likeness; and I felt the same disbelief I had then, when Jim'd assured me of its accuracy. Too awed then to claim it, I'd put it down as the product of his creativity—a combination of artistic liberty and craftsman's bias; for though the features were mine, the noble demeanor—the strength of mind and air of refinement, the clarity of purpose and vision—were those of a far loftier man; and I couldn't begin to own them as mine.

But now I realized we'd become one, I and this figurehead that never went to sea; recognized that I had somehow caught up with what Jim had two years ago perceived; and curious, awestruck, I peered into the mirror, trying to grasp what had happened. Aye, that was my hair, hard as ever to tame with a brush, bleached out by the sun and now touched with grey; my same broad mug, permanently weathered, albeit with beard unusually well-trimmed; and the eyes looking out were familiarly mine—the eyes most definitely of a man in love, barely able to keep his mind on his business.

But infusing the lot and informing it all were the authority and bearing of a master, the mind of a shipwright and aim of a voyager, and something more I couldn't name; and I caught my breath at what I had become. No awkward mariner, nor failed merchantman, this man looked august—the equal of any Crowninshield or Astor, trial and loss of livelihood notwithstanding; looked comely, in a rugged, manly way; looked like a lover on his way to a ball, or a groom on his way to—

Then with a shock I knew what I was; knew what had eluded me a moment ago; and more dumbstruck than ever—remembering the hopelessly ill-prepared youth, barely come of age, who'd waited, flustered, at the foot of the stairs for Anne, nigh onto a decade ago—I bowed, lips parted, at the mirror; and plucking a small white rose from the bouquet on my table, I tucked it into my lapel, and squaring my shoulders, stepped into the hall.

By chance we all came out of our rooms together—Stephen and Rowan just down the way, Jacob next door to them and Jim and Eben, arm in arm, across from me; and thank God that we did, for as soon as our eyes collided, Jim's and mine, we both knew—knew as plainly as if we'd met to walk down the aisle; and the presence of the others helped censor our abashed awe. As shy of each other as if we'd just been introduced, we snatched nervous side-glances as we walked—me scarcely daring look at him after that first hasty encounter, so striking was he in the artful flair of a Rom costume; while as soon as he saw me, his eyes flashing the confirmation of what I'd seen in the mirror, his gaze fled, and returned for only quick peeks at my appearance, like the forays of a darting sparrow.

For a mercy we did not have to speak to each other, besides our brief exchange of greetings—Stephen and Rowan at once monopolizing the conversation with inquiries about Jim's garb; and my throat too tight for a word of my own—Jim's jaw set against his emotion, as he manfully tried to answer questions—we soon found ourselves in the midst of the ballroom, where Eliza and Claire were already beginning to receive, and guests were flowing in through the doorways. Taking up his post near the refreshments, Jacob made himself available for the courtesies of newcomers; while Stephen and Rowan plunged into the crowd, introducing Jim as they went—my heart yearning for him as guests closed between us, and foisted their attentions on me.

From time to time I could glimpse him shaking hands across the grand room, his poise seemingly rattled by neither the fine names nor the elegant fashions that assaulted him; and though he was always so surrounded I could only catch glances—dancing figures in low-cut dresses, erupting foliage and oriental screens frequently barring the space between us—I could see he was obeying Eben's instructions, neither dancing nor staying on his feet long, groups simply sitting down with him when he needed to rest. With his dark, brilliant looks and the exotic allure of his costume—the black and white as formal as any evening wear, yet flowing with the aura or romance—he was easily the most fetching man in the room; and I was aware of the magnetic feel of his presence, even when I couldn't see him.

Sometimes as I made the rounds I found him beside me—knew, by some growing warmth or attraction, that he was near, even before my eyes found him; and we stood shoulder to shoulder, arms brushing, as we reached out to greet others. Responding to their queries, making light of his experiences, tactfully refusing to be drawn out on occasion, he deftly managed to remember names and professions, and the names and relationships of family members as well; and the object of sympathetic attention from the older matrons, and of the romantic regard of their daughters, he navigated those pitfalls as well. Protesting his health when they angled for dances, sidestepping overtures that were coquettish, he was usually out of their sight—and mine—before he could be nailed down; but he would resurface at unexpected moments, sometimes nearby me; and I made up my mind to have him alone, even if only for a moment.

Testing a glass of Jacob's punch—not as dangerous as the champagne, but in every way a credit to Melchett anti-temperance tradition—I felt fortified from within; and ladling a fresh cup for him, I dodged the intervening sashes and fans, and snatched a rare instant when he was alone. Touching him on the arm—feeling his sudden start—I got his undivided attention; and the company swirling unnoticed around us, we at last took a long look at each other, as I offered him the sweating glass.

"Ben, I don't know as I should," he protested, as disconcerted by me as I was by him; and delighted at his flurry—taking in every detail of him close-up, including the flash of discomfited blue eyes—I couldn't resist a challenge.

"Come on, mate—down the hatch," I invited; and our fingers touched as I gave him his glass.

"You know I ain't drunk a thing this past year except that bit o' wine the other night—what's in this?" he asked, suspiciously cautious.

"Somethin' bully enough t' make you let down youhr guahrd," I grinned, taking an appreciative sip of my own cup.

"That's what I'm afraid of," he said dryly; but he accepted the glass, looking over the rim at me, and measuring me with his eyes;

and we drank silently together, taking in quiet snatches of one another, till Claire swept up to claim his attention, and tugged him off for another introduction.

*   *   *   *   *

Unaccustomed now to strong drink, I felt the effects at once, the warm glow of the liquor magnifying the heat of my heart, and sharpening my sensitivity to the sights and sounds all around, even as it began to dull my defenses. It was a sweet night, though still hot—the humidity making curls cling to damp foreheads, and bringing out the headiness of perfumes; and the tall, arched ballroom windows were wide open to the breeze, which stirred the heavy brocade of the curtains.

Rejoicing that Ben finally understood the evening—knowing that somewhere in the ballroom he celebrated in silent communion—I moved about, shaking hands and nodding; and I could feel his eyes from afar as I wandered, flickering on my face and shoulders. Knowing that he was watching me—deliberately turning my back at times, so I could feel his glance behind me, whenever there was a break in the crowd—I accepted his gaze as a cat absorbs warmth, sunning itself in the lee of a porch; and occasionally, to up the ante, I answered stare for stare—meeting his gaze with such open meaning that overcome, he broke away.

Watching him in return, I was so struck by his bearing that I could seldom keep my eyes on him for long; and I frequently broke away myself, actually glad at times for interruptions. Readily the tallest and most commanding figure in the room—though he didn't know it, his disinterest in himself and his unawareness serving to make him all the more striking—he moved from group to group with far more engagement than he had shown at *Abigail's* launch ball, when he'd given up on conversation and simply hauled out the charts; and occasionally he even danced, choosing partners who were predictable and safe.

Though he never attempted anything more difficult than the waltzes, he danced those well, making an eye-catching picture with his cousin Claire—her small, fair form, dressed in layers of light blue, dwarfed by his broad-shouldered, dark-clad frame, not unlike a forget-me-not by the bulk of a rock; and I longed to dance with him myself—yearned so fiercely to feel him lead me, to find out how we'd match in rhythm, that I had to seek the semi-privacy of the windows to cool my face in the open night air, and focus my thoughts on the vagaries of the city.

∗   ∗   ∗   ∗   ∗

Fueled by the desire to provoke him further, I couldn't resist the opportunity to meet up with him again, this time by the refreshment table, where I'd stepped up to replenish my glass, he to fetch squares of cake for some ladies; and as I gave him an inviting nod at the punch bowl, he emphatically shook his head, answering,

"Ben… one more, an' you know what'll happen."

Eyes tempting, I offered him a sip from my own glass instead; and again, he shook his head.

"Not from the same glass," he reminded gently; and dumbfounded, I gaped at him.

"F'r Christ's sake, Jamie—y'mean we can't drink out o' the same cup—even *married?*"

"A' course not," he returned, as though I ought to know as much after all these years of association with him, and an actual visit to a Rom camp to boot.

"Why in thunderation not?"

"It's not proper."

"It ain't propeh!" I exploded with laughter—several heads turning to look at us in my outburst; and lowering my voice in an attempt to suppress mirth, I teased him, "An' I s'pose it's propeh for two men t' marry?"

"I've got no control over that," he said dryly. "I can't choose not t' be in love with you. But I c'n choose what t' do about the cup—an' I'm telling you, we're supposed t' drink together only once, when we actually jump the broomstick."

"Well, damned if we didn't drink from the same cup just the

otheh night!" I reminded.

"We did?" he gaped, fumbling back through the mist of the punch.

"Aye, on youhr balcony, when we shared the wine."

As if cascaded by the memories of touches and kisses, he flushed, "Well, you made me forget."

Heedless of others, I exploded again into laughter, the glad, frank guffaw of a man in love. "An' damned if I can't do it again," I challenged, as once more I offered him my glass; and giving me a long, thoughtful stare—a look that was at once a return dare, and a warning—he accepted a swallow, letting his fingers slide over my hand so that he caressed each separate knuckle, before leaving me with a backward look over his shoulder.

*　*　*　*　*

Trying to attend to the many who met me—endeavoring to catch, in the flurry of my nerves, not just their names and occupations, but some semblance of what they were actually saying—I netted an earful of gossip and news: sometimes overhearing speculation about Ben's trial, or questions about his judgment on the Pacific, even as merchantmen introducing themselves coquetted me about *Abigail* and her sale price. Realizing that some were angling to buy her— knowing that Ben wanted her to say in Maine hands, to lessen the chance her speed would eventually turn her into a slaver, or land her in the opium trade—I offered nothing in the way of information, referring them all directly to Ben himself; and my protectiveness increased as the evening passed, along with my suspicions as to their motives in meeting me.

But it was when I met Charles Snow, a junior partner in the shipping house managed by the Crowninshields, that I stumbled on the real news of the evening; and caught all unawares, I almost backed into the fern bank.

"So—will you be heading back t' sea with Ben when he ships out t' the East Indies in August?" he asked me, by way of making conversation.

As taken aback as a brig in a squall, yet determined to reveal nothing of my reaction, I got out truthfully enough, "I haven't really thought much about it"—managing to keep my face blank from long practice; but within me my thoughts were racing in turmoil, as I struggled to absorb the news without losing the thread of conversation. Only seven weeks away, the voyage loomed like an unlooked-for cloud over the moon; and knowing that I had neither the strength nor the heart for it—overcome that Ben hadn't told me—I craved the chance to be alone with him, so that we could talk about it.

"How about the cargo this time—light enough t' permit a fast run?" Snow was asking, again as though making idle chat; and realizing he was fishing for information Melchett Bros. was probably trying to keep under the hat, I rose again to Ben's defense.

"We haven't had the time t' talk much about it, Eliza's kept us so busy," I answered as graciously as I could; and doubly on guard now, lest anyone gain from me a chance word that might hurt him, I actually began to seek out the ladies—preferring their coquettish games, when all was said and done, to the hard-nosed panderings of business.

Still trying to digest Snow's news as I wandered, surrounded now by a maze of chaperones and charges, I avoided Ben for all I was worth; but he caught up with me as I stood unattended a moment, and offered me a fresh glass of punch. Having accepted one from someone else in the meantime, and recognizing my lowering guard—more determined than ever to keep up my wits, not just to prevent some indiscretion with him, but to forestall any play to compromise Melchett Bros.—I refused; but he insisted, holding out the glass with a grin, and searching my eyes as if already alert to my disquiet.

Trying to hide my answering smile—keeping my voice lower than the violins, and the rushes of conversation around us—I murmured, "Ben, if I do, I'll...I'll make a pass at you... I won't be responsible for what I'm doin.'"

Still holding out my glass, he assured me, "*I'll* be responsible... now, drink it."

Throwing back my head at once in laughter, I countered, "Melchett, you know you've drunk twice as much as me… You couldn't be responsible for a cat."

"Don't matteh," he said blithely, like a groom on a fine night; "I c'n carry a drink better'n you… always could."

Meeting his gaze with a mix of doubt and affection, I accepted the glass in silent contest, my fingers this time frankly caressing his wrist where the cuff had fallen back; and he at once responded in kind, sliding his hand along my arm to my elbow, and holding it there as I drank. This time it was Eben who interrupted us, joining us with a cup of his own; and definitely light-headed now—feeling engulfed by the waves of violin music, the gusts of my nerves and the gushes of conversation—I took refuge in him: Ben regretfully withdrawing his fingers, which dallied on the sheer cloth of my sleeve.

*   *   *   *   *

For a while I watched Jim again from afar—watched him mingling with the guests, or finagling to bypass the dancers, an easy man to spot in his costume, and his warmth a sure draw for my compass. Feeling my gaze he caught sight of me once as he paused at the refreshment table—my eyes falling at the same time on the cup in his hand, testimony to the allure of the punch bowl; and throwing back my head, I laughed freely. This time it was he who—with a roguish, daring grin—offered his glass, and me who unhesitatingly responded—finishing the drink, then fetching us both dainties from the table; and we munched on pastries together in silence, exchanging glances, but saying nothing. At length I suggested, "Let's get a breath of air—how about it?" and nodding, he leaned toward me in answer—covertly slipped a hand past my open jacket and rested it for a fleeting moment on my thigh; then turning away with a suggestive half-smile, he headed for the balcony nearby—leaving me suddenly speechless in his wake, to follow when I gathered my senses.

On the balcony we looked out on the city—me slipping an

arm about Jim's shoulders as I came up to stand beside him, and the two of us hushed in the hot, breezy darkness. Though the long, narrow space was comparatively crowded—couples and groups having sought it for relief from the heat, or for a chance at a private flirtation—there was a circle of quiet about us; and I turned to him and gazed at his profile.

Strong and clear in the lantern-lit night—flushed with the hue of the rose-colored lamps, hung above the balcony on strings, and touched with the damp of the heat and his fervor—his face was a mix of eager restraint; and his shoulders revealed the same inner tension, as if braced against a wind he yet craved. In the sweet, stirring air I felt my head clear a little; felt the warmth of his back through his waistcoat; saw he was just reaching round with his own hand to touch mine, when again we were interrupted. Now it was Stephen and Rowan who approached us boisterously, wending their way through the crowded ranks on the balcony; and hearing their coming before we saw them, we instinctively stood apart, me regretfully withdrawing my arm—but not until my hand dropped a little, and brushed the satin curve of his hip.

Coming upon us half-intoxicated, intent on sharing a story or jest, Rowan and Stephen didn't notice, nor did anyone else around us, deep now in the lures of their own romances; but Jim turned away with a jerk of his chin. Anxious to dispatch my cousins—sensing that I'd pushed Jim too far, and feeling my head clear even more with my concern—I heard them out with ill-concealed impatience, casting about for some way to get rid of them; but bent on the unfolding of their own hilarity, they observed neither my irate brow nor Jim's discomfiture as he stood, half-turned away, tensely looking out on the city.

Feeling a rising wrath at the intrusions that had plagued us the whole month, and now threatened the sweetest night of our lives—wondering vaguely if this was how it would always be, and more impatient than ever at the idea—I became downright hostile; but still they remained blissfully unaware of my anger, refusing to take their belated departure. In the end they were spared my plot to throttle them both; for Jim took matters into his own hands, and abruptly excused himself from our midst. As he swung past me I caught a rapid glimpse of his face—saw him lower his gaze and square his jaw, sure signs he was fighting both need and strong feeling; then he was gone, heading across the crowded ballroom; and Stephen and Rowan were left wondering in his wake.

Goaded to action, I excused myself as well; was just making my way across the balcony to the ballroom when I began to hear the scraping of chairs, and noted the halt in the music and dancing. Perceiving that something had caused an intermission, I just as swiftly came to the realization that Eliza'd caught Jim, and asked him to play; and wondering how on earth he would do it—both of us having forgotten his music was ever on the agenda for the evening, indeed was one of Eliza's pet schemes—I drifted toward the back of the ballroom, where I found a seat near the hall door and sat down, sweating in silent sympathy for him.

Stepping onto the platform he bowed at her introduction, as composed as if he'd been preparing for the chance to play all evening; graciously accepted the violin she offered him, as if nothing had happened to upset him; and propping it under his chin he tuned it a moment, poised with the easy charm of his nature. Tall and straight there alone on the stage, the black and white of his costume giving him an elegance that was striking, he was the image of poised grace and restraint; and his gold neckerchief stirring in the breeze of a hundred fans, he played whatever came into his head, as relaxed as though he was alone with me in our room. Slipping from fanciful and teasing to fervent and yearning, now dancing, now twirling, now tendering in the moonlight, he released the allures and longings of the evening, taut with the reins of intrusion and constraint; and I listened entranced with the others, half-hidden in the back so no one could observe the uncontainable pain of love on my face.

Creeping out one by one from behind the screen, the musicians slipped forward so they could watch him, some sitting on the stage, others taking their places near guests, forgetful of their station as they looked on; but even without their reverent delight I knew his playing was graced with genius, the instinctive mastery of his people; for the ache of my heart as it leapt over moors, then danced before tents in firelit celebration, was the ache of the recognition of greatness.

From my place at the back it had been all I could do to control my emotion as he played the violin; so when they rolled out the great harp, two of the musicians helping, and he obligingly took his seat before it, regarding its splendor with quiet awe, I knew at once I was going to cry; and I hunkered down even lower in my seat, my hand half before my face to shield me. As soon as his fingers swept over the strings they leapt to life with the swell of his touch, rippling, shimmering in curtains of music which glistened about him in gossamer layers, then fell to his feet in cascading folds: glimmering layers which unveiled one by one the inner peoplings that were his—now the sailor, now the courtesan or carver, now the merman or musician or lover, each bodied out like his figureheads from their concealing mantles of wood.

Listening, I saw he had become fully himself—not just fully my mate, but fully who he was, a nomadic man sure of his heart; saw he'd taken the place here he'd never take at the festival at Bala; and the sting of triumph which seared my heart caused the tears to drop unconstrained on my gloves. Unable to bear the ache any longer, I slipped out of the ballroom before he finished, down the hall to the little supper room where we'd had dinner, then onto the private balcony beyond; and there by the screen of twining jasmine, sweet and vivid in the dark, I gave way to the fullness of my heart.

*   *   *   *   *

I knew where to find him as surely as a pigeon knows where to home, or a pilot to make landfall; and as soon as I could escape from the response of the others, I hastened down the hall to the supper room in the family quarters, and out onto the deserted balcony there. Quietly locking the French doors behind me, I crept up on him as he sat by the jasmine, his gloves in his lap and his head in his hand; but he gave no other sign of deep feeling, swiftly slipping his handkerchief into his pocket as he hurried to his feet to greet me.

As we gazed with compassion on one another, secluded at last from the intrusions of the crowd, fresh music came wafting in to us from the ballroom, the musicians now settling the dancers down for dinner, and embarking on a succession of waltzes; and we recognized at once the strains of the sea chantey which'd rung out at Toby's just before he stepped in, that blustery March night three years ago. As if conveyed back to the decks from which they'd been sprung, hauling in line hand over hand in the wind, the crowd took up the haunting verses, seamen all, despite fine silks and satins; and "Shenandoah, I long to see you, way-aye, yon rolling river" came sweeping in over us from the ballroom, trained voices intermingling with the rough ghosts of Toby's.

Putting his hand over his heart, he bowed from the waist as if I was royalty, and asked "Will you do me the honoh?"; and stung with sweet pain I went at once to his arms, as naturally as if we'd danced together every night of our lives. One big hand at my waist, the other cupping my fingers, he guided me in the simple rhythms, in and out of the fragile shadows of jasmine; and I sheltered against him as I'd longed to years ago, in the promenade of *Abigail's* launching— luxuriating in the bulk of his shoulders, the brace of his arm and the warm hush of his breath, as he bent his head tenderly toward mine. Gravely tracing the steps in the innocence of a first dance, we discovered how we moved together; shyly trusted ourselves to the lure of the music; dipped through the shadows like a vessel through moonlight, in the intricacy of promptings and responses.

When the music fell still he stopped with me near the jasmine, and plucked a sprig to adorn my hair; then silently, purposefully, he undid my neckerchief, the gold Turkish *diklo* Eben had bought me, and solemnly re-tied it in a marriage knot. Understanding at once I stifled hot tears, even as steps sounded in the hall just beyond the supper room door; and taking my arm he sat me down in the chair he'd vacated when I came in, his hands insistent and sure at my shoulders. Half-frozen there we waited for silence—the steps passing by on down the hall, perhaps a servant's on a mission for Claire; then kissing the fingers clenched in my lap—the prickle of his beard vivid on my palm—he let himself quietly out the door, slipping back to the ballroom lest anyone detect we'd been long away together.

Returning myself when I was calmer—counting down the minutes remaining till supper, when at last we could take our departure—I encountered a totally unexpected new threat; for across the ballroom greeting Eliza was a fresh arrival, just in time for the midnight meal and german: a young man I recognized at once from Creek Lane. Why he was here, I couldn't fathom; but who he was I knew at once; and my stomach lurching as if it had been kicked, I hurried directly to the ballroom balcony to recover—bypassing inquirers after my music, and Claire, finagling for the supper dance, almost rudely. Catching sight of me as I hastened past, Ben followed, faster and firmer than anyone who might be inclined to trail me; and meeting up with me at the rail, his voice low at my ear, he murmured, "What is it, matey—someone you recognized?"

Still trying to snatch my second wind, I quavered in awe, "Aye… how did you know?"

Smiling gently, he said, "I know you."

Half-reassured already just from his nearness, I drew a deep breath, keeping my back to the French doors; and giving me time he waited close by, instinctively turning his shoulders to screen me.

"Who is it?" he asked then, seeing I'd grown calmer.

"I don't know, I—I only know his first name—I—" Flushing miserably at what he must think—not wanting him to conclude the newcomer'd once been a lover, yet not eager to confess what he *had* been—I stammered, "He's over by the door, still talking to Eliza… he just came in."

Turning so he could survey the ballroom—taking a step or two closer to the French doors, then returning calmly to my elbow, as at ease as if he'd just fetched a drink, in a continuation of the game he'd outlasted me at earlier—he informed, "That's the Chamberlain's son, they're up here from Boston… D'ye mean t' tell me he visited Lomond's?"

"Aye, he—it's not that we were ever t'gether, but—" Flushing painfully again at what I had been, and at the way my past had intruded on this of all nights, but determined to be honest, I plowed on, "He—you see, he drew me."

For a moment he looked confused, as if he had no idea what

I meant; but then a light seemed to dawn on his face, just as I'd wretchedly concluded I'd have to explain; and to my amazement a smile appeared too. "Oh," he said simply, as if we were talking about some feature of decoration, "you mean the sketches b'hind the bar stools?"

Too floored to say much, I dumbly floundered, "You mean…you noticed?"

"A' course," he said dryly, as though I'd implied he might miss a cloud bank, or some other indication of the weather. "I spotted youhrs right away… Did'je imagine for a minute I wouldn't?" His smile widening and his eyes almost nostalgic, he added, "I figured then it'd be the only chance I'd eveh have t' see you that way…so I made sure t' pick out one o' the best when I left."

My amazement at him at its utter limits—my astonishment exceeded only by my consternation, as I combed my memory for recollections of my poses, each posture undressing me before him and the whole ballroom—I managed to stumble on, dumbfounded: "Ben, you mean you…you've *got* one of those drawings?"

"A' course…locked in my trunk." Seeing my mingled shame and incredulity he added, "I think it's beautiful… It's all I had for a long time, more than I eveh thought t' have when I found it." Taking my hand in a swift grip he squeezed it, as I struggled to master the hot sting of exposure; then quickly letting it go he simply smiled at me, grey eyes misted with compassion.

"Ben…I don't want you t' think…I'd ever do anything like that again, I—" Hurrying out the words now in the commotion around us, I struggled, "When we say our vows, I don't want you t' imagine… I'd ever let anyone see me like that, except you…or worry I wouldn't be true to my promise, just because of what I was like in the past."

"Is that what you was readin' the otheh night, when I came int' youhr room t' see how you was feelin'?" he asked, his eyes as knowing as if he'd seen me with the service.

"Aye," I confessed, gaze lowered.

"Jamie, look at me," he urged, his voice strong and kind in the tumult of dance noise.

Obeying him I met his eyes, wide and tender in the halo of

lamplight; and in their depths lay an unshakeable sureness. "I've got no doubts," he said serenely.

Nodding I braced my hands at the rail, struggling to control their telltale quaver—striving to remember we were surrounded by watchers who might, in the midst of their own secrets, hear ours. Seeing my battle, Ben caught my hand, sheltering it from the eyes of the others; stroked my palm with a covert thumb; but before we could slip away to a quieter place, any place, we were again interrupted, this time by a colleague of Ben's in shipping; and blind to anything else save my need, I abruptly struck out across the ballroom, risking even an encounter with Albert in the determination of my exit.

*   *   *   *   *

Seeing him drop his gaze and bite his lip as he hurried off without an excuse, I felt a rage rise hotly within me, fiercer than the heat I'd felt for my cousins; and I all but unleashed it on the hapless Wingate, who merely wanted to commence bidding on *Abigail*—he being one of the few I'd actually have wanted to see buy her. Putting him off—not having a care as to how curt were my words, or whether I looked as wild as I felt—I followed Jim across the ballroom and toward the kitchen on the other side of the hall; hastened through it, finding it lighted, but vacant; and so happened into the darkened pantry, where he had taken instinctive refuge.

Determinedly closing the door behind me, I found myself in pitch darkness; but having glimpsed him standing, elbows braced, at the one of the tall cupboards, I crossed the pantry sure-footed towards him, and seized him fiercely in my arms. Responding at once—hurling his arms about my neck, and pressing himself to me with a cry—he offered his lips before I could say a word; and swept away by his abandon, I took his face in both of my hands, and kissed him again and again.

As his hands came up to clutch my back—as they slid beneath my evening jacket, and eagerly came down my sides—I felt an unleashed thrill of power; and pressing him with all my strength to me, I claimed him over and over, my hands clutching at the hot silk at his shoulders and clenching the satin at his hips. Moaning even in the midst of our kiss, he at last broke away, and hid his face against my shoulder; and about to kiss his damp, tumbled hair, I was just twining its strands in my fingers, when all at once voices erupted in the kitchen, and pots and pans began to rattle.

Stifling Jim's little sound of despair—hurriedly trying to gather my thoughts, to come up with a satisfactory story to explain our presence—I stood a little apart from the door, holding my breath at every footstep and clatter. At least two or three servants were bustling nearby, probably preparing to carry things in to dinner; and whether or not one of them would burst into the pantry—whether some need for a salt cone or a sherry or sugar would drive one or more of them to enter—was entirely an open question.

For at least fifteen minutes they rattled and clattered, chattering enthusiastically about the party, and whispering and hissing bits of gossip; and as the moments slipped by slowly—as footsteps started out time and again for the pantry, only to stop short at some dry sink or cupboard—I waited, frozen, conscious of him motionless nearby me. Aching to touch him, to reassure him—wild to be off with him, free of the others—I at last perceived a lessening of sound; heard two or more servants go off with a clangor, a rattle of cart wheels and conversation, their voices drifting back lower and lower as they made their way down the hall. One servant remained, bustling about in unnerving dashes, putting things away with a clank and a clang on a wagon; but at length she too departed, her footsteps shuffling off down the hall, leaving the kitchen in overwhelming silence.

Going at once to the door, I opened it a crack; peered out into the still-lighted room; and seeing it was vacant, I flung the door wide, and crossed compassionately to Jim. Finding him trembling—gently smoothing back his hair—I adjusted his waistcoat, and straightened his *diklo*; and he—bringing his chin up in his old game, forthright manner, taking a deep breath and giving a smile—reached out in turn and righted my collar. Tenderly brushing his cheek with my hand, I said—speaking for the first time since we'd entered the pantry—"Come on," my voice resolutely controlled and quiet; and leading the way through the kitchen and down the deserted hall, I ushered him back into the ballroom, with the unspoken determination to bow out at once.

The dance before the supper waltz was in progress, couples spinning with the importance of the moment; while out on the margins of the floor, others were preparing to file into the dining room, only waiting for Eliza to lead them. Spotting Eben not far from the refreshment table—thinking to enlist his aid in our departure, and cornering him while Jim was again engulfed by the crowd—I managed to begin the painstaking round of goodnights, Eben backing me up with reminders of our early start tomorrow; but our progress was slow, what with Eliza, Jacob and my cousins scattered to the far ends of the hall, and business colleagues constantly intervening.

Growing more impatient by the moment—catching sight of Jim's drawn expression, as he tried to avoid the waters near Albert—I barely managed to be civil; but done with my obligations at last, I turned around to search for him, thinking to escort him out before dinner—only to find he'd made his own excuses, and already fled to his room. Furious with Eliza for delaying her exit, I waited around till the end of the supper dance, treading water near the door; then carried down the hall by the tide of dinner-goers, I ducked out like a man diving from a sinking vessel; and making my way round the corner to my room, I admitted myself with a vast sense of escape, tiptoeing at once to the half-open door which communicated with Jim's chamber.

Before I was even close to his room I heard his inquiring "Ben?"— heard, with a catch at my heart, the anxiety and longing in his voice; and throwing open the door, I crossed at once to the chintz-covered sofa, where he—minus waistcoat and pumps—had been anxiously waiting. Taking in his looks in a swift gaze—the brace of his arm on the back of the sofa, the curve of his hip as he sat a little sideways, in a wait half-graceful, half-strained with tense hope—I slipped back to his bedroom door and latched it, then directly sat down beside him. As I drew him into my arms—as I took his face in both of my hands, and triumphantly scanned his eyes and lips—he averted his gaze and whispered, "The hall locked, too?"; and with a leap of the heart at his quaver I firmly answered "Avali," and drowned his response in my kiss.

*   *   *   *   *

Taking my hands one at a time, he finished unhooking my wristbands—kissed the bare, open skin of my wrists, exposed where my shirt cuffs had fallen back; then easing me forward, drew off my shirt, brushing it from my back and shoulders. Half-bare in the curtained breeze from the window, I gave myself to the glance of his hands; waited, hushed, while he drew the sash from my trousers, then slipped them past the curve of my hips. Fingers brushing the slope of my thighs, I felt their lingering slide at my feet; then leaving my side he crossed resolutely to the bed, and drawing back the covers, threw them down on the floor. An urgent light blazing high in my chest, I watched as he finished stripping the bed, not stopping till the mattress lay bare; then tenderly, he came to me.

XXIX

MELCHETT, ROBERTSON & McCABE
New York—Cape Damaris, June, 1845

When I woke the next day—not to the servants' knocking, which'd entirely failed to rouse me, but to Eben's insistent, forceful tugging—I merely looked up in recognition, not caring what he thought of my appearance; and understanding at once—if he hadn't already from my return to my room, which had locked him out from our nightly switch—he withdrew, coming back in a few minutes with a tray. Unloading first a pot of coffee, he set it down with a cup by the bed; then picking up the steaming pitcher, he filled the vessel on my stand, and backed out of the room with a nod.

Wordlessly grateful, I managed to sit up, haul on my dressing gown and move to a chair; and gradually downing a cup of coffee, I stared about my chamber vaguely. As I slowly came to my senses I took anxious note of the state of the room, observing it through the eyes of the others; and finding it miraculously in order—finding even my clothes arranged as they would be, had I come in and slept after the party—I uttered a sigh of relief. Whether the servants had entered or not—whether they'd peeked in my unlocked door, which for a mercy I'd remembered to unlatch—I hadn't the slightest idea; but relieved that my night's final efforts had returned things to a state of normalcy, I continued to sit in my chair, sipping my coffee and staring out the window.

Pouring another cup, I tentatively got to my feet, and carried it to the dresser mirror; set it down by the water, and peered into the glass; and seeing that I had a job before me, I painfully went to work. Only now did it dawn on me that this was our last day in New York

—that we were due to leave for the cars at eight in the morning; and turning anxiously to the clock—seeing it was just past six—I donned the sack suit I'd set aside in my wardrobe. The rest of my gear having already been packed, I stuffed a few final items in my valise; then unable to allow Jim to sleep any longer, I re-crossed the room and entered his chamber, tiptoeing noiselessly to his bedside.

Gazing down, I found him exactly as I had left him, lying crumpled on one side and covered—looking for all the world as if I had struck him; and conscience-stricken, I sat down beside him, then smoothing back his hair, whispered "Jamie."

At the sound of his name, his lashes trembled, then lifted as I repeatedly called him; and taking in the sight of my face, he roused, with a smile which sprang from drowsy contentment. Not wanting to rush him, I smiled back, waiting for him to more fully waken; and basking at first in my quiet nearness, then rousing enough to reach up his arms, he invited my embrace. With a hasty glance at the unlocked door, I slipped my arms quickly beneath him, and crushed him fast to me for a moment; then as I broke away he drowsily murmured, "No," and tightened his clasp about my neck.

Smiling into his hair, I gently told him, "We've pushed oweh luck about far enough for one night, mate; time t' get this show on the road." Reaching for his nightstand, I handed him a glass of water, and braced him to it while he drank it; then—seeing his eyes sleepily close, and his slumbering smile gradually fade—I told him: "In a minute or two I'll be back with some tea, an' a pitcheh of hot wateh for washin'. Don't you go back t' sleep on me, now: we got the cahrs t' catch in two owehs."

When I returned ten minutes later with a decanter in one hand and a tray in the other, he was sitting in a chair by the window, wearing his dressing gown and dreaming out on the city; and pouring tea for us both I handed him his cup, the two of us drinking together in silence, a companionable silence which spoke our feeling.

Now and again it was our eyes, meeting over our cups, which carried on our conversation; sometimes it was our hands, brushing over the cream, which gave voice to our belonging. With the servants beginning to knock and enter—with them setting out towels, those we'd used even now hidden in the bottom of my valise—discretion was more needed than ever; and under the pressure of restraint, our quiet communion was sharpened and heightened, till the room seemed to throb with its hidden presence.

Helping him pack his last-minute belongings, I carried his valise down to the drawing room, where I waited for him while he dressed; and watching him reappear, freshly shaven, handsome in his new suit and cravat—bidding goodbyes with him to Eliza and Claire, Rowan and Stephen and all the servants—I took leave of the townhouse, scene of my unlooked-for wedding celebration; descended the steps on which I'd welcomed him home, and saw him up into Jacob's carriage. With Eben beside us we made the short drive through the city, re-tracing the routes along which we'd searched for him; and as they blurred past me each mile spoke the hopes with which we'd invested our days.

But it was not till we'd arrived at the cars, in the luxury of Jacob's brougham, and bidden goodbye to him as well, drenched in the radiance of a summer's morning; not till we'd seen our luggage aboard and sat down, Jim and I, with Eben across from us, that I realized the full sweep of all that had happened, and the liberty that was before us. Free at last from the confines of Jacob's—even if on our way to new constraints at Elkanah's, and surrounded by the watchful eyes of the car's crowd—we settled in like a couple eloping; and feeling the warmth of each other's nearness—our shoulders brushing as we sank in the plush seats—we took in the details around us.

As we pulled away from the station and began to move through the city, I felt the tensions of Jacob's fall from my limbs; reveled in the sensation of travel, however noisy and intermittent, without the accompanying motions of labor. Feeling his unspoken yearning to touch me, I was swept by a fresh surge of power; felt not just physically strong but intellectually buoyant—all of my senses, indeed all of my impressions, swinging into poignantly sharp focus. The clarity of the brass lamps, despite the smoke film of whale oil, the purity of the whistle and the eloquence of chatter, all cut me with their painful clearness; while the man beside me alerted my whole heart with the confiding warmth of his nearness.

Out of the corner of my eye I could see the curves of his thighs, hard and blunt beneath the sharp crease of trowsers; could glimpse the sturdy lines of his shoulders, clothed now with his show of restraint; could catch the new, dusty blue of his suit and the crisp cut of his hair, as he gazed ahead or glanced out the window, and fought the need to put his head on my shoulder—

And then with an impact, an actual bolt, I knew—knew we'd fallen into my dream, or it had fallen into our present; saw he knew it too, as if he'd felt my jolt, his alert eyes colliding with mine as they fled to the window. Stunned, I turned away, not knowing for the time whether we were in my dream or no; while he stared wordlessly out on the city, fighting the yearning which claimed me as well. As if he understood Eben rose, and unfolded a lap robe over us both—it having been provided to keep off the cinders; and under its cover I took Jamie's hand, nearly crushing it as I sought some control; took it and held it for long miles of our journey, till gradually he relaxed under my touch, and dozed with his head back against the seat.

*   *   *   *   *

When Jim come to, the outskirts of Portland was at hand, farmsteads softly twinkling with lanterns; and Ben was gathering up the day's newsheets, while passengers scooped up dust cloaks and children. If we thought we'd have a quiet jaunt to Elkanah's, in a private carriage down lamplit ways to Congress Street, before the inevitable din and display of reunion, we soon discovered we was dreaming; for there on the gas-lighted platform was a throng, fully half of which looked to be earmarked for us; and picking out from my window sundry Howlands and Melchetts, and even some loafer who looked suspiciously like a news agent, I was thankful that Jim'd rested. Peering out the smoke-besmeared panes at the crowd, Ben—who'd written Elkanah pleading for a quiet welcome, and the chance to sleep off the stresses of the journey—scowled visibly at his kith and kin; but the reason for the mob soon made itself plain; for word come down the aisle that *Abigail* had just docked, discharging a boatload of Howlands and Melchetts; and the skylarking was clearly in full swing.

Looking down at the melee we recognized Reuben, pompous as ever in coattails and tophat, and Jim's old smug-faced rival, Sal Howland—the two of them jostled by a dozen shipmates; and realizing that not till now had they discovered Jim was alive, or that their cousins was dead or that Ben's trial had come off, or even that the ship they'd made port in was for sale, I knew they'd swoop on us like a swarm of locusts, and probably eat Jim alive with their questions. Looking acrosst at Ben I cocked an alarmed eyebrow; but intent on assisting Jim to his feet—the two of them glowing like they had been all day, despite Jim's obvious fatigue and Ben's tense face— he didn't catch my quick warning; and the three of us surrendered to the crowd like fresh bait, Jim leading the way with a game smile and set chin.

Organizing itself into a swarm of carriages, the mob descended on hapless Elkanah's, where most of Ben's Portland kin, especially the women, had remained to await the onslaught. Overflowing from the drawing room and library onto porches, and so into the gazebo and gardens, they held forth in a blaze of candles and whale oil; and debarking from broughams, wagons, even carts commandeered earlier from the wharves, we swelled their ranks in a commotion of noise.

Meeting them all with his best stab at aplomb, Jim struggled to respond to all hands— to thank those in the know for letters sent to New York, and to sort out the astounded questions of those just arrived; while feeling doomed, Ben and me too mingled, bracing ourselves with Elkanah's best scotch. The deaths of Roan, Ephie and Paul, Jim's heroic survival, the financial disasters of Ben's trial and the sale of *Charis* and *Abigail*—all these his old shipmates devoured like vultures, oblivious of the wounds they caused him; and outraged by this evidence of their ill breeding, Ben sent them packing whenever he was within hearing, like a bully mate with a belaying pin.

Finding our room upstairs at last—discovering we'd been housed on the third floor, the returning tribes having already taken over the second, and even the third mostly given over to Howlands—I slipped into our chamber to see Ben and Jim, already laying claim to one of the big four-posters; then saw, stretched out like a beached whale on the other, a ludicrously snoring John Howland. Realizing I had a drunken leviathan for a bunkmate, I shoved him over to the edge of the bed, attempting to free up some of the covers; meantime saw, out of the corner of my eye, Ben and Jim climbing in under theirs—Ben screening Jim with his broad back as he murmured some tender reassurance, and Jim's answer drowned out at once in a kiss, snatched under cover of Howland's snoring.

*   *   *   *   *

Established in a deserted warehouse this past month, Jackson was helping set up a seaman's home like the one he'd started up in Boston; and welcoming us with open arms the next morning, he spent a long time closeted with Jim, talking about the meaning of baptism and listening to Jim's experiences on the Pacific. What they said together I couldn't hear, out in the lobby on my packing crate, catching up on the shipping news in Portland; but when they emerged Jim's face was smiling, and Jackson's was alive with respect; and over an early tea together we planned tomorrow's ceremony. Agreeing to meet down the bay by my rosebush—Jim insistent that my cove be the site of the service, not any traditional altar or setting—we parted ways till the morning; and wordlessly moved that he'd remembered my landmark, the place where I'd read his letter and realized I loved him—I drove him to Jacques' rooming house in silence.

Greeting us royally at the door, Edna and Emma—elderly twins grown so alike I could scarcely tell them apart—ushered us into the cheerful downstairs parlor they'd turned over to Jacques in his illness; and finding him reclining, frail but alert, on the sofa, we celebrated a poignant reunion. Already fatigued from his visit with Jackson, Jim turned swiftly ashen at the sight of his old friend, before checking his reaction with his ready wit and quick laugh; and they were at once in each other's arms, Jim catching up Jacques' thin shoulders, Jacques flinging his arms about Jim's neck, face joyous.

Embracing him next, I looked carefully at him—saw that he'd lost little ground since spring, and seemed likely to weather the summer; and glad to the heart for his reprieve, I sat by while he and Jim talked for an hour, babbling like brooks after a spring thaw. Listening to them chatter, half in French, I realized I'd seldom heard Jim talk so much—saw that it drained him almost as much as Jacques' decline; but Jacques saw only his bright, handsome face; looked marveling at him, then at me.

"You're a lucky man," he said to Jim, his rich Flemish accent belied by his frail voice; "you found what we wanted."

"Aye, I know it," Jim acknowledged, his smile awed; then generously he added, "I'll share him with you"—as if he'd understood completely the relationship that had sprung up between us, ever since the night I'd rescued him from Slater's.

"Merci," beamed Jacques with a quick glow, and the bashful look he used to show that he loved me; then they were off with a clatter about New York, our upcoming gadje wedding and plans for the summer—not looking too far ahead in their gazing, and plotting plenty of visits to Portland. At last, knowing from the glint in Jim's eye and the tautness about his jaw he was exhausted—hearing Jacques beginning to cough, and noting the hectic rouge at his cheeks—I insisted that we return home to rest; and embracing each other in farewell, they kissed. It was the first time I'd ever seen Jim hold or kiss another man; and filled with the odd sense of proof it gave me that he was a lover of men, *my* lover—chagrined that I'd never perceived it before, plain as it must have been these past years—I too embraced Jacques, with goodbyes till tomorrow.

*　*　*　*　*

Finding Elkanah's in another uproar—Agatha's family from Augusta having arrived a day early, and turned the place upside down once again—we tried to slip covertly up the back stairway, Ben and I; but spotted by Agatha herself in full cry, we had no choice but to step into the parlor, where we encountered the assembled tribe. Unable to keep my mind on a word, I only allowed myself to be introduced, before I excused myself and disappeared; took to the stairs in the haste of my pain, thinking only to hide myself in our room. Anxious for my distress over Jacques, Ben tried to follow me at once; but accosted by Agatha's mother, an immense woman in satin and jewels, and her glad-handing brother, a state senator home on recess, he found his route of escape cut off; and we were once again split apart by the others.

Coming in when he could—sitting by me on the bed—Ben determinedly braced me to a glass; cuddled me to a strong shoulder and urged "Down the hatch, matey—all of it." Knowing it was some gadje concoction or other to make me sleep—knowing it would come between us and any chance we might have for the night—I nonetheless obeyed him; drained it off without a protest, then lay back in his arms with a shudder.

"If it hadn't been for you…if I hadn't found you…that'd be me, dyin' like Jacques," I quavered.

"Matey, I know it… If I hadn't found you, I know what I'd look like, too," he told me.

Startled out of my grieving, I gazed up. "Ben…you never…who was he?"

"Oh, he was a man I haven't told you about…sitting alone at Slateh's tavern….a homely fellow past his prime, waitin' for someone t' join him for life. Probably he's waited for yeahrs…probably's still there…probably always will be." Unaware he was crying till he saw my face, contorted with distress for him, he drew his cheek close beside mine; and caught up in the fearful joy of our chance, we clung to each other; held on to each other till, relaxed at last, my fingers loosened in the peace of sleep, and he slipped me tenderly under the covers.

*   *   *   *   *

With the arrival of morning came the overland mail, including a letter from John containing news of Jim's adoption; and like another piece falling into place came his baptism hours later, Jackson meeting us by my cove shortly before noon. Carrying a hamper filled with Agatha's best cooking, Eben and I set out our repast, then with Jim and Jackson we stripped off shoes, rolled up trowsers, and waded out into the cool waters of Casco Bay. Shimmering deep blue in the summer sun, its islands dark green with pink granite ledges, the bay stretched before us like a broad embrace; and sailor-clad in duck pants and red cotton jersey—not unlike the man I'd first beheld aboard *Charis*, those warm, spicy days in the spring tropics—Jim gave himself up to the sparkling waters, kneeling before Jackson beneath a benign sky. Standing close by Eben and I looked on, while Jackson, dressed more like the seamen he tended than a preacher, explained the ceremony so Jim could understand.

"Jim, you went out to the sea almost to the point of death, and experienced there the presence of the Lord, the Creator, whom you yourself came to know as a crone, rocking your boat like a cradle… as a porpoise, which like Christ the Redeemer gave you its life-giving juices…as the Spirit walking to you on the waters, carrying a basket and bestowing assurance… am I right?"

His face contorted with feeling but his voice calm he answered, "Aye."

"And what was in the basket the old crone showed you?" Jackson prodded.

"A tent," Jamie told him, voice thick.

"And what did you understand about that tent?"

"I don't know, I… Sometimes I've though she meant Jesus, b'cause he pitched his tent amongst us…an' sometimes I've thought she meant a journey, that she an' we are on the road, like the Rom…an' sometimes I've thought she meant a promise, that she was showing me *my* tent, my home yet t' come."

Casting a quick glance at us full of awe and delight, Jackson smiled as he continued, "Do you undehstand from this experience the Christian idea of leaving behind your old self, and taking to the road in the tent of a new life?"

Again he calmly answered, "Aye."

"And are you ready to let go of that old life you saw die out on the Pacific…to be born again into the promise of Christ, and received into the world-wide tent of faith?"

Without hesitation he replied, "I am."

"Then James Gethin," he pronounced, using both his English and Welsh names as I had begged him, and scooping cool waters with each phrase, "I baptize you in the name of God, the Father-Crone, O Meero Duvel, the one who rocks our earthly cradles… in the name of the Son, who pitched his tent amongst us in order to save us, even at the cost of life, like your porpoise…and in the name of the Holy Spirit, who will come walking to you with the promise of home all your days."

His pleasure at hearing Jackson name God in his own tongue, and in his own experience aglow on his face, Jamie rose from his knees and immediately hugged me; and claiming him too Eben took him in his arms, while Jackson playfully scooped water at us, great cool splashes reminding us we too were baptized. Then plowing our way to the shore we sat down in the sun, drying off in the heat of the day while we ate; and no meal tasted finer than that humble repast by the bay, in the sweet-smelling wafts of scent from my rose.

*   *   *   *   *

That night in Elkanah's parlor—our last in Portland, since we were due to take the steamer to Cape Damaris next morning—we put on our best face with Ben's assembled kin; sat talking business with Elkanah and his brother-in-law, a state senator from Augusta, or singing sea chanteys at the piano: Ben poised on the edge of his chair like a man ready to jump ship, and Eben smoothing over his brusque responses.

Climbing over our laps and in and out of our arms, Elkanah's youngest were enjoying our attention; and though not noticeably affectionate toward any children besides his own, Ben was tolerating them as he talked of cargoes and tonnage; was putting up with them as they scaled his limbs the way his own young ones did, attracted by his burly size. At his chest, on his lap, against his beard, they crawled about as on a brawny oak; climbed and laughed with the public permission of play; and I looked on with envious understanding, barred as I was for all time from such freedom.

Breaking in on my thoughts Elkanah suddenly put down his pipe, and turned the conversation toward *Charis;* caught us completely amidships with his offer to buy her, meeting not only Ben's price for his half-interest but also his condition she not be used for illicit trades. Torn between his desire to keep her in the family—between his recognition that the Melchett yard couldn't afford to buy her, and his distaste that Reuben would ultimately command her if Elkanah did—Ben's face was a study; but after a swift mental review of other offers—none of which guaranteed she wouldn't end up a slaver, or in some other disreputable trade due to her speed—he quietly accepted the deal.

Upstairs in our room I sat with him by the window, trying to get him to speak his mind before we were once again invaded; and he was still stalling with his bullheaded pride when Eben stepped in, and presented us, bowing, with his wedding present. "I was goin' t' wait till afteh the weddin'," he said—meaning next week's gadje ceremony—as he offered the flat box; "but t'night seems like the propeh time t' give this."

Curious, Ben opened the box at my nod; lifted a paper from bright-colored tissues, fishing meantime in the litter by the lamp for spectacles; then clapped a swift hand to his face to shield it, so that we couldn't see his reaction. Picking up the paper from his limp fingers, I saw at once it was Eben's eighth interest in *Charis,* signed over to Ben that we might still own a piece of her; and heartstruck, I knew it was worth a fortune, well onto eight thousand dollars—all the kindly man had besides his small interest in *Abigail,* and his inconsequential share of *Idris.* His face contorted, Ben tried to refuse, handing back the paper with mute hands; but waving it aside, Eben insisted he keep it, with a gruff "It's all in the family anyways, mate"; then blessing us both with a homely cuff, he left us alone in the room for a spell.

With strong arms about him, I held Ben at last, trying to soothe the night's pains with sure hands; nursed him so tenderly against my breast, smoothing his brow and broad back with slow strokes, that I never even heard Reuben's step in the hall; and at the rap of his knock we had scarcely a second to lurch apart, before we were once again invaded. So furious was I at this trumpery pest for bursting in on our private moment that I straightaway bore down on him with hands clenched—Ben clutching my arm in a fierce grip to stop me; and thinking no doubt I was about to take revenge for past insults, Reuben unceremoniously backed away, slamming the door before he could crow at us over *Charis*. Looking at each other, Ben and I grinned, then threw back our heads in hearty laughter; and we were still chuckling when all hands tumbled up to bed, the senator's children next door thrashing in bright glee.

Across the pillows from one another, we lay awake long after Eben was snoring, and his bunkmate—Agatha's brother—had settled; and so sublime was it to lie beside him—to feel the warmth of his hardy bulk, and the tantalizing closeness of limbs—that pretending to sleep I turned away, and luxuriated in his burly nearness. As I had aboard *Charis* that wretched night off the Horn, I drank in every detail of his presence—cherished the hush of his breath, the warm tang of sweat, the depths to which he sank in the ticking, till even my teeth ached with my need.

How he sensed my mute pain I couldn't have said, since I hadn't made a sound; but presently his big hand laid claim to my shoulder, in silent sympathy and knowing; and I pressed my fingers on top of his. Caressing my shoulder, the curve of my ear, the hairs at my neck till I could bear it no longer, he turned me to face him on the pillow; cast a swift look at the others sleeping nearby, then shifting his broad back to them, traced my lips with slow fingers. Too roused for caution I reached for his thigh, roaming it with suggestive touches; expecting him to stop me, felt him instead stroke my hip, then slide his hand up under my nightshirt; then swiftly making up his mind he tossed back the covers, reached for his dressing gown and tiptoed to the door. Making sure I followed behind him, he led the way down the darkened hallway, stopping before the cupola door; and picking his way up the tower stairs he tred lightly, so as not to wake the baby with our senator's wife close by.

Shutting the cupola door behind us, we found ourselves in a small room—the look-out at the top of the house, ringed with wooden benches and fitted out with a telescope, that viewers might spot the house flags of incoming ships; and alone together in the secret dark, we clasped one another as if it had been years; grasped shoulders, faces, damp hair; flung ourselves to the feel of hot cloth and hard curves, and to the sounds—sweet, urgent, fast—of our kisses. Sitting down with fumbling haste on the bench—not even feeling its unyielding hardness—twined together, hands gripping at cotton, we were struggling to throw off our night shirts when the high, piercing wail of a baby's cry met our ears.

Holding our breaths—not knowing whether the whole floor below might waken, and discover our obvious absence—we listened, Ben's arms rockhard at my tense hands, and my body quaking with suppressed laughter, the hilarity of an anger beyond tears. From below came the murmurs of a soothing voice, reminding us how vulnerable we were to sound; then quiet followed, the sheer release of silence; and victoriously seizing me by the shoulders, Ben bent me urgently over the railing.

*   *   *   *   *

Leaving Agatha's brother to sleep off a late night, the three of us dressed and trussed up our luggage, anxious to make the Cape Damaris ferry; and with Eben going ahead to see to the carriage, Jamie and I followed with our valises, wordlessly making our way down the stairwell. Pausing a moment on the landing—finding ourselves temporarily alone—we exchanged quick, guarded glances, sharp with the moments wrested from last night; and obeying impulse, I fumbled to touch him, to seal with my hand this fleeting moment—this instant beneath the wings of white curtains. From somewhere above us, sudden footsteps broke in; and seeing him blindly grope for his luggage, then make his way hurriedly down the stairwell, I suppressed an onslaught of fury; met Elkanah, now passing, with the barest of greetings, and followed him wordlessly down the stairs.

Aboard the steamer to Cape Damaris we were once again surrounded—not only by strangers, but by acquaintances in banking and shipping; and after a mute exchange of glances, we settled to windward of the great funnels, shoulders and knees occasionally touching. Finding in that light pressure enough to sustain him, Jamie surrendered before long to sleep, despite the confounded noise of the boilers—too worn by the long journey down from New York and all that'd happened on the way to wed us, and too aware of the turbulent welcome which waited him in Cape Damaris to miss an opportunity to rest; while I sat beside him with unseeing eyes on my newsheet, too beset by exasperation to concentrate on shipping.

Having devoted the whole of the past month's efforts to getting him home and marrying him—having never once looked further into the future than our week or so alone on the island—I was just now beginning to realize how obstacle-ridden our marriage would be; was just commencing to see—as the miles slipped slowly by— how rare the mornings we'd wake side by side, or complete a caress by a stairway window. Overcome by a sadness that was part regret, part rebellion, I stared blankly at my paper, or snatched brief looks at the hushed man beside me, asleep with a quiet, trusting expression; glanced restively about the deck, my gaze flitting from tophats to bonnets to strawbrims, as if I could find in the faces beneath the solution to my unspoken questions.

Should I break from my past, leave my family and work, and carve a new life for myself farther north, in some place Jim and I could live undisturbed? Should I take to the sea—in the manner of Ezra—and never again know any permanent address, sailing with Jim more or less by my wits, in a schooner small enough for us and Eben to man? Or should I muddle on as at present, compromising my own and Jim's needs, facing invasion of our private moments, and only partially fulfilling my obligations to family and home, shipyard and business?

And what did *he* want, this enigmatic man beside me? Flitting from scene to scene in my mind, I tried to imagine how it all looked to him, these stages of our unfolding wedding; tried to picture what he hoped for in the future, if he had an aim beyond the charm of the moment.

What did he yearn for in partnership and marriage, beyond the passion that compelled us at present; where and how did he see us living? I, who'd learned to read his face like a chart—to see defiance in his jaw and need in his eyes as plainly as a shoal in the waters— looked him over like a pilot now; saw that his mouth was tense with frustration, with fatigue from intruders and distress for Jacques; but about his brow there was an unmistakable glow, the serenity of love and satisfied pleasure; and I guessed he was much more accepting than me of the odd places we'd had to meet, and of the practical challenges to our future.

Rubbing my brow with a weary grimness, I suddenly felt his eyes on me, as if he sensed my thoughts in his sleep; and looking over at him, I met his gaze.

"Penny for your thoughts," he murmured, pitching his voice below the engines.

Encouraged by his sympathy, I drew a deep breath. "I'm thinkin' that I need t' do betteh by you in the way of a weddin'," I blurted, tackling our immediate needs.

Straightaway he looked appalled. "What's wrong with it?" he challenged.

"We can't just keep on like this, y'know, Jim, goin' from pantries to cupolas," I said dryly.

Wrinkling his brow, he puzzled "Why not?"; and I saw full well he was perfectly satisfied with whatever privacy we found, just so long as we found it.

"B'cause we need oweh own berth, gawddam it, a place with a bed an' a lock on the doohr…an' I aim t' see that we find it," I burst out, lowering my voice when I saw his raised brow.

"There's our room at the cottage, y' know…we c'n sleep in your bunk," he said dreamily, as though he'd already imagined us there many times.

"Then we ought t' make it biggeh," I returned, my voice absent; for it didn't look to me anything like a long-term solution to the obstacles that beset us.

Looking at me, he was again plainly appalled.

"What is it now?" I asked him.

"We need t' leave your bed just the way it is," he insisted.

"Just the way it is? Why, Jamie, it's too small, almost too snug for me; with you an' me both, we'll be so…"

His smiling eyes told me he'd already won; so I had the wit to shut my mouth, and tackle matters from another direction.

"I s'pose that, for you, this is all pahrt of the 'charm of goin' in circles,'" I said dryly.

"Aye, exactly—*avali*," he returned; and I knew from his serene brow that each of the days past corresponded in some way to a Romany wedding—to the stages which led, like a circling dance, to a destination without end.

"An' you ain't distressed about whehre all this is headin,'" I went on.

"A' course not—so long as it keeps headin' into a bed somewhere; an' I know that it will," he affirmed.

He was so sure of himself that I looked at him, suspicious. "An' you know that how?" I challenged, beginning to guess I was being managed by some heretofore undetected Rom wiles.

"B'cause I took the necessary steps t' see to it."

"James Robehrtson, just what is it you've done?" I demanded, looking back in my mind over the possible pitfalls of the past days— over the moments when I might have left myself vulnerable to some Rom intervention by this man, supposedly now Christian.

"I cahn't tell you exactly, or it'll lose its poweh," he dodged, underscoring he had the upper hand by aping my accent.

Exasperated, I insisted, "You've put somethin' in my soup, or spoke somethin' oveh me while I was asleep—is that it?"

Smiling, he confessed, "You guessed it right with the soup."

"You Romany weasel, look at me: what did you put in it?"

"Just a hair or two…with substances from private places," he answered vaguely.

"Jamie Melchett, you mean you—you mean I've eaten…?"

"Worked, didn't it?" he smiled, the corners of his lips twitching; and serene, smile still twitching, he closed his eyes dreamily in sleep.

Rousing again in the mid- afternoon—looking eagerly about him, and recognizing all the familiar approaches of the Mussel Ridge

Channel—he went to the rail as if to get closer; stood looking out on the buoys and islets, while his dark hair blew freely about his forehead, and his face grew tense with the taut look of landfall. When at last we rounded the Point and beheld the quaint, steep slopes of Cape Damaris, he gazed out from the rail with quick, stricken glances, as if he scarcely knew where to look next; and like a runner poised for the crack of a gun, he waited, braced, as we backed water at the end of the Ship Street pier, then dropped anchor in the blue ripples of the bay.

Before he could even set foot on the pavement he was swamped by the crowd mostly waiting for him; was engulfed as he marched— tall, straight and steady—down the gangplank by a mob that seemed to stretch all the way back to the Seven Seas Inn. From its foremost ranks a joyous shriek went up, the shrill piping and dancing of childish glee; and he was surrounded first of all by my children, screaming and circling about him like gulls. Stunned to find himself in their midst—not having expected to see them till later this evening—he dropped to his knees in the pain of his greeting, nearly crushing them in his embrace; but before he could begin to take in their welcomes, he was surrounded by a deluge from the Inn, Jimmy himself—white-maned— in the forefront. As the crowd swept in and he spotted Keziah—as he received bear hugs from my brothers, and stooped his head to Mother's swift blessing—he looked overcome not just with homecoming, but with gratitude for the town's tribute; and though clearly beset by growing fatigue, he nonetheless maintained his poise, till the moment he caught sight of Rose Talbot.

His gaze suddenly falling on her still features—on the grief-worn face of her mother beside her—he sagged as if borne anew by Paul's loss; and engulfed by their sorrow he hurried to them as their son and brother. Forgetful of others he embraced Rose, then stooped to her mother, and buried his face in her hair; and brought to a hush by their wordless reunion, the crowd looked on spellbound for a moment, then tactfully began to disperse.

In the thinning ranks I suddenly spotted Damaris, on the fringe of the crowd as she apparently had been all along, watching Jim walk off arm and arm with the Talbots; and at her telling face my old jealousy dissolved, as swift sympathy for her rushed in its place. Following her with my eyes while she fell in step behind him, far enough back so as not to be noticed—gazing after her with fellow feeling, an almost man-to-man spark of heart—I became aware all at once of someone beside me, someone who'd struck me vaguely as a stranger, albeit with oddly well-known bearing; and shifting my attention to her unfamiliar attire—peering into her face, at the foreign style of her hair, and her unexpectedly matronly features—I recognized with a start she was Anne.

Face to face with her for the first time since my wedding— confused that I hadn't at first even known her, changed as she was, or as I was myself—I felt shaken with guilt, hardly knowing what to say; and struck amidships by the thought that it was *she* I was going home to—that my children lived with her, that it was *their* table I was expected to sit at tonight—I simply gaped at her, speechless. Awkward as if I hadn't met her for years—at a complete loss for what to say or do—I tried to be gracious as I walked her to the carriage, and told her I'd be helping Eben open the cabin before coming home to a late supper; and saying she would look for me sometime around nine, she climbed in beside Mother and the children—the driver whipping up the horses with a clatter that left me alone on the cobbles of Ship Street.

Still disoriented I drove off with Eben, not far behind them in our borrowed buggy; opened his cabin and built up a fire, with a fervor that tried to blot out confusion. Postponing home as long as I could—visited abruptly with the realization I'd be staying the night there, not just for supper but breakfast, and wondering what on earth I would say all that time, or where I would sit or what I would do—I borrowed Eben's horse and rode back to the Inn; raced up to the third floor to Jim's old room, to ready it for him after his visits to Ephie's family and Roan's, throwing open the windows to the warm summer tang.

From the street below came the glad ring of greetings, or the clang of rigging at the mastheads; and thinking it time for him to head home—listening for his step on the stair, and yearning to have him burst in the door, to scoop him up in my arms and sit with him on the sofa, where I could ease him and myself at the same time—I wandered restlessly about in the twilight, setting out water and making things shipshape. Taking out a note sheet at last, I scribbled "Mande kamro tute" across it, and set it in plain view on his pillow; then with a sigh I rode Eben's horse back to his barn, and trudged slowly through the woods to Anne's house.

So small was the doorway—so much smaller than I remembered—that I actually had to stoop to get in, or so it seemed to me when I got there; and the rooms seemed shrunken too, as they had on the night of the shipwreck. The big country kitchen with its long pine counter, walk-in hearth and massive cupboards was a tight fit for me as I stepped in; and I thanked God for the cheery presence of Sadie and the piping of childish voices as I tried to find a chair to squeeze into. With the twins on my legs pretending to ride horses—with Jean on my lap softly patting my beard, as if she knew full well that I suffered—I managed to get through the discomfiture of the evening; and when at last Anne retired with the older children, leaving me a few moments by the fire—when at last I was alone in my own private berth, which I'd set up in the library two years ago, long before I'd understood I loved Jim—I felt reprieved.

Tossing and turning in the aftermath of the day's stress—feeling trapped in my bunk, as if I'd outgrown it as well, and worrying about the pressures on Jim—I realized around midnight I wasn't going to sleep; and pulling on my clothes I slipped out the front door, and galloped the mile or so back to the Inn.

Noiselessly turning my key in his door—seeing at once that he was in bed, not just from his shadowy form under the covers, but from the characteristic trail of his clothes, tossed here and there as if he'd undressed walking—I directly slipped off my shoes, and tiptoed silently to his side. That he was deep in sleep was at once apparent, from the rhythm of his chest and breathing; and knowing straight off that I could not wake him—knowing that he was wholly spent, that he'd come here because he hadn't the strength to make it all the way out to Eben's, or to rendezvous with me tonight—I turned away with a stab of regret, and tiptoed softly to his desk. Taking out another sheet of paper, I scratched out an invitation to noon dinner, and placed it on the table beside the bed; gently fondled his hair, smoothing back a sweet, damp curl; then noiselessly crossing the room to my shoes, I swiftly caught them up in my hand, and silently slipped out the door.

There being nothing else for it, I went on 'Change at eight next morning, cross as a bear needing a meal after winter; tried to pin my mind on freights, consignees and shipping, never hearing a word that stayed with me more than a minute; then giving it up after a quarter hour, left the jabbering mob without notice, and fled to my office at the shipyard. Though there was a mountain of mail sprawled across my roll top, the place was at least for the time quiet, the tick of the clock and the more distant clamor of mallets actually soothing my nerves after the commotion on 'Change. Working my way blindly through bills of lading, I plowed along in relative silence, the early morning sun my only companion; and not till visitors began their confounded knocking—haranguing me now about *Abigail,* now about *Charis,* and worst of all, my yet-unposted orders to the East Indies, or their plot to send me to Boston for business—did I reach the limits of my poor patience, and slip back over to the Inn.

Going directly to Jamie's room—listening for sounds, then hearing him move about, a welcoming bound animating my heart—I knocked commandingly on the door; and as if he recognized my rap, he eagerly called out "Come in!" Standing before his mirror he was shaving for dinner, half-dressed in trowsers and gauze undershirt, his face still mostly covered with lather; and as soon as he saw my compassionate eyes he rushed straight to my arms, soap brush and all; threw his hands about me and buried his face against my beard, while I crushed him demandingly to me. Overjoyed that we were actually alone for a moment—heedless of the door and the parade of visitors on my tail—I murmured "Jamie," tendering him in my arms; and burrowing in my clasp, he mournfully asked me, "Why didn't you wake me?"

Stroking his hair and half-bare shoulders I gently murmured "How could I?—when I could see from youhr face how bad you needed sleep?"; then hushing his protest by taking his lips, I hungrily laid claim to his mouth. Heedless of the shaving soap now all over us both, we laughed as we kissed, laughed with abandon—laughed away the strains of frustration, the demands of the past day's needs and intrusions—laughed with such unchecked rejoicing that we only heard steps at the door at the last moment; and springing apart, we ducked for cover still laughing.

Slipping into the little alcove he'd set up for dressing, I went to work on my suit coat and beard, while he caught up a nearby towel; and deftly wiping his face he opened the door for Jimmy, come to invite him to a free dinner. Waiting for his retreating steps to trail off, we peeked speechlessly at each other, bits of lather still adorning Jim's lashes; and exploding again into laughter we tried to make ourselves presentable, then set off arm in arm for the dining saloon.

*   *   *   *   *

Though we were surrounded by well-wishers and curiosity-seekers who'd still not had a word with me; though we could scarcely get in a word to each other, we were at least able to share a meal together: me searching his face for news between bites, and he in turn taking measure of me. Walking together as far as the Talbots, Ben leading his horse as we strolled streets I hadn't trod for over a year, we snatched another half hour of company; then leaving me with a regretful squeeze of the elbow, he rode on to meet Anne and Eben, and escort them to the church.

Sitting only a row or so beyond him, I accompanied my lost shipmates' families to their pews; saw him sitting stiffly beside Anne, like a stranger who'd come by to escort her; and torn between my sympathy for my shipmates' kin and for Ben in his awkwardness by Anne, I could scarcely concentrate on a word of the service. Longing for the right to sit beside him, to ease him with my nearness—fighting the unspirited droning of Brewster, and my realization that this could have been *my* funeral, that Paul could as easily have been here in my place—I could hardly wait to get back outdoors; and only pausing long enough to pay my respects to Rose, her mother and the rest of Ben's kin, I hurried out to the refreshment tables on the lawn, and drew in great gulps of sea air in the sun.

Heading back to his office till sometime in the evening—determined to clear his desk so that he could get away next week for the island—Ben begged me to stop by his house for supper; and awkward with Anne myself, I nonetheless hurried out, thinking we could rendezvous later at Eben's. Stopping there on my way I changed to sea gear, then joyously re-united with Dee; and riding her on to Ben's I met Anne at the door, and wrangled an hour on the shore with the children.

Tousling with all six, even Becky—Anne and Sadie willing to get them out from underfoot, as I'd hoped, after the stresses of cooking and dressing for the funeral—I put in a golden afternoon; and they were still shrieking and darting around me, teasing and dancing and climbing on my shoulders, when I sensed Ben watching us from the landing, and hailed him with a jaunty wave. Signaling he'd be down in a moment, he hurried up the walk to the porch; and returning in ten or fifteen minutes—wearing his work clothes, and carrying a tray in his hands—he passed out lemonade to the children, and handed me a brandy and ice, with a longing look and lingering fingers.

As we tangled together with the children, rolling them in the warm, drifting sand; as we sat together, alone for the moment, I felt myself relax for the first time since we'd made port; and I lost myself in the ease of the present. It was the same sitting with him at supper, and afterwards as he settled me down in the library, poured me a drink and picked a chair beside me; for I saw I'd come home to the same place I'd known two summers ago, when I'd lived with him here as his mate for a fortnight.

With Bo'sun purring away on my lap—with Sam nuzzling my feet on the rug, and a fire on the hearth before me—I looked speechlessly about me, finding again in the charts and half-models, the battery of clocks and barometers, the very sum and substance of him; and seeming to see his house through my eyes—looking less awkward and cramped by degrees, as if the rooms had swelled to admit him—he sipped his drink without speaking, seeing no need for words between us. When at last I'd downed my drink, and the fire had fallen to sparks and embers, he rose and bent over me; and taking my glass, he offered gently, "Be glad t' walk ye t' Eben's, mate."

As I looked up and nodded at him, an expectant light taking leap in my heart, he added protectively, "You remembeh t' bring a jacket?"; and at the rueful shake of my head, he ducked out of the room for a moment, and swiftly returned with two of his own. Finding an odd joy—a badge of belonging—in wearing something of his, I donned it; then we called the children and kissed them goodnight, me fondling each one of them; and stepping out the front door into the cool evening wind, we took the path to Eben's cabin.

*   *   *   *   *

Taking our time along the way—walking close together, Jim's arm about my waist, and my hand firm about his shoulders—we admired the early June foliage and flowers, or took deep lungfuls of tangy sea air; walked slowly, savoring our anticipation; and not till we came in sight of the cabin did we slide our arms from one another, briefly holding hands, then breaking our clasp. Stomping our boots on Eben's sandy porch—bursting into the hall and looking into the sitting room—we were stunned to discover a houseful of guests, all guessing that Jim would show up this evening; and it being too late to beat a retreat, he exuberantly stepped into their midst, pumping hands as if he'd expected to meet them.

Taken aback as always by his transitions—too bitter myself at the loss of another evening to demonstrate half of his grace or tact—I reluctantly shrugged and entered, briefly nodded and tipped my cap, and made my way at once to the kitchen, where a busy Eben was mixing drinks. Helping myself to a hearty whiskey, I sent Eben an exasperated look, and received an apologetic response; and united by an unspoken determination to pack the lot off at the earliest opportunity, the two of us braved the sitting room together.

Seated in the place of honor by the fire, Jim was patiently fielding questions, tackling stories and casting retorts, all with his quick-witted charm and humor; and only his gaze as I handed him his drink confessed his fatigue and regret. Though it was as fine a gathering of doughty downeasters—of seamen and shipwrights, lobstermen and riggers—as ever had gathered under one roof; though there was a score of stories in the memories of all to match every tale of Jim's, I had nothing but anger for it; had eyes only for the lines of Jim's face, which I could read as plainly as sea swells or clouds. As the hour grew late and the company rowdy—as a number of others tried to take the floor, inspired by Eben's potent mixes—Jim slipped more and more into silence, his expression restrained and drowsy; and thinking it high time to end the party, I got up and cornered Eben in the kitchen, with the idea of spurring a plan of action.

Returning to the sitting room, I found Jim absent, and the company more boisterous than ever; and leaving it to Eben to clear the decks, I ducked out of the room and headed for the stairs. Convinced that I'd find Jim in his room—longing to snatch even a few minutes with him alone at his window, welcoming him to his occasional chamber—I paused for a moment in the hallway, disappointed to see his bed empty; but in the chair downstairs by Eben's hearth, curled up and sleeping, I discovered him, a spent calm on his features.

Twitching into a smile in the midst of frustration—thinking how much a sailor he was, able to sleep anywhere, under any conditions—I at once crossed over to him, bent down and whispered, "Jamie"; and instinctively rousing and looking up, he leaned appealingly toward me. Keeping him discreetly at bay, I helped him to his feet and steered him determinedly to the stairs, no one in the sitting room— now a sodden scramble for caps and jackets—noticing our covert departure; then reaching his room and closing the door firmly behind us, I took him straightaway in my arms. My back to the door I seized his face, his hands tearing at my collar and shirt; then scooping him up in my arms I sat us down on the bed, struggling to strip off our confounded boots.

Fumbling and trembling at the buttons—too obstinate for my big, clumsy fingers—I gave up on the job in exasperation, Jim seizing my hand and pulling me urgently on top of him; and gasping our pleasure—laughing as our clothes came down to our feet, and tangled there in a jam at our boots—we clung to each other, at last free of restraints. Fingers clenching me to him he sobbed with a fierce "I just want you all t' myself the whole night"—the words buried at once in my kiss; and barely able to manage him with all of my strength, I thrashed with him through the throes of the night, till at last we had spent our passion, and the early dawn peaked in the window.

*   *   *   *   *

Up early I concocted a big breakfast, ready to bet Ben'd be by to help pack it away—even though he'd slipped out barely before the birds to make some pretense of waking at Anne's house; and sure enough— just as I was frying the fishcakes—I heard the scrape of his boots on the porch, and the slam of the screen as he stepped into the entry. Short on sleep, worn with the pressures of the yard and home, and all used up by a barn burner night, he looked about as bad as old cod; looked almost as rugged as Jim had last night, torn with the stresses of weddings and funerals. But his eyes was aglow and his step was light as he claimed a seat on the kitchen sofa, and his manner brisk with sudden decision.

Helping hisself without so much as a by-your-leave to the coffee, he launched straightaway into what was on his mind, characteristically by-passing a greeting: "Mate, thehre's a southwest wind blowin' straight off the harboh; I want ye t' sail Jim out t' the island t'day, an' get him away from all this till the weddin'."

Having already hit on the same idea myself, in my worry Jim'd relapse from all the commotion, and relieved I didn't have to do battle to convince Ben, I said simply, "Makes sense t' me," ready to press on with the notion. "We could open the house, Jim an' me, an' have it all set for the weddin'…could get all the hullaballoo of meetin' an' greetin' out thehre oveh with, while you catch up on things at the yahd."

Nodding agreement he tackled the fishcakes, then plunged on. "That'll get us by till the weddin'…but what about the week after? If we can't get an oweh alone t'getheh here, how're we goin' t' manage out on the island, where folks're even more in each otheh's business? All Jim wants is time for us alone at the cottage; an' whateveh comes afteh, I'm determined t' see we get that."

"Oh, I've been thinkin' about that angle," I said easily, going to fetch my black satchel; and digging into its depths, stocked with apothecary bottles, I held up a quarantine sign.

Looking at it for a nonplussed moment, he suddenly burst into laughter, a glad guffaw such as I hadn't heard for days; and slipping the sign back into my bag, I went on, "I figured I might as well use my rights as a doctoh…We could give out that Jim'd had a relapse; nobody'd dispute that, or come within a mile o' the doohr… An' just t' be on the safe side I could work on the porch roof, where I c'n keep a lookout on the road…that is, if you boys'd want me around."

"A' course we want you around, you'hre part o' the family…an' a crack hand at the stove b'sides. We'll need ye t' concoct a meal now an' then, an' ferry it up t' the bedroom doohr; 'cause I'll be damned if eitheh Jamie or me'll be comin' down t' do any cookin.'"

"Just so's I'm not in the way," I told him, pleased that they still looked on me as family, and that I had a role to play in the household; and putting our heads together, we began to tackle a plan to convince Jim.

*   *   *   *   *

They made me rest while they unpacked supplies—Eben leaving some of the boxes for me, knowing the pleasure I took from tending this cottage; then Ben and I said goodbye at our bedroom window, the last time we'd see each other before the ceremony on Monday. Though that was now only six days away it already seemed like a month; and it took all the room's cheer to buoy up my spirits at the prospect of parting. Our hands at each other's shoulders, we looked one another over, the breeze from the bay billowing around us; then as if he'd read my needs from top to bottom, Ben murmured,

"I want y' t' rest as soon as I'm gone…not just t'day but all o' t'morrer…Ye've only slept a couple hours."

"Not any less than you," I reminded, knowing full well what these next days would mean for him.

"That's different," he pronounced, stubborn as ever. "I ain't just recoverin' from scarlet feveh, an' three months to sea in an open boat."

"No, I countered, "but you're goin' back t' the stresses of home, an' the pressures of what t' do about Boston."

He cocked an astonished eye at me. "How on earth didje know about Boston?" he barked, brought up short as I'd intended.

"Oh, I know what's goin' on," I said dryly.

"Well, that project's neitheh here nor there...a minoh matteh of arrangin' business...an' I c'n manage it a lot betteh if I know that you'hre restin'," he huffed, closing the door once again on my help. "At least with you here I'll know that it's quiet, an' there ain't fifty people bustin' in on youhr sleep."

At the very thought of such privacy I flowed with relief; and before I could wipe it from my face he saw my release: release not just from the intrusions of shipmates, old worthies like Eli or my lost friends' families, but from the relentless pursuits of Keziah's set, seeking to pick up from where they'd left off. Worried about his stresses, I'd kept my own from him, as obstinately as he'd tried to keep his; but alert to me now he caught my chin, and prodded me with quiet knowing.

"They give you a rough time already, did they?"

"Aye...even Damaris," I quavered.

Searching my face he at length said gently, "Matey, why on earth didn't ye tell me?"; and flooded by all that was still unspoken between us, I looked down to shield my eyes.

"Ben, you know there ain't been time t' talk—not a minute."

All the obstacles that had plagued us—the intrusions on our private moments, the trap of social expectations, my compromised past and Ben's obligations—suddenly broke forth and stood between us, as if to bar us from one another; and looking past me as though he saw them, Ben braced himself as for a burden. "I wish I could tell ye this'll be oveh Monday, when we're married propeh an' 've come t' this room," he told me, acknowledging facts in his straightforward way; "but the truth is, the frustrations of past days 're all nothin' compared t' what waits yet with Anne, an' the children. We've got a week t' ourselves, then we've got t' face it... Eben told me that was the one condition he had t' marryin' us."

"Aye…fair enough," I said gamely, aching for his hurt.

"Jim, I…" he began and floundered, "You undehstand that this is one time when I don't have any of the answers…when I'm sailin' half-rigged without a compass?"

My eyes hot, I confidently nodded.

"You sure you want t' go through with this?"

My incredulity that he should ask actually snatching my breath, I nodded more emphatically still; and overcome by my trust, he caught up my hands to cover his face. "Ben," I pledged, finding my voice, "whatever happens, I'm already married t' you… I've… I've been married t' you since the first night I met you… An' there's nothin' that c'n ever undo it…not Anne or Damaris or the town or the children….not sailin' or buildin' or workin' or dyin'…Monday noon just makes it official."

Giving a gasp which was half-laughter, half-sob, he kissed me with sureness and sorrow; then drawing apart—pulling my two hands away from him—he left me without a backward look; and I listened to his footsteps till they were so soft they blended in with the soughing of the pines.

Down on my knees, I prayed for our marriage, there for an unknowable time at our window; prayed for resilience and endurance, the way one prays for the hold of a mooring; prayed as for an anchor chain in the deep, pleading for the sturdiness of its links. Then worn out as if I'd ridden a storm, I rose to find the tide breeze dwindling, and the afternoon mist gathering at sea.

I slept the rest of the day and straight into the evening, not just because he wanted me to, but because I was spent; curled up on his bed, newly made with fresh linen, and dozed at once, one of his flannel shirts close to hand. As evening came on it started to rain, pattering on the eaves over my head; and rising only long enough to partake of supper, a fine chowder Eben had rustled together, I crept back into bed to sleep through the night. The rain on the eaves, the wind in the firs, the snap of sparks on the dying hearth, all combined to lull me into a peace; and crooned to, I slumbered with a profound sense that I, the most restless of men, was home; I and my gypsy feet were home.

*   *   *   *   *

As soon as I opened my eyes I felt it around me—the wind, the irrepressible wind; and fully awake I sat up in my bunk and watched the dawn light toss in the room. It was Saturday, the 13th of June; and the wild, tangy wind that touched my lips invited me out and away from my work, away from the cares of shipyard and kin. Scrambling to the library window, I saw it was gone, the past week's fog; and restless to roam I pulled on my shoes and slipped out the door, the first one abroad. Racing back and forth I paced the shore, even ran for a stretch—a boy again, summer free; paced back and forth with an inexplicable glad laugh, till I heard a shrill "Papa!" and Jean was beside me.

Sun-browned, slight, grey-eyed, impish, her tow hair cut short again in spite of Anne's protests, she might have been the very spirit of the place, dancing beside me in her cotton dress; might have been the ambassador of the wind, given the shape of a sprite by the sea. Dancing as one, twirling in and out of the waves, or catching the spindrift with shrieks as we fled, we splashed together, father and child; then as if she understood—as if she knew it was taking me away, this irresistible, tumbling wind, like an autumn gust sweeping up a stray leaf—she tucked her hand in mine as we walked, bent on turning back to the house; tucked it firmly, securely, as if it could hold me down, this miniature grip the size of my palm.

Almost unable to put two thoughts together, I made it through breakfast and so out to town, drawing rein at the counting house in the yard; stood vacantly looking at my cluttered desk, ears still attuned to the stir of the wind; took a futile stab or two at the mail, then gave thanks when I heard the sweep of a broom, and knew it was Fan come for Saturday cleaning. Peeking into the main office with its tall desks and stools, I saw her scrub gear and, near the door, a pasteboard box; and making conversation, I asked her what was in it. Looking surprised —as well she might, since I'd never spoken but two words to her before—she proudly opened the folded top; and there lay an ornate gold and silver cake, made for the church raffle later this noon.

As soon as I saw it I knew it was mine—knew it was our wedding cake, as plainly as if it held a tag; and barking "Fan, what d'ye hope it might fetch at the raffle?", I paid her three times the amount that she named. Triumphantly setting the prize on my desk, I knew I needed a bottle of champagne; realized I needed dozens of other things, including an immediate way out of Boston; and feverishly thinking of staging a raid on the Inn, I was just barging headlong out the door when I collided with Will Coombs, an old schoolmate just off the Boston steamer. Wanting to know if there was work for him at the yard, he confessed he was down on his luck; and grabbing at him with a manic laugh, I gave him my Boston tasks with the promise of double wages if he'd do them in my name, and sent him straight back to the ferry.

Needing to make it appear it was I who was leaving, I galloped back to the house and grabbed a valise, stuffing whatever came to hand inside it; said goodbye to Anne, who'd expected my Boston departure, albeit not so abruptly; gave a kiss to Jean, with a pledge to take her out to the island on my return; and glad of the sparkle that sprang to her eyes, I tore back to town in time to filch some champagne, and hitch a ride with a trawler bound for the Banks.

Slipping aboard with my load of contraband goods—slinking to the bow to keep out of sight of the crowds, gathered to wave off friends at the ferry—I watched the town fall astern like an old life, jettisoned with the rag ends of a voyage; stood flowing with the wild pulse that was Jim's, a-throb with the delight of the moment; then wondering what on earth I'd packed in my valise, I leaned on the rail and laughed at myself, not unaware of the dubious regard of my shipmates. Looking out from the bow I put my thoughts not on Boston, not on my orders to ship for the East Indies—still unannounced through looming large in just six weeks—but on the broad, gleaming back of the sea, and the vista of my upcoming wedding; bowed my head to the windy reaches before me, and gave myself up to their bounding grandeur.

*   *   *   *   *

I was just finishing up preparations for noon dinner when I heard the crunch of a buggy in the drive; and my heart giving a leap as if it understood before my head, I says to Jim at work beside me,

"Unless I miss my guess that's Ben, an' he's here for an early weddin.'"

Giving a whoop Jim raced out the door, nearly knocking Ben down as he hopped from the buggy; and twirling him round and round in the dooryard, Ben hollered out with his quarterdeck bawl, "How about it, mate, feel like havin' a weddin' t'day?"

For an answer Jim gave his glad, ringing laugh, still in Ben's arms as they came to a halt; and barking loud enough for me to hear, Ben pressed him,

"You ain't afraid o' gettin' spliced on the thirteenth?"

Shaking his head with another frank laugh, Jim rang out at him "What about Boston?"; and Ben shrugged it off in genuine Rom fashion.

"Oh, I bribed Will Coombs t' go in my place, then sneaked a ride here on an outward bound trawleh—nobody on earth b'sides them'll eveh know the difference."

As if celebrating a wit as sharp as his own, Jim rollicked out a laugh with glee—then dashed off to find something that would answer for broom, there being an abundance of huckleberry down the road; and it fell to me to help unload the buggy, Ben having crammed a regular wedding cargo in it. In his plainest twill pants, sack coat and pilot's cap, he soon found he'd packed nothing more suitable for a ceremony than what he was wearing—his valise chock full of a useless assortment of work gear; and realizing he'd have to stand up in a plain skipper's rig, he broke the news to Jim when he breezed in the door. Glad to the heart for it, Jim dropped his branch, then dashed upstairs to get into his own gear—a Romish affair he'd finished up yesterday, whilst resting on the sofa as per orders; and waiting for him, Ben and me wrapped up dinner—trying to set the roast so it wouldn't dry up, or burn the place down whilst we was to sea.

Catching up the champagne and several glasses, Ben clattered together a box for the boat; and half-witted myself, I rushed about in his wake, scavenging for salt and twine and a knife, a pottery cup and Jim's huckleberry—all the indispensable props of a gypsy wedding— to add to the prayer book I scooped up at the last minute. Already down at the dock readying *Idris,* casting down lines right and left in no order, Ben stowed my gear for a mercy safely; and ready at last the two of us took our places—Ben erratically pacing the deck, or blindly inspecting my knots and turnings.

At the slam of the porch door he fumbled and dropped lines, his hands trembling so plain I could see them; and turning instinctively to face the house, he watched Jim come down the path towards us. As he gazed all the awkwardness of past years was wiped from his face, leaving a wonderful softness; and love and pride blazed out from his features. In his dark velveteen breeches, white figured shirt, and brightly embroidered scarlet waistcoat, Jim come walking sure-footed towards him; and on his face was an answering delight as he looked on Ben's seafarer timbers.

Wordlessly reaching for his visor, Ben slipped his cap from his head; and as I silently handed Jim aboard, Ben took his arm in quick fingers, and helped him step down onto the deck. Standing side by side in the stern, they exchanged quick, searching glances; then casting off the bowline from the piling, Ben took his place at the tiller.

Sailing round the southwest tip of the island, we coasted along the eastern shore, thick with stands of spruce and birch, and bare of cabins or fishing vessels; and finding the cove we'd agreed would be private, we tacked our way into the middle, then dropped anchor in several fathoms of water. Coiling up the lines and clearing the deck, we at once made our way to the stern; and with Jim and Ben bareheaded and silent, standing hand in hand at the tiller, I come and stood before them.

"B'fore we b'gin, mates," I says, taking the prayer book, "I been savin' some words t' speak t' ye, as friend t' ye both an' longtime shipmate." Standing solemn-eyed in the sun, they listened obediently—Ben's open collar alive to the wind, and Jim's neckerchief adrift with each gust; and looking into their eyes, I launched my say.

"This weddin' we'hre about t' celebrate's actually been goin' on for a numbeh of days…or even years, dependin' on how ye look at it," I went on, seeing the smile tug at the corners of Ben's mouth, and the glint of appreciation light Jim's eyes. "Ye might even say it's already happened—happened three years ago when ye two met, an' begun t' travel each otheh's lives, in spite o' the odds of character an' custom. That's certainly one o' the main reasons why I'm standin' here b'fore ye t'day, t' make things official as a captain o' the merchant marine.

"But there's otheh considerations b'sides. The plain fact is, I neveh met a couple… a man an' a woman, more suited t' be joined than you two men; neveh met a pair that's endured more hardships for each otheh, stayed trueh t' each otheh, seen more deeply into each otheh's hearts, or loved each otheh more fervent than you two. It ain't my place t' wondeh why it's so, or t' figure how it is that oweh two cultures, along with the religions that uphold 'em, 've failed t' acknowledge what's plain t' me, that your marriage as men is equal t' any otheh, an's as worthy in God's sight. It's only my job t' testify that it's so, since I've seen it with my own eyes these past three years; an' by marryin' you t'day, I'll stake my claim t' eternity on it."

So a-flood was their eyes that I could only bear to meet them a moment; and I hurried on with the rest of my say. "But it's only fair t' say there's certain things I expect in return. I expect ye t' tend your marriage with care…expect ye t' resolve mattehs with Anne an' the children, with consideration for all hands…expect ye t' treat one anotheh, different as ye both still are, with respect…t' guahrd against your impatience, Ben, an' your high-handed manneh…your tempeh, Jim, an' your wanderlust.. in short, expect ye t' conduct your marriage in such a way that if God was t' grant us t' stand here fifty years from now t' consideh what we've done t'day, we'd all say it was the right an' honorable thing."

Having never heard me speak in such a fashion before, Jim and even Ben respectfully bowed their heads; and seeing they'd sincerely weighed my remarks, I opened Ben's seaworn prayerbook, and embarked on the marriage service.

"Benjamin Galen," I begun gently, "wilt thou have this man to be thy wedded mate, to live togetheh afteh God's ordinance in the holy estate of matrimony? Wilt thou love him, comfort him, honoh, and keep him in sickness and health; and forsaking all othehs, keep thee only unto him, so long as ye both shall live?"

His voice husky with the promise, Ben firmly responded "I will"—his grey eyes unswerving as they looked at Jim; and as if undone by his honest sureness, Jim gave way to pain, his face working against it.

Giving them a moment I turned to Jim, my eyes on his still-struggling features; waited till he'd mastered himself, and given me his gaze. "James Gethin," I says kindly, using both his English and gypsy names as Ben had begged me, "wilt thou have this man to be thy wedded mate, to live togetheh after God's ordinance in the holy estate of matrimony? Wilt thou love him, comfort him, honoh, and keep him in sickness and health, and forsaking all othehs, keep thee only unto him, so long as ye both shall live?"

His serene answer rang out "*Avali,*" rich with Welsh tones in spite of his quaver; then as if overcome by the power of the pledge, this man of few words bowed his head, silent.

Understanding at once Ben instinctively turned toward him, and reaching into his pocket, pulled out a rose, a white sea-rose he'd plucked from our bank; and though it was somewhat the worse for wear, he placed it fumblingly at Jim's collar, whilst Jim set his jaw to still its tremble.

Then repeating my words in strong, measured phrases, Ben straightforwardly pledged to him from the service: "I, Benjamin Galen...take thee, James Gethin...to be my wedded mate...to have and to hold...from this day forward...for betteh or worse...for richeh or pooreh...in sickness and in health...to love and to cherish...till death do us pahrt..."

His voice quivering like a sail in the wind, and breaking so often that mine faltered with him, Jim begun to speak the same vow: "I, James Gethin...take thee, Benjamin Galen...to be my wedded mate..." Almost unable to speak he come to a halt, Ben taking him at once in his arms; and there he finished the rest of his vow, words stumbling in Ben's ear: "to have and to hold...from this day forward…for better or worse…for richer or poorer…in sickness and in health…to love and to cherish…till death do us part…"

Waiting for Ben to raise his taut face, and for Jim to catch his voice, I hunted around for my well-worn cambric, and unceremoniously blew my nose; then searching the prayer book for the place I'd just lost, I returned my attention to business, whilst Jamie and Ben slowly drew apart, wiping their eyes on the backs of their hands.

Turning to Ben, I asked for Jim's ring, which he pulled out proudly and handed to me; and blessing it with the prayer that was given, I returned it to him, placing it on his broad palm. Repeating the words forthrightly after me, Ben triumphantly said, "With this ring, I thee wed… In the Name of the Fatheh, and of the Son, and of the Holy Ghost"; and so saying, he slipped the ring on Jim's finger.

Wordlessly touching the broad, gold band, cut like a porpoise with a sapphire eye, Jim cupped his left hand in his right, his features working; and catching both his hands in his own work-hard ones, Ben kissed the ring, then Jim's hands together.

Bowing my head, I prayed for their marriage, haltingly searching for the words I needed, while the rigging rang its chimes at the mast: "Lord, hehre are two mates, spliced now for life… bless their voyage…chahrt their course…smooth the watehs b'fore them…" Then raising my head, I joined Ben's right hand to Jim's right; and over them two hands, hard-twined, weathered, I gravely concluded, "Those whom God hath joined t'getheh, let no man put asundeh."

Gathering Jim into a mighty embrace, Ben kissed him as if no one was watching; then breaking their clasp, they turned to me, and generously cast their arms about me. Victoriously hugging first Jim, then Ben, I indulged in their celebration; then calling an intermission in the stern—hunting about for the twine, salt and bread, and all the other implements of a gypsy wedding—I prepared to launch the second part of the service.

Sitting down by the tiller, Jim played his harp, brung aboard by Ben at the last minute; plucked some Romany melody, lilting and fervent, whilst I hauled up our gear from the cuddy, and Ben sat listening, chin in hand. Slipping into a sea chantey, Jim strummed

"Shenandoah"—the tears springing unabashedly to Ben's eyes at the first bars; and understanding that I was hearing something special between them, I stopped my scavenging and set down to listen. Over the blue of the waters and the sweep of the boat, the chords strummed out with a yearnsome roaming, as from hundreds of capstans or crowded taverns; and as though re-living the places of three years—the smoke of Toby's or the heights of Rio, or the strands of Cuba or Anjier or Whampoa—Jim and Ben exchanged wistful glances, flickering with the shifts of scene.

Then the harp falling silent, they got to their feet, and once again stood ready before me; and standing at the tiller I commenced the Romany rites, aided and abetted by Jim. Rich with rolled r's and French and German twists on top of the tortures of Welsh, Jim's dialect was a poser; and so badly did I botch the opening phrases that they broke into rollicking laughter, and thereafter simply spoke to each other. All symbol and action, not unlike Jim hisself, the Romany service needed few words anyway; so I confined myself to giving directions, whilst they obeyed with occasional remarks to each other.

Following custom, I told Jim to fetch the bread, salt and water; and bringing the basket with its fresh-baked loaf, a bag of coarse sea-salt and glistening pitcher, he set it before me, eyes sparkling, whilst Ben found the pottery cup and filled it. Sharing the cup—Ben first, Jim second, the only time they was ever supposed to sip from the same container—they drained it off; took turns with murmurs of thanks, "*paracrow tute*," and the mingling of fingers as they served each other; then they smashed the cup, dashing it against the teak rail, so signaling their break from the past.

Opening their cuffs, they then rolled back their sleeves; and holding out their wrists, they waited while I pierced their skin, then bound them together with a silk cord. With the length that was left I tied three knots—one for constancy, one for pleasure, and one for long life in marriage; and as I made fast the last Jim told Ben: "*Kaulo ratti adrey tute*"—"Now you have gypsy blood in your veins." His face shining Ben rang out "*Avali*...like there's Yankee in youhrs"; and there with their wrists in the air they laughed, laughed away years of hardship and waiting.

Unwrapping the cord I prepared to cut it, and give each a half in case they ever wanted a gypsy divorce; but Ben resolutely refused to let me, stopping my knife before it came down; and taking the cord now stained with their blood, he tossed it out into the sea.

Lifting the bread from the basket, I then broke it in half and salted both parts, giving one to Ben and the other to Jim; and taking these tokens of bliss they exchanged them, feeding each other, eyes dancing. While they ate I took the bag of salt and tossed grains over their left shoulders, that they might be favored with good fortune; and as they bowed their heads to the blessing I sealed their luck with a bit of a gift, a *kharvie-saster*. As soon as he seen the traditional present—the heart and soul of camp and tent, the kettle-iron from which black pots simmered over gypsy dinner fires—Jim cried out in joy; and Ben was still holding him, tenderly calling him "*chav*," when I brung forth the huckleberry, and held it invitingly before them.

Hand in hand they stood before it; and jumping together they crossed over to a new life; met on the other side and, fully married at last, cast their arms about each other. Embracing first Ben, then me—hurling hisself back at Ben, then standing awed at the tiller, unaware he was both laughing and sobbing—Jim reached for his neckerchief, untied it, then let Ben tie it again in the marriage pattern; and though he had been wearing it so for a week, Ben took him by the shoulders and kissed it.

Breaking open the champagne, I poured three glasses, and offered an impetuous toast; and settling ourselves about the hatch, we helped ourselves to the celebration, me passing around some day-old confections, and Jim and Ben filling each other's glasses. With the sun warm about us and the waves lapping at our bow, we basked away a blissful hour, me sitting Indian-style on the deck, and Jim reclining against Ben's shoulder; shared memories amidst shouts of laughter, or drifted in sunny spells of silence, whilst the offshore wind ripped the harbor, and flashes of sunlight danced in the hollows. Now and then fondling Jim's ring or feeding each other tidbits, they indulged in the foolishness of lovers, not forgetting to include me in their antics; then gently stroking Jim's hair, Ben eased him aside, and led us in getting underway for our own dock.

Jim and me at the ropes, and Ben—who'd never sailed any way but sober—somewhat shakily at the tiller, we managed to negotiate the Point, and luff successfully up to our landing; then straightaway fishing in my bag, I hauled out the quarantine sign from its depths, and triumphantly nailed it to the porch, whilst Ben stoked the fire up in the stove, and victoriously unpacked his valise.

As we savored the magnificent dinner—for a mercy, none the worse for postponement; as we piled our plates high with prime downeast fare, them two exchanged meaning glances, as if harking back to what they was years ago—as if understanding they'd carved each other out like craftsmen, chipping away at the figureheads in their workshops. Watching their eyes flicker—watching Ben's hand fumble with his silver, and Jim's impulsively lay down his fork—I harkened back to days past myself; remembered, as Ben got to his feet and offered Jim wedding cake, the sight of him feeding a straw man off Argentina, four months into Jim's disappearance at sea; remembered, as Jim fed Ben in return with a touch to his face, the sight of him peering into a steam tent, and stroking with joy Ben's living brow. Fumbling myself, I laid down my fork, and tugged at the corners of my napkin in silence; and when I looked up their eyes was on me, the eyes of shipwrights smiling on their work.

Thanks by chance to the weather, by chance to my sign, we was interrupted neither by visitors nor tradesmen; and we finished our dinner at a leisurely pace, lingering at the table with wine glasses, and the noble remains of the wedding cake. When at last it was plain there'd be no intrusions, and Jim and Ben traded off testing glances, I begun to clear the table, and shooed them away for the evening; and getting apologetically to their feet, they abandoned me to the clean-up. Not looking at one another, they made for the stairs, Ben fumbling for some moments to lock the stair door behind him; then firmly, swiftly they mounted the steps, passed into their bedroom and locked it as well; and I scarcely seen them again for a week.

* * * * *

Our stay on the island lasted a week; and for the first five days we dwelt in seclusion, in the intimacy of a cell or cocoon: seldom coming downstairs even for meals, never once venturing outside the house, but spending the whole of our time in our room, glutting ourselves on one another. From the first moment Jim came to me out of the spare room, slipping his dressing gown from his shoulders, to the final hour when we debated our course, we scarcely moved more than ten or twelve feet in one direction or the other; but in passion and memory we traveled miles, indeed boxed the compass through our bodies and lives.

All over the bed as we were in our travels—now by the window, reminiscing together, now sideways near the head, bracing Jim's feet on the roof slope—I came to see it almost as transportation; and as I'd once used his trunk or wardrobe or vardo to access the mysteries of his heart, so now I used our bed to know him. Rumpled from one end to the other, its coverlet tangled as any gypsy wagon's, and its pillows tossed wherever needed, it was the vehicle that yielded him to me; and he knew full well that, once I'd caught up with him there, I'd finally have the upper hand.

Looking into his eyes after one such encounter—lingering over his damp face, sweet with release, and the curve of his bare hip tucked in the moonlight—I murmured to him in the candor of pleasure: "Oh, God, *chav*, I knew it'd be good…but I neveh dreamed or imagined it'd be like this, or I would've taken you that first night at Hannah's."

Smiling, he shook his head. "It wouldn't 've been like this," he told me, realistic with what he knew of himself. "I wasn't ready…an' even if I had been, I certainly wouldn't 've let you know then."

"When would you have?" I challenged, dryly.

"When I was sure you'd chased after me as long as you could," he returned with a devilish sparkle.

Gazing into the dark blue eyes beside me, I saw a deep wit, a profound intelligence of the heart—an intelligence far out front of my own, beckoning and plotting and waiting, then taking run and darting ahead. As an archipelago or chain of islands resolves itself as one draws nearer, only to draw one into its channels, and on to more islands on the horizon, so he had drawn me on with the beyond; and the vivid eyes that were laughing into mine now, confiding a shoal, the guess of a shoreline, were plainly concealing the rest of the waters—were already making me wonder whether I'd ever indeed won the upper hand, as they held out another isle for some future revelation.

*   *   *   *   *

If what he needed from me was horizon, the mariner's quest for a shifting compass, what I needed from him was landfall, the unshifting ground of a sure anchorage; and we were perfectly mated to provide for each other. Broken from years of unruddered direction—craving the heat of a constant passion, the bedrock of a solid companion—I healed under the steadiness of his handling, whilst he flourished under my impulsive migrations. Yet though the two of us moved in response to each other—though our give and take was as rhythmic as the back and forth of a seaman and vessel, or the to and fro of a pair of jugglers—I knew that the advantage was his; knew it even though I hid it from him, indeed led him on with the subterfuge of the chase.

Yearning for his strength more than I'd ever shown him, I yielded myself to it in rare moments—relinquished myself as I had in New York, or off Cape Horn that bitter night; and the thrill of finding I was overmastered was as keen as that of any pleasure. As our nights slipped into hushed, tranquil mornings, into wakings with his arms about me—as our noons faded into wind-gusty evenings, into murmurings taut with desire—I came to discover a finish, a completeness that encompassed us both; and no place spoke of that wholeness more than our bed. Wholly ours, wholly shaped by us, it was the uttermost home I'd sought—the place where I could test his power, taste my own strength in submission; and unbeknownst to him, far into the night, whilst his broad chest rose and fell in sleep, I cherished the simplest rumplings of the sheets, the most mundane crumplings of the pillows.

*   *   *   *   *

On the dawn of our sixth day on the island, I was the first one to wake, coming to consciousness with the preoccupation which'd been troubling me when I fell asleep: that this was the last day but one of our stay, the day I'd set aside for talk and direction. Though I'd said nothing to Jamie about my sailing orders—though I'd never once referred to my growing intent to leave Anne, nor the half-dozen plans which had shaped themselves in my fancy—I knew he understood we could travel no further without a course choice; knew he understood today was the day I'd reserved for decision.

Lying in the early morning half-light, I waited for him to waken; gently eased an arm about him, and felt his instinctive slumbering nestle. Stroking his hair with my other hand—watching the light grow stronger in the room, as the smooth, dark tangles slipped beneath my thumb—I finally whispered, "Still snoozin', mate?"; and giving his head a drowsy shake, he turned more fully into my arms, and rested his face against my throat. Feeling the gentle brush of his lashes, the warmth of his breath as he slowly wakened, I tightened my arm about his shoulders, and buried my lips in the thick waves of his hair; then quietly disentangling our limbs, I resolutely got to my feet, shrugged into my dressing gown, and went to fetch coffee.

Finding a pot already prepared—as I had each day—and a plate of fresh muffins set out by Eben, I set the lot on a tray, then carried the meal back up to our room; and pouring out coffee, I sat down by the window, and waited for Jamie to emerge from the hallway. Though we'd lived together in intimacy for a week—though we'd shared close quarters frequently for years, and knew each other's every habit—he still persisted in maintaining the code of etiquette imposed by Rom standards; and I knew by now he'd slip off without notice to use the hall chamber we'd set up as a water closet, and return washed and shaved without reference to his actions. Amused by the compromise between Rom and gadje customs which he had unconsciously worked out, I smiled into my coffee; glanced benignly at the cup which was his alone, and gently touched the curve of its handle.

As he entered the room he caught up his cup and sat down on the sofa, then gave his attention to our breakfast; and sensing my mood, he said little, his expression thoughtful above the dark cloth of his wrapper. When at length I set down my cup and stretched out—propped up—on the bed, he finished up his muffin and followed, settling down by me with his chin in his hand, and an expectant, watchful air to his features.

Never one to beat around the bush, I got right down to business; gave him a sober, serious look, heaved a great sigh, and launched into my thoughts with: "We've got a decision or two t' make, mate."

Looking down at his hands—now both playing with the coverlet—he gave me a quiet nod, knowing perfectly well what I was going to say; and reading his understanding in his averted gaze, I determinedly persevered.

"In a day or so we'll be back in town, tryin' t' get on with oweh jobs and oweh lives…but b'fore I c'n bear t' pack up my bags, I've got t' know what we're goin' t' do, an' exactly how we're goin' t' do it." Seeing his jaw tighten against his emotion, I paused to master my own feeling, then calmly, stubbornly pressed on, saying: "The way I see it, we c'n keep on as we have been, carvin' out time for owehselves afteh workin' or sailin'—me at the yahrd or at Anne's with the children, an' you at the joiner's or McCabe's or the Inn… It wouldn't eveh be like it has been, this past week or so here on the island: we'd have t' pretty much play things by eahr, an' snatch time t'getheh at night or on weekends."

Searching his by now inscrutable features—longing to find, in some quiver or tenseness, a clue to his desire for the direction of our marriage, but discovering only a patient attention—I unsteadily continued, "Or…if I was t' leave Anne…we could live t'getheh… not here, perhaps, but elsewhere in Maine…Canada…Wales… whereveh we wanted…We could pack up a wagon an' travel an' hunt, all the way from here t' the West…or take t' the sea like my old Uncle Ezra, an' travel the globe, Romany fashion." Still finding no flicker on his face—his countenance as still as an inland pool on a windless night—I concluded, "It's got t' be one choice or the otheh…this ain't no time for the 'chahrm of goin' in circles,' mate."

Looking up with a quick, comprehending glance, he wordlessly nodded his assent; but reserving his thoughts, he glanced back down, and tugged at the fringes of the blanket. Waiting for him to speak, I looked at his face, saw signs of the struggle taking place within; perceived that he was groping for words; and at last forcing the issue, I caught him by the chin, and gently told him, "I can't make this d'cision without you, Jim."

Meeting my eyes with a swift, piercing glance, he wavered, then softly responded: "Ben, I…you see, I…can't help you choose what t' do about Anne. It… it just wouldn't be fittin' for me t' decide her fate."

Looking into his honest gaze, I perceived the truth of his statement; looked down at my own hands, folded beside him; then raising my eyes—finding his waiting—I informed him gently but frankly, "Just the same… if I'm t' make a choice… I've got t' know what you want t' do."

His jaw squared and tense and his eyes averted, he offered in a low voice, "I c'n tell you what I think we *should* do."

Shaking my head, I said firmly: "That's not what I asked; what we *should* do c'n come lateh. Right now, I've got t' know what you *want*."

His face even tenser, awash with his feeling—his hands quivering as they toyed with the blanket—he shrugged, then whispered simply: "I want t' wake up b'side you every day for the rest o' my life… I want my socks in the same drawer as yours." His voice breaking, he halted, raising a hand to ward me off—swiftly engulfed as I was—from a hasty, emotional rejoinder; then gathering strength, he ended firmly, "But what I want's not necessarily what I think we should do."

Still wordlessly awed by his confession—one of the rare moments when he spoke with direct candor; overjoyed that his longing matched my own yearning for a life shared under one roof, I gratefully met him head-on: "An' what d'y think we *should* do, then?"

A tug of resistance tightening his jaw line and battling his disciplined effort at fairness, he at last managed to say: "I think that we should keep on was we have been…that we should go back t' Cape Damaris, an' lead separate lives at Anne's house an' Eben's."

Taken utterly aback, I cried out, "Jamie, d'ye realize what you're sayin'?"; and nodding his head, he looked down, and listened while I gathered steam to combat him. "It's not just that we'd almost neveh be alone t'getheh," I began, my eyes scanning his averted face. "It's not just that I'd have t' slip out at night t' see you, an' back home again b'fore I was missed... not just that we'd always be interrupted, or worse yet, run the risk o' bein' discovered, unless Eben continues t' look out for us. It's the charade of me pretendin' t' be married t' Anne, an' you pretendin' t' be separate at Eben's—all that, plus the barriers we'd face at sea, even if you shipped aft as steward. It's...it's me gettin' my sailin' ordehs for a few weeks hence," I blurted, "when I can't bear t' so much as leave this room."

Looking swiftly up at the break in my voice, he knowingly met my eyes; and seeing not just understanding but the utter lack of surprise in his gaze, I wonderingly murmured, "You knew about the Indies all along," while he gave a game smile and a nod. "How'd you heahr?" I asked then, marveling at his silence and tact; and shrugging a shoulder, he answered,

"That night at the ball, talkin' t' one o' the Crowninshields—he knew all about it, an' was tryin' t' trick information out o' me about the consignees."

Touching his face, I looked down, and considered my next words for a moment; then raising my eyes—meeting his sureness—I obstinately tried him again: "Afteh hearin' all this—afteh hearin' about the Indies—you still think we should go back t' Cape Damaris, an' carry on oweh marriage b'tween voyages an' shore jobs?"

His face drawn but calm, he nodded; and scanning his features, I persisted, "You don't think I should even approach Anne on the subject, an' sound her out about divorce or separation?"

Biting his lip, he trembled, but stubbornly shook his head; played with the coverlet for a long moment; then determinedly looked over at me and tried to explain: "You see...it's not just that I know she'd say no to divorce, or...that you'd never feel right if you left your responsibilities." Seeing the conflict on my face—the desire to protest warring with the conviction that there was justice and truth in his words—he huskily persevered, "It's... the children, Ben, especially the young ones." His voice dropping so low that I had to draw near to hear him, he struggled to express his meaning: "B'cause...I can never have a family...not that I'm complainin'; I never wanted t' be anything other than what I am...but b'cause.. we'll never have our own children...let me give you yours...a second time...by keepin' them with you."

Understanding the whole of his sacrifice in a moment—seeing the clarity with which he'd foreseen Anne's reaction, and intuited my dance on the beach with Jean—I closed my eyes in the pain of his gift, in an ache so deep that I could neither speak nor look at him. Lying beside me, he waited, gradually fighting back the tautness which had captured his throat; and when at last I looked up he insistently whispered, "Promise me you'll weigh what I said... Promise."

Getting up on one elbow, I took his chin, and gently kissed his lips in answer; then climbing out of the bed, I pulled on my clothes, and wordlessly left to make my decision.

*   *   *   *   *

Knowing perfectly well that he'd head for the mainland—that he'd probably spend the day by the lighthouse, weighing his thoughts on the rock shore he loved—I crossed over to the north window; watched him till he was but a speck on the road, bound into town to hitch a boat ride; then collapsed into the chair beside me, and gave way to the pain which had swept me since waking. Overcome by the inevitable course before us, by the path I knew without doubt he would choose, I abandoned myself to the flood of my feeling; and hearing my sobs or maybe just guessing them, Eben soon turned the knob and entered our chamber, and sat down by me on the arm of the chair.

Putting my head on his lap, he heard the whole story, which fell out exactly as he'd expected; offered futile, well-meaning gestures; even laughed with me when I managed to gasp out, "At least this way, he'll always be hot"; then lapsing into a tender silence, he stroked the tumbled strands of my hair, and sat with me late into the morning.

*   *   *   *   *

Making for the wharves, I caught a boat into Cape Damaris, doing my best to make it appear I'd just arrived back from Boston; then heading for the Point before anyone spotted me, I sat down on a rock overlooking the channel, and struggled to take command of my thoughts. For a long time I was pulled first one way, then another: now considering the justice of Jamie's words, the inevitability of the children's needs and my own sense of failure, should I ever leave them; now weighing my need for a genuine marriage, or Jamie's for my unbroken attention. Complicating these demands was the factor of my work: the necessity for six months out of every twelve at sea, and for time-consuming extended family relations the remaining six at the yard. Every time I came to the point of abandoning the entire structure—children and wife, career and business—which I'd mistakenly put together, the integrity which was at the core of my nature forced me to reconsider; and every time I reconsidered, the outrage of my own denied person, of Jamie's sacrificed mornings and evenings, exploded to protest and accuse me.

Wrestling with the options before me, I sought for some combination of choices which would permit compromise; tried to imagine persevering at Anne's house till our youngest were done with their schooling, then gently shifting to Jim's without divorce or scandal. Yet the very idea of postponing living with him for fifteen years—the very concept of starting our life together when he was thirty-six, and I myself was well into my forties—caused a violent inner surge of rebellion. Were there any way to deal out the fifteen years in question so that both Jim and my family received a fair share—were there any way to spend long stretches with him on the island or at sea or elsewhere, then return for stretches to dwell with my family—the period of time could be made tolerable; but as life at sea offered neither privacy nor time together, and life ashore offered spells too brief even for my family, I could perceive no satisfactory division. For an indeterminate time I speculated and searched, while the shadows shortened, then gradually lengthened; but finding no solution which would answer the needs of all, I took to staring about me, my thoughts empty of words, ideas and actions.

At first I stared at the tumble of rocks, the tidal pools and crevices and ledges which comprised this shelf of land at the Point; then shifting my gaze, I took in the lighthouse, the outbuildings and stunted spruce and fir which for decades had characterized this headland.

Lifting my eyes, I gazed further, scanning first the gradations of silver and blue near the breakers, the swirls which denoted roadways of currents, and the patches which pointed to sandbars or shallows; then settling at last on the horizon, I took in the sapphire blue of deep water, the utter clarity and precision of the line between sea and sky.

Following its sweep toward the harbor—descrying a whirlwind of gulls, wheeling and diving round some minute vessel—I came upon a magnificent sight, all the grander because unexpected: the *Charis Spooner* outward bound for Rio, every stitch of canvas drawing, and her whole clear-cut form bowing down to the wind gusts. Though I'd known she was outward bound today—though I'd seen the crowds gathering at the Ship Street wharf, even as early as my arrival—it hadn't struck me till now she was leaving, or occurred to me I should have bid her farewell; and I watched her now with a practiced eye, the intimacy of a skipper and shipwright. As she serenely made her way down the passage between the headland and St. James Island—as she progressed with the majesty, swiftness and balance her trim lines offered—I was swept with an intolerable pain, an ache compounded of pride, awe and memory; and watching her with unspeakable regret—seeing her decline on the distance—I suddenly knew I'd never helm her again

With this knowledge came an indescribable clearness, lightning-swift and wholly unlooked-for, which blazed in my mind and heart: a clarity of vision which, like a sudden storm-flash, illumined the hills and dells within me, and revealed both purpose and direction. As if these contours had resided for years in some obscure seat of my imagination, I recognized their pattern—sensed that I'd all along known my own landfall, and joyously took in its well-known approaches. Springing immediately to my feet, I knew exactly what I needed to do; and heading for the house, I went to confront Anne.

Finding the kitchen unnaturally quiet, I hunted about till I spotted her in the sitting room, mending a dress by the open window; and understanding from her that Sadie was in town, and that the children were spending the afternoon at Mother's—the older ones, no doubt, at the very departure of *Charis* I'd just missed; understanding that some unknown force was at work, opening the way for my new direction—I waved aside her exclamation at my supposed return from Boston, heaved myself into a chair and said, "We have t' talk."

Looking up in stunned surprise—as well she might, having never heard me utter such words, or invite her into a frank discussion— she immediately put down her work, and gazed at me with wary attention; and seeing again how much she'd changed—noting the signs of stresses and time—I watched her carefully as I launched into my say. "Anne," I began as she folded the dress, "I've been weighin' my course whilst I've been away…an' I've made up my mind just t'day what to do. I'm goin' t' leave my berth at Melchett Bros…am on my way right now t' resign my commission."

She couldn't 've looked more dumbfounded than if she'd been stove by a whale. "Why, Benjamin," she gasped, giving a tug at the folds, "You mean…you won't be sailing this summeh, you…? Ephraim as good as told me yestehday, they'd be putting you in masteh for that East Indies voyage."

"I won't be shippin' for the East Indies, or anywhehre else eveh again, Anne; I'm all done with the sea," I said firmly.

Her face was a study as she tried to adjust. "You're…you're retiring as a captain, you…why, Ben, you'hre just turning thirty, you…"

"It's the age many a skippeh retires," I reminded.

"I know it, but you…you've got such a promising career, in spite of what just happened, you…You're one of the best mastehs on the coast; an' you've said so often yourself, with clippehs just coming into their own…there's almost no limit to what they could achieve, an' you with them."

"I know what I've said…an' it's still true. For those as c'n stand the pace, there's a fortune t' be made in the clippeh trade, an' a name b'sides, eitheh shippin' as masteh or buildin' designs. But I tell you again, my aims've changed; an' I don't intend anymore t' follow the sea."

"Ben, you...this isn't just because of your trial, or bad feelings you have right now for Melchett Bros.?" she prodded, still tugging at the folds of her dress. "Because if—"

"Anne, without the trial an' all that came b'fore it, I'd still have reached the same conclusion... It's time for me t' leave deep wateh, an' stahrt a new life on land that's more... simple. I... I don't mind tellin' you, I've had my doubts about the whole thing eveh since Jackson preached about riches a ways back...an' seein' the greed an' indifference t' human life that comes with makin' a fortune at sea— seein' what even friends of owehs was ready t' do to *us*, oveh a cargo of *tea*, for Christ's sake—ain't changed my thinkin' any. I'd far ratheh spend the rest o' my life earnin' my livin' in a more honest fashion... an' I need t' do it independent of Melchett Bros."

"You're...you're not even going to *build*, Ben?" she boggled.

"No, I'm done buildin' clippehs...done sendin' out ships t' make the rich richeh...at the risk o' common seamen."

Her distress was real and not just for me, as she began to see clearly she'd no longer be the wife of a noted sea captain and shipwright. "But, Ben, you're...the best buildeh on the Gulf of Maine, you...the name you've made for yourself, an' the yahrd, is as good as any in New York...you...you know it's your genius."

"I know it is...but I plan t' turn it t' otheh uses."

"What...on earth will you do?" she gaped, looking as if she was bracing for anything, including that I'd taken a notion to farming.

"I'm goin' t' build what I feel confidence in, fishing vessels, small coastal craft that c'n carry lumbeh...the essentials of life, Anne, not the riches; an' I'm goin' t' build 'em on my own, on the island."

She was so struck amidships she simply stared; and to give her time to adjust to the idea, I filled in the picture of what I proposed—a partnership with Jim and Eben; at first; a bare bones shipyard with a building or two; but eventually, a thriving business, big enough to create work for many, and provide an alternative to fishing, especially in the off season.

"What...what on earth will Melchett Bros. say to all this?" she asked finally, her eyes clearly seeing our family diminished—mere fishing boat builders on some obscure island.

"What can they say or do t' stop it? I won't be workin' in competition with them…in fact, I'll be in a position where I c'n throw business their way, an' they mine. They've plenty o' shipwrights an' skippehs without me…the family is big, and business is wide open. An' finally, I don't owe them a dime…have taken the entire loss of *Abigail's* cargo t' ensure their capital's sound."

"That's…just my next point, Ben; what'll you do for money?"

"Jacob offered me ten thousand as a personal loan, when I was in New York earlieh this spring… I don't know if he meant t'was free t' be used as seed money for a new venture, ratheh than a new ship; but if he's still willing, I'll take it."

"We'll be in debt," she pointed out.

"Aye," I said, unflinching. "The reality is, Anne, I'm no longeh a wealthy sea captain an' shipwright, but a simple laboreh stahrtin' oveh."

A simple laborer starting over had never been in her plans when she married into the Melchett family, and her face showed it; but she had in reserve—as she'd demonstrated the night of the shipwreck—a considerable mettle of her own; and her chin came up to announce it. "Well, if it must be, then let it be so, Ben… I know you well enough to know you'll make a success of it."

"I will, an' while I'm at it, you an' the children won't lack for anything, you c'n bank on it."

"Why eveh did you choose the island for the location of the new yard?"

"That's the otheh decision I came t' talk t' you about," I said, up against it at last. "I chose it b'cause I want t' live thehre…I've come t' love it…it's home, Anne."

"But….home is here in Cape Damaris."

"For you it is; but not for me, anymore."

For a moment we stared at one another, as if, in this simple conflict over home, we saw the wide gulf that'd always flowed between us; then drawing a deep breath, I plunged,

"What I'm leadin' up to, Anne, is… I think that we should

separate."

To my amazement, she burst into laughter—into a merry peal which held neither rancor nor surprise. "Why, Benjamin," she said, getting the better of her mirth, "I thought that we've been separate for yeahrs…eveh since the very beginning."

That she spoke true was certainly no surprise; but that she had always known—as I had—of the complete disunion of our life, took me totally aback; and whilst I was trying to catch my breath, she hastened,

"Oh, I don't mean that like it sounds…You don't go long voyages, like most do…haven't eveh been gone for long spells, except the last. My sisteh's daughteh was nearly two before she sawr her fatheh the first time… And when you're here, you're more attentive than most fathehs—-most of my friends envy your care of the children. It's just that, with respect to you and I… we've always been separate, even when we're togetheh."

So baldly put, her words whipped like a lash, even though I'd always known them—had lived for years with the failure they named. "I know it's true," I said without protest, flinching still at her assessment. "You should have married Joe, Anne, when you had the chance."

Again she laughed, but this time her laughter was touched with the futility of regret. "I shouldn't have married eitheh of you…at least, not so young as I was… I shouldn't have let the expectations of othehs decide for me what course I should take. If I'd married Joe, I'd be in the same situation—mistress of a big house, but not of my life. Far from having a marriage, I'd be a widow… No, I don't envy Elizabeth her life, or wish that my life had been traded with hers."

"What *do* you wish, then?" I got out, floored to hear her speak so directly, and of the same traps that'd always boxed me.

"Now, you mean?" She drew a sigh, and I saw with a sudden sympathy she was pretty—still handsome despite the stresses she'd borne. "I could say I wished for things to be different, for eitheh you or I to be more like the otheh…that's what I wished for in the beginning. But now, recognizing we're too set in oweh ways, both of us, to eveh change…I just wish for what *you* want, a place where I belong."

More stunned than ever, I simply looked at her, mouth agape.

"Oh, you can't be surprised, Benjamin," she smiled; "you know I've wanted a house in town for yeahrs, and all the social life which comes with it."

"What would you do if you had it?" I asked, wondering at my long resistance with a sting of reproach; and she looked at me as if astonished I'd asked.

"Why, I'd…I'd be able to go to preaching every week, I and the children…neveh have to worry about the roads being passable afteh a rain. I could go to all the Ladies' Aide meetings, really help them to plan things, including the suppehs… The children would be close to the district school; we could go to every spelling bee, no matteh the weatheh… I could…there's so little culture in the town, besides the lectures the temperance clubs provide… I could stahrt up a literary guild, and folks could come to meet at oweh house… Maybe we could finally have a piano, and the children could take lessons… Even—you'll laugh, I know—but I could even stahrt up a small orchestra, and we could play once a month for social events."

Hearing her out with silent patience; surprised, in fact astonished by her hunger for music, and by the vivacity which livened her face at its mention; guilt-stricken by her obvious need for more freedom— not just for more money as I'd expected, but for a far greater latitude of activity—I confessed, "I…. Anne, I had no idear you wanted all this… I mean…I knew you wanted t' be closeh t' town, but—"

Seizing the moment, she poured out her frustration—her weariness at her pattern of living, and at the conventions which shackled her spirit. Seeing for the first time her view of our marriage, and comprehending its utter collapse—recognizing, in her resistance to the treadmill of duty, my own exasperation with Melchett Bros., and feeling the first bond of kinship I'd ever felt with her as a result—I said to her, voice hushed,

"Anne, I thought you *wanted* all this… I thought you wanted *more*—more children, more rooms, more carriages, more relations, an' all the responsibilities that come with them."

Touching her handkerchief to her eyes—one of the rare times I'd ever seen her cry—she responded gently, "I did. I did want all this, and more. But I wanted something of myself in it…something of myself in my marriage, in my obligations to my house and children."

Heretofore I'd only known of my own need—of my own bitter incompleteness in marriage; had only guessed at her lack, and imagined my inadequacy for her. Now that I heard her in plain words, I couldn't duck the totality of defeat; and stunned that what had begun as a business proposal had led to this confrontation with failure—torn between an oppressive guilt, and an indescribable release we'd at last aired our feelings—I asked her gently, "Do you want a divorce?"

Her face registering neither shock nor dismay, she responded simply: "No. That's not a solution. Even if the church accepted it— even if the town could—even if your family and mine undehstood, I could neveh do that to the children. They'd be the only children in town who came of divorced parents… We've had oweh chance; now they deserve theirs…and what we've done, we've got to deal with."

Seeing in her an adherence to responsibility even fiercer than my own—an acceptance of reality even stauncher than Jim's prediction—I leaned toward her and insisted, "If we're not divorced in letteh, then we are in spirit; and I won't go one step furtheh till we both face it."

"I undehstand," she said wearily, but with acceptance.

"You may undehstand," I flashed, "but I can't… I can't undehstand how we can both, with one breath, damn the town an' convention for the yoke we've put oweh necks into, an' then, with the next, knuckle undeh t' them, ratheh than break the tie when we can."

"If it was you and I only, Ben, I wouldn't hesitate—even though I can bear up undeh the judgment of othehs less well than you. But thehre's the children to consideh… They have to be able to hold up their heads—and they've already, this month, seen their fatheh go to trial, and emerge without a penny…are about to hear of your move to the island, which is bound to confuse them, no matteh how we disguise it."

"Do we agree, at least, that we're separate, whateveh we might be in name?" I kept at it.

"You know we do," she said, unflinching. "It's… how we look to othehs that mattehs to me at this point…especially how we look to the children."

"Then what c'n we do t' make oweh lives betteh?"

"You mean…more bearable to us while the children are growing?"

"Aye. I've told you what I need t' do… begin a new business an' live on the island, most of the time at least, while I get things stahted. What about you? I… If we was t' buy a house in town, would that help?"

"Benjamin, are you serious?" she gasped.

"Neveh more so."

"I…why, it would change my life…almost overnight."

"Have you thought of a place?"

"Why…the half-moon house is for sale."

"The half-moon house?" I puzzled.

"Yes…that's what Courtney calls it; the one on St. James Street, with the half-moon windows in the attic—Charley Percival's fatheh's."

"You'd like that?"

"I'd… I'd love it."

"Then we'll do it."

She looked around her, stunned. "How?"

"Well, this house is for sale, ain't it? I'd thought, you know, that whoeveh bought it…might continue t' rent it to us, till I'd saved enough t' buy it back; but…if you could hang on till I've saved enough t' buy in town…"

"I've got a betteh idear."

"What on earth is that?"

"Release my funds, which you've refused to touch all these yeahrs because of some silly notion about 'only men should provide'…and I could buy it for us myself."

Aghast, I gasped, "Anne…it's…it's *my* job t' buy the house."

"Why?"

"Why? Well…amongst otheh things, you know…"

"'Only men should provide,'" she mimicked.

"It's not just that, it's… My Gawd, Anne, folks'll say I've not only failed with *Abigail,* but with my family, an' now you've got t' pay your own keep."

"Oh, you mean those same folks we were just condemning for putting oweh necks in a yoke, and that I was afraid to rile with a divorce?" she jibed.

Silently, we looked at each other; then—perhaps out of strain, perhaps sheer logic—the comedy of the situation so overtopped every other aspect that we burst into hearty laughter.

"All right," I capitulated, "I'll release your funds…with the undehstandin' I'll pay you all back."

"Half."

"All."

"Half."

I would have protested far longer, but her eyes were so bright with hope and animation—the taste of life I'd won for myself, with Jim, and never would have begrudged to her—that I subsided. "Well, we'll dickeh about that lateh," I said, bringing one boot up to rest on my knee. "I'll sign the papehs t'day, an' we'll buy the house t'morrer… on one condition."

"And that is?"

"I want my own room in this place, just as I have hehre—a room I c'n come an' go to as I please, when I'm in town…a room that'll have my books an' chahts an' bunk, all laid out neat without them freaks o' chests with claw legs…an' all the otheh truck I know you'll fill the place up with."

"I'll store oweh family things carefully in the attic, and I won't clutteh up your room with any new things I buy, any more than you'll force me to deal with whateveh you've got out there on the island."

"Fair enough. I won't be needin' it often… I'll be honest… I'll be most of the time on the island…What I'm about t' do there'll be a king-sized job, an' it'll keep me on the spot for the most pahrt. But there'll be spells when I'm in town for business…an' I'll be around often enough t' keep down talk, an' help take care o' the children."

"Fine," she agreed, brighter with each minute. "May I…may I use enough of my money to hire anotheh maid to help Sadie?"

"Anne, the money's youhrs; if it'll help you an' Sadie, do it."

"I know the money's mine, but I want to use it in a spirit that won't come back to bite us lateh… You wouldn't object if I bought a piano?"

"It's a fine idear… If it pleases you, do it."

"Violins for the girls?"

My eyes smarted so suddenly with tears that she looked at me sharply; but before she could question me about my swift feeling, I hurried on, "I'd be pleased if you did… I'd…like t' heahr them play, one day…an'…that orchestra idear… I…don't know much about music of that sort; but it certainly couldn't hurt the town none."

"Then I'll do it… I know that there's talent in town, folks who can play the flute or horns."

"And I know where you c'n borrow a mighty fine harpist… Now, you undehstand, Anne, as long as we'hre not officially divorced… I consideh it my job t' pay for the runnin' of this household. Youhr money's not goin' to last foreveh, an' mine's goin' t' be slow t' come in at first; so you'll have t' show sense in divvyin' funds out."

"Haven't I always, till now?"

"Aye; I've got no complaints, so far."

"Do *you* have what you need, in that relic of a camp out there?"

"Whateveh ain't there, we c'n build, assumin' Jim an' Eben stick around t' live with me. I won't be alone… We'll eat good grub an' work well t'getheh…which is about as simple as my needs have b'come. There's just one last thing I've got t' have… If we're t' do this—go oweh separate ways, so t' speak—I…I want the children in my life, out there, just the same as you want them here. May we…once a yeah anyway, during the long vacation…may I take them out for a spell?"

This was hitting her where she lived, as I knew; but I was emboldened by my need and Jim's; and I had given her so much ground already, she couldn't but respond in kind. "You mean, you'd look afteh them…as you did when I went to Portland that one August?"

"Aye."

"You'd take them to preaching?"

"Didn't I b'fore?"

"See to their Sabbath School lessons?"

"Regulah."

"You'd"—she was careful with her words, but I knew exactly what she was thinking— "you'd protect them from bad influences?"

"Anne—"

"Oh, I don't mean Jim; I—since he was baptized, I don't worry so much about him. I mean—"

"Who told you he was baptized?" I asked sharply.

"Why, he did."

Checking a smile that he'd outfoxed me again, that Romany weasel—that he'd been a step ahead of me again, and was probably, even now, well down the road—I said simply, "Well, I just wondehed. Anne, you know he's a betteh influence on the children than most, an'—"

"I wasn't referring to him, if you'd just let me finish. I meant—will you see to it they don't all come and drink, all those island fishermen, and utter profanities and carry on and such, around oweh young ones?"

"I've always protected 'em that way hehre—betteh than you know; you c'n depend on it, I will thehre as well," I promised, checking my ire at her notions of class.

"Well, I know youhr word is good... So if you want to take them in August...especially if you have some hired girl who can help, some *good* girl now, whilst you're at work by day...then...it's all right by me."

"Out to the island they go, then, next month... An' *you*...you should go t' Pohrtland."

Her face was so keen at the idea I thought I'd have to pin her down in her chair; but she managed to sound calm. "I will at that... I'll find a piano...and violins for the girls."

"You c'n ship 'em back on Elkanah's schooneh...he's got a cargo bound this way then."

Her face softened till it was almost sympathetic. "Ben, you...do you think you can manage to stay friends with them all, with that you're about to do?"

"I'll try," I said firmly, albeit grim at the prospect. "How about you, for youhr pahrt? D'ye think you c'n manage all the talk that's sure t' erupt, what with you buyin' a house an' me buildin' a yahrd?"

"I'll give it my best," she promised, chin up.

"Then we have only one last matteh b'tween us, an' I'd say we'd squared the yahrds well enough for one day."

"What is it?"

"It's…the children, Anne…not just right now, but oveh the long haul. I've always given you free rein with their raisin', an' you've done a fine job, bringin' 'em up obedient an' all. But I'm determined t' play a hand now, betteh than I done b'fore; an' there's certain things I want t' see to, an' have you agree on right from the stahrt."

She looked so alarmed that I couldn't check the grin which twitched away at the corners of my mouth.

"Oh, I don't mean encouragin' the boys t' drink when they come of age, or stowaway whilst they're still to school," I went on. "I'm talkin' about…. their education, an' their outlook on life. I… I don't want them t' suffeh from the conventions that brought us t'getheh, Anne. If the boys don't want t' go t' sea, they shouldn't have to…an' if the girls want to, I…I don't want you, of all people, t' stand in their way. I want *them* t' decide where their course lies, so they c'n get off t' a betteh stahrt than we did. D'ye undehstand?"

"I should," she replied, her voice husky.

"Jean, for example… She's got the brains of a navigatoh. She should be able t' ship with one o' the family, if she takes the notion—- like Keziah did a few voyages ago. An' if she wants t' go t' college t' get the education she needs, I… I don't want any of us t' prevent her goin', just b'cause she's a girl. And finally… I don't want t' see none of 'em sportin' attitudes, Anne, about bein' betteh than folks down to the Point, b'cause they live in a fancy house in town, an' play the violin an' such. D'ye see what I'm sayin'?"

"I undehstand… I'll try t' do betteh to guard against it," she vowed.

"It ain't Christian, for one thing, all them notions of class… It's been a load around oweh own necks; I don't want it t' be so around theirs."

She swept her eyes over their portraits near the mantle, and I saw that she understood; saw the tenderness that lighted her eyes, and softened the regret that tightened her lips; so getting to my feet—feeling suddenly that she was my comrade, that failure had brought us, ironically, to friendship—I said gently, "Thanks, Anne… I'll…I'll talk t' John, an' release your account this aftehnoon…probably catch a boat oveh t' the island t' make some plans with Jim an' Eben…then come back int' town with the mail boat t'morrer, so we c'n buy the house."

Nodding, she got to her feet as well; then for all the world like my business partner, she held out her hand; and taking it, I gave her a bow—a bow of deepest respect—before I put on my cap and stepped out the door.

Buoyed still by the wave of clarity and purpose that had carried me through my conversation with Anne, I went to the shipyard, where I found both my uncles; sent for John to join us, which he did forthwith; and calling an impromptu meeting, I turned down my orders for the East Indies, resigned my commission as skipper, and withdrew from my partnership in Melchett Bros., all before they could get a word in edgewise. Though aware for some time—ever since the Pacific—that I'd been less than keen on my duties, all my hearers were nonetheless astounded; astonished as much by the unprecedented nature of my actions, as by my intention to start my own business.

Though what I intended to do in no way competed with them, nor caused any loss, save for my resources and talents, they were wholly taken aback that one of the family should leave them, and go off on his own for any reason; simply couldn't fathom—even after my trial and all that went with it—why any Melchett wouldn't stick with the business. Not since old Ezra sailed off into the blue a decade or so ago in his schooner, had Melchett Bros. lost anyone through any means save death; and anxious to bring me to my senses, they postponed tea, and struggled to make me see my madness.

Offering higher wages, a greater voice in decisions, a change in responsibilities or patterns, they tried to augment my already generous arrangements—even John, who as my lawyer knew my changing priorities better than any; but patiently turning down each suggestion, I strove to make clear my direction, and my determination to pursue it. Unwilling to accept my resignation—insisting on seeing me tomorrow, to talk the matter over further—they leapt at my offer to stay in the picture, at least as a liason to the small craft business; and agreeing to meet them—not to discuss my decision, which I emphasized was closed, but to explore the relationship between our two yards—I arranged to join them for the noon dinner, and bowed at their carefully cordial goodnights.

Checking a smile at their solicitude—which was greater by far than it ever had been in the past—I made for John's nearby law office; signed the release to Anne's funds, which John promised to file with the counting house; then set in motion the dissolution of my partnership, and the liquidation of my few remaining investments. Still trying to dissuade me, John filled out the papers, insisting he'd hold them till I'd thought matters over; but assuring him I'd thought matters over for years, I penned my name firmly to the bottom of each page. Then marveling still at how plain it all seemed, as if I'd always known this was what I must do, I plucked down my cap from the stand by the door; and turning my back on all that I'd worked for since I'd come to manhood—turning my back not just on the headaches of the yard, or the hated complexities of the business, but on my success as a deepwater skipper, and any satisfaction I'd found as a builder—I headed for the waterfront traffic, and looked for a ride out to the island.

*   *   *   *   *

I was looking out for him by supper; had spent the past hours cooking up a big meal, convinced he'd forget about eating all day, and now—with Eben gone to the village to buy supplies—was standing alone in the deepening porch shadows, watching for him on the sandy road. Not long ago Charlie's ketch had swept in, her running lights playing on the grey harbor; and instinctively sure that he was aboard her, I'd started counting the minutes till he'd be home.

Torn between my hope that he'd settled his mind, and my pain at his anticipated verdict—dreading the trek to the Indies and the breaking up of our household, yet knowing that home was wherever he went—I scanned the village road in the twilight; searched the greys and taupes for a figure, for the abrupt, stubborn motions of his stride.

Picking him out at last in the shadows of nightfall—getting to my feet with the old leap in my heart, and going to the door as if it'd been days since I'd seen him—I watched him come up the roadway; noticed at once his firm erect bearing, and straightaway knew he'd reached his decision. As he came up our path with steps that were buoyant, and a head that was raised with resolve and purpose, I tremulously opened the porch screen; and seeing me there in the dim light of the doorway—taking in at a glance both my hope and my fear—he took me at once in his arms, and burying his lips in my hair, hoarsely whispered: "I've found us a way, mate."

Drawing back till my hands rested on his shoulders, I looked up at him half-wondering, half-fearful; and reading my unspoken question, he went on, "We're stayin' hehre for the summeh...stayin' here most o' the time, from now on; we're home."

My heart a blaze of hope and confusion, I found my voice and asked, so halting and low he had to lean toward me: "Ben, but...what about the Indies...what about the yard?"

"Thehre ain't goin' t' be any Indies...ain't goin' t' be any more of the yahd. I've just quit my berth with Melchett Bros...directed John t' dissolve my partnership, an' resigned my commission as skippeh."

The breath knocked out of me, I managed to stumble, "But... Ben...what'll you do instead?"; and serenely smiling at me in answer, he told me,

"I'm goin' t' build fishin' boats...right here on the island. I'm goin' t' stahrt up a yard of my own, with you an' Eben as partnehs... that is, if you'll have me."

Feeling my knees give way beneath me, I tightened my grip on his shoulders; flashed back to the man who'd stomped into Toby's, more like a fisherman than a master; and knowing that I'd just met him again, fought back the hot flood that sprang to my eyes.

Tightening his own grip above my elbows, he calmly and firmly explained, "I figured with sailin' out o' the way, I could clear time for us on the island—could stahrt up a yard here, without hurtin'

Melchett Bros., an' when business took me t' town, stay with my family for a spell."

Seeing the whole of his plan in a sweep—understanding, along with its sheer suitability and rightness, the unstated sacrifice of his career on deep water—I collapsed onto the kitchen sofa, and hid my face with my hand.

Sitting down by me and drawing me into his arms, he swayed with me a wordless moment; then stroking my hair, huskily murmured, "It's the only way for us, matey; b'lieve me, I searched."

Struggling to steady my voice, I managed, "I can't bear for you t' leave the sea."

"You made youhr sacrifice... I had t' make mine." Forcing me to meet his eyes, he went on, "If this thing's goin' t' work, we've got t' meet in the middle—an' I'm damn determined it's goin' t' work. Buildin' a yahrd here'll mean we c'n live t'getheh, while still stayin' close t' the children like you pleaded; it'll mean I c'n still keep up a pretense with Anne, from a distance, an' only have t' be separate from you when we're in town. It'll even mean I c'n maintain a link with Melchett Bros.—once they get oveh my leavin', which they will. What with sailin' back an' forth t' Cape Damaris, or up an' down the coast t' deliveh boats, it won't really be like I'm leavin' the sea, or turnin' oveh the helm t' anyone else...just concentratin' on things from the shore end."

Trying to still my hands in my lap, I nodded; and seeing me begin to subside, he determinedly went on, "B'sides, Jim, you what what's comin'. The ship we've got on the ways now is already twice as big as *Charis*; an' there's no reason otehs couldn't build one biggeh. In five or ten yeahrs they'll be two thousand, maybe three thousand tons with a crew t' match 'em: a hundred men whehre we once had twenty. I can't imagine us tryin' t' carry on a marriage amidst such a mob, or competin' with oteh such mobs t' make a buck. An' I *won't* tolerate the thought of watchin' you anymore, fistin' a frozen topsail a hundred feet above the deck...that's flat. Whateveh we do, we'll do at ground level, an' for a purpose we c'n live with...that much's been clear t' me for some time."

Carefully absorbing his words, I heard him out without comment;

then raising my voice in one final protest, I wistfully interjected, "But you...you couldn've made your name as a skipper...could've been famous for the ships you'll never make now. You're already known from here t' New York, you...you could have a place in the history books when they write 'em."

The smile on his face neither pained nor heroic, he forthrightly answered, "I ain't interested in makin' my name; I might of been once, but I ain't anymore. I'm interested in makin' a marriage; an' if the only way I c'n swing that, an' my otheh obligations, is by givin' up clippehs an' plyin' these watehs, then I'll ply 'em unsung the rest o' my days."

Lifting my eyes I saw, not the face of the men who'd commanded the ships I'd crewed since I'd first sailed down the Mersey, nor even the face of the man who'd once paced the quarterdeck of the *Charis Spooner,* but the face of the fishermen I'd watched in Wales; saw, looking at his weathered features, a patience I'd never beheld there before, a surrender to diminished dreams, a simplicity of mind in keeping with the shores around him. Giving me time to take in his words, he touched my hair with a comforting gesture; then sensing my gradual calming and easing, he said as lightly as if he'd been fishing:

"I ain't had a bite since daybreak with you, mate. Come set with me a spell at the table, an' I'll tell ye the whole story from the beginnin.'"

Touched that I'd spent the majority of the day cooking—that I'd known where he'd been and when he would return, and prepared his favorite supper in welcome—he put away three or four helpings in a row, sharing his story in between bites, and holding my free hand with his while we ate. Now and then rising to fetch him more bread and tea, I sat across from him at the table; listened while he traced his debate on the rocks, and the decision which came with the passing of *Charis.*

Seeing my pleasure at his conversation with Anne, he re-told his conclusions with her, and the agreements he'd worked out with Melchett Bros., with a confidence and pride of his own. Then having disposed of the events of the day, he turned his attention to the future—outlined his hopes for our business, and the ketches and yawls taking shape in his mind; spun dreams as brightly as a boy, while I fed him bits of pie for dessert.

Dazed by the vistas stretching before us—by the dawning realization of my own hopes, only just now breaking through the day's fears—I plotted in concert with him; imagined August morns with the children or afternoons building or moonlit nights by him on the pillow. Of the difficulties which lay before us—of the compromises of marriage or the tasks of the new yard or the challenges of establishing a business—we gave little thought as we dreamed; only indulged in our exultation for home, our exhilaration at a shared household.

Drawing a bath for him after supper I bathed him in our old copper tub; washed the burdens of years from his broad back, and kneaded the tensions of months from his shoulders. The cottage dark except for two oil lamps—Eben still somewhere down at the village, probably surrounded by folk asking about me—we had the place to ourselves yet a time; and I took care of him as I'd longed to, holding him while he leaned back on me, or soothing him with watery strokes. The greys had gone from the western rim of the bay, and our lamps were shining bright with the night, before he stepped at last from the tub, and drew on his dressing gown and slippers; and tidying the room out of sympathy for Eben, we headed for the staircase together.

Taking a lamp in one hand, he led the way—slinging the ditty bag he'd brought home over his shoulder; and looking at it for the first time as we climbed, I inquired what he had in it. In answer he stood me before our chest of drawers, built into the wall much like the cabin of a ship; opened the top drawer, then untying the bag, poured in a cascade of stockings and socks—a waterfall of hose, his and mine, of every kind and condition and color. "I fetched them b'fore I left town," he explained, while I stood gaping at him in wonder; then understanding all at once he'd remembered my words—realizing full force I'd be waking in his arms, be finding my socks in the same drawer as his—I completely gave way beside him.

Collapsing abruptly at his feet on the floor, I cried for joy, indeed stormed, till he took me anxiously by the shoulders, and—lifting me to my feet—pinned me to the wall.

"Whyn't you tell me how much this meant t' you?" he hissed fiercely, pinching my arms in the force of his feeling; "why'd you let me think we should do anything else but live hehre in this house t'getheh?"

"I had to," I gasped in answer, "had to…if I was t' make you find a way for Anne an' the children."

"Don't you eveh leave me in the dahrk again about how strongly you feel, or what you need…sweahr it," he shook me.

"I sweahr," I promised, taking on his accent in the intensity of my vow.

"Neveh again leave me in the lurch when we're making' a decision, or let me set a course without you….promise."

"Promise," I vowed again, eyes on his.

Gentling his grip he tenderly held me, while I sobbed out my joy in his arms; then together we returned to our socks, waiting for us in their glad inter-tumbling. Scooping them up in our hands, we cupped them like water, then let them ripple and pour and mingle—cotton socks with ribbed tops and stout toes; striped silk stockings, ready for dancing; cashmere half-hose; merino tweeds; hunting stockings thick enough for the arctic: scooped them up and let them fall, laughing at their homely beauty. Then making sure they were well-mixed, Ben closed the drawer; and reaching out, he turned down the light.

XXX

EBEN MCCABE
Spooner Bay
Epilogue: 1845-1877

As in winter when the ice builds along the shore, then breaks and shifts with the tide all which ways, so it was with our belongings that summer: on the way back and forth between house, yard and cottage or shuffled off into heaps for a time, till it appeared a whole ocean of stuff was migrating. If it looked like chaos to me and Ben, who was used to doing things shipshape—if it seemed a bit of an upheaval even to Jamie, who preferred things in a volcanic clutter—it must of been a regular hurrah's nest to the town, watching the spectacle unfold from the sidelines; and since it went on for months on end, them folks on their porches taking inventory, or simply wallowing in our circus antics, had plenty of chances for free entertainment.

First Jamie's gear was all moved out of my place and marched down the road to his room at the Inn—where he planned to stop whenever we was in town, doing business or biding time with Ben's children; and there was nothing easy even about that, since—though he hadn't much—it was all of a tangle, and prone to be scattered hither and yon. Some of it, like his tools at the shipyard, or his prize horse Dee, who he thought of almost as much as Ben, had to be hauled to the docks and shipped off to the island, then herded further on to our cottage; and if Ben wasn't ready to throttle him for his lack of organization the first week, he certainly was by the second.

Then my gear followed on down the road out of my cabin and was carted off to my new spot at the Inn, across the hall from Jamie's,

353

the only other room on the floor; and there it piled up even along the hallway. When every nook there was crammed to the gills we hauled the rest in boatloads to the island, then discharged the unending tide to our cottage; and. since I was actually breaking up housekeeping— selling the cabin me and Ben had built, and emptying it of years of stowage—we was still packing up cellar and pantry, and shipping off gear in all directions, when the autumn winds swept in in September.

But Ben's belongings—sprawled from his house on the Point to his office at the yard to half a dozen spots in between, not to mention, spread over four generations—was even more monumental in scope; and getting it all into boxes and crates and so to wherever it was migrating was a colossal undertaking. Some of it was earmarked for his room at Anne's house, newly bought from Percival on St. James Street; and whilst folks watched from porches sipping lemonades or calculating his living arrangements, we hustled it into the back kitchen door, and so through the pantry to its new home.

Originally meant for a borning room, the spot pleased him because it was out of the way; and we packed it with everything he'd need in town, books and charts and business papers, shore togs and bedding for the bunk he'd built in—the whole lot needing to be unpacked before he could move on, and in an order only he had mapped out in his brain.

Then down to the wharf we hustled the rest, herding tools and chart boxes, sextants and rolltops in a mammoth flock of gear; and up waiting gangplanks we ferried it to the island, where it couldn't be crammed by near half in the cottage, nor stowed in the carriage house, since we'd already commenced building a boat there. As he was the opposite of Jamie, needing everything labeled and kept track of, his move was an even worse trial than ours; and we was both ready to brain him, Jamie and me, by the time we'd got all his ducks in a row.

If we hadn't all three of us been moving our jobs, in fact changing the whole means of our livelihood at the same time, it might of been more manageable even with Ben's truck; but there we was in the midst of it all carrying on business—liquidating stock and borrowing money and turning ourselves into a corporation, even as we was buying and selling houses, or picking out a spot for the new yard on the island. Though we could only afford to break ground in a small way, we went right to work on a boatshed and mold loft; and before long we was creating an upheaval in Spooner Bay—or at any rate, overseeing one, since to save time we'd hired out the construction— to equal the commotion we was making in Cape Damaris.

Shipping lumber, milling keel knees, building the smithy and steambox, all had to go on whilst we was still moving; and our own carriage house had to be converted for boatbuilding, and the loft cleared away for chalking up the new ketch. His mind made up on his course at last, Ben steamed ahead full throttle, making up in one summer for the years he'd tread water; and every minute we could spare from moving our gear, we was tracing patterns and planking.

But even re-locating our work wasn't the crown of it all; for Anne's move had to be carried off at the same time as ours—and hers was the one that won by a mile. The three of us together, even with our new business, owned nowheres near what that woman did—especially since her freight included six children's; and no transfer in the town's history equaled her shift to St. James Street. They was already, the townsfolk, primed by the news that she'd bought the place herself with the funds Ben'd freed up; and half-rabid with gossip and speculation—hot with envy for her and doubts about Ben and dire predictions for the future—they was all but out on the rooftops when her circus load come down the street in wagons.

Bureaus, wardrobes, sideboards, tables, enough kitchen gear to host a city a week—it all come parading in the heat of summer; and most of it marched up into the attic, whilst down from Portland or Boston or New York flowed fancy mahogany replacements. The fact that it was all bought with her money heightened the spectacle even more; and we could almost hear the columns added up in folks' minds as we grunted with highboys and chests and pianos, shifting them here and there in the parlors midst flowery drapes and laces and carpets, till their settings finally pleased her. When the dust'd finally settled from her gear—when Ben's was all neatly tucked away in his sane room, a cabin-like refuge to which we repaired often—we

might of drawn a deep breath, and deserved it; but all this was a
sideshow compared to our real work, finally taking shape in the form
of the ketch.

Going at it hammer and tongs, Ben led us through the familiar
stages—chalking up patterns and laying the keel, then setting the
ribs and pounding on planking; and it was a job for just three alone,
even with his skills as a shipwright, Jamie's genius with wood and
mine with a mallet. Yet as the ketch took shape and our moves along
with it, you could say we was shifting into a new form—a partnership
that included our house chores; could even say we was shifting from
the inside, where our real moves was going on round each other. No
longer shipmaster and first mate and second, we'd no idea what we
was now to each other; and we fumbled around our company duties,
trying out our new roles as partners.

Though still at the helm, Ben gave ground in some ways—not
only to Jamie, who was his match in carpentry, but even to me,
thanks to my years in a dory; and there was a pooling to his decisions
that'd never been there before. Still wayward alone, Jamie worked
hard amongst us, almost harder than Ben in his desire to help him;
and me, the jack-of-all-trades of the group—I knew perfectly well
where this was all heading; knew clear as a bell that my all-around
skills marked me out as the foreman of our yard down the road.

In the house it was the same, each of us shifting into new duties
that made it possible for the whole show to run; and though I
conjured breakfast and Jamie cooked dinner and Ben puttered with
the makings of tea, we was all, all three of us, merging parts of the
whole.

If it was a summer above all for wedding, for the mating of lives
and goods and employments, it didn't bypass me even though I was
gooseberry; for it was a time for my unique strengths as mediator—
my role as a go-between one of the few things that was unchanged
between us. Far from being the odd man out, I proved myself a
mainstay once again, not only in our domestic arrangement, but in
our fledgling business endeavor—keeping accounts for Ben, aiding
Jamie in spar and sailmaking, and passing on to them my years of

experience at the helms of sloops and ketches.

As I'd once stood between the two of them, helping to draw them closer together, so now I stood between them and the town, guarding their privacy from invasion, and lending credibility to a living arrangement that might of otherwise raised questions; while at the same time I threw my weight behind the business, taking on the deskwork Ben hated, and managing the new start at the yard. As the days passed I thus become as much a part of their marriage as the business plans and belongings we shared; and they come to look upon me as a sort of guardian spirit—as a provider of guidance and the kind of acceptance the rest of the world couldn't give.

In the midst of our efforts to launch marriage and business, we was preparing as well for the children's August visit; and if there was anything that was needed to complete our sense of family, it was the arrival of them six little hellcats, tumbling over each other on our sitting room floor. Having built bunks for them in the spare rooms upstairs—stacking berths up the walls like the tiers of a forecastle— Ben hired a cousin of mine to do laundry, then braced hisself for the ruination of what little order he'd managed to create; whilst Jamie took matters in Romany stride, him having been one of such a mob in Wales.

And as for me—scaring up extra chairs, or stocking mountains of provisions—I threw my weight behind Ben's quarterdeck order, much like the old days when I was mate; saw, amused, that they too slipped into their old roles of skipper and steward, now that there was a crew to manage. Anxious to hide their real relations, Jamie moved back to his old bed, and left the door to their room determinedly ajar; and less convinced that they needed to carry things that far, Ben got out of bed in the middle watch every night, and locked the door on their privacy a few hours. With our roles thus mobilized as for a sailing—with the children's gear scattered from one end of the place to the other, high chairs and tops, nappies and dolls strewn stem to stern despite Ben's best efforts—the house had the atmosphere of a ship deck on launch day; and if there was anyone who had doubts we was family, they lost it within a minute of arriving at our place.

Allowed to work on the ketch by day, the oldest ones soon fell in with our routine—Tom and Jean, at nine and eight, old enough now to be a real help, and Ben never one to let hands lay idle; and some measure of order was thus created by dividing ranks. Barking orders from aft, he had them caulking and paying, till they was as disreputable-looking as any tar on the Line, slushing down the masts for home; and it was a mercy Anne was a hundred miles to the south so she couldn't see what'd become of her daughter, short-haired again, in Tom's pants. At six the twins was eager enough to assist, even if they wasn't as useful; and Seth was taught to pound trunnels and sand whilst Courtney went about with her basket, picking up chips for the kitchen fire. Not liking the mess, she left small improvements everywhere, usually in the form of colorful yarns she'd braided, then tied round the doorknobs and cleats and what-not; and as August wore on we come to relish them doo-dads so much they become a permanent part of the craft.

Too small to be anything but underfoot, Nat and Becky was banned to the house, where they clung to Jamie's pockets whenever he showed up to cook, or to lend a hand with the laundry tub; and after dinner he'd take them down to the shore to get them out of Lou's hair for a spell. Though he loved them all, Jim especially adored Nat, for he was the spitting image of Ben: sturdy, hearty, sandy-haired, grey-eyed—needing only a pipe and a beard to pass muster; and Jamie spoiled him for all he was worth. Remembering perfectly well how he felt about Sacki, Ben seldom put a stop to it like he might of; and no sight pleased him more than to see them together, picking up shells or tussling each other.

One August afternoon—after an especially hectic day, Ben having cracked the whip even harder than usual—I come upon Jamie curled up in the sun, his bed the great coils of an anchor cable; and tired out from their sport, Nat and Becky napped with him, Nat with his head pillowed on Jamie's hip, and Becky half-sprawled athwart his chest, for all the world like goslings in a nest. Creeping away, I brung Ben at once, fetching him from the timbers of the new ketch; and his face struck with love, he set down on a half-barrel, watching them with the tears sliding into his beard, whilst I respectfully tiptoed away.

Taking them to Sunday preaching—even though all six was as

bored as we was, our island preacher being a far cry from Jackson—
Ben kept his promises to Anne and then some, scrubbing up even
Tom and Jean to look decent; but Sabbath afternoons was Rom to the
core, spent sailing if the wind and tide was with us, or lying on rocks
to the smells of a clambake. Digging clams, hauling rockweed, taking
a splash off the dock, we put in hours that was nigh perfect on earth,
the gulls mewing above as we tossed off shells and corn husks; then
with night coming on Jamie'd bring down his harp, and favor us with
some fancies on strings.

Though they was only with us a month, they seemed to thrive, them
children—to say nothing of how Jamie and Ben and me did; and
pleased beyond words at how they'd all flourished, Ben scarcely
could bear to let them all go when the time came, whilst Jamie was
crushed by their departure. Touched, I found that they didn't want to
leave even me—Jean tucking a handful of stones in my peacoat, and
Courtney tying a braided band round my wrist; and the thunderous
silence of their fresh absence was louder than any nor'easter we'd
faced.

It was the beginning of what proved a hard fall for us, what with
all of us going off in every direction in the big build-up for launch-
day and winter; and we lost some of the sense of home we'd enjoyed
in August, even as we finally wrapped up all the loose ends of our
old lives. At least a couple times Jim and Ben sailed to Portland to
drum up orders and visit with Jacques; and most every week found
Ben in Cape Damaris on business, sometimes with Jim and me,
sometimes without. After the summer together at close quarters,
elbow to elbow in the cottage and boatshed, it was a shock to be in
separate apartments, Jim and me at the Inn and Ben at Anne's; and if
we two suffered Ben did even more so, for we could keep each other
company in our rooms, whilst Ben was alone in the social whirl at
Anne's.

Though he kept to his corner as much as he could, went on
'Change and hung out in counting rooms and chandlers', in the
evenings he had to go home at some point; and what with Anne's
social calendar in full swing, he couldn't duck out of every to-do she

held. Many a night he come by Jamie's around nine, unable to put up with clubs or guilds any longer; and keeping close to home hisself so as to be ready for him, Jamie'd give him a drink or a roll in the hay before seeing him back on his way to Anne's. Keeping an eye on the stairs, I tried to protect them, waylaying any late-nighters looking for a ramble with Jim; and by day I did what I could to create home, working with Jim to make sitting areas in our rooms, and setting up a desk for Ben to keep accounts at. Cutting back on his night life, once as a-flitter as Anne's with taverns and sociables and beech-nut parties, Jim shored up my efforts by camping on his hearth, now a family man shunning bachelor friends; but all in all, what with the unsettled pitch of our fractured base, Jim's unspoken ache and Ben's frustration, we felt the head winds of our new venture.

If it was rough on them when they both was in town, it was harder still when one was to the island—which happened when we was at critical stages on the ketch, and couldn't spare the two of them away; and they took to hitching rides to and from the mainland with fishermen bound for supplies or discharge, in order to get back together sooner—the mail ferry only sailing at whiles in the autumn. As if to remind them of old disasters—of the perils you didn't have to go round the Horn or out to the Pacific to face—it was Jamie who late October sailed to town on business, and Ben who stayed behind to step the masts with me; and on the return trip the Kalkman boys he'd sailed with met up with foul weather athwart the shoals, the boat going to the bottom within sight of Spooner Bay.

As soon as we knew it—the signal flags going up at once, and the volunteer crews combing the beaches—Ben raced to and fro with anxiety for him, too harried to be any use on the shore; but next day, the seas calmer, Jim stepped off the Shields' boat, not having an idea as to what'd happened. "You know you taught me not t' sail on a flood tide when the wind's cantin' round t' the west," he protested, when he seen what a total wreck Ben was; and "Know I'd taught ye—didn't know you'd listened," was all Ben could manage, still green round the gills. Quickly seizing hands, they gave their fingers a squeeze—the only show they could make in all the hullabalu on the wharf; then as quickly letting go, they turned away, and gave their attention to the commotion of others.

Nor was that our only trial our first fall; for Jamie was gone over a week to Portland to finalize our winter orders and stop over with Jacques, who was slowly failing; and Ben seen him off with many misgivings, not least about their separation. Though he could take the Portland ferry, which still run to and from Cape Damaris, and though the season'd been an unusually mild one, the fishing fleet still plying Jeffries Bank, the risk for November gales was increasing; and Ben wasn't any too easy either about how Jim'd handle the business climate in Portland, or manage large sums of debit and credit. But to prove us wrong again back he come in time for Thanksgiving, with an unexpected contract for our first schooner—and $150 in cash to boot, not to mention, gifts for Ben and me and the children; and delighted as much by the money as by the contract, Ben asked him how on earth he'd come by it.

"Oh, I bought a sailfish," he said airily, munching contentedly on the lobster rolls he'd fetched home for our luncheon from Jimmy's.

"You bought a *what*?" Ben bawled, lobster roll mid-hoist.

"A sailfish," he breezed, as if tropical schools of them was something you snapped up every day. "One of the hands on the ferry had one all mounted on a board, ten feet long, with a wonderful fin; an' he wanted t' sell it t' pay his fancy man. So we fell to dickering an' in the end, I offered him five dollars for it."

"Five dollahs!" Ben groaned, that being a week's wages.

"When I saw what a commotion folks on the wharf made over him," he went on, ignoring Ben as he munched away, "I d'cided t' charge admission t' see him; an' I set up a booth by the side of the road, an' asked 25 cents a crack the whole week."

Completely took aback by this tactic—supremely Rom in its mercenary instinct, easily outshining Yankee wiles to make a buck—we burst into an explosion of laughter; and still paying no heed he proudly informed us he'd made over $200, even after hiring a boy to mind things so he could be about his business, which plainly involved more than the missions he'd been sent on. Hauling out a fine sample of worsted, he showed us the winter suit of clothes he'd bought for Elkanah's tailor to make up—which he needed, and which Ben never would of begrudged him anyways, him being the first to appreciate how Jim looked well-dressed; then unpacking our gifts—including a sailor's valentine for Ben, a fanciful box festooned with shells from Anjier, a sign of devotion which moved Ben to tears—he described his artful dealing on 'Change, and the maneuvers by which he'd landed our contract.

Hearing him out with the realization that Rom blood was going to be our bonanza—as much an asset to business as to home and marriage—we listened while he wrapped up his story, with the news the fish now was at Jimmy's: breaking into fresh gales of laughter when he asked us how much we thought he could make there, and how much he'd owe the Inn in commission.

It was such moments as these—spontaneous and unlooked-for, and usually brung on by some freak of Jim's—that seen us through the lean times that fall: through the days away from home and the trials of trying to launch a business and the painstaking labors of rigging and sailmaking. Though Ben and me rigged the ketch the canvas work fell to Jamie, not only because he was fast—averaging fifteen yards an hour—but because he did the finest work in the county, splicing the thimbles with intricate cringles that practically made an artwork in thread; and though he hated the monotony of sewing as much as we did the fussy exactness of rigging, we had the ketch in the water by mid-December, just before the ice set in for winter. Behind the helm again for the first time in almost a year, with Jamie and me at our customary deck posts, Ben tried her out every whichways before delivering her in person to Belfast: on the wind, off the wind, round ledges and buoys, down channels and close in to headlands and capes; and he was already sketching the lines of Jamie's schooner on a pad on his knee on our stage ride back.

Besides the lifts we got from the money the boat fetched, the heartening orders beginning to come in, and Jamie's irrepressible spirits, we had the children in pairs off at on, at least while the weather held that autumn: Anne finding we hadn't sent them home permanently damaged, and willing we should take them in turns on weekends. This last was an unexpected bonus, as dear in its own way as Jim's fundraising success; and nothing pleased the lot of us more than when contrary winds held them over a day longer. Beginning to see that the children would be a part of our lives at other times besides August—starting to find that we could make a living, even short-handed, and that the business was coming to life, with orders enough to tide us over the winter—we begun to settle into our partnership; and though Jamie was pained to see Ben reduced to such work as making the deck boats for the ships he'd once built, Ben loved his little boats, and showed it.

But what lifted our hearts most of all, and kept us on track through the stiff times, was the freedom we had to set our own course; and none of us felt it more keenly than Ben. Rid of his old ties to Melchett Bros.—and more important, the family expectations that went with them—he was like a young man heading west; and nothing had taken the years from him faster than his agreement with Anne to go their separate ways—to end what the town now ironically called the area's "most perfect marriage." Aware that folks'd come round from thinking of them as the partners from hell to the ideal couple, him and Anne was baffled by the reaction; could never see themselves as anything more than business partners who'd struck a bargain. But what the town seen was not two contrary souls finally coming to terms with each other, but confederates who flourished apart, and who was blissfully happy whilst they was at it: Anne at least as sunny as Ben in her newfound freedom and purpose.

Independent in her house on St. James St., where she'd always wanted to live—in the center of her social doings, and in control of her own money as well as her household—she was the envy of all the town's ladies; was envied all the more for Ben's support, him being willing to stand by all her harebrained schemes, including the starting of an orchestra—folks now tooting away once a week at the town hall in preparation for Independence Day, and all them ice cream socials in the park next summer. Though he had his own life out on the island and only come home at intervals to do business didn't make him any less the perfect husband—rather more so; for in his coming and going, she had the best of both worlds—independence and support; and folks translated his distance into confidence and respect. Having all the benefits of family without the daily wear and tear, Ben was even more envied than Anne—men coveting his partnership with a capable mate, and his freedom from the conventions that trapped them.

What they looked like together, in the parlor at Anne's house, was not a woman who hated the seafaring life and a man who comically dwarfed his frail chair—a brocaded and carved bit of toothpick from Boston—but a pair of satisfied associates, not like each other, but bound by mutual respect; and since folks never seen them nights he fled from Anne's, completely worn out by the social chitchat, or guessed the sacrifices he made for the children and the noble way Jim held him to it, it was easy for them to conclude this was a match made in heaven.

That the real marriage was his and Jamie's, and no one but me could know it, was what drove Ben slowly over the edge; but at least early on—as Jim was contented with secrecy, and both of them found a pat on the back from me—he bore with it; and if that fall in public was hard on them, it was more than made up for by our private winter. Though the children was separated from us for a long spell, all but deepwater traffic having come to a halt by Christmas, we was already looking ahead to spring weekends; and in our cut-off coziness by our kitchen fire, we had our happiest moments yet.

Carving a block of applewood, Jim was in raptures—the kitchen littered with wood shavings from a figurehead he wanted to try out, in between baking us pies; and as the face come to life—a Turk complete with turban and sash, and a come-hither look Ben said should be censored—we seen again what a gift he had, and began urging him to sideline his own business. Carving along with him, Ben pegged the lift-model for the schooner, shaping the contours as tenderly as a lover; and knee-deep in their mess I baked biscuits and beans, and swapped yarns with the few folk who dropped by between storms.

So hard did it snow—reminding us we was blessed not to be out on deck, looking out for her under short sail in blind gales—that there was days we didn't even make it out to the carriage house, our temporary mold loft, to lay down the lines and commence making patterns; and cut off from the world, stocked with provisions, self-sustaining as a ship stowed for a two-year tramp, we held forth by our homely fire—nobody more pleased than the gypsy rover who'd at last settled down by a hearth.

A gypsy rover was what Jim's figurehead turned out to look like—Jim's own beckoning, eye-catching sketch of male beauty. To the splendor and dash and swarthiness of the Turk, he added the strengths he recalled of his father, the dignity and grace and seasoned charm; whilst the Romany flair for colorful glad rags was made plain in the bright waistcoat and billowing sleeves. With dark eyes and brown skin, the flash of a red smile, and a wild head of hair half-blown in the wind, the face was the gist of unbridled romance—a look Ben swore seduced him every time he walked by; and the bold neckerchief and plum-colored sash both added to its dash and appeal.

But it was the simple gold pendant on a chain about the neck that somehow captured and held your attention, if once you got past the frank come-on; for its clear, bright design and obvious value, along with its flaunted shine on the gypsy's chest, suggested somehow a lover's attachment. It was the way Jim announced his own commitment, the way he handled the secrecy that so plagued Ben; and it was Ben's favorite part of the carving, a touch that frequently caused him to draw out his own locket and tenderly press it to his lips. Altogether it was a striking carving; and finding in it roots and themes which shot down deep into Jim's past, we watched it take shape with pleasure, and the certainty it was his surest effort.

With spring come the usual burst of commotion: our yard bustling forth with a new sail loft and sawpit, and the purchase of workhorses and oxen to stable; the children arriving in pairs in fair weather; the granting of Jim's citizenship, another piece of their marriage, which come in time to celebrate with the fourth anniversary of their meeting March 31; and above all the framing of the schooner, Ben having for the first time hired a couple of hands so we could wrap up the deck boats, and get her off the ways by late summer.

Having finished the ways on site at the yard, we commenced operations there: Ben laboring fore and aft as a shipwright, me managing day's work as a foreman, and Jim serving as ship's carpenter and joiner, with a billethead for the bow in the offing. As she took shape in the public eye, Ben's skill was again the talk of the town, and much to Jim's satisfaction, further abroad: his bevel board, intricate with lines and angles, as much a testimony to his fine mind as a shipwright as ever his logbook was to his seamanship.

Planes and adzes, broad axes and dumb irons, bevel squares and caulking mallets—they come to his hand as apt as brushes to an artist's; and he grew even hardier with the hard work, him and Jamie both pleasing me with their strength. Snatching sandwiches in the sun on the stage, eyes bright with their keenness at construction, sleeves rolled up above their elbows in the heat, they looked hale and hearty as they stood side by side; and no contrast to their ruggedness was more touching than when Ben's big hand, rough and work-hardened, come down for a moment on the back of Jim's neck, or when Jim's strong fingers, bronzed by the sun, kneaded the kinks from Ben's burly shoulders.

This was the pattern we kept up for years: building fishing sloops or coastwise schooners of a summer, more often with the children as their skills improved—Tom turning out his first dinghy at ten; launching vessels and stocking provisions in autumn, not just for ourselves but for our next orders; designing and laying down lines in winter, then transferring them to patterns and selecting wood; and commencing on keels and ribs in the spring.

The yard was completed our third summer, with lofts and equipment enough to work on two larger vessels at once; and we made the final moves of all the tools and machinery from our carriage house to our site on the other side of town—our sign, Spooner Bay Shipyard, never failing to make our hearts leap. Though Ben never ceased the most common labor, nor Jamie and me neither, despite our evolving roles as carpenter and foreman, we hired on a number of permanent hands—two or three at first, then upwards of two dozen; and we come to be a real source of income on the island, particularly as we was self-sustaining—our sail loft, riggers loft, and eventually even rope walk, all supplying us like a ship on a voyage.

Each autumn we ventured brief spells at sea, delivering vessels up coast and down—the three of us skimming blue bays, spray flying, or harboring in tidy inlets, beneath black vaults ablaze with stars; and each winter Ben modeled our upcoming orders, often in concert with a figurehead from Jim. What with smart management and able shipwrights, and plenty of labor, Melchett Bros. kept afloat even through the Panic of '47, turning out crack ships for other houses or putting in their own masters; and as they often returned our favors, sending us orders for craft too small for them to handle, we barely felt that first big recession.

When the major Panic of '57 struck—ships hauled up all along the coast, business dull and freights flat or nonexistent, due to a merchant marine badly over-extended, and ships too extreme and expensive to operate—many yards, including Melchett Bros., almost went under; and it was us, simple and practical, that was able to keep Ben's family above water. Pumping money and small orders their way we kept them alive: a heaping of coals that satisfied Jamie especially, since he'd never stopped blaming hisself for Ben's lawsuits, or resenting Melchett Bros. for cutting Ben adrift.

Each year a different note was sounded against the backdrop of this rhythm: one year, the second, it was our loss of Jacques, all three of us shutting down operations to be with him, and seeing him off— quiet and peaceful in Ben's arms, as he'd wished; another, the fifth, it was paying off Jacob's loan, and clearing ourselves altogether of debt; another still, the sixth, it was Tom's first voyage, sailing off as foremasthand for his namesake uncle. At regular intervals, there was trips to Wales—Ben and Jim going the fourth year, Ben following his heart at last to see Sacki, and me staying behind to run the yard: the two of them taking a steamer and having a honeymoon of sorts, though Jim told me later Ben almost drove him to distraction, second-guessing the captain and finding fault with the sailors. Better on land than as a passenger aboard someone else's ship, he followed Jim through the maze of his old haunts, listening rapt to John Roberts' harp-playing at Bala, and kneeling at the cool edge of the waters; and they come back healed in many ways, having visited the places they'd last seen in pain, and re-carved their initials on Tomen Bala.

The seventh year I finally went with them, and seen it all firsthand for myself: the steep hills and rugged moors with their outcroppings of heather—the horse fairs and music festivals frequented by Jim's kin—John Roberts hisself, handsomely turned out, unaware of his son standing silently nearby—and young Sacki, free-spirited, dark-haired, a-dance on the moor as Jim had been at ten.

Through the years there was constants midst our routines and changes, constants that knit the two together: the quality of our work, the progress of the yard, and the success of Ben and Jim's marriage—their faithfulness to one another and the children, in spite of the obstacles that plagued them, making me proud of my matchmaking venture. Not that there wasn't transformations that come to them or their marriage, or to the parts they played in it. Consistent as Jamie was over the years—still drinking from his own cup, and avoiding anything *mukado*, down to separate laundries for the boys and girls; still indulging in his love of fashion, spending most of his spare cash on garb that caught his fancy; still up to all this, Jamie nonetheless was changeful, not just with the restlessness that was his nature.

Never tiring of his experiments, Ben looked forward to working with a different character each day; and we never knew who would come down to breakfast—sometimes a Welsh gentleman, sometimes a Rom dancer, and sometimes an American sailor, or some weird combination of all three. But in truth what was shifting was not just his moods and the garments that showed his frame of mind, but his role at home and in the yard; and one of their early struggles was his stressful wrestling with hisself as a man in his work and marriage.

To all appearances he was a man's man, proud in the tradition of Rom men, and independent as anyone can be in a marriage; but that wasn't what he was in private. In private what he was was a wife; and though that'd always been the case, it took him years to come to terms with it. Able to take on any job and frequently called to do so at the yard, this big, hardy carpenter just wanted to make Ben dinner, and steward the house the way he once had *Abigail*; and he didn't hardly know what to do about it. The first year or two, we was so busy, there wasn't time to consider our druthers; but by the third year he was aching for change, and though Ben didn't see it, I did.

Opening up to me as he always did with the right ploy, he poured out his yearning for time in the house, and greater freedom to explore his carving; and he already had in his head a blueprint for his role: a blueprint that included his staying home of a morning, cooking dinner and carving figureheads in his own shop off the carriage house whilst he was at it, then working at the yard in the afternoons, carrying on whatever stage of carpentry was required. Afraid of letting Ben down, especially them crucial early years, and confused hisself about his passion for home, he kept his dream to hisself till I nudged him to spill it; and when he seen not just Ben's acceptance but his support and understanding, he was so overjoyed he forgot his own fears.

In short order he got his shop off the kitchen, him and me building an ell between the carriage house and the cottage whilst Ben carried on without us for a spell; and whilst we was at it we constructed his other yen, across the hall from his shop in the same ell: a water closet like Jacob's in New York, big enough for any ten men—a place with a commode, a great brass tub, a stove for warmth and heating water, an overhead tank with perforated head for a shower, and even a padded bench for massages—the sort of furnishing you'd find in a bathhouse in Boston.

Watching it take shape, Ben was a bit leery, insisting it was lewd enough to get us arrested; but it turned out to be the room in the house we used most, besides the kitchen: the three of us finding, in the hot baths or cool showers, the conveniences of indoor plumbing, and the delights of a rubdown by Jim, not only all the essentials of living we'd missed, but a streamlined way to take care of the children. Nodding approval, Jim declared we met Rom standards—cleanliness being the antidote to *mukado*; though I noticed that when it come to actually cleaning these instruments of cleanliness, the job usually fell to a gadje.

Nor was our home improvements the only result of Jim's plan; for coming home of a noon, we'd find dinner ready, usually some combination of downeast and Rom that took in all the staples we loved. With dinner over we'd peek into his shop, to check on the progress of the figureheads and trailboards he was carving out now on a regular basis; and the explosion of colors, shapes and designs carried us as on a crest into our afternoons at the yard, where Jim always worked harder than any of us to make up for his morning absence. Out of that shop came a magnificent succession of figureheads over the course of our years together—angels, mermaids, dancers, sea gods, buccaneers and seekers of fortune—marching in and out of our rooms not unlike the medley of characters that paraded in and out of Jim's person; and with this expression added to kitchen and marriage, Jim at last arrived at the hearth of his soul.

If Jim struggled mostly with private issues—his wifely nature, his artist's needs, and the means to fit them into our patterns—Ben struggled with matters that was public: the competing claims of his family, the burdens of birthing a new business, and above all his relationship with Jim, which he did not want to keep secret. Though from time to time we rode through Thomaston, where the state prison sat bold and dark as a dungeon, and I pointed out its reminder of what'd happen if folks knew, he rebelled against that reality like a bear in a cage; railed that society, and church especially, recognized marriages not half so deep as his—marriages of convenience like his and Anne's, even hostile relationships like many we knew—but gave no sanction to a jewel like his and Jim's. As in love with Jim as he ever had been in Anjier, successfully over the hurdles of them first years together, Ben wanted to publish the news far and wide; and Jim's acceptance of their secrecy drove his almost as crazy as society's denial.

All too familiar with the disasters of open knowledge, Jim carefully guarded their relations in public, keeping up the old disciplined restraint he'd shown round folks from the start —never allowing more than a cuff on the shoulder or a quick, wary catch of the hand, once they'd stepped out the front door; and exasperated by his reserve in public Ben complained to me, "I sweah t' Gawd, sometimes it's like we've neveh even *met*."

Forthright as a gale and twice as persistent, it wasn't Ben's nature to keep things so hid; and the news crept out at times the way the tattoo on his upper arm—where Jim's initials was twined with his in an anchor—peeked out from under his rolled-up sleeves, or the way his ring, long explained as a Rom heirloom, set quietly on Jim's hand. But what really smoked him out in the open was them moments of crisis that come with accidents or storms, as on the day when, after too many hours in the August sun, Jim suddenly fell of a heap by the steambox; and he was lucky that, in the midst of their own panic, folks didn't really take note of his, as he went rushing pell mell and dropped to his knees to anxiously fondle Jim's hair. Struck by nothing worse than a bit of a sunstroke, Jim noticed though, when he come around; and half-glad, half-fearful, he was smiling gamely at Ben, "D'termined t' give us away, ain't you?", even as I held the water to him—Ben's hand only then falling reluctantly in check.

The energy from the marriage Ben couldn't make public had to go somewheres, and it did—into the shipyard, business and boats. The opposite of Jim's shop, the yard was shipshape as ever *Charis* was, a berth and a loft and a cuddy for every box and tool and timber; and there was enough of everything to supply every need and every last, unlooked-for disaster. Competitive as ever, though less impatient, Ben was determined to make us a success; and gradually he begun re-making his fortune, our increasing wealth changing him no more the second time than it had the first.

Looking at him, you'd no more guess he was monied than he was married; for in his laboring clothes above the sawpit, he was as unpretentious as he ever was on the quarterdeck, taking the sun or setting day's work. The succession of boats that come off of our ways was a testimony to him as a shipwright; and it matched in its way Jim's procession of figureheads: ketches, schooners, sloops, dories, cutters—all made not just to order from as far away as Boston but in answer to an interior design, their fairness and function a model of his mind.

Under Jamie's influence he was far more willing to spend what we made than he had been; and once we'd safely established the yard, and paid back Jacob for our start-up, he gave it in many directions: supporting Anne's household and orchestra, the children's schooling, and Melchett Bros. during lean spells, or buying back shares of *Charis* and *Abigail*, so we could help sway what trades they plied. Not forgetting Jim's plight as a stranded seaman, or as a rudderless tar in New York and Boston, he had me send drafts to charity hospitals and seaman's homes, Jackson's especially, establishing a memorial there in the name of Jacques; and every few months checks went off to Misericordia, long after Sister Leonora had passed away.

As over-indulgent of Jim as he was over-protective, he regularly urged money his way, so's he could spend it on fancies like cologne and toilet soap, or newfangled inventions for carving; and as determined to of fairly earned it, Jim usually figured his share to the dime—a good part of their squabbles sparked by such mathematics. But on hisself he spent as little as ever, tramping about in the same scarred boots, ragged jersey, and pilot's cap he'd worn for years— Jim, who secretly loved them, once setting up a museum display of decades-old relics as one of his ceaseless practical jokes, and labeling them with carefully etched cards, "circa 1836" or "worn at Bowdoin commencement."

And our cottage too was plain and simple, still looking like a camp years after it'd become a home. Except for the ell which connected carriage house to kitchen, we built only one addition, a chart room off the sitting room and a room above it, to accommodate Ben and Jim's privacy and Jim's expanding wardrobe; and cozy as the interior was, it was humble. Filled with keepsakes as varied as Ben's shell collection, Jim's figureheads and the girls' beeswax dolls, it had all the earmarks of a place long lived in; and no doryman ever failed to find comfort in the big, roomy sofas, braided rugs and blazing hearths. Though from the outside it looked like the rocks it was built on, grey-shingled, weathered, unbroken by shrubs, on the inside it took after the cabins of a ship, pine-paneled, practical and warm; and what with Ben's wall of barometers and charts or the telescope mounted at the sitting room windows, the whole place looked like she was about to set sail.

In quiet succession they celebrated their anniversaries—March 31, June 3 and 13—the only couple I ever knew to have a double wedding anniversary; and usually they popped a cork at home, Jamie less and less likely to show up at a tavern, even our own Fiddler's Green, or anyplace else where he couldn't show frank affection. On their first anniversary they cleared the sitting room, drew the shutters, dressed to the teeth and danced a few waltzes—the music, if it could be called that, coming from me, Jim having learned me to play some tunes on the fiddle, though it was no easier a job than my learning him higher mathematics that first voyage aboard *Charis*. Often we celebrated our birthdays that way as well, locking the doors, building a fire, and discouraging what few folk would ever be likely to drop by after dark: even Jim's coming-of-age our first summer passing quietly with champagne at our hearth.

But in later years, when business took us afield, we celebrated wherever we was—in Boston more than once, Ben and Jim putting on dress coats and sharing a fine dinner at the Tremont, or sprawling in sea gear at Toby's on March 31, all three of us swapping yarns of years passed. The heights of Corcovado, the red dawn at Anjier, the harpers' chords on the autumn winds at Bala—these wove in and out of the chanteys around us, interspersing the rude choruses like verses, or wafted above in the smoke-filled rafters, drifting like sea mist down tidal bays. Never rid of his anxiety about Slater and Lomond—always anxious about some chance encounter with someone he'd met, some exposure that would bring disgrace to Ben, or compromise our name at the yard—Jim set with his back to the room as we talked, only turning around when the door popped open: almost seeming to catch then, in the swirl of the snow, some long ago glimpse of Ben Melchett, stomping in on the eve of *Charis'* sailing.

To the end they was devoted partners: Jim's fire and passion constantly taking new forms, and Ben's faithfulness as steady as trade winds—him down the years able to bend Jim with a sweet word, and no one was ever better at it. Their room was a mixture of their odd mating, Jim's fervor and flash with Ben's steady embers; and as you picked your way through Jim's discarded clothes, past the rumpled heap of his bed, always unmade to keep up appearances, to the islands of order that was Ben's, you felt like you was in the midst of their marriage. Never changed or enlarged, it was as snug as a forecastle aboard a tight ship; and their bed was the same, never much roomier than a captain's bunk. One time when I asked Ben if they wouldn't like a bigger space, and offered to help re-construct the room, he shook his head, saying "Jim likes t' sleep close—an' I can't say as I mind"; and I seen it was true, there never being a morning—unless Jamie was sick, and Rom-like, in his own bed—when coming up with hot water, I didn't find him anchored in Ben's drowsy arms.

That isn't to say they never fought, for better fighters there never was; and as I'd expected from the beginning, there was plenty for them to wrangle over. The new roles they shifted into come slow, even though by their marriage they'd met in the middle; and there was ample occasions for backsliding, even as their old roles died away. Though a team player in new ways, Ben was high-handed, used for ten years to ordering men, not to mention children and critters, to do whatever it was he wanted done; and that didn't disappear overnight, anymore than Jim's hotheaded pride did. There was still flashes of both for years after; and when Ben'd take to flinging orders, in the heat of framing up a vessel, then Jamie—who'd certainly never regularly obeyed even as a seaman, when he was legally bound to do so—would fling back a round of Romany curses, the sort of rude sailor's blessings you'd hear on the waterfront. Like a peek into his past you'd see his rude fire, the way Sal did in Rio when Jim flashed his knife; and when Ben'd lose his head in return and try to control him like a seaman, instead of softening him up like a lover, there'd usually be a shoving match for me to hose down.

If they wasn't fighting over control—a specially touchy matter for Jim as his role changed—they was oftimes wrangling over money, or for the upper hand when one was ill or over-worked. All the usual sorts of things folks brawl over—religion and politics, amongst others—never caused them to lock horns; for Jamie was never remotely interested in politics, always trustfully voting as Ben did, and Ben showed extraordinary tact towards Jamie's strange mix of Romany and Christian faith. But money and health was a different matter—the former a matter of pride and control, the latter of surrender and caring; and I once seen Jim actually go sit on Ben, to keep him from working when he had the ague.

Sometimes when Ben'd confront Jim the same way, Jim'd be off in a flash on Dee—only stopping to hitch up the *vardo* if it was handy; and somewheres on the island he'd come to a halt and cool off while he camped by a tree. Getting better and better at reading his moves, Ben'd track him down in short order—once completely unnerving him by showing up where Jim was going before he got there hisself. And once—the only time Jim thoroughly scared Ben, and made him wonder if he'd gone back to his old ways—Jim quit the island altogether, jumping the ferry and heading for Portland: coming back on the return run shamefacedly cooled off.

By that time, a' course, Ben was on *his* way to Portland, having hopped aboard a lumber barge—the only vessel he could flag down at short notice; and to prevent this relay from going on till kingdom come, I set Jim on his hands and took the ferry, hunting Ben down before he could make a fool of hisself looking for Jim in some Portland dive. Finding him a day later—wandering the wharves, grey-faced, wondering if, at forty, he'd lost his powers—I simply put an arm about him, and brung him home on the return ferry; and I never seen much of that reunion, since it went on upstairs for hours.

If I'd ever thought these fights was completely spontaneous—as they seemed—that was changed altogether one time when I went up to soothe Jim, who'd stomped upstairs after a bout with Ben. Expecting to find him on the brink of tears, I discovered him reading by the fire, for all the world serene as a sunrise; and when he seen my consternation, he burst into hearty laughter. "Nothing more boring than a smooth sail, pal," this Romany fox informed me, writhing with inward merriment; and already you could almost see him hatching the circumstances of the next round.

Making up was as vital as their brawls was; and they made up every way ever invented by man. Sometimes if was Jamie who, unexpectedly yielding, simply gave way with a sweet shrug— sometimes so suddenly Ben almost fell on his face; and other times it was Ben who apologized, though there was nothing more comic than his gruff grace. But the dearest reunion I ever seen—not just because it made things up, but because it was a public declaration, the sort Ben'd been yearning for all along—occurred at the Portland ferry, when all three of us had been to the city on business, and Jim decided to quit our ranks early. Still miffed by his desertion, Ben put him on the steamer, then watched him off from the dock with the usual mob of farewellers; and hanging over the rail, Jim looked down to spot him. Catching sight of him all at once, Jim simply hollered—in all the hullabalu of departure—an impulsive and unmistakable "I love you"—not in Romany or Welsh, but bold English; and so taken aback—and so moved as well—he couldn't find his tongue in return, Ben wordlessly tipped his cap in answer.

There was tensions too that sprung from women, though not in such a way as to divide them—tensions that, like their enforced secrecy and compromises from the past, simply become part of their lives together. Though he'd settled down to home and work and dropped out of the social circles he'd once traveled, Jim never stopped being a draw to the ladies; and since there was no wife actually on his arm, and no further details of his ties in the past, some never really gave up on his heart. Damaris was one who hung on to the end, her having been serious enough to of proposed to him herself; and the extent of her devotion was obvious when, over the years, she never married anyone else.

One by one all his other admirers—Sabrina, Kate, even Ben's sister Keziah, who I'd always suspected had more than a sisterly eye on him—went to the altar with skippers and shipwrights; but Damaris took up schoolmarming, and gave her affection to a generation of students. That she never found in anyone else what he had in his life with Ben, cut him with dismay and regret; and an unspoken source of distress for him—the kind that sent him off on Dee, to ramble the shore road alone for a spell—was them times when he bumped into her by chance, and realized afresh no one'd answered her feelings.

But no woman afflicted them both as Anne did; and year after year I seen what it took from them to discipline their lives to hers. Though capable and independent, she insisted they keep up appearances, maintaining at least the look of a marriage; and if Ben ever wavered—if he ever shrank from them weeks in town, or entertained thoughts of packing up altogether—Jim held him to it for the sake of the children. When at last he come home, wide-eyed and shaken, from one of his weekend stints at Anne's, and told us she'd taken him aside to confess she'd fallen in love with a retired colonel—when at last she declared, ten years after his marriage with Jim, that she too wanted to be free to marry, and had pleaded with him to help her find a way—there was a celebration at our place like no other; and plans went forward for him and Jim to re-marry, though there was months to go before things between him and Anne was final.

Months indeed, and what months they was—the town exploding over the decision: not least because Ben and Anne was both so obviously at peace with it, and so friendly in how they went about it. Never wanting her to have anything less than he did hisself, the pleasure and support of a well-matched partner—respecting Jeb Snowe as the perfect mate for her, which he was, a gentlemanly widow both cultured and monied, and sociable the way she was in town and church circles—Ben stood up for her to the bafflement of all; whilst Anne, the most hot-headed defender of old school morals, confounded folks by not only ending her marriage—that "perfect" arrangement they'd coveted for years—but straightaway embarking on another.

Though he kept in the background, waiting for Anne and Ben to settle matters, everyone knew Col. Snowe was waiting for her; and his quiet patience only fanned the flames higher. Divorce being almost unheard-of—a frowned-upon civil procedure—Anne and Ben went the route of the courts unblessed, leaving the church to decide how they felt about it; and how the church felt about it was loud, pronouncing judgments heard in the next county. That any institution would want to prison together two people who was so fundamentally unfit for each other staggered a few, me not least amongst them; but there was plenty who felt marriage was till kingdom come, and argued it chapter and verse, trumpet volume. In the end the congregation actually split, some taking Anne's side and supporting the right to divorce, others not; and a new congregation was born, taking up a subscription and laying a foundation even whilst Anne was building a new life.

Never having wanted to be the center of a scandal—having avoided it for years, even at the price of an empty marriage—Anne weathered it the best she could, showing again the stuff she had in her—the sort of steel she'd revealed the night of the shipwreck; and so much did he respect her for her persistent courage that Ben at last become friends with her—even prayed with her when things was at their worst. Helping out with the children—taking them out to the island to get them away from the heat, and give them a chance to sort matters over—he lightened her load every way he could; and she leaned on him the same way as the young ones—the way you lean on a steady compass.

Though Tom by then was mostly on his own, and Jean was gearing up for college—though the younger ones was all into their teens, and old enough to explain things to—it was an adjustment for them to see Ben pack up his gear, and to welcome a new face at the table; and it took all the steady-handedness he'd built up over the years to keep things on an even keel. Seeing him happy with Anne's choice and content with his own life stabilized things most for the young ones; and one of the best gifts he ever gave Anne was the careful steering he did for their children, whilst she was re-constructing her life.

She become Anne Melchett Snowe—the name the town gave to the music academy she established, and later on to the new library she underwrote—in a quiet ceremony with few attending; and so pleased was he for her that Ben showed up at her invitation, sitting bold as a skunk in the fog with the children, whilst Jamie and me camped nearby him. As if such a benediction was the final straw, the town almost collapsed under the weight of its blessing, even more scandalized by it than the divorce; and in after years it become local legend that Ben handed his wife over to another man at the altar—a tale recounted by young and old long after all the true events was forgotten.

But unbeknownst to them all, that was not the final chapter; for in October of 1855, on a fine Indian summer day when the blue waters was sparkling and the shore was an autumn riot of color, we cast off *Idris* and returned to our cove, Ben at the tiller and Jamie and me crewing; and there they repeated their vows, at last completing the splice begun over ten years ago. Commencing his forties, Ben was showing his age the way an oak beam shows its weather; whilst a decade younger, Jim had the look of a warm and seasoned ripeness, the sort you see in a September apple. In words they'd written themselves they staked their common future, celebrating a mating that claimed every corner of their lives; then—having worked on it secretly for months—Jim gave Ben a ring, a bit of scrimshaw intricately etched with an outline of *Charis*, framed in a plain gold setting and band; and Jim in return got his diamond, which he wore on a chain round his neck, Ben's sapphire-eyed porpoise never once having left his wedding finger.

Sharing a meal by the tiller—concocting stories to fool others about Ben's ring, the only note in the day that upset Ben, who ached for a public declaration like Anne's—they fed each other tidbits and enjoyed my audience; then sailing back to the cottage on a generous fair wind—making the sloop fast to the pilings, and ferrying the remains of our feast down the worn path—they headed for the house, and closed the door for all time on separation.

From time to time the children still stopped with us—Jean, during her college years, the month of the long vacation in August, and Seth and Nat, whole building seasons, as they finished up their secondary schooling; but mostly we was launching them the way we was vessels. Tom, following his father's earlier footsteps, took his master's papers and doubled as shipwright, going into partnership with Melchett Bros. and, not long after, a marriage with Gillie Coombs—buying back, to Ben's quiet delight, their old yellow homestead on the Point; whilst Jean decided on a career in navigation, charting first for Tom and later her husband, Dory Winslow. With time Seth worked up to a position at our shipyard, a course that settled him onto the island; and Courtney hitched up with the youngest of the DeMille brothers, moving into a small house on China St. The only one who went out to the war between the States, Nat trained as a medic under me, then come back to help manage Ben's latest venture, a salvage operation we'd started up as a sideline; whilst Becky, the youngest and most musical of the lot, learned on the violin and taught at Anne's academy.

For each of them Ben made generous financial arrangements—the Panic of '57, which all but shut down Melchett Bros., hitting even those as young and financially uninvolved as Tom; but with Ben's help he made a swift personal recovery, Melchett Bros. meantime changing course and orienting more toward coastwise vessels. Never going in for steam, they built 3- or 4-masted schooners, not so grand as the square riggers of the Fifties, but good workhorses that attracted freights; and their speed and maneuverability kept them competitive for years. Having seen the family yard through its crisis and his oldest son onto his feet—having witnessed at last the twilight of the great ships foreseen by him more than a decade ago—Ben wrapped up all business in Cape Damaris, saving only our two rooms on the third floor of the Inn for visits.

If our old place seemed empty without small fry underfoot, it wasn't so for long; for there was soon a shipload of grandchildren, all six of Ben's young ones producing their own. Twenty-three of them there was that lived, of varying ages as they come along over two decades; and though never at our place all at one time, there was usually a goodly number of them to climb over Ben and pull his beard, or bend knots with me or ride in Jim's *vardo*.

Ever on the lookout for new ways to tap sea life, Ben started up our salvage operation in the mid-sixties by a fluke, one of Hull and Lombard's ships coming to grief on our shoals, and Ben going into high gear to rescue the cargo. Winning not only quick money and a reputation for shrewd action but a fascination for sunken treasure as well, he went to work with his usual gusto, pinpointing wrecks and stockpiling equipment; and though there was nothing our place needed less than another wall of charts plotting ship bones or another boatshed full of tackle, he steamed ahead with his latest venture. Needing divers, he turned first to Jim and me; but now in my mid-fifties, I couldn't see myself as a seal; and though a decade and more younger, Jamie flatly put his foot down. "Melchett, y'know I'd do just about anything for you," he declared, hands on his hips in the midst of Ben's tackle, "but I'll be damned if I'll go down there in the dark on a rope; an' I ain't goin' t' let you do it either—I'll cut all the lines an' let off all the tanks first."

Getting nowheres with us, Ben turned to the younger generation, finding eager recruits in two of his nephews and later on, Nat; and buying up an old tug—which he renovated as lovingly as ever he did *Idris*—he stood out to sea with cigar, cap and seaboots, holding forth with as much pride as an explorer bound for new worlds.

Managing things topsides, Jamie and me hauled up cargo, everything from Chinese jade to rusty anchors—our harvest now brass, now a plate-filled strongbox, now a crate load of nails or porcelain shards; and though our catch was more often bizarre than practical, and more often practical than lucrative, we was one with Ben in our anticipation of whatever would next break the surface. Of course it all had to be stored somewheres—hauled to a warehouse we'd managed to earmark at our shipyard, then sent on to owners or dealers in salvage; and of course it all had to be categorized and sorted, requiring a separate set of books which was of course kept by me. But there was an enchantment to even the most commonplace gear, once it'd been transformed by a few years of sea change; and many a night we spent round the kitchen table, pouring over old logbooks and plotting coordinates, with an eagerness for what might be in the next load.

Helping stock the tug for one of our expeditions—coiling up lines and stowing tanks, or making up beans and salt pork in the galley— Jim and me would watch Ben and Nat on the dock, Nat hauling his diver's rig and Ben lengths of tackle, weathered as an old piling in his oilslicks. Seeing in the two of them the Ben of old, embarking on a deepwater voyage in his twenties, and the Ben of now, still farming the sea in his fifties, Jim would frequently turn away, eyes blurred; for without photographs of them early years of their marriage—with little more to go by than a portrait or two he'd made Ben set still for, and the figurehead he'd carved the year they'd first met—there was only Nat to provide a look back on the young Ben, a living picture of the man who'd first taken him to mate.

Of all of Ben's children, Nat was as well most their own, the closest to being both of theirs as parents, since they begun together with him as a babe; and it was a crushing blow to both of them when he was lost in a diving accident off Foster's Ledge in '72. Comforting Jim—accepting comfort—Ben simply murmured, "I c'n stand anything so long as it ain't you, mate"; and the salvage operation went on, as island business always did despite hardships, two of Nat's cousins taking his place.

There was other hardships as well, though their outcomes was less disastrous: nights of storm, when one or the other of them was out to sea, or times of illness on top of harsh work; but nothing was more touching in the midst of such trials than the tenderness they used to ease each other, even as middle-aged men. Seeking port in the sloop in a thick of fog—after a day at sea in the pouring rain—Jim once found his way steering by compass and the foghorn Ben sounded for hours on our dock, like some forlorn, searching birdcall of homing; and there was no end to the hot baths and blazing fires and chicken pies Ben had waiting for him at our house. Battling a lame back or a bout of fever, Ben was fussed over the same way, Jamie nursing him with tricks gadje and Rom; and Ben never slept without hot bricks and compresses and the soothing touches of Jamie's hands.

Nor was I forgotten when ill, or home from the yard with wet feet of a cold March; for many a time I slipped my blue toes into slippers toasted by Jim at the kitchen fire, or ate the hot meal of cod and potatoes dear to Ben and me since childhood. At such times I found out what it was like to be one of them—what is was in each other that so attracted them, even after years of living together; for Ben would take charge in such a way as to make you feel he'd taken the world off your hands, a release every man should know now and again to keep sane; and Jamie's hands flirted in ways you could sense even when sick—in ways young and old, men as well as women, most likely even dogs and horses, could feel as suggestive no matter the task.

It was such hardships that forced even Jim out in the open over the years—though you had to be me to see the small changes in him, or appreciate how an unlooked-for moment, ordinary from every point of view except his, overcome him with feelings he couldn't hide. Watching Ben tromp down our dock with a bucket of clams, his perpetual pilot's cap like the bill of a duck in the twilight, and his seaboots a-ooze with mud, bait and brine, Jim'd be as moved as one hailing a lover back from some faraway adventure; and he once took off like a shot for Ben's arms, running to meet him in a public welcome that would of been seen by one and all but for fog. Anxious, Ben cried out "Jamie, what is it?"—Jim sobbing, "You, walkin' down the dock with a bucket o' clams"; and "Hell, I'll walk down the dock anytime with a bucket o' clams, for a welcome home like that" Ben chuckled, kissing him there in his briny arms.

Alert at once to where they was, Jim looked over his shoulder as if expecting an audience in the fog; and smiling, Ben told him, "Honey, I'm fifty; ain't nobody goin' t' put these old bones in jail now." Knowing full well all the penalties—ranging from violence to ostracism—that waited them as readily as prison, Jim simply smiled against his shoulder, "You old fool"; but they walked down to the house arm in arm together; and it was a rare occasion after, no matter how many folks was present, when Jim didn't venture to let down his guard in some small way.

Our last trip to Wales come in '73, the year we learned of John Roberts' death. All our journeys you might say was bittersweet—not just for Ben, who seen in young Sacki the Jamie of old, but for Jamie too, who watched from afar the traditions he was no longer part of, and the kin that must never see him in return. But this last was the most poignant of all our visits; for John Roberts' passing brung more than loss with it. Though I'd never once heard Jim regret that he was who he was, or that he was no longer home with his kin, his father's death brung home to him the bargain he'd made for all time with his secret, the news of life and marriage that could never be shared now; and for the first time he was face to face with the frustration that Ben's battled for nigh onto three decades.

Besides the honesty he could never lay claim to—the openness Ben'd championed for years—there was the additional fact of his aging that come plain to him with the old man's passing: the realization he was in the front trenches, now that the last of the old generation was gone. Unnerved by that—though he didn't say so—he struggled to absorb it along with his loss; whilst Ben, who'd grown as accustomed to picturing Jim in the future—through his father—as in the past through Sacki, wrestled too with the stark void that stretched now before him.

Caught up in their loss, they each reacted in ways you would expect: Jim taking off on his horse for four days, leaving us in the lurch at the Inn in Bala, and Ben—sensibly letting him go—turning to track down the place where John Roberts had been laid to rest. Since we couldn't name him out loud to Jim's kin, due to the taboo that sealed names in death, or publish how we knew of him in the first place, it was no easy job to find the churchyard outside of which he'd been buried in Bala; but Ben kept at it till he'd found the new grave, and had had it out with the rector who'd refused to bury him inside, with the Christians. For a long time he paid his respects at the site, planting a holly bush and a stone in farewell; and when he left there was not just them things to mark the place, but a bottle of ale with a straw leading down, a parting shot for the old man's voyage.

When Jim finally hauled up to our door at the Inn—still wearing the worn tweeds he'd made off in, and the tourist's cap of the type we always donned, to give us the look of gentleman travelers—he homed in on the sofa and a seat by Ben, who was deep in the Liverpool shipping news as per usual; and neither of them said a word to the other, Ben slipping off Jim's cloth cap and stroking his dark hair, still without a trace of silver, and Jim pillowing his cheek with a sigh on Ben's shoulder.

Before we could adjust to John Roberts' death or do more than get our feet under us that autumn, we was brung up short by another haymaker, this time one that threatened Jim. It was one of them falls when Line storms was a-plenty, even so far downeast as us; and the hurricane winds that swept the West Indies lashed up the seas all the way out on the Banks. Caught on the fishing grounds, dozens of schooners parted cables and collided or dismasted; whilst closer to us an Appalach vessel making from Bangor with a cargo of lumber went aground on the shoals not far from our Point. Responding to their flare our lifesaving service—still a matter of volunteers and Lyle guns—wheeled surfboats down to the shore till they was opposite the wreck; then with night coming on and a gale of wind blowing—with sheets of rain thrashing our gear as we worked—we tried to set up a breeches buoy.

Too far out for the success of a taut line—the vessel over 400 yards distant, and the whip sagging in the water even when we did manage to connect—the breeches buoy had to be abandoned; and we readied the surfboats, preparing to send out a pair with four or five hands in each craft. Keeping close together as they plowed into the waves—planning to row out together, and take their chances in the same boat—Jim and Ben was just ahead of me, manning the gunwales to meet her head on; but in all the scramble of trying to board her, Ben was launched at the steering oar—his fearsome strength even nigh sixty making him a prime hand at that post; whilst Jim got cut off by a sea at the last minute. Watching Ben's boat mount straight up a comber, fall off, then labor on even as a sea breeched her, Jim suddenly dropped to his knees beside me; and letting go the next boat, I groped for him in the foam. Whether it was the night's exertion or the stinging shock of Ben in that surf without him, it'd happened too fast for me to say; but I knew even as I clutched at him that it was his heart.

Abandoning the rescue—unable to carry him, not having Ben's strength, but managing to drag him through the tide wrack to the sand, and so through the sea grass to the back shore—I hauled him to the nearest refuge, a survival hut built twenty years ago for such a night; and scrambling for the blankets and matches—finding, for a mercy, they hadn't been looted—I went to work warming him by the rude hearth. Soaked as he was—blue from the cold, and worse—it was no easy job to fight off the chill; and not having my bag with me I'd no medicines to give him. Urgently needing the stimulants always packed in my satchel, I had to leave him long enough to fetch it; and back out into the storm I flew on my mission, his hushed face the last thing I seen as I made off.

Driven by that look I battled the wind—punctuated by the thunder and boom of canvas, the break-up cries of a dying vessel—till I reached the point where we'd hauled the boats off their carts, my satchel still hanging where I'd left it; then plunging into the surf I managed to find Seth, still trying to launch the second boat. Having capsized twice, it was now far behind Ben's, the one it'd been meant to companion; and at the steering oar hisself, Seth was marshaling a third try, having no more idea than me where in all the chaos Ben was. Hollering to him to send Ben to the hut when he made shore—bent only on the imperative of saving Jim, with no notion how Seth'd ever deliver my message, even if they did both return—I made off with my bag through the drenching commotion; and shutting out the distant mourning of timbers, I raced the windy mile to the hut.

Responding to the brandy Jim gave me a wan smile, once along about the first watch; then repeatedly he asked for Ben, with mounting anxiety as he became conscious; and I was just weighing the risks of leaving him again—hardly able to bear the waiting myself, and anxious that my word'd miscarried—when the door blew open and Ben hisself busted in. Dropping to his knees beside Jim—catching the point of my hand at his heart—he hovered grey-hued, wild-haired over him, the spent peace of a successful rescue swiftly chased from his face by the tumult of fresh fear; and sensing his presence at once in his sleep, Jim stirred and looked up with wordless relief. Gazing down on Jim's face, unmistakably bluish beneath his night's beard, Ben whispered hoarsely, "Don't you leave me"; and giving a game smile—making an effort to respond, in a voice so low Ben had to bend to hear him—Jim murmured, "Ain't goin' nowheres… without you."

His recovery was slow, not aided any by that long, hazardous night, or the rough ride next morning in the boat cart Ben'd rigged up, its makeshift tent only partially shedding the rain. Weakened by survival at sea and the harsh demands of life before the mast, by fever and the intemperances of the city, his heart didn't rebound like it might of, given his native physical strength; and his intense emotional nature undermined it as well. Putting him to bed in my room at our place, I didn't give Ben any guarantees; and climbing in beside him—not just to comfort him, but to find rest hisself, his big, burly limbs a-shake with worry—Ben took care of him with hands that was sure, his touch better than any medicine I gave.

In the days to come he built Jim a special bed in the kitchen, one that could be raised up at the back so he could look out on the bay, and still see all the activities of the hearth. Not allowed to walk, Jim read and drew, often leaning on Ben's shoulder of an evening, the two of them wrapped up in comforters like a cocoon; and when he did get back on his feet—when I told him he was done with the yard for the year, and wouldn't be doing any more heavy labor—he didn't put up a fuss, settling down instead in the household he loved. Mixing Romany potions, he drank them with mine, long after he was up and around; and setting up headquarters in his shop he carved all winter, baked dumplings and looked after grandchildren. The wood shavings flying, he modeled toys—rocking horses, doll beds, striped tops and trains—in between his figureheads and pies; and I always thought after it was the best year he ever had.

At Ben's request, he carved hisself as a merman, the bewitcher in an old dream of Ben's, then carved Ben as a retired sea captain, grey-haired, grey-bearded, but hale in his timbers, an old-time quadrant held in his hand. The two best works he ever done, we kept them with our others—his Turk, bought back when the *Song of the Orient* was decommissioned, and Ben as a young skipper, Jim's first effort. There was even a figurehead of me, lean-faced, weathered, mending nets with a length of sinnet; and it stood in the line with the rest in the ell hallway, for all the world like a gallery of portraits, or a row of ancestral frames in a mansion.

In his leather apron, Jim shaved and chiseled, his health improving with each order he filled; and when requests lagged he made shadow boxes, or ships-in-bottles for the grandchildren. With the light of the lamp on his face as he painted, or outlined the form of a tinker or sailor, he appeared to finally be what he was, a master artisan and craftsman: a man swept with images like a heath swept with wind. Yet the man in his apron, bent over his workbench, was but one of a dozen or more that we knew; for what he was above all was a medley, a gallery of faces like the figureheads in our hall, or the storied prows that arched over Ann Street.

At last handing over the reins to Seth, Ben kept Jim company all winter, organizing his logbooks and charts in between shaping lift models, or overhauling our salvage gear and tackle. As spring come on and hardship struck again, this time in the form of the loss of Jean's husband, on the high seas off Diego Ramirez—as Jean brung home the ship with the mate, Dory's brother, and made fast in Cape Damaris with two small children, and little more than the shares they owned in three ships—Ben diverted funds again to support her, setting her up in Boston where she found a berth teaching navigation. Finding ourselves in more modest circumstances as a result—deriving an income primarily from the salvage operations, and our share of the shipyard profits—we took to fishing to beef up our funds, throwing in our lot from time to time with my cousins.

Constitutionally unable to stay off the sea, even nigh sixty as he now was, Ben took to this new form of farming the waters much as he done when he was my sternman in his teen years, with a passion for scouting and hauling live cargo; and since Jim could sail with us as steward and deckhand, it was the logical next step for us three, the last stage in our partnership together.

Them being the days when cod was so plentiful it was laid out to dry on the hakes by the thousands, there was no lack of work for us in the summer; and there was money and security in the job for the season. Never one to look down on honest employment, no matter how demanding or briny, Ben made the shift from shipbuilding and salvage to setting and dragging and hauling in nets; and though we never strayed far from local waters, letting younger cousins stand in for us on the banks, we reaped cargoes a-plenty, both haddock and cod.

Still far from a poor man, he nonetheless took on—as them last summers passed and he turned sixty—more and more of the unsung look of our shipmates, saltwater farmers and lobstermen all; and his face, like his garb, reflected the economy of his condition and tasks. Though his eyes still showed the nobility Jim'd seen long ago; though his features gave voice to a sharp mind and wit, his prevailing look called to mind the austerity of the seas he worked, or the plainness of them that labored with him. Hale, weathered, windblown, hearty, he visibly portrayed the tides which'd carved him; but nothing of his tasks or surroundings was responsible for the glow in his eye; for that sprung from the hidden flame of his marriage, which burned on through storms and calms alike.

Never getting over the scare of Jim's heart, his one great anxiety was his loss; and haunted by the thought of years without him—spooked equally by his own passing, and Jamie's subsequent bereftness—Ben struggled to come to terms with their aging, and with their inevitable separation. Characteristically responding with action, he lectured me again on the precise terms of his will, and on his instructions as to how Jim was to be looked after, should he be the first to pass on; and when Jean arrived for her customary summer visit, he went over the same ground with her. Nor was that the extent of his business; for he went into committee with hisself, and when he emerged he sailed off to see John, to file some document even I hadn't seen.

That John hadn't read it either I soon understood, for he hounded me to remember it was to be opened before his will, and that John mustn't be allowed to forget its existence. His mind lifted in some way by what he had done, he seemed more summery after, especially as Jim's health begun to improve; but I knew by the way he looked after him—by the way he drank in his comely looks or small pranks, as if to savor every minute of the present—that his mind was never wholly off their separation.

As they'd once battled other forces that worked to separate them—different cultures, different values, different definitions of manhood, previous relationships and pride and social threats—so now they wrestled with the final challenge of death; but when it ultimately come it was as none of us had expected, for all of Ben's efforts to be prepared for it. A fortnight earlier, the ice still thick on the millpond, we'd gone skating together with much of the town—

Ben, who'd always felt too big and lummoxy on blades, tending the roaring bonfire on the shore, and Jamie and me gliding along together, him rhythmic and sure, me carrying the lantern, the snowflakes falling gently about us.

Finding myself sick the next day, due to a chill taken that night, I laid by with the ague whilst spring come to a degree; and when my cousins hailed me from their ketch for our first haul, I tried to rally my old bones for the run. Having cossetted me day and night for two weeks —Jim with food, Ben with fires, the two of them keeping up a regular relay there in the kitchen—they wouldn't hear of me dragging nets, going off without me for the haul; and I watched them from the window that mild April morning as they hopped aboard with Alden and Jeb.

So it was that, not long after the 35th anniversary of their meeting at Toby's, they put out to sea without me; and lonely without them—the house suddenly empty as it always was without Jim's ringing laughter, or the quarterdeck bawl of Ben's bluster—I fussed in the kitchen in small fits and starts, clearing away our hurried breakfast. Springing up out of the northeast, a gale of wind swept the bay, churning the seas beneath sheets of rain; and unreasonably restless—finding it impossible to keep still—I finally up and threw on my oilslicks, and headed for Seth's place just down the road.

Home hisself for the birth of his son, the eighth and last of his brood, earlier in that hectic week, Seth took me in and set me by the fire; served me a hot toddy to settle my ague, and tried to argue me back to bed. Swept by a succession of chills and flushes—too nervy to be the product of fever—I obstinately refused; endeavored instead to convince him to walk out to the Point, and have a look at the horizon. Finding my edgy foreboding catching, he at length caught up his glass, and made for the door with a word to his in-laws, there to keep house during his wife's confinement; and too restless to remain by the fire, I stubbornly departed with him.

The squall having lifted, it was windy and rainy, but clearer than it earlier had been; and reaching the Point, we scanned the seas, slate-colored and heavily running. With Seth's glass we could make out one or two of the islands and the rain-enshrouded haze of the mainland, but no sign of traffic, coastwise or deepwater; and returning to my place for supper, we warmed up and dried off and debated our options. Uneasy at not having sighted the ketch—alarmed at the lateness of the hour, which, with the inclement weather, should of fetched its arrival—the two of us braved the mud back to town, scared up a spare hand and put out in Seth's sloop, scouring the shores of the nearby islands.

With twilight coming on and the seas running high, it was a difficult expedition, and in the end, entirely unproductive; for not only was there no sign of the ketch, in waters she was known to be headed, but no other sailing vessel either. Making fast to the wharf, we found Kalkman's trawler, having returned from outside in our absence; but from his hands there was no news of the ketch, nor anything else save hard work and rough weather.

Returning to our cottage alone, I walked almost witlessly through the rooms; tried to suppose the ketch was hauled up in some eel rut, as'd happened any number of times in years past. Climbing the stairs, I turned toward the front room, and tremulously halted on the threshold; seen the bedclothes and drawers in upheaval, in the disarray of an early morning departure, and the curtains billowing in the wet wind. Closing the window—blown open and banging—I looked about in desolation and panic, their surges gusting through me like wind squalls; but the patient attitudes of the chamber—the quiet tangles of clothing, the still arms of the sofa, the waiting jumble of pillows and blankets, all looming in the shadows and moonlight—unnerved me even more than my terror, and drove me back down to my chair in the kitchen.

Alternately drinking strong coffee, walking the room and pacing the seafront—all the way from the cottage to the Point—I spun out the unending night watch; took to the shore when the sight of Ben's pipe stand, or a half-finished wooden toy on the mantle, compelled me to flee the unspoken waiting of the cottage; then returned to the house when the raw wind and breakers took on the rush and swirl of lost voices. At the first sign of daybreak I threw on my oilslicks and went to meet Seth at the end of the dock, already swarming with deckhands and neighbors; and at dawn we put out in a flotilla of vessels, each of us taking a different direction.

Scouring the shores of the mainland, the shoals round the islands, and the stretches of open sea in between, we covered the course the ketch must of taken, allowing for the squall and driftage; hailed passing schooners and smacks for news, and alerted shore folk to the missing vessel. By noon the overdue signals was flying from semaphores in Cape Damaris, Spooner Bay and the inside islands; and some of the mainland fore-and-afters had joined in the unproductive searching.

There being no sign of vessel or wreckage, nor any reports of possible sightings, the day wore on in frustration and worry; and Seth and me was about to turn back to Spooner Bay to check for word there, when a signal went up on the staff at Mast Island. Signaling the search craft around us ourselves, we hauled the mainsail and put her about; and with one or two of the nearby boats following suit, we bore down on Henry Pinkham's wharf. Finding Henry hisself on the wet planks to meet us, we made the lines fast and leapt down with questions; but when I seen Henry take Seth aside and put a comforting arm about him, I knew very well, without words, what he'd found. Suddenly old, I groped for a seat, and doubled up for a time on a cask; then getting to my feet, I jumped down from the wharf, and followed the others up the shore in silence.

I was prepared to find one, but not both; and when I seen them together on the bit of beach at the point, with planks and pieces of wreckage around them, I fell of a heap on the shore beside them. Tangled together, they was tied with a rope, a stout length of hemp that bound them at the waist—as though, in them final moments before things broke up, they'd found a sure way to brave it together; and their limbs too was locked in the last throes of life.

Tenderly brushing the hair back from their faces, then witlessly plucking at the rope, I blindly confronted the knot, and made futile efforts to unloose it; but so sure was the tie, an anchor bend, and so steady—as if Ben'd bent it, not minutes from death, but on some sunny dock in the harbor—that I didn't have the heart to undo it; and suddenly understanding it wasn't meant to be undone, I dropped it and announced we'd move them together. Too stove to argue, Seth gave consent, Henry fetching Seth's sloop round and helping us ferry them in the dinghy; and so it was we made for Spooner Bay with them still bound, Henry's sons kindly sailing us home.

When word reached Cape Damaris, late in the evening, that bits and pieces of the ketch had fetched up on Mast Island, and that the bodies of all five'd been recovered, either washed ashore or picked up at sea, it was too late for much of the town to descend on Spooner Bay; and I found myself, that unreal April night, with mostly islanders at the cottage, grieving or sitting in stunned, hushed restraint. Besides Jamie and Ben, two of my cousins, both McCabes, and one of the Pelhams had been aboard; and the whole of the island shared in the misfortune. Moving about from house to house—bypassing Seth's, where his wife'd just given birth, and coming together instead at our place—they wept and prayed and comforted and talked, or stood around in stoical silence, till—torn between a longing to be left alone, and a dread of the total aloneness that waited—I felt almost mad from pain and exhaustion.

Gruff and impatient—nearly hoarse from my own withheld grief—I spent the night guarding their bodies, for fear somebody'd take a knife to their rope; fought with Seth—when his senses come to—over how they was to be laid to rest, and thanked God I had Ben's directions to back me. However they'd died, however many years apart, he'd wanted them to be laid in the same grave, if their bodies was recovered; and since I had the papers to prove it, I could squelch Seth's insistence they be divided, so long as I kept awake.

Nor did the dawn bring any respite; for with the coming of light an armada of vessels, bearing every one of my mainland relations, the whole of the Melchett clan now in port, and dozens of sundry Pelhams and townsfolk, descended on our little island village. Ben's brothers and sister, his children and grandchildren, more distant kin and shipyard comrades, lifelong companions of his and Jamie's, shipmates, dockhands and tavern cohorts all made their way to our cottage that morning; and most, along with a throng of McCabes, required food and care for the day—more grub than I, in my grief, could of managed, even if I'd been free to cook it.

Sticking to Jamie and Ben as if I too was knotted, I kept up my guard in the tent I'd created—the two of them, with their rope, having been left on the sloop, it being too hard to move them together; and lying thus side by side, with a ship's lamp above them, they lay on the deck with the light on their faces, whilst the town paid its final respects beside me.

But it wasn't the sight of them locked together—not the sight of their tangled limbs, nor even the sight of the extraordinary rope, that begun to unsettle folks that looked on—not yet; for most of them, naive and sheltered, found in that knot the sum of a deep friendship, a bond heralded far and wide for decades; whilst others, old cronies who might of suspected, held their peace out of respect or unsureness. "David and Jonathan," many murmured, stung almost as much by their loyalty as by their death; and I done what I could to encourage the notion.

No, it was the burial in a common coffin—which I'd already asked old Jorab to construct, him being the undertaker of sorts on the island, when he'd come to tend them on arrival—that so begun to agitate others; the burial in a common grave, that smacked to them of something unchristian. As if these arrangements wasn't enough, folks was disturbed as well by how the men looked; for not only had I refused to have the rope severed, but their garments exchanged for fresh suits and linen—insisting that Ben'd always wanted to die with his boots on, and that the integrity of their looks be honored.

Unable to abide either the "heathen" burial or the laying to rest of the men in anything less than their best, Seth—as strong-willed as ever his Pa was, and ferocious now he had his kin to back him—fought with me over and over; and stamping my foot in my grief and anger, I held my ground with as obstinate passion. Finding in their rope, their rough boots, their fishermen's jerseys and seamen's trowsers the very gist of the men I loved, I was desperate to leave them untouched; was loath to either alter or cancel the statement of their last, simple moments. Crushed by the talk and the senseless habits—enraged by others' attempts at control, when it was I who above all was family—I broke down and cried in the midst of my anger; and so stunned was they by my display of emotion—the only outburst they'd ever seen from me—that Seth backed down again in silence, and relented his say in the day's preparations.

Not one at this point to compromise or dally, I sent to Jorab's for the plain double coffin, as simple as any fisherman's last bed; and with the help of Longworthy and Eli and Haggai, I laid Jamie and Ben to rest in it, and set them again in their tent on the sloop. Going to their room—from which I'd barred the whole village—I risked fetching some bedding whilst Seth went home for a spell; brung down their comforter and some of their pillows, flung off just two days ago when they come down to eat; and arranging these familiar comforts around them, I again took up my post by their side.

I might of pulled it off yet if it hadn't been for John, calling us together in the sitting room after supper; for he had a document in hand to read us, the paper Ben'd wrote after Jim's spell with his heart; and the words he now spoke changed things forever. Thinking I'd finally get the support I needed in a more official way than Ben's wishes, left in an informal file in his rolltop, I'd set down beside John front and center; and so I was there in the midst of all hands when Ben's final message was held up before us, and John broke the seal, explaining Ben'd asked him to do so before services was held or his will was read, so long as Jamie'd passed away before him.

Nigh seventy now, his hair thick and white, his looks lawyerly still as he hooked spectacles to his ears, John smoothed the brief paper kept secret from all, even him; and he read it through to the end despite rising incredulity and doubt, the lawyer in him winning out over the brother:

> "I, Benjamin Galen Melchett, being of sound mind and body, do this day the 27th of November, 1872, take pen in hand to inform you of the marriage I have kept hidden for the past several decades. If this message is read, it means that we are both gone now, Jim and I; and with our passing I do not want to have pass away the truth

of our relationship. If I'd thought we'd have
had your understanding in life, as we did
Eben's, I'd have shared this information
long ago; but my hope is that in death,
sorrow will bring with it acceptance. 'The
truth shall set you free' it says in the Bible;
and in truth I do feel set free writing these
words. May our marriage be recognized at
last by all, not just by one, as Jim and I join
each other in the hereafter; and may our
legacy be that our love was honest."

Set free the truth did—not understanding but outrage: an uproar
of shouts and questions and dismay, an explosion of embarrassed
confusion ricocheting the room from mantle to rafters; and most of
it was directed at me. Engulfed like a ridge by an army's onslaught,
John tried to gain control of the mob long enough to remind that
services was tomorrow, and the reading of Ben's will in his office the
day after; but he was barely heard in the tumult, all hands turning
on me in their outcry; and refusing to get caught up in apologies or
defenses, I simply repeated Ben's words in a sane way, and strove to
find the means to calm things.

Crushed that Ben hadn't thought there might be one left behind
to bear the storm he'd unleash—wondering how he could of forgot
me in his plans, one minute outraged at him, the next realizing he had
only me to defend them, the next even suspecting the old buzzard'd
intended it that way—I was heaped with abuse and derision, the
more so as the full import of Ben's words come clear to them; and
"Sodom and Gomorrah" was hissed round the room in place of the
tenderly spoke "David and Jonathan." Refueled by the news, the
debate over the burial flared up again in the midst of folks' passion;
and for the rest of the day battles was fought and re-fought over the
shape of the final arrangements.

Sticking to my guns I declared things'd go on, including the shared
funeral tomorrow, even if I had to dig the grave myself; and dig it

I later did, the church refusing the churchyard, and the preacher refusing to lead the service. The coffin already having been delivered, Jorab couldn't very well take it back; but he sent word to one and all he was ashamed that he'd made such a sinful bed; and sharing his feelings all hands begun leaving, departing the house for the town wharf and tavern. Abandoning Ben and Jim in their disgust, they marched off in irate ranks and battalions, even Ben's brother Tom and his children and best friends; and I found myself in a smaller and smaller circle, till finally there was only me left, and Jean.

Having arrived that noon on the mail boat—her young ones left in Cape Damaris—she'd held the fort in the kitchen for hours; and at the sight of her eyes now, clear and steady like Ben's—at the touch of her hands, warm and soothing like Jim's—I at last gave way to grief, and bowed my head at the kitchen table. Sitting beside me, she took my fingers, and stroked them a bit in mute understanding; and seeing my hand in her firm, young fingers, I seen it was old, old and gnarled, as knotted and broke as a doryman's paw. Touching my shoulder she stroked it as well, almost of a size with me as we sat; and in her sheltering ring I seen I was frail, as fragile and slight as a bird in a palm. Wracked as I was, my shoulders quivered beneath the capable curve of her arm; and though she too—her father's favorite— must of been aching with unspoke sorrow, she waited in hushed pain for me to quiet.

When at last I steadied, she rose a moment, and fetched me coffee from the pot on the stove; and accepting the cup with a dazed silence—wiping my eyes with the lost feel of a child, cut adrift from all kin by some unforeseen blow—I shook my head in disbelief and murmured: "Jim….Jim's hair'd scarcely begun t' gray yet…an' Ben… he had yeahrs of haulin' left in his ahrms." Schooled for four decades to the will of the sea—tutored most recently by the loss of her husband, swept overboard off Diego Ramirez—she glanced grimly out toward the harbor; then bending, she kissed my weathered fingers, and wordlessly sipped her cup beside me.

What we had to do next we both knew, me taking the shovel and telling her I thought the place on the bit of a rise near the house—the place where two or three pines come together, in such a way as they looked like one—might be a spot where they'd like to rest; and her taking the spare as she hoisted her skirts, the two of us worked well into the night.

Whether her life in Boston had opened her mind to a broader understanding of others, or whether her unswerving love for her father'd simply made way for the acceptance he'd sought, she had no argument with him and Jim, speaking lovingly of them both as we rested on our shovels; and when we retired at last, hard on midnight—when I prepared to take up my vigil on the sloop, secretly slipping my flintlock into my gear—I seen she was as ready to defend them, taking down Ben's rifle and calmly setting it by the door. Catching her eyes—as steel grey as Ben's ever was at the rudder—I could tell she was fully prepared to use it; and patting her shoulder, I said "Don't worry, the dog an' me'll wake first; an' we'll give folks somethin' t' remembeh if they try an' disturb them."

We'd expected a small crowd at the funeral next day, and we wasn't disappointed; for by noon there was only Fan to join us, her being the widow of Ben's son Nat; and by one o'clock—as the mail boat made fast from its morning run—there was but a single carriage on the way from the wharf. Making towards us slowly in the mud, it at length pulled up at our dooryard; and stepping down from it, John helped Damaris, her face sweet and calm beneath a black hat. Her hair streaked with grey now, she was still pretty, not unlike the young woman who'd set her cap for Jim; and she embraced Jean whilst John shook my hand, as stiffly distant as one sent on business.

Then turning from me, he helped one more from the carriage; and moved to the quick, I seen it was Anne. Widowed by now, silver-haired and frail, she'd come all the way on the water she hated; and as her black silk and bonnet—fashion-plated like always—blurred with the hot sting of my disbelief, she took my hand and said simply, "He stood by me in my trouble."

No one else having come to honor the captain who'd steered their boats or built them for decades—no one else having come to pay tribute to the craftsman whose toys even now was delighting their young ones—we picked our way past the house to the sloop, and gathered round Jim and Ben on the deck, us six. There being nothing else for it—the preacher still adamant, and Jackson, shot years ago in a wharf side crossfire as he tried to aid a runaway slave, sleeping peacefully above Boston Harbor—I took up the service and read it, the cool April wind from the sea on my pages.

Having married them three decades ago now, it was perhaps fitting I bind them in death; and trying not to look back on that June day in the cove, I bid them off on their final journey. Subdued in the mist, folks stood about me: Jean, close by, her hand in my elbow; Fan, beside her, as though they was sisters; Anne and Damaris on the other side of the coffin, each of them with an unreadable face; and off near the cuddy, John in his frock coat, looking as if he wished he was elsewhere.

Then closing my book, I bowed my head, whilst Jean gave voice to their favorite chantey, "Shenandoah" trembling out on the breeze; and following the notes to a hundred places—from the humpbacked upsweep of peaks in Rio, to the dark burst of palms in the red Anjier dawn—I sailed the words as if they was vessels. Unable to look up, I stared at the ground whilst Damaris took up a Romany ballad, singing out in a clear, trembling rhythm words Jim must of taught her on a lark long ago; and as the journey wound down from the steep lanes of Wales to the peninsula roads of Maine, I caught a vision of towheaded children, their hands waving from the bright gates of a *vardo*.

Then standing in everyone's midst once again—struggling to find my voice in the silence —I begun to close the service; spoke a few words in memory of my friends, with the wind hissing past my bare head and collar. Longing to convey the honesty of their mating in such a way as these five could fathom, I spoke of the journeys that'd joined course in Boston; traced separate wanderings down the glens of Wales and past the foggy banks of the Mersey, or down from Cape Damaris launchways, and brung them together at Toby's one March night. Tacking, mooring, navigating, salvaging and shipbuilding and trawling: with these well-known motions I mapped their friendship, triangulating their discoveries with mine; whilst such homely images as campfires, compasses and sextants and landfalls, helped shape the face of their devotion.

My voice trailing off in the hush of my feeling, I spoke of the unity of a ship, in harmony with its crew and the sea; spoke of the hard-won medley that'd made us into such a unit, us three—then bowing my head I turned away, and readied the ropes that would convey them home.

Lowering the lid, we slipped in tokens of farewell—Damaris sliding a lock of her hair in Jim's pocket, and Jean small keepsakes fetched from home. I'd already, myself, brung things I wanted them to have for the journey, going through their belongings the past day: Jim's Havana shell, given to him by Ben, then given again by Jacques at his last; and Ben's journal of Wales, with sundry notes and confessions I couldn't destroy, but feared others would find. They was already wearing the most intimate signs of their union, Jim's locket—which'd never left its place at Ben's throat—and their rings, which I'd anguished somebody'd try to remove, even at the cost of breaking their fingers, so bitter was the outrage at their marriage.

So now I gave them their final gifts, Jim his boyhood harp, and Ben his grandfather's quadrant; then reaching into Ben's pocket, I slipped a final message from Jim. Going through Jim's papers—including his will, a hastily scrawled paragraph that consigned his belongings to me and Ben—I'd found two sealed notes, one for each of us, to be opened at the time of his death; and now relinquishing Ben's—still longing to read it, wondering what final word this man of few phrases had chosen to say to his life's mate—I patted my own, still sealed in my pocket, and gently latched the lid of the casket.

Having done his duty—a task I understood better later, when Ben's will was publicly read—John was about to take his leave; but when he seen they was going to help me, these women, to guide the coffin as the horse hoisted it from the sloop and hauled it to the gravesite nearby, he took off his frock coat and helped with the labor, till—lowered by means of a rope and tackle—the box rested in its final home. Then turning away he strode back to the carriage whilst Jean and Anne and Fan and Damaris in turn spoke their words, and cast in their handfuls; then they too turned away, Jean leaving me alone for the night as I'd asked her.

By myself in the cottage for the first time since my loss—dreading aloneness, yet craving the chance to give vent to my feelings—I felt my way through the kitchen and front room; stared about me half-dazed in the silence, and touched the chairs as if unsure of their presence. Setting down on the sofa—tentatively feeling the cushions—I found Jamie's cup on the table at my elbow; and reaching out towards it with trembling fingers, I touched its cool, abandoned handle. Seeing the unfinished dregs—the tea he'd left behind him, as Ben'd hurried him off that last morning—I unsteadily got to my feet; and witlessly wandering about the front room, I opened a window and admitted the sea breeze. In the failing light of the sunset hour the curtains billowed and fell with the rain gusts; and as they flapped and idled like canvas I touched the mantle, where a host of memories assailed me.

Ben's humidor, his penknife and matches, a half-smoked cigar in a tray by the chimney—Jim's neckerchief, his keys and paintbox, a half-finished top for Ben's latest grandson—my fingers wandered and quivered on these, like the fragile antennae of some restless insect; then halting before the model of *Charis,* they contemplated the small, carven figures—the captain and mate who conferred near the wheelbox, and the seaman who hauled a line on the main deck. Suddenly collapsing, they slid from the mantle, and fell to my sides as if stricken; and dangling there whilst I drifted and wandered, they alternately trembled and twitched, or reached out to stroke some surface nearby them. Ben's boots and oilslicks, his yellow sou'wester, the sleeve of Jamie's navy pea jacket: they fondled these as if they was feet, the tresses of hair or the slope of an arm; then falling limp again at my sides, they swung quietly as I walked the room, and took to the rail as I mounted the stairs.

Unlocking the bedroom door, they fell still again, as I stood uncertainly on the threshold; then responding to the waves that engulfed my frame, they violently quavered and shuddered, and clutched one another in spasms. Reaching out, they touched the chair, the seat by the window where they'd long ago soothed Jim; lifted Jim's soiled linen, Ben's worn flannels, then dropped them where they'd earlier been let fall; made futile efforts to pick up the towels; fluttered at the bedside lantern, at the fragile frames of Ben's spectacles; then fumbled amongst the cool, tangled bedclothes. Struggling to smooth the counterpane and linen—tugging at corners, then stopping, uncertain—they halted at attention like the ears of a rabbit, poised to catch fleeting sounds in the twilight: a low, drowsy sigh, a needy murmur, a bawdy chuckle or jest or comment—the sounds of three decades of trust and devotion, lingering still in the bedclothes and rafters.

Then animated again, they kneaded the blankets, burrowed and clutched the folds and wrinkles as my groan pierced the hush of the evening, and echoed within the abandoned chamber. Plucking, tearing, they wormed themselves in and out of the blankets, tugging and wresting with my weeping; till at last, trembling and wearied, they took to tapping, to stroking with a rhythmic thumping, as the passion slowly ebbed from my sobbing.

It was Jean who seen me through them next days—through my cousins' funeral, from which I was sent away as unwanted; through the turning aside of old friends; and even through the reading of Ben's will, though it put her as much in the midst of controversy as me. Calling us together in Cape Damaris, John set us down in rows in his office, lined with calfskin books and ledgers; and there he read out Ben's final wishes, penned after Jamie's spell with his heart. Though I'd never seen it, I'd assumed it was like the rest before it; supposed he'd made only small changes in it, like he done over the years as family or business matters grew.

Intoned by John, it named me as executor, as expected; transferred his shares in our shipyard to me and Jim, and disposed of his stock in the salvage company the same fashion; set aside bequests to Misericordia and Jackson's sailor's home in Boston, pretty much like he always done;—then boldly disinherited all his children not present at the funeral, save those too ill or far away to reach it—and those as well if they'd turned against him; cut off too any beneficiary from the town for the same reason, leaving his estate to be shared by those both named and at the graveside. Understanding at a swoop why John'd been there, to oversee attendance and forestall any groundswell to contest the will—understanding Ben's foresight, the old buzzard having seen exactly what'd happen, once John broke the seal on the truth of matters at his death—feeling in some uncanny way he was present, enjoying at last the frank justice he'd craved—I gathered up my old bones and went out into the afternoon, that I not witness the break-up of the family we'd worked so many years to unite.

Jean weathered it well, having inherited Ben's grit, a commodity that stood her in good stead the next weeks; immediately shared half her legacy with Fan, her being Nat's living representative; made arrangements with Seth to sell him the shipyard, which I'd directly passed on to her; and went into business with Fan with my blessing, managing the salvage company on the island.

Moving into the cottage, she spared me aloneness; settled into my old room whilst I moved into Ben's and Jim's, taking Jim's old bed and merging my clutter with theirs; bedded her children across the hall, so the place, for a mercy, held the scampers of young ones. At ten and eight, they was not unlike Tom and Jean'd been at the same age, Dory hardy and bright, Charis dreamy and slight; and the years so blurred for me now that I frequently mistook them, calling out for them to tumble out of bed as if Ben would, any moment, swarm down from the poop, and bawl orders at them as we worked towards Anjier.

Insisting on keeping Jim's workshop intact—insisting that his gear and Ben's be left out, that even their linen remain on the bed and the still-damp towels stay at the washstand—I nonetheless allowed, with the passing of time, for the tidying up of the workbench and dresser, for the making of the bed and the putting away of clothes. Taking care of one small thing at a time—washing up Jamie's cup, restoring it to its hook in the kitchen, or setting Ben's pipe in its rack—Jean sensitively sorted out the downstairs; lifted items from their mute, helpless settings to places on pegs and shelves and mantles.

Having settled into my room, she helped me move my few wants upstairs, and into spare drawers in Ben's and Jim's chamber; and nestling into Jim's bed by the dormer, I tentatively adjusted to my losses. With the wind at the curtains and my own clothes on the chair backs—with my mates' belongings present yet straightened, no longer helplessly waiting where dropped —with Ben's logbooks neatly stacked on his rolltop, and Jamie's drawings scrolled up beside them—above all, with children in the rooms across the hallway—I found that I could bear the cottage; and in time the place took on the pace of the present, without sacrificing the face of the past.

At 64 a worn waterdog—an elderly man for my day and age—I discovered I was all done with fishing; concentrated on wrapping up Ben's business and giving Jean a fresh start, and taking Ben's place as grandfather to the few young ones permitted to stop by. Cut off as finally as if we was a continent apart, and not just down the road from each other, Seth kept his brood away from our dooryard, and managed the shipyard so all on his own that I never seen any of them again; whilst Tom and Becky and Courtney, not far away in Cape Damaris, kept to themselves as if we'd never met. After a day in town buying supplies from folks who wouldn't speak to me either, I found it a blessing to play with Nat's boys, Fan bringing them to stop often as she did business with Jean; and at least that much of the family survived, enough of a remnant to get on with.

Respecting my need to keep the cottage the same—throwing away not even the waste in the basket by Ben's desk, leaving me to sort the crumpled papers, amongst them Ben's infernal lists, and Jamie's quick, impulsive sketches—all hands filled in around the edges, seldom leaving me alone; and if I wanted solitude I had to go out to the grave, where I'd pitched a bit of a tent to stay near, and watch over them for the summer.

To those outside the immediate family I become, I suppose, something of an eccentric; for though I faithfully appeared in town for supplies—never allowing their spite to prevent me from commerce, nor letting Jean take the heat for me neither, especially since she suffered no small meanness herself; though I often clattered by at the reins of Jim's *vardo*, with Dory and Charis and Nat's boys at the windows, I was more and more of a recluse, and never set foot again on the mainland. In addition to known oddities of behavior—especially with regard to my devotion to Ben and Jim, and my preservation of their belongings—I couldn't escape their reputation as well: Ben's controversial will, their common burial, their marriage, Ben's divorce and Jamie's mysterious past, all inexhaustive topics for gossip.

Nor was I especially inclined to quell things, or distance myself from the conflict; for with both my friends gone and the children grown—with the word already out and its surgery done—I discovered in myself, as my own end neared, a desire a keep their story alive. The truth divides, as Ben'd foreseen; and so the unity that we three had shared become all the dearer to me as my days waned, and all the more important to tell. Carving their gravestone—a mighty boulder I'd used the team to drag in place, square in the middle of their grave, lest any plunderer seek to disturb them—I chiseled therefore the painstaking announcement:

Here lie
Capt. Benjamin G. Melchett
1815-1876
and his mate
James Robertson Melchett
1824-1876
United in life; undivided in death

At the bottom I couldn't resist adding—since Ben would of liked it, and there was no reason anymore to pussyfoot around: "What God hath joined, let no man put asunder"; and I didn't cut it in small letters neither. Off to one side Jean fashioned a ship, a clipper under a full press of sail; whilst off to the other I cut my own name, Capt. Eben McCabe, 1812— . Not a carver myself, it took me the whole summer; but it pleased me to have the truth cut in stone; and when the last letters was cast I struck my tent, and moved into the cottage for autumn.

When I took to my chair in failing health in October, the cold rains lashing the seas with dense fury, I followed my heart and told Jean the whole story; and setting at my side them chill afternoons, she listened with patience and understanding—with the look of one who sees old friends more clearly, or a child who hears a tale of far places. Nodding at my words or knitting or sewing, she listened to stories of Ann Street and Rio, to tales of knife fights and shells and hurricanes, to yarns of crimps and seamen and shipwrights, and gypsy harpists by campfires at Bala.

As I emptied myself of memories and vistas—as I dreamed on, eyes closed, scarcely aware I was speaking, or smiled over at her with the brightness of fond days—she received my yarns as a jug receives cider, or a ship the cargo waiting on dockways: storing them firmly in her mind's hold, and later on, in the evening, recording them in her logbook. Promising me to preserve the story—to keep it with Ben's charts, which she was arranging to publish, a move that would of mightily pleased Jim—she granted me the only wish I desired, save that I be laid to rest by my mates; and I listened to the voices tumbling in the chimney with contentment as we sat by the hearth.

Yet the last of my words did not end the story; for one day in late autumn, when the season was far advanced, and the ducks in the bay was skimming the waters, so close that they seemed to kiss their reflections, a disreputable sloop made fast to our dock; and there come a knock at our kitchen door. Opening it, Jean was blowed down for find Ezra, the old shellback nigh onto eighty at least, and dead for all we knew the past decades; for the last we'd had word of him was Whampoa, when some Boston skipper said he'd spoke him near Hong Kong. With a bird on one shoulder and a seabag on the other, he looked like he'd come to stay for the winter; and his words immediately bore out the impression, for with a marbley "I been lookin' for a place unconventional enough t' call home; an' from what I heahr tell, this hehre is it," he moored seabag and parrot onto our hearth.

His bursts of impulsive, eccentric spirit, so like Jim's, and his gruff, forthright manner, kin to Ben's, gushed over me like a healing river; and on its flow I traversed the next days; set nodding as I gave ear to his traveler's tales, yarns of places even I had never seen. Under the influence of his words the walls rolled away and I was at sea again on a fresh voyage, unloading my gear once more in my cabin; was tumbling on deck where Jamie already stood, giving a playful gibe at Ben's orders; then it was ringing eight bells and the watches was changing beneath the hoarse, deep throbbing of canvas, and the hills was sliding astern on a keen wind.

Finished this day 18 April 2000
Steuben, Maine

Begun March 1978 — Beirut, Lebanon
Completed April 2000 — Steuben, Maine
Typescript completed 10 May 2004
Third revision completed 6 August 2009
Converted from Works to Word 17 July 2011
Revised conversion completed 23 October 2011
Vol. I edited/ published February 2012
Vol. II edited/ published June 2013
Vol. III edited July/ August 2013

About the Author

KIM RIDENOUR RAIKES is a member of the faculty of Maine Maritime Academy in Castine, where she teaches writing and humanities. An important aspect of her teaching career, which began 37 years ago in Marjoyoun, Lebanon, is global education, and she has led numerous study abroad programs for American students in Ireland, Great Britain, and India. As an ordained minister and student of world religious traditions, she has long incorporated spiritual themes in her writing and academic researches.

Beginning in Beirut in 1978 and continuing over the course of the next 30 years, Raikes worked on this novel daily, drawing not only from primary researches into historical records and sailing ship logs, but also from her personal experience of the working waterfront. Though these outer resources were important shaping influences, the key inspiration for this story came in the form of the three narrative voices which emerged from within, and the historical places which took shape though unseen.